Nicole looked up as her door opened, and Jake walked inside, closing the door behind her.

"Busy?"

Nicole sighed. "Yes. Does that matter?"

Jake smiled. "No."

"I didn't think so," she murmured. "I thought you wanted to talk to Catherine."

"I did. I also wanted to talk to you."

"Well, Detective, I can spare a few—"

"Let's stop this, Nicole," Jake interrupted.

"Stop what?"

"Stop this bullshit. Stop pretending we don't know each other. Stop pretending that we . . . we haven't seen each other naked. Stop pretending that we're damn strangers."

Nicole stared at Jake's flashing eyes, trying to ignore that she was aroused by her words.

Visit

Bella Books

at

BellaBooks.com

or call our toll-free number

1-800-729-4992

The Killing Room

GERRI HILL

Bella
BOOKS
2006

Bella Books, Inc.
P.O. Box 10543
Tallahassee, FL 32302

Printed in the United States of America on acid-free paper

First Edition

Editor: Anna Chinappi
Cover designer: Sandy Knowles

ISBN-10: 1-59493-050-3
ISBN-13: 978-1-59493-050-8

Dedicated to Stephanie Solomon-Lopez. Many, many thanks for all you've done, including your help with The Killing Room.

About the Author

Gerri lives in the Piney Woods of East Texas with her partner, Diane, and their two labs, Zach and Max, and a bucketful of cats. Hobbies include any outdoor activity, from tending the orchard and vegetable garden to hiking in the woods with camera and binoculars. For more, visit Gerri's Web site at www.gerrihill.com.

CHAPTER ONE

Jake McCoy drove along the Taylor River, her Land Cruiser packed to the brim for a few weeks of unexpected solitude. She glanced in her side mirror, smiling as Cheyenne's face came into view. The dog hung out the open window, anticipation on her face as she realized where they were headed.

Jake had owned the tiny cabin near Tin Cup for eleven years, fixing it up little by little. At first, when she lived in Gunnison, she could come out every weekend. But living in Denver for the past five years had put a damper on her visits—and her renovations. Not that she regretted the move. Her salary had nearly doubled. Four or five more years of padding her saving's account and she'd be ready to move back permanently.

As the thick stands of pine, spruce, and fir flew by, she felt the familiar peace settle over her. With her own window open, she hung her arm out, loving the feel of the cool mountain air as it rustled across her body, bringing a smile to her normally impassive face. She watched the water glisten in the afternoon sun as the river almost roared down the canyon, bouncing off boulders on its way to Gunnison and the Black Canyon. She climbed the winding canyon road, finally reaching the dam where Taylor Reservoir spread out beneath the shadows of the Collegiate Peaks mountain range, the blue, blue water splashing against the shoreline on its haste to tumble over the dam and down the canyon.

Watching the handful of anglers that lined the shore, she realized that in late August, most of the tourists were gone. She turned right on the forest service road, bouncing along the dirt road as it made its way deeper into the forest, crossing several streams and wooden bridges. They climbed slightly when they reached the tiny community of Tin Cup, and she slowed as she passed the old general store, waving at the locals. She'd like to think that most knew her by now, but she realized it was really Cheyenne they recognized. She usually brought her supplies with her and seldom ventured into the store. Just a mile outside of Tin Cup, the forest road turned into a four-wheel drive road, and she downshifted, bouncing over the rocks that now lined the road. She drove past the cutoff that would take her over Cumberland Pass and continued on until she came to Mirror Lake, one of the most picturesque lakes she'd ever seen, the reflection of the mountain peak behind it shimmering clearly on the still water. Crossing over the dirt-packed dam, she headed around the canyon with Cumberland Pass hovering over to her right. She would top nine thousand feet before she reached her cabin. Even though the days remained warm and comfortable, the nights would drop into the thirties. She hoped there was enough firewood. She doubted she'd be able to cut any on this trip. Rubbing her injured leg gently she thought she might just give it a try. She'd been laid up so long already, she was starved for physical exercise.

She met her eyes in the mirror, frowning slightly. She'd promised her lieutenant she'd take it easy. That was why he'd agreed to let her spend the beginning of her "desk duty only" assignment up here. He knew she'd go completely insane being tied to a desk for a month, perhaps longer if her physical therapist had his way. Well, she was stronger than she looked and much too stubborn to let a bullet to the leg keep her out of commission for months. Two weeks in the hospital had nearly done her in, another full week in bed with that psycho therapist insisting on flexing her leg once an hour. Grudgingly, she knew it had helped. It just hurt like a son of a bitch. Last week, he'd finally had her walking, first using a walker that embarrassed her to no end, then finally a cane. At least with the cane, she could use it to threaten him when he pushed too hard. She let a small smile escape as she recalled how she'd whacked him across his shoulder two days ago with the cane. He had been adamant that she was not ready for this trip, that she could not possibly get around in the mountains by herself.

"Like hell I can't," she said out loud. Cheyenne moved from the window to the space between the seats, standing on the console and nudging Jake with her wet nose. "I know, girl. About there."

Most of the land along Cumberland Pass was public, but there were pockets here and there that were privately owned. Her own cabin sat on just two acres, but it was surrounded by the national forest, and when she stood on the huge boulders and surveyed the mountains around her, she felt like she owned it all.

She downshifted into low as she made the last climb, finally stopping at the small wooden gate that marked her property. Cheyenne danced excitedly, urging her to hurry. Opening the door, she gritted her teeth, knowing that the last three hours of driving without a break would have taken their toll on her leg. Using the cane to support herself, she gingerly straightened up, putting more weight on her injured leg. She gasped as the pain shot through her, and she gripped the cane tightly. The pain passed as it always did. For probably the thousandth time, she wondered if she'd ever fully recover. If not, well, she could either accept desk duty for the rest of her career or take the disability package and retire. She looked around her, breathing deeply the fresh smell of the mountains. If she didn't love her job so damn much, she'd take the disability in a minute. But once she did it, that was it. Wasn't like she could go back into law enforcement after that. No one would hire her. And at thirty-eight, she was a little young to retire up here and hide out in her cabin. She'd turn into a bona fide hermit before she knew it. She liked being alone too much to turn out otherwise.

After taking a few steps, being careful not to trip on a rock, the feeling in her leg returned to somewhat normal. She grabbed the padlock, inserting her key and turning, listening for the click that was about to open up her world. She swung the gate open, then hobbled over to secure it so she could drive through, knowing she'd just have to do it all over again when she stopped to close it. She'd close it and lock it and . . . finally, after nearly a month of being waited on by nurses, she'd have complete solitude. She and Cheyenne. They'd only been together two years, but they'd bonded like no other dog she'd ever had. She often wondered if Cheyenne could hear her thoughts. She had no doubt the dog understood her spoken words. A high-pitched bark urged her to hurry and she laughed.

"I know, I know." She crawled back inside and drove through the gate, stopping once again to close the gate and lock it. Cheyenne was nearly dancing by the time she got back inside. She ruffled the dog's fur, then sat still as a wet tongue swiped at her cheek. She drove on, curving to the right as the tiny road was nearly swallowed by the forest. Just a short distance later, her cabin appeared. "Here we are, Cheyenne."

The small cabin looked like it could have easily been built in the 1800s. It was as rustic as it could get and still have plumbing and electricity. And that was why Jake loved it. Of course, when she bought it, there wasn't plumbing and electricity. She'd made do with the old outhouse and hauling in water, but that soon got old. So, she spent a small fortune on a well and having electricity brought up the pass. But the other renovations, like the new porch and the added bedroom, she'd done herself. Mostly. It was just a one-room cabin when she bought it. Now, eleven years later, it had a separate bedroom and bathroom, and a real kitchen. The original part of the cabin was now entirely a living room, with one whole wall composed of a rock fireplace and nothing else.

She opened the back door of the Land Cruiser, and Cheyenne bolted out, nose to the ground as she sniffed around the cabin. Jake walked slowly to the porch, taking the first step with difficulty. Using the cane and the handrail, she pulled herself up. She felt nearly disgusted with her inadequacy and had to push it aside, knowing it would pass. But she was impatient. She paused on the porch and looked back at the Land Cruiser, wondering how in the world she was going to unpack it.

"Very slowly."

Well, she had nothing but time. A slow smiled formed as she stood on the porch. She let the familiar smells of the forest relax her and embraced the peace she felt as she stared out at the mountains. Yes, nothing but time.

CHAPTER TWO

Nicole rushed down the sidewalk, dodging others who obviously were not running late. Her gym bag bounced on her hip, and she tossed an "excuse me" over her shoulder as she bumped an older gentleman. Standing impatiently at the elevators, she punched the button six times, then glanced around, just daring anyone to say something smartass.

A tone sounded, the doors opened, and she pushed her way on, knowing there was no way all twelve of them could fit. But she was late. She glanced at her watch. Jesus, was she late. Catherine would kill her.

And as expected, her secretary was pacing in the lobby when she walked in.

"Do you *know* what time it is?" she demanded.

"How long have they been here?"

"Twenty minutes. There is no telling what they've talked about in twenty minutes."

"We're in . . . what? Week nine? They're fine." Nicole shoved

6

her gym bag at Catherine and walked confidently to her door. Only quiet murmurs were heard from inside, and she nodded. Yes, they were fine. Swinging the door open, she smiled at the eight women who were waiting for her. "Did you start without me?"

"Dr. Westbrook, no, of course not," said Patty, the group's normal spokesperson.

Nicole walked slowly to her desk, pausing before sitting down. "Sorry I'm late. I know we only have a couple of sessions left. Let's make the most of them, shall we?"

"Beth would like to go first today," Patty announced.

Nicole nodded, her mind already beginning to wander even before Beth started speaking. She'd heard their stories a hundred times, and she wasn't sure how much more she could endure. Each group was the same. Eight to ten women, all various ages and from different backgrounds, thrown together because of a common cause. Violence. And every ten weeks or so, a new group would come, all telling their stories. And this group was not unlike the one before them or the one before that. They all came because they were victims—rape, assault, domestic violence. She'd heard it all. And she realized she was no longer shocked by what she heard. It had become nearly commonplace. And that's why she knew it was time to stop. Mentally, she couldn't take it anymore. For the last five years, she'd been conducting group sessions, eight to ten weeks long, meeting three times a week. She found the women were more apt to open up in a group.

Normally, they felt no one could possibly have it as bad as they did or no one could relate to what they've gone through. But in a group setting, they listen to other women whose stories mirror their own and most times eclipse theirs. They find support where they thought there'd be none. The group sessions had been a huge success, but they had taken their toll on her. She felt like she'd lived every rape, every beating, every tear that was ever shed.

"Dr. Westbrook?"

Nicole blinked several times, focusing on Beth. "Good, Beth. Who would like to comment?"

And so it went. One by one, they told their stories, over and over again. The anxiety that Nicole had been feeling for the last week seemed to manifest itself tenfold. She felt nearly suffocated, and she reached for her glass of water with trembling hands.

"What's wrong, Nicole? Catherine's afraid you're having a breakdown of some sort."

Nicole wanted to laugh it off, but Dr. Peterson would see through it in a heartbeat. The older woman had been her friend and mentor for more than ten years. If there was anyone she could confide in, it was Dorothy. She settled down on the couch beside her and took a deep breath. "I don't know how much longer I can continue to hear about their abuses. It makes me want to find one of their husbands and beat the shit out of him."

Dorothy laughed and reached over, squeezing Nicole's hand. "I tried to warn you. One-on-one sessions are hard enough. But groups?"

"The group sessions are the most helpful," Nicole reminded her.

"Yes, I agree. You've done wonderful things for these women. I've no doubt they're able to ease back into society with a confidence they never could have imagined before. I'm talking about you, Nicole. You relive everything that happened to them, over and over. Ten of them at once? I can't imagine the burden you're carrying around."

Nicole rolled her head along the sofa, meeting the other woman's eyes. "Dorothy, I'm not sure I'm in the right profession."

The other woman only smiled. "We all go through that, Nicole."

"We're trained to be objective and to separate ourselves from our patients. But all I hear is their pain and their fears, and I realize there is so very little I can do for them."

"That's not true and you know it. By the time they finish with you, they are ready to head out that door and take life by the horns. You've instilled confidence in them, Nicole. Every one of

8

them leaves here knowing that what happened to them was not their fault. And you do it in a mere ten weeks time. I have a patient that I've been seeing for over a year. She was raped by her neighbor, and I'm no closer to having her accept it than I was on the first day. You have a way with them, Nicole. Don't throw that away just because you have . . . burnout."

"Burnout? I think that's too mild a word for what I'm feeling. Do you know I was twenty minutes late for our session today? I was at the gym, and I knew I was late, but I just couldn't make myself . . . go."

"Because you were exercising and you weren't thinking about them or their problems, and it made you feel good."

"Exactly."

"Well, good for you. Most of us just turn to alcohol."

Nicole laughed. "I've tried that, too." She turned sideways on the couch, facing Dorothy. "I feel like I have this tremendous weight on me, and I can't shake it. I have two more sessions next week with this group, and Dorothy, I don't think I can do it."

"Of course you can do it. You know why? Because when you're done, you're going to take a vacation."

"Vacations are hardly stress-free. And at the end of them . . . it's back to work."

"I happen to know that your most favorite thing in the world is to backpack into the mountains. When's the last time you've done that?"

"I've only been able to get away once since I started the group sessions."

"Exactly. You used to tell me that the only way you could reconnect with yourself was to go out alone into the mountains."

"There's never time."

"Well make the time, Nicole. Next week, when this group is done, take the time. Go out alone, forget about all this and focus on you."

"And just like that, it'll all be better?"

"No, it won't. I'm going to recommend that you limit your

9

group sessions to two per year. Get back to doing one-on-one. I know that family violence is your specialty, but perhaps you could broaden that. There is always marriage counseling."

"The divorce rate would soar, I'm afraid." Nicole sat up. "But Dorothy, I'm doing five group sessions a year now. Cutting back to two . . . that eliminates about thirty women that I could possibly be helping."

"If you don't cut back to two, you'll be eliminating fifty women, not thirty. You said so yourself, you can't keep this up."

Nicole nodded and squeezed the older woman's hand. "Thanks for coming by. I think I'll take your advice and get away. After that, I'll see how I feel." She stood. "Regardless, Catherine has already scheduled the next session."

"As a colleague and a friend, I would recommend you cancel it, Nicole. Take on a few of them for individual sessions if you must, but don't take on another ten-week group session."

"Thank you, Dorothy. I'll take that under advisement."

Dorothy let out a laugh as she stood. "I'll take that to mean I should mind my own business."

"Not at all. I appreciate your concern. And Catherine's."

"Don't be hard on her. She's just worried about you."

After Dorothy left, Catherine stuck her head in, albeit a bit hesitantly. "Are you mad at me?"

Nicole motioned for her to come in. "Of course not." Nicole pushed away from her desk and leaned back, relaxing as she stared at Catherine. "Sit down. Let's talk."

"I've just been really worried about you. I've never seen you this stressed," Catherine said, taking a seat in one of Nicole's visitors' chairs.

"You're right. I have been stressed, and it is hardly professional to be late to an appointment. You were right to call Dorothy."

"What's going on?"

Nicole gave a forced laugh and shrugged. "Too much pain and suffering, not enough love, I guess."

"This group's been hard, I know. Two of them lost children, one . . ."

"I know," Nicole said, interrupting her. "God, I know."

"Sorry. Is that what's bothering you? That you have to . . . absorb all that?"

"That's a good way of putting it." Nicole leaned forward, resting her elbows on her desk and closing her eyes. "Every day, every session, hearing about the horrors they faced," she said quietly, "has taken its toll, yes. I would never admit this to Dr. Peterson, but I've been having dreams about it. And that scares me. I'm too close, and I have no outlet."

"What do you mean?"

"I'm single, I live alone. I don't even have a damn cat."

"You can talk to me," Catherine offered.

"Thank you, but it's not the same."

"Well, I won't bring up your love life, I know *that* subject is off limits."

"I date. I don't have a love life."

"You date. So, at least . . . you know."

Nicole shook her head.

"You're not having sex?" Catherine asked loudly.

"No."

"Since when?"

Nicole looked away. God, it was so . . . weird to talk to Catherine about this. "Since Rachel."

"You're kidding? Nicole, that's been . . . what? Three years?"

"Something like that."

Catherine shook her head. "That's just not normal."

"Why thank you, *Doctor* Catherine. However, I'm afraid to sleep with someone. The last time I did, they moved into my home within a week and stayed a year and a half."

"You know what you need?"

"No, but I'm sure you're going to tell me."

"You need to go out . . . and just . . . have wild sex. Meaningless

11

wild sex. And don't tell them your name, and certainly don't tell them where you live."

"And what exactly would that solve?"

"Well, it would certainly let out some of the pent-up energy I'm sure you have." Catherine leaned forward. "Just let loose for once. Let your hair down. You're always so controlled."

"I have to be."

"I know. So go out somewhere where you don't have to be. Surely you people have sleazy bars you can go to."

"I will *not* go to a bar, thank you."

"Well, you need to do something. My God, your dates have to be *so* boring."

Nicole let out a deep breath. "You probably won't think of this as letting my hair down, but Dorothy suggested I take some time off and maybe . . . well, get away into the mountains."

"Backpack?"

"Yes."

"But that's great. You love doing that, you should go."

"There are only two weeks between sessions," Nicole reminded Catherine.

"I can stretch it, no problem."

"I really would like to have a break. Can we stretch it to three?"

"Of course. Only two more sessions with this group. Which ones are you going to hold over for individual meetings?"

"Sara, of course. And I think Lee Ann. I'll know for sure after next week."

"Okay." Catherine stood. "It's late. Why don't you go home?"

"I just have a few more notes to make."

"Fine. Make them. Then go home."

Nicole stared after her, a little envious that Catherine had someone to go home to. Well, maybe not envious. It wasn't all that long ago that Nicole longed to go home to an empty house. Rachel had come to stay one weekend and never left. But even at the beginning, what she'd had with Rachel was never anything close to what she imagined a relationship would be like. In reality, Rachel was the first time she'd even tried. At first, she'd been so busy with school, she didn't want the complications of seriously dating someone. Then, when she was building her practice, she certainly never had time. Most of the dates she went out on now were discreetly set up by well-meaning friends. She felt like she'd been out with every eligible doctor and lawyer in the city. Unfortunately, second dates usually meant sex and so far, she'd been able to resist. None of them stirred her libido, and she just didn't see the point in faking it.

She twirled around in her chair, staring out the eighth floor window at the lights of downtown Denver. Now . . . now that she was settled in her practice, now that she was well respected in her profession . . . now, she felt the emptiness in her life. But after Rachel, God, she swore she'd *never* do that again. No. If she were to meet someone now, someone that she was attracted to enough to consider a second date, she would never live with them. In fact, she wondered how anyone found the courage to take that step.

The professional part of her knew that it was simply the dreadful experience with Rachel that deterred her. Well, that and the constant horror stories she heard about failed relationships turned violent.

She took a deep breath, forcing herself back to her desk and away from the lights of downtown. A vacation? She smiled. Yeah. One more week, then she'd get away. And reconnect, as Dorothy had said.

CHAPTER THREE

Jake stood on her porch, a blanket wrapped around her shoulders as she sipped hot coffee. Dawn had brought her outside and even though it was cold, she couldn't resist the sunrise. She leaned on her cane, head cocked slightly as she watched the first pink rays cross the mountain tops. Before long, the colors changed, the dark green of the pine and spruce trees nearly glowing as the light touched them. She stood still, her eyes fixed as the orange globe rose over the Collegiate Peaks, casting light and warmth over the mountains.

Cheyenne nudged her and whined softly. She gently brushed the dog's head.

"Hungry?"

A quiet whimper followed.

"Okay. Let's do breakfast. Then we've got to finish unpacking." She looked at the frosted windows of the Land Cruiser, knowing that she'd only managed to bring in the bare minimum yesterday. She'd been too tired to finish. But she felt much better this morning. In fact, she'd only had to take one pain pill. Hopefully, in a few days, a week, she could wean herself off them completely.

After a hot bowl of oatmeal and a scrambled egg, she showered and slipped on a thick pair of sweats. For wearing jeans, they had given her a padded bandage to put over her wound but with sweats, she didn't bother with the bandage. She stood and looked at her reflection in the mirror. It still startled her. She brought her hand up and rubbed across her head, the very short hair popping back into place. After a week of lying in the hospital with no one to wash her hair, she'd gotten pissed off and had a nurse call up a hairstylist. The dark hair that normally reached below her shoulders was gone in five minutes, replaced by a close crop that needed no brushing. She stared at herself, thinking that she actually liked it better this way. Definitely no fuss. But she'd always worn her hair long, going all the way back to college. Well, it was past time for a change. She rubbed her head one more time, then grabbed the cane, walking slowly through the cabin, Cheyenne right at her heels.

She knew the dog couldn't understand why they weren't out hiking. Normally, the first morning, they would have been out before dawn, hiking to the rock pile that overlooked the canyon behind Cumberland Pass. Across the canyon were the Collegiate Peaks. If she hiked high enough on Cumberland Pass, she could see all the way to Mt. Harvard. Actually, she could see six of the peaks at once. It was a favorite spot, but she knew she wouldn't be climbing up there on this trip. If fact, it would probably be awhile before she climbed it. But she would do some hiking. Her doctor told her that the best way to strengthen her leg was by walking.

"Come on, girl. Unload first, then a short hike."

Cheyenne cocked her head, her intelligent eyes staring directly into Jake's. It was at moments like this that Jake would swear the dog understood perfectly what she'd just said.

She made three trips from the Land Cruiser to the cabin, carrying as much in one hand each time as she could. With the other, she still used the cane for support. Most of her supplies consisted of food items and a fifty-pound bag of dog food. Having the young man at the grocery store load it for her was fine, but now, she was on her own. The dog food would have to stay in the truck. She'd have to get it little by little as she needed it. Again, she hated the helplessness that she felt at not being able to function as normal. But . . . at least she was alive. She squeezed her eyes shut, trying to get the image of the little boy from her mind. It had been haunting her. She'd had her standard sessions with the police shrink, and she'd lied her way through them. *Yes, it was tragic that the little boy had died but no, she didn't feel like it was her fault.*

"Yeah, right," she murmured. "Then whose fault was it?"

But she would deal with it herself, not on the couch of some shrink. Yes, goddamn it, she felt like it was her fault. She was the fucking cop, she was supposed to protect him. The fact that she took two bullets didn't matter. The little boy was still dead.

She took a deep breath, refusing to think about it. Right now, she wanted to get out in the forest and forget. She filled up a water bottle and clipped it to her waist pack, then checked her cell phone, surprised that she had service. Normally, she would turn the damn thing off while she was up here, but not now. In case . . . well, in case she fell or something, she could at least use it to call the local sheriff. She and Chad Beckett used to be poker buddies when she still worked in Gunnison. Wouldn't he get a kick out of her calling for a rescue?

Cheyenne was dancing at her feet, knowing the waist pack meant a hike. Jake nearly laughed, something she'd not come close to doing in the last month. "Let's go. Lead the way." That was all it took. Cheyenne was out the door in a flash, her bushy tail held high as she shot into the forest, following the trail that they always took.

Jake took her time, using the cane and trying to put as much weight as she could stand on her leg. It would be throbbing like hell by the time they got back, but that was okay. She needed this, even if it was only a short hike, she needed it. She'd been treated like an invalid for the past three weeks. She didn't care how much it hurt, she was going on a hike.

16

CHAPTER FOUR

Nicole leaned her pack against the rental car then looked inside one more time, making sure she hadn't forgotten anything. She manually locked the door and slammed it. The rental car was a dud, but she wasn't about to drive her Lexus down here and leave it parked for a week or more.

Struggling to lift the heavy pack onto her shoulders, she walked past the trailhead, pleased that hers was the only car in the tiny parking lot. She needed time alone and the last thing she wanted was to walk up on another hiker or two and have them ask her to join them. Even if she declined, they were obviously on the same trail. She remembered her last trip, four or five years ago, where she and another woman had crossed paths at least ten times over the course of five days. She finally gave up trying to avoid the woman and simply hiked with her the last day.

But not this trip. She would go off-trail if need be. This time, she craved solitude. And this late in the season, she would likely get it. Labor Day was right around the corner and the campgrounds would be full, but she doubted the backcountry would get that much activity. Checking her trail map one last time, she set out on the Colorado Trail, heading southwest to Cottonwood Pass. From there, she would take old Forest Service trails to the ghost town of St. Elmo. There was an old mining road that was now simply a trail. She would take that to reach Monarch Pass. Nicole figured five or six days to reach Monarch Pass, another two to hike down the mountain to the highway. Once she reached Salida, she'd grab a motel for a night, then hire a taxi to drive her back to Buena Vista and her rental car.

"Simple enough," she murmured. She shoved the map into the back pocket of her jeans, steadily climbing the trail that would take her high into the Collegiate Peaks mountain range. She hadn't been in this area in years. But with September only a few days away, she didn't want to chance a trip into the northern mountains and get caught in an early season snowstorm. So, she'd studied the map for a more southerly route. And the Collegiate Peaks, with their numerous hot springs, seemed the logical choice.

She felt a spring in her step and she actually smiled when she hit the first switchback. Switchbacks meant she was climbing and climbing meant she was leaving her life behind, if only for a week or so.

CHAPTER FIVE

Jake tried to stretch her leg and nearly cried out from the pain. She reached blindly for the pain pills beside the bed and swallowed two. Cheyenne shifted next to her, moving around on the bed until she rested her face on Jake's arm.

"It's okay, sweetie. Just too much hiking."

Cheyenne nudged her arm until Jake reached over to pet her, gently scratching behind her ear. "Spoiled rotten," she murmured.

A short while later, she felt the pain pills kicking in, and she finally relaxed. She'd felt so good after their short hike on Saturday that she thought they could hike down to the rock pile overlooking the canyon. The hike down was fine. It was the climb back up that nearly did her in. She wasn't afraid to admit that there were a couple of times that she wasn't sure she could make it. She had cursed herself last night as she lay soaking in the tub, trying to stem off some of the soreness she knew she'd feel. It was a stupid thing to do, and it would probably take her a whole day to get the strength back. But . . . she had time. Her eyes finally closed . . . the pain pills had taken hold. She threaded her fingers into Cheyenne's fur and fell asleep.

She held the gun tightly, finding him in her sights, but her hand trembled, she was shaking so. The boy was too close. Too close.

"He's going to shoot him," Perkins said as he knelt behind her.

"No he's not."

"Back off, bitch! I'll do it! I mean it."

"No! He's done nothing," she yelled.

"He's dead! I mean it," the man threatened.

Jake met his eyes. Even at this distance, she could see his fear, see his anger. She walked closer, her weapon still pointed squarely at him.

"Backup's coming," Perkins said urgently. "About fucking time."

They heard the sirens in the distance, and Jake saw the man's face twist in anger. "I said no more cops, bitch!" he yelled. He had the boy around the neck with his forearm and he pressed the gun to the boy's head, pulling him along as tried to round the corner into the alley.

Jake moved with him, staring him down. "You're not going anywhere," she yelled. "You're a dead man."

"Fuck you!"

Jake's eyes widened as she saw his index finger tighten on the trigger.

"No!" she yelled. She felt the perspiration drip down her face, could feel the rapid pounding of her heart. "Don't fucking do it!"

"Take him!" Perkins yelled as the boy screamed.

CHAPTER SIX

Nicole sat cross-legged on the boulder, staring toward the east as the sun finally showed itself, peeking above the mountains, chasing the shadows from the canyon and engulfing her in light. Her eyes widened as she took it all in. She hadn't realized how much she'd missed this, the simple pleasure of a sunrise on a clear morning in the Rockies. Amazing, but for the brief moments that it took for the sun to scale the highest peak, Nicole's mind had ceased its tumultuous churning and racing and simply stopped to enjoy the show.

Yes, this trip would be good for her. She'd ended her last session with the group only three days ago, holding over Sara and Lee Ann for future visits. The others she set up with support groups if they felt the need, but the last session told her that they'd accepted what had happened to them and were ready to move on. After ten weeks together, meeting three times a week and sharing the most intimate details of their lives, most of them had formed the bond necessary to be each other's support. Nicole knew that was one of the best benefits of doing group sessions. It produced long-lasting friendships that would endure long after their therapy ended.

But she didn't come up here to hash over her practice. She stood and brushed off her jeans, then went about the task of taking her tent down. The morning wasn't exceptionally cold, so she would forego coffee and a hot meal and make do with a breakfast bar instead. She was anxious to get on the trail and put as many miles between her and her life as possible.

She rolled her eyes. God, if Dorothy could hear her thoughts, she'd set her up for a counseling session in a minute. And it wasn't like she was really running from her life. In fact, she had a good life, a successful practice at a relatively young age, and she was well respected by her colleagues. She paused, looking up thoughtfully. *Was thirty-six considered young?* She shrugged. Young enough, and it didn't really matter. The point was, she had a good life.

Then why did it feel so . . . empty? She refused to even consider that being single contributed to her feelings. Lots of people were single. Not everyone had to have constant companionship to feel complete. She, of all people, should know that. But still, sometimes, she wished there was someone to confide in, share things with, *be* with.

And therein lay the problem. It had been so long since she'd been intimate with someone, she was afraid it had become a habit she couldn't break. Maybe she needed to take Catherine's advice and just let her hair down and . . . and what? Anonymous sex? Jesus, the very thing she preached against in her sessions! Besides, that just wasn't her. She was too . . . too conservative for that. She'd like to say that she was from the old school and wanted to have some sort of commitment before entering into a sexual relationship, but that wasn't really it.

"Hell, I'm shy, okay," she said out loud. *Jesus, now I'm talking to myself.*

Shy and . . . embarrassed. It was silly, and she knew it was silly but she still saw herself as the fat teenager with thick glasses *nobody* wanted to go out with, much less see naked! She'd poured herself into books instead of friends and graduated valedictorian, much to the dismay of Crissy Piper, who had wanted to add that to her long list of accomplishments, as if class president and head cheerleader weren't enough.

Nicole pulled the heavy backpack onto her shoulders and adjusted the straps, recalling their fifteen-year class reunion. She didn't know what possessed her to go, but she was awfully glad she had. There wasn't a single member of her high school class she'd kept in touch with, but her mother received the invitation and urged Nicole to go. Nicole knew it was mostly her mother wanting to show her off. The fat teenager had grown up. Nicole wasn't sure if her mother was more proud of the fact that she had "doctor" preceding her name or that she'd turned into a fitness freak with a toned body. Regardless, both caused quite a stir. That and the fact that Nicole now sported a chic blond hairstyle instead of the mousy brown ponytail of her childhood. She had seen the envious looks from her classmates and the appraising eyes of most of their husbands. Yes, she was awfully glad she'd gone. Especially when Crissy Piper showed up, looking every bit the married housewife and mother of three that she was.

As Nicole walked along the trail, she wondered why she was taking a trip down memory lane. It wasn't like those people were a part of her life. But the therapist in her knew that those years had shaped her life and because of them, she was who she was today. Corny, but true. Had she not been a fat teenager with glasses who got teased mercilessly, she may have been a cheerleader dating the quarterback and stayed in Grand Junction and gotten married instead of going to college. Well, that probably wouldn't have happened. She knew even back then that she was gay. She just didn't do anything about it. In fact, she didn't do anything about it until . . . *God, was I really twenty-four?*

"Suzette," she murmured dryly. They had been in medical school together. And to this day she's convinced it was her encounter with Suzette that caused her to abandon medical school and settle on psychology instead of psychiatry. Her world had been turned upside down, and she simply couldn't handle that and med school at the same time.

Again she rolled her eyes. Dorothy could have fun with her thoughts today. She might even make a case study. But she knew it wasn't really Suzette's fault. It was just a good excuse at the time. The reality was, she didn't want to be a physician. She wanted to be out helping people, counseling them. Not studying medicine.

Nicole stopped suddenly and looked around. She'd been hiking for over an hour and had been so lost in her thoughts that she had no idea where she was. Thankfully, she was at least still on the trail. Loosening the straps on her pack, she let it slide to the ground as she rested on a boulder the size of a small car. Unfolding the map, she spread it out across her thighs and tried to determine where she was. She hadn't started the switchbacks yet to climb to Cottonwood Pass. Moving her finger along the map, she found a small stream she would cross before climbing higher, and she was fairly certain she'd not crossed a stream. Surely she'd not been that out of it. After a quick drink of water, she again shouldered her pack and walked off, this time making a point to acknowledge her surroundings instead of getting lost inside her own mind.

CHAPTER SEVEN

"Drop your goddamn weapon!" she yelled.
"Come any closer and he's dead! You hear me?"
"Drop your fucking weapon . . . NOW!"

Jake sat up quickly, her heart racing. She touched her face, feeling tears still fresh on her cheeks, and she rubbed vigorously. The dream. Always the fucking dream. She wiped at her forehead, feeling the perspiration that had formed. Taking a deep breath, she lay back down, running her fingers through Cheyenne's fur to reassure the dog everything was okay. She'd hoped that the damn pain pill would knock her out enough so that she wouldn't dream. Sometimes, it did. But more often than not, the little boy would visit. She wondered how long it would be before she slept through the night. A part of her feared she'd never be able to sleep through the night again.

Rolling over onto her side, she reached under the covers and touched her wristwatch, checking the time. It was only three. Too early to get up but too late to try for a good night's sleep. She closed her eyes, willing sleep to come. But forty minutes later, she was still awake.

She tossed the covers off and, with difficulty, managed to swing her leg over the side. She sat there in the darkness, one hand absently rubbing along her thigh, feeling the scar tissue that remained after her surgery. Small price to pay. She could have lost the whole damn leg.

Cheyenne moved closer, nudging her with a cold, wet nose. Jake rubbed behind the dog's ear, wondering what she would have done these last few weeks if not for Cheyenne. She was a comforting presence, a silent presence. Every person in her life had asked the same question: Do you feel responsible for the little boy's death? Even those who didn't ask, she could still see the question in their eyes. The question and the accompanying sympathy. And in others, she saw relief. Relief that it was Jake who was first on the scene, not them. All but Rick. Her big, macho partner blamed himself. He should have stayed with her. But instead, he'd chased down a guy running from the scene, a supposed accomplice. He turned out to be an older cousin of the boy who was shot. By the time Rick caught him, gunshots were already sounding in the alley. He'd rushed back to Jake, only to find her shot and bleeding profusely . . . the uniformed officer Perkins and the little boy lying dead, not five feet apart. Perkins had taken a shot to the neck. The little boy, a single gunshot to the head.

Jake squeezed her eyes closed, trying so hard to forget that night, knowing that she never would. The hardest part was waiting. Waiting to find out if it was her bullet that had killed the little boy.

"Come on, girl. Let's have an early breakfast." Jake grabbed the nightstand next to the bed and used it to steady herself as she put weight on her leg. It was stiff but actually felt much better than she thought it would. Apparently the soak in the tub had done wonders. Reaching for the cane, she walked through the dark room and into the kitchen, flipping on the overhead light, then closing her eyes against the brightness. Cheyenne, too, turned away from the light. She walked into the living room and climbed upon the sofa, curling into a ball in one corner.

Jake lit the propane heater in the living room to chase away the early morning cold, then put coffee on. Leaning one hip against the counter as she waited, she surveyed the small cabin, her eyes lighting upon objects quickly, then moving on. The Navajo rug she'd picked up in Santa Fe years ago. The old wooden snow shoes that hung over the mantel, she'd found in an abandoned cabin high up in the Wet Mountains near the Spanish Peaks. Handmade pottery—vases and bowls—littered her bookshelves and tables. The few prints that adorned the walls were mountain scenes, painted by a local artist in Crested Butte. Jake had stumbled upon her studio one summer when she'd ridden her mountain bike from her cabin to the ski village some forty miles away. She was out of water and had gone begging. Serena, with her long shiny black hair, had offered her kitchen in the back of her studio. Jake smiled at the memory. She'd stayed three days.

"Oh, to be young again," she murmured lazily. She wondered if Serena was still around. Jake hadn't run into her in years.

The smell of coffee brought her thoughts back to the present, and with automatic motions, she poured coffee and added a teaspoon of sugar, closing her eyes as she sipped the hot liquid. It was far too early to plan her day, but at least she felt well enough to plan a day. Last night, as she'd struggled with the pain, she imagined she'd be laid up all day, recovering. But, as she flexed her leg, she thought she might even be up to a short hike.

Although, if it was as warm as it had been yesterday, she may simply choose the lawn chair on the deck and sit with a book, soaking up the sun while she still had the chance. Which would be fine. It wasn't like she made a habit of lounging on the deck.

She crossed over into the living room, turning on a lamp as she went. Cheyenne opened her eyes, then closed them just as quickly. Apparently, she hadn't recovered from the hike yesterday, either. Jake eased into the recliner and stretched her leg out, careful not to spill her coffee. She sat facing the large windows that over-looked the Collegiate Peaks. Still a couple of hours before day-light, she stared into the darkness, seeing nothing. It was at times like these that she was most frightened. Awake and alone with no distractions. In her mind, she saw the little boy's face, the scared look in his eyes. And later, the look on his mother's face, the tears, the accusing eyes. Telling herself that she'd done all she could do wasn't helping anymore. She was to blame. She should have taken a shot earlier. She shouldn't have tried to talk to the bastard.

Closing her eyes, she ran her hand over her injured leg, reminding herself that she hadn't come out totally unscathed. No, but she was still breathing. She leaned her head back, bits and pieces of that night flying through her mind in no particular order, the gunshots sounding just as loud in her mind as they had that night.

"Goddamn it," she whispered.

CHAPTER EIGHT

Nicole emerged from her tent well after daybreak, the sun already warming the day. She stretched her arms over her head and bent back, loosening up her tight muscles. She couldn't remember the last time she'd slept through the night. It had been glorious. And she wasn't in any hurry. No reason to get up at the crack of dawn and hit the trail. She had time to relax. She'd allotted seven or eight days for the trip but if that stretched to ten, no big deal. Catherine would cover for her.

She lit the small stove she carried and heated water for coffee and oatmeal. Sitting cross-legged on the ground, she looked overhead at the blue, blue sky and took a deep breath. Yes, she would take her time. And if the fates were being kind, she would stumble upon one of the many hot springs that dotted the Collegiate Peaks.

She could already envision it, stripping naked on the spot and submerging into a crystal clear, bubbling hot springs. "Heavenly," she murmured. She pulled the folded map from her jeans pocket and opened it, her eyes searching for the black dots that signified hot springs. They were more numerous around Mt. Princeton. More numerous and more populated. No, she was looking for something a little more secluded. And for that, she'd have to get off the Colorado Trail and . . . pick up Cottonwood Creek. The trail followed the canyon into the mountains, crossing over Cottonwood Creek six or eight times along the way. And she counted . . . four hot springs. From there, she could follow Ptarmigan Creek which met up with a Forest Service trail that would take her to Cottonwood Lake. She could pick up the main trail again there.

She picked up a small rock and turned it over in her hands. Two days. It would add at least two days to her trip. Was hiking out of the way to find four obscure little hot springs worth it?

"Absolutely."

CHAPTER NINE

"I know it doesn't look like it to you, but I am hurrying," Jake said, looking Cheyenne right in the eye. Yes, she swore the dog understood every word. Cheyenne cocked her head once, then walked on, turning back occasionally to make sure Jake was following her.

She'd decided on a relatively easy afternoon hike, one in which she might be able to catch the sunset over Cumberland Pass. That is, if she hurried. After only four days up here, her leg felt much stronger, but she continued to be cautious and use the cane. Especially out in the forest. One slip on a rock, and she'd go down. But it had felt really good that morning to walk around the cabin without the aid of the cane. It wouldn't be long, she knew. Whether or not she ever regained one hundred percent strength back, she had no idea. The doctors had seemed happy to tell her she'd walk again. And her physical therapist, although a little quirky, had pushed her hard. She was actually looking forward to seeing him again. She knew he'd be surprised at the progress she'd made.

But she didn't want to get ahead of herself. That was why, after the longer hike yesterday, she'd settled on a short, easy one today. Now, she paused at the base of the hill. An easy hike, except for this last part. It involved climbing nearly straight up to reach the ridge—the ridge and her sunset. Cheyenne was already up the trail, a trail Jake had made years ago when she'd first found the ridge. She hesitated, wondering if she should be satisfied right where she was. But the cirrus clouds overhead promised a colorful show.

So, with a determined effort, she put all of her weight on her left leg, pushing off the rock and holding onto the limbs of a young spruce as she brought her injured right leg up. She felt the shooting pain as soon as she put her weight on it, but she pulled herself up. Cheyenne, as if sensing her discomfort, came back down the trail, waiting.

"It's okay, girl," Jake murmured. "I'm still coming."

And one step at a time, she pulled her way to the top, managing to catch only the last pink rays as they reflected off the clouds. The sun had already disappeared. But it didn't matter. She'd made it. She slid down the side of a boulder, resting on the ground as she stared out to the west, watching the daylight begin to fade from the sky. She'd be hard-pressed to make it back to the cabin before dark, but again, it didn't matter. She felt a sense of accomplishment as she sat on top of the ridge. After just a few minutes rest, she made herself get up. If nothing else, she at least needed to make it back to the main trail before dusk.

But she need not have worried. The trip back down was easy and quick. Once back on level ground, she leaned heavily on the cane, following Cheyenne back to the cabin as darkness surrounded them.

And once safely back inside, she was pleased to notice that her appetite had returned. For the past three weeks, she had to force herself to eat. But tonight, she felt like . . .

"A steak."

She took a thick T-bone from the freezer and put it in the microwave to thaw as she drew her bathwater. Another hot soak, a steak on the grill, bottle of wine, maybe a few chapters of the mystery book she'd brought along. She felt almost like she was getting back to normal. And if she could sleep through the night, it'd be an added bonus.

CHAPTER TEN

Nicole stood at the small stream, looking in both directions, then back at the map. The trail on the map crossed over the stream and continued until it reached Cottonwood Creek. However, across this stream was . . . a mountain. Nicole leaned her head back, looking up high to the top of the peak, then back down to the little stream.

"Shit," she whispered. *Am I lost?*

She let her pack fall to the ground as she turned a circle, wondering where she'd taken a wrong turn. As she looked around, she noticed that she wasn't really on a trail anymore. This, obviously, was not Grizzly Gulch. "Christ." She unzipped a side pocket on her pack and pulled out her compass. Well, she was facing west. At least she thought she was. Turning a complete circle, she watched the compass needle turn with her. Yes, sure enough, she knew which direction was north. Great. And if she only knew where she was on the map, the fact that she knew where north was might help her. She'd been told numerous times that there was an art to using a compass. An art that she'd obviously not mastered.

"So I'm lost."

Saying the words out loud caused a mini panic attack, and she leaned back against the trunk of a Douglas fir and closed her eyes. She couldn't really be that lost. Surely. An hour ago, she would swear she'd been on the right trail. Or so she thought.

"Okay, okay. Talk it out. You're an educated woman. How hard can it be?" She pushed off the tree, pacing next to the bank of the tiny stream. "I'm on the east side of the Continental Divide, so, I would turn south and follow the stream. It's going to hook up with . . . maybe Grizzly Gulch." She looked at the map again. No, Grizzly Gulch should be . . . *God, like I know*. She rolled her eyes. "When in doubt, follow a stream. It's got to go somewhere. Or, you can backtrack." She looked behind her. If only there was a real trail to backtrack to.

She shouldered her pack again and started walking downstream, pleased to see that there was somewhat of a trail there along the bank. Apparently, she wasn't the only one to hit this dead end.

But an hour later, when the sun crept behind the mountain, leaving her in shadows, she felt another wave of panic. The trail was nonexistent and the creek was flowing steadily downward. It was slow going as she maneuvered over the rocks that littered the banks. And now that the sun's rays had left the canyon, she felt the evening chill.

"Couldn't walk upon a hot spring, could I? *No*."

Well, it was too early to stop for the day. There was at least another good hour of daylight left. Then she'd find a nice level spot in the forest to pitch her tent. Hopefully, she'd be too exhausted to worry about being lost. And surely to God, tomorrow, this creek would take her somewhere.

CHAPTER ELEVEN

A part of her knew she shouldn't be doing this. But the stubborn part, the part that won, would hear nothing of it. So, as Cheyenne danced excitedly around her, Jake added a couple of extra dinners to the pack, just in case. Two nights out on the trail, there was nothing wrong with that. She'd be careful. She'd take her damn cane.

It wasn't so much being out on the trail, it was the lure of the hot springs. She felt like Grizzly Gulch was her own personal spa. Few people knew of the springs and those who did found the hike difficult when coming up from the Colorado Trail. If they were smart, they would simply hike the Mt. Princeton trail. The hot springs along the river there were so numerous, if one was crowded, you simply moved downstream to the next. No, the hot springs that bubbled up along Grizzly Gulch were primitive and secluded. Only twice in the eleven years Jake had owned the cabin had she shared the springs. And once was with a black bear that chased her up a tree.

Pulling the backpack tight on her shoulders, Jake closed and locked the door to her cabin, then dutifully leaned on her cane as she walked down the three wooden steps that took her from the deck to the forest. She figured the normal four-hour hike to the springs would take six. Still plenty of time to get there before dark. Plenty of time to enjoy a soak before bedtime.

"Oh yeah, Cheyenne, we'll be living the good life tonight," she said, smiling as the dog tossed her a look before continuing down the trail. With luck, she added silently. Her leg felt pretty good. Not normal, certainly, but not the constant throbbing pain she'd felt the first three weeks. Still, part of her knew she was overdoing it. But even then, she didn't care. She just couldn't stand being confined.

So, instead of worrying about her leg and the subsequent aches and pains she'd feel after this hike, she focused instead on the mountains around her. After eleven years of hiking these trails, she knew every rock, every tree, and every mountain peak. It brought her a sense of peace that she could never explain to anyone else. It was the smell, the crispness of the air, the sounds of the birds, the whisper of the trees as the wind kissed them. All simple things, insignificant alone but playing off each other much like a well-rehearsed orchestra. Her footsteps on the rocks blended in with the other sounds and soon she was lost in the magnificence of it all. She forgot about her injury, she forgot about her dreams, she forgot about the damn job and just drifted away. Yes, this is what she'd hoped to find up here. Peace. For however long or however brief, she would embrace it.

Because once she left the mountains and went back to Denver, it would hit her full force. The shooting, the boy's death, the questions. And she would be ready to face them. All she needed was . . . a little time.

CHAPTER TWELVE

"Jesus Christ," she murmured. The wind coming off the water was biting and Nicole hurried, dutifully grabbing the toilet tissue she'd tossed aside as she pulled her jeans up. She had hoped for an early morning campfire to warm her up, but the wind was too strong, and she decided not to chance it. Instead, she'd have coffee and oatmeal and hit the trail.

"What trail?" she asked, unable to keep the sarcasm out of her voice. Of all the stupid things she could do, getting lost had to rank right up there. She liked to think that she had a general idea of where she was but, the truth was, she didn't have a clue. She was somewhere in the Collegiate Peaks Wilderness, of that she was certain. But the stream she was following? The compass said she was traveling southwest. The map showed streams going west and streams going south. There were no streams going southwest. *Obviously the map lied.*

But she would not panic. The stream had to go somewhere. And she had enough food for three weeks. So, there really wasn't a problem. She rolled her eyes. *Of course there is a problem! You're freakin' lost!*

Nonetheless, after a quick breakfast, she folded the tent and tied it to the bottom of her pack and bravely set out again, following the stream into the canyon. With luck, she'd hit a river or a larger stream that she could find on the map, and she might figure out where she was. If not, she'd hike the stream until she came to civilization or met another hiker. Which, again, surely to God, would be soon. Not that she was afraid of being alone. In fact, she liked nothing better than being alone in the mountains. Of course, that was when she knew where the hell she was. But, being lost like this, she had a strange feeling of being disconnected from the world. And a part of her wondered if that was such a bad thing.

Jake rested against a tree, leaning heavily on her cane. She could just make out the stream through the trees but knew she had a good half-hour hike to reach it. Closing her eyes, she rubbed her leg lightly. The throbbing had started nearly two hours ago.

"Maybe this wasn't such a good idea." Jake affectionately rubbed Cheyenne's head as the dog rested on her haunches next to Jake. Oh, she could make it down to the stream. That wasn't the problem. It would be the return trip home. Even if she stayed two nights at the springs, she still didn't think she could hike back to the cabin in one day. Mostly uphill . . . she'd be lucky to hike it in two days.

"Got nothing but time," she murmured. Giving Cheyenne a pat on the head, Jake pushed off the tree, grimacing as pain shot through her leg. "Goddamn," she whispered. She gripped the cane tighter, leaning heavily on it as she moved carefully down the mountain.

"Where the *fuck* am I?" Nicole whispered as she bent forward. She stood on a rock, watching as her little stream disappeared over the edge of the canyon and tumbled down some thirty or forty feet before landing in a beautiful spray of water and continuing on its way.

With an exasperated sigh, she shrugged off her backpack and let it fall as she rested against the trunk of a spruce tree. The map that she'd folded and unfolded a hundred times that day was spread out once again on her lap. Unfortunately, the topographical map didn't mark insignificant waterfalls on unnamed streams. She fingered the compass in her right hand, turning it over and over before looking at it. So she was facing south. And? She looked again at the map, shaking her head. She still had no idea where she was. She'd been in the mountains three days. Surely she couldn't be *that* far off course. Surely, she was following one of the hundreds of streams on the map.

Again, she tried to tell herself it didn't really matter. So she was lost. She had food, she had water . . . she had time. Might as well enjoy it. She found it funny, actually. Had she known exactly where she was on the map, she'd be enjoying herself a hell of a lot more. But since she didn't, that tiny, nagging panic attack that she'd managed to keep at bay was rearing its ugly head. She should be enjoying the solitude, the quiet, the peacefulness. Instead, she was studying the damn map, wondering where the hell she was.

"Well, forget it," she murmured. She hastily folded the map and shoved it back in her pocket, vowing once again to simply enjoy the mountains and not worry about where she was. Eventually, she would turn up somewhere. After all, Colorado wasn't *that* big.

With a clenched jaw, Jake took the last few steps down the trail, holding onto a tree limb as she balanced on a rock overlooking the stream. The fallen log she'd pulled up last year to help cross the stream with was gone. Apparently, last spring's snowmelt had flooded the stream, moving her log. On a good day, it wouldn't matter. She'd simply hop across the rocks to the other side, moving upstream to the hot springs.

"But it's not a good day."

Cheyenne was already in the water, splashing across to the other side, waiting expectantly. Jake studied the area, knowing that she couldn't cross here. Not with one bum leg. So, with the cane digging into the soft earth near the stream, she pulled herself farther upstream, using the trees for support. There was a natural pool around the hot springs. If nothing else, she'd hike upstream that far and simply walk across the flat rocks.

Easier said than done. This side of the stream was steep and rocky. The other side, the side that Cheyenne was walking along, flat and padded with spruce needles.

"Fuck it." She was tired and way past ready to submerge in the hot springs. So, using the cane to support herself, she stepped into the ice cold water, sinking to her knees as the mountain stream rushed by her. The current pulled at her and she used her left leg to brace against it as she moved slowly through the icy water to the other side. Her injured leg felt nearly numb as she maneuvered over the rocks, her thoughts simply on making it to the other side. Cheyenne waited anxiously as Jake pulled herself from the water. Her jeans were wet up to her thighs and the late afternoon shadows cast a chill over her as she limped after Cheyenne. The dog, as if sensing her pain, walked slowly, turning often to look at her.

"I'm okay, girl. Lead the way." Damn dog. Her intelligent eyes acknowledged that Jake was in pain. Jake didn't doubt that if the dog could talk, she'd have blasted her for making this trip in the first place.

The springs were as Jake had remembered. A large pool carved out of the stream, steam rising as the afternoon temperatures dropped into the forties. She felt a grin slash across her face at the sight of the springs. Yeah, she could easily spend the entire day tomorrow soaking. It was picture-perfect—the water, the steam, the trees surrounding the hot springs, the sun setting over the mountains.

Jake let her pack fall, bending to unlace her wet boots. She kicked them off and shed her jeans, walking toward the water as she pulled her shirt over her head. Stark naked, she limped to the edge of the pool, bending down to support herself as she pulled her right leg over the rocks and into the water.

"Oh . . . *God*," she murmured as she submerged up to her neck. She let out a satisfied moan as the hot water washed over her and she bent her head back, wetting her hair. She relaxed under the water, stretching her legs out in front of her and closing her tired eyes. The throbbing pain, constant for the last two hours, eased somewhat. Despite her vow that she didn't need pain pills any longer, she was thankful she'd brought them along. No doubt, she'd need one tonight.

Keeping her eyes closed, she listened to the water, hearing the constant roar of the waterfall farther upstream. Tomorrow, she'd hike to the falls. It was a beautiful sight, watching the water drop off the mountain some forty feet above her head, crashing on the rocks before continuing on its journey south. It was a beautiful sight, but, tucked way back here in the wilderness, few ever saw it.

Nicole spent the better part of the afternoon climbing down the canyon, trying to reconnect with the stream. She could hear it, she just couldn't get to it. The steepness of the canyon dictated her route, and on more than one occasion, she slipped, landing on her backside as she bounced down the rocks. But finally the rocks lessened, and the trees thickened as the ground leveled out. Resting, she got her bearings as she listened to the rush of water over the rocks.

She pushed on, walking toward the sound of water. It was nearly deafening as she approached the falls. Lifting her head up, her eyes followed the stream of water high up the canyon, finding the spot where she'd stood earlier that day, the spot where her small stream had disappeared. And ended down here.

"Wow." *Beautiful.* Nicole wasn't one to carry around a camera but she certainly wished she had one now. The sight was nearly breathtaking. *See, getting lost has its benefits.*

She stared a little longer at the falls, then moved on, feeling somewhat comforted by being next to the stream again. It, at least, was familiar. So, she followed its rocky bank, taking the time to admire the scenery around her; the sounds, the smells of the forest. Even though she was lost, she was determined not to waste this time. The day was too perfect.

Jake watched as Cheyenne raised her head, ears pointed forward as she stared upstream.

"We got company?" Jake asked quietly. Cheyenne growled low in her throat, then stood and walked quickly along the bank. Jake followed the dog with her eyes, finally seeing movement in the trees.

"Oh, shit," Nicole murmured as the large brown dog bounded up to her. She stood still, her earlier excitement of seeing steam rising from the water—a telltale sign of hot springs—vanished as she was being stalked by this . . . "Nice doggie. I hope."

It was only then that she saw someone in the water. Again, her elation at not only finding a hot spring but another human as well, was curbed by the curious dark eyes watching her.

Nicole froze as the dog walked closer, sniffing her pants and boots, then nudging her hand with a wet nose. "Please don't bite," she whispered. Finally, the dog shook herself and turned, trotting back to her owner. She watched as the woman in the springs reached out a hand and affectionately rubbed the dog's head. Nicole cleared her throat, deciding she better ask first instead of just walking over.

"Is it safe to come closer?" she yelled. "I mean, with the dog."

"Cheyenne won't hurt you."

Nicole stared. "I guess that's a yes, then," she murmured. As she walked closer, Nicole politely averted her eyes. The woman was naked, casually sitting on a rock as the water swirled around her waist. *Great. A naked woman. A naked woman with . . . perfect breasts.*

Nicole looked downstream, she looked at the dog, she looked at her own damn feet. Finally, she looked at the woman, struggling to keep her gaze from lingering. "I . . . I don't mean to intrude," she finally said. *Jesus! You'd think you've never seen a naked woman before!*

"You're not intruding. This is public land," the woman said. Nicole noticed the amusement in the woman's voice.

Nicole shifted uncomfortably. "Actually, I'm . . . well, I'm sort of lost."

"Oh, yeah?"

"Yeah." Nicole finally loosened the straps on her pack and let it fall to the ground behind her. "Actually, I'm really lost. I'm assuming I'm still in Colorado. Other than that, I don't have a clue."

The woman's laughter rang out, and Nicole relaxed for the first time in what seemed like days. "I've been following this stream for two days."

"Grizzly Gulch."

"This *is* Grizzly Gulch then?"

"Yep."

"The map showed the trail crossing over Grizzly Gulch and continuing on until it reached Cottonwood Creek. But when I got to Grizzly Gulch, there was a mountain on the other side. No trail."

"Maps have been known to be wrong." The woman shifted off her rock and submerged under the warm water, a satisfied look on her face as she resurfaced. "Why don't you join me? There's not much daylight left."

Nicole hesitated. A few hours ago, she would have given her right arm to walk up on some hot springs. But that didn't involve stripping naked in front of a stranger. A quite attractive stranger with . . . perfect breasts.

"If you're shy, I'll turn my back," the woman offered.

"That'd be nice," Nicole said. "Thank you." *Jesus, you're being silly*. But as the woman dutifully turned her back, Nicole wasted no time in stripping off her clothes, dropping them in a neat pile next to her pack. As she walked into the water, the dog watched her every move. She had no doubt that, if instructed, the animal would attack. So, she slowly reached out and petted the dog's head, pleased that it didn't bite. She settled into the warm water, a quiet moan escaping before she could stop it. "You can turn around now."

"Great, huh?"

"More than great. I've been dreaming of this for three nights. That's the reason I'm lost."

"Oh, yeah?"

"I had this bright idea to leave the main trail in search of hot springs." Nicole stretched out, not caring that the crystal clear water did little to cover her. She dipped her head under water, smoothing the hair away from her face as she surfaced. "Two days of being lost is well worth it." Then she smiled. "Provided, of course, that you tell me where we are."

Again, the woman laughed, and Nicole couldn't help but stare. Her hair was cut short, brutally short. But it did little to distract from the attractive face. In fact, it most likely enhanced the woman's features. Clean, smooth complexion, nicely tanned for this time of year, dark eyes framed by thick eyelashes, and full lips turned up now in a smile. *Jesus, Nicole, can you get any more obvious?*

"We are between Cottonwood Pass and St. Elmo."

"St. Elmo? The ghost town?"

"Yes. A good three-day hike."

"My original plan was to hike the Colorado Trail to the base of Mt. Princeton and then head up the mountain to St. Elmo."

"Lots of hot springs around Mt. Princeton."

"Yes. But I was looking for solitude."

The woman shrugged. "Sorry."

"Anyway, I didn't count on getting lost. Once I made St. Elmo, I was going to hike around Mt. Shavano to the highway and down to Salida."

"That's quite a trip. Especially alone."

"Yes it is." Nicole looked away, sinking a little lower in the water. "But I needed some time alone." She felt the woman watching her, but she didn't care. The water felt too good, and she closed her eyes, sinking below the surface, letting the warm water surround her. When she lifted her head out of the water and slicked her hair back, the woman had moved away. Nicole watched as she rose out of the water, catching her breath as the woman stood, water dripping lazily off her body. Nicole's eyes, of their own accord, traveled down the sculpted body, resting briefly on the . . . *Jesus* . . . nicest ass she'd ever seen. *You're a pig.*

"I'll give you some privacy, since you wanted to be alone," the woman said. "I'll get a fire going."

Nicole wanted to protest, but she'd lost her voice. The woman was . . . beautiful. She told herself it was extremely impolite, but still she stared. Long legs moved through the water and the woman sat on the ledge, swinging both legs out of the water at the same time. Nicole frowned, catching a glimpse of a red scar. Then the woman moved, standing on the bank, water dripping from her body. Nicole tried to summon just a small portion of her professional side and failed miserably. Unabashedly, she stared, eyes moving over the well-toned body, resting again on the nicely rounded backside.

"There's plenty of room for two tents. You're planning on camping here, right?"

"If you don't mind."

The woman nodded and walked away, still naked, clutching her clothes to her body. Nicole noticed the slight limp and dutifully turned her eyes as the woman bent over to retrieve her backpack and a cane. The dog walked obediently beside her, following the woman into the forest.

"What is wrong with you?" Nicole whispered as she turned away from the woman. *God, try to act like you're not a total idiot!*

Jake tugged sweatpants from her pack and slipped them on. From the side pouch, she pulled out thick socks and her moccasins. The warmth she'd enjoyed in the springs faded as soon as the cool, crisp air hit her. She unrolled her tent, using the cane to steady herself as the clasped the rods to the ends.

Unable to stop them, she found her eyes wandering to the naked woman frolicking in the hot springs. *Her* hot springs. "She's cute, Cheyenne. Don't you think?"

Cute . . . and damn sexy. You could tell a lot about a woman when she was soaking wet. And with the blonde hair slicked back from her face, the woman appeared nearly angelic. Flawless skin, sparkling blue eyes. And even though Jake had turned her back while the woman undressed, she'd managed a quick peek before the woman sunk under the water. And that quick peek afforded her a lovely sight of a small, yet muscular frame. Yes, there was nothing like soaking with a naked woman.

"You're such a guy sometimes," she murmured. Even so, she still stared as the woman rose from the water and hastily pulled on her shirt over her still-wet torso. Like Jake, she searched in her pack for something, pulling out gray sweats much like the ones Jake was wearing. Jake swallowed hard, watching as the woman pulled the sweats over her naked body. "Cheyenne, did you see that?"

It was then that she realized that she hadn't even started gathering wood yet. She'd been leaning on her cane . . . staring. She finally turned away, walking under the trees in search of fallen limbs. There were plenty. However, bending over and grabbing them was easier than it looked. She was struggling with the first piece when the woman spoke next to her.

"Maybe you should let me do that."

Jake wanted to protest. She wasn't a fucking invalid. But, the woman, this stranger, was only offering a helping hand. "Yeah. Kinda hard to maneuver with the cane."

The woman bent down and collected an armful of sticks and a larger limb. She dumped them near the fire ring, then went back for more. Jake felt the woman watching her as she broke up the sticks and piled them on top of the pinecones she'd already tossed in. Any minute now, she's going to ask, Jake mused.

The woman came back, dumping another armload beside the others. Jake looked up and smiled. "Thanks. This ought to last us."

"I take it you've camped here before. This spot looks well-used."

"Yeah. I camp here quite a bit. Actually, I've got a cabin over near Cumberland Pass. It's about a four-hour hike, on a good day."

"Wow. That must be great. Do you live there?"

"No."

The woman nodded then hesitated. Finally, "I couldn't help but notice your limp. A four-hour hike must be difficult."

"Like I said, that's on a good day. It took me six hours today."

"Forgive me for asking, but what happened? You seem incredibly fit. Is it a recent injury?"

Jake nodded. "Yeah, I . . . I was in an accident. Had surgery on my leg. But it's coming along."

Nicole had been in enough sessions to know when someone didn't want to talk. Which was fine. Nicole wasn't exactly in the listening mood. However, she did want to know the woman's name.

"I'm Nicole, by the way. I just realized that I don't know your name."

"Jake."

"Jake?" Nicole raised an eyebrow. "Either your mother hated you or they really, really wanted a boy."

Jake laughed. "Some of the kids I hung around with in the sixth grade gave me the name. My mother detested it."

"What's your given name?"

"No, no, no," Jake said, shaking her head. "That's not something I say out loud."

"Can't be that bad."

"Oh, yes, it can be. I had my name legally changed when I was twenty."

"To *Jake*?"

She shrugged. "It's what I've been called since the sixth grade."

Nicole noticed that the entire time Jake spoke, her hand was threading through the dog's fur. She didn't want to analyze, hell, she was on vacation. But, she suspected the woman was single and childless, and the dog was her constant companion. Judging by the protectiveness of the dog, who was leaning against Jake's leg, it was a mutual affection.

"I don't know about you, but I'm starved," Jake said.

She got to her feet with the aid of her cane, and Nicole had to force herself not to hop up and assist her. She sensed that the injury was fairly new, and no doubt the woman was struggling to regain her independence. Why else would she hike six hours through the mountains? So, instead of offering help, Nicole went to her own tent. She always packed her favorite meals, and she debated between the stroganoff and the chicken spaghetti. The stroganoff won. When she returned to the campfire, Jake was already lighting her stove, with a small pot full of water sitting nearby.

Nicole sat on the opposite side of the fire and attached the small propane canister to her own stove, occasionally glancing up at the other woman as she poured water into a pot. She finally sat down on the ground, crossing her legs. Through the smoke of the fire, she watched Jake. She was a striking woman. Tall, lean . . . powerful looking, even stark naked. *Especially stark naked.* Her smooth face and full lips had Nicole mesmerized. As her gaze lifted higher, dark eyes captured her own and refused to let go. Through the smoke of the small fire, their eyes locked and, for the first time in her life, Nicole was afraid of another woman. Not physically afraid, but, with difficulty, she pulled her eyes away, impatiently tucking her still-damp hair behind her ears. It occurred to her then that had she met this woman in the city, Nicole wouldn't have given her a second look. Not that she wasn't attractive, she just wasn't Nicole's type. Nicole tended to date professional women, like herself, whose appearance didn't scream *lesbian*. She wondered why, then, she found this woman physically attractive if she wasn't her type.

Jake lifted a corner of her mouth in a smile as Nicole turned away. If she were so inclined—and had the energy—this impromptu camping trip could turn out to be fun. There was just something about sharing an intimacy with a total stranger. No inhibitions, no worries. Just . . . sex. Well, perhaps she was being a bit presumptuous about this woman. You couldn't put a whole lot of stock into looks. But still, pain pills and fatigue weren't the best ingredients for a brief, anonymous sexual encounter. The mind might be willing, but the body was definitely dragging.

Well, it didn't matter. For all her professed desire to spend some much-needed time alone, she found the other woman's company enjoyable. And that was enough.

"How long have you been on the trails?" Jake asked, startling Nicole.

"This is day four. I think. Being lost sort of turned days into weeks."

Jake nodded. "I can imagine. Although I don't recall ever being lost."

"No? There is a well-marked trail from your cabin, six hours away?"

Jake smiled. "No trail."

"Then how on earth did you find this?"

"I found it about ten years ago. I had hiked all around the cabin, up to Cumberland Pass. I knew the area pretty well. The topo maps from the Forest Service are pretty good, if you can use a compass."

Nicole rolled her eyes. *Of course.*

"I wanted to find some hot springs that were relatively close, but still off the beaten path. It took me three days to find these. But they're beautiful. And in ten years, you are only the second person I've ever seen here."

"You're kidding? You mean I'm *that* far off a trail?"

"Well, yeah. You're two days from a trail."

"So, this is all really your own private resort?"

Jake grinned. "I like to think of it as my private spa." Jake pointed upstream, where the constant roar of the falls had faded into the background. "You came by way of the falls?"

"Yeah. I was following the stream. When it tumbled over the side, I almost went with it. It took me several hours to find a way down the mountain and into the canyon. But I didn't want to lose the stream."

"Yes. It's a steep drop. But beautiful."

"Oh, very. And if I wasn't so concerned with being lost, I think I would have camped there, by the falls."

Jake put another small log on the fire, then stirred the embers. "If you're up for a little hike in the morning, the falls are great for sunrise." Jake pointed over her shoulder. "There's a gap in the mountains where the sun shines through. It hits the water perfectly. The colors are out of this world. Every time I see it, I always wish I could paint."

"Camera?"

Jake nodded. "I've taken several shots, at different times of year. But it's never the same as seeing it in person."

Nicole smiled across the fire. "I think I'd like to take a look. Of course, that would mean being *up* by sunrise."

"I won't have that problem. Because after I eat, I think I could lay down and sleep the night through."

"Does your leg stiffen up?" Nicole asked.

Jake shrugged. "Some."

Ahh. Off limits. Okay. Instead, Nicole lifted the lid on her dinner, satisfied that it was done. She turned her stove off, watching as Jake did the same.

"What about Cheyenne?" Nicole asked. The dog was staring intently at Jake's food.

"Yeah. I usually split it with her." Jake reached behind her and pulled over a canvas pouch. Inside was a dog bowl and some dry food. She filled the bowl, then added part of her dinner to it. Cheyenne sat obediently, never taking her eyes from the bowl. "Spoiled," Jake whispered.

Nicole saw the tail wag and wondered what Jake had said. Obviously, the dog understood. "She's very pretty."

"Yeah, she's a good dog. Smartest dog I've ever seen."

"How old is she?"

"She's only two. And you don't need to be afraid of her. She won't hurt you." Then Jake grinned. "Not unless I tell her to."

Nicole smiled, too. "So, I need to stay on your good side?"

Jake was about to say she didn't really have a good side, but no sense scaring the poor girl. Besides, a month ago, she did have a good side. But, well, the shooting had pretty much ended that. She closed her eyes for a second, then forced them open, meeting the pleasant blue ones across from her.

"How's your dinner?"

Nicole looked at the untouched pot in her lap and twirled her fork a few times before stabbing some noodles. You're on vacation, she told herself. Don't meddle. But the nearly pained expression on the woman's face made Nicole want to ask a hundred questions. But she didn't. And Catherine would be very proud of her. For once, she shoved her professional side away and tried to simply enjoy the evening, the campfire, the outdoors, and the company of this very attractive woman.

"It's good," she said as she chewed. "Yours?"

Jake shrugged. "Cheyenne appears to like it." Jake twirled her own fork in the fettuccini and took a bite. It tasted like freeze-dried fettuccini.

"You should try this beef stroganoff. I swear, I can't tell the difference between this and homemade."

Jake peered across the fire, eyebrows raised. Nicole finally offered her pot and Jake stole a forkful of noodles.

"Good," she murmured. "Better than mine."

Nicole smiled. "All we're missing is a good bottle of wine."

"Yes, that would be nice." Jake took a couple more bites, then emptied the rest into Cheyenne's bowl.

"Was it that bad?"

"Wasn't great. But I took a pain pill earlier. It kinda kills my appetite."

Nicole glanced at the woman's outstretched leg. "Is there anything I can do?"

"No. I'm fine. It's just the hike today was probably too much. I'll hang out here tomorrow and soak and rest it."

Nicole stood up. "At least let me wash out your pot. I'll take it with mine."

Jake protested. "No, you don't need to do that. I can get it."

Nicole took the pot anyway. "I'm sure you can."

Jake watched her walk away to the stream, feeling the heaviness of her eyes as she attempted to remain focused. Damn pain pill. She struggled to stand, using her cane to push herself up. Her leg hadn't felt this bad since . . . well, since she got out of the hospital and started walking again. Hopefully, after a day of rest tomorrow, the pain and stiffness would subside. And, she would hike back to her cabin in two days, not one.

"Need some help?"

Jake turned her head, quickly meeting Nicole's eyes before looking away. "No, thanks. I'm going to turn in. Please make sure the fire is out."

"Of course."

Jake knew she sounded abrupt, and it had nothing to do with the other woman. She just hated feeling dependent on anyone and appearing weak. So, she paused at her tent, looking back at Nicole. "Don't forget our date in the morning."

Nicole flashed a smile and nodded. "Sunrise." Her smile faded as she watched Jake struggle to get into the small tent. Cheyenne sat patiently outside until Jake was in, then, with a wag of her tail, followed the woman inside.

Nicole couldn't understand why some people were so fiercely independent that they wouldn't accept help from anyone, regardless of the circumstances. And she imagined this woman fit that mold perfectly. Well, she wouldn't push. If the woman wanted to struggle to get up instead of accepting a helping hand, that was her business.

But it was eerily quiet now that the woman and dog were gone. Beyond the crackle of the fire, the constant roar of the falls seemed almost muted by the darkness. The breeze that had been blowing down the canyon all day had subsided, and she leaned back slightly, her eyes following the smoke of their fire as it rose into the night, disappearing in the trees.

CHAPTER THIRTEEN

Jake stretched, then cautiously rolled over, careful not to bump her leg. She'd slept like a rock. Apparently, the exertion from the hike and the pain pill had been enough to keep the damn dream away. For one night, at least.

Sitting up, she rubbed her face with both hands, then unzipped the tent. It was still dark. Plenty of time for coffee before they attempted the short hike to the falls. She slid her cane out of the tent with her, using it to stand. Surprisingly, her leg, although stiff, felt pretty good. She couldn't say the same for her head. She always felt hazy the morning after a pain pill. But, coffee and a hike usually brought her around.

She put water on to boil, then took a discreet trip into the woods. No sense squatting too close. Wouldn't want the woman surprised by her bare ass this early in the morning. But Jake needn't have worried. The woman's tent was still zipped.

It would only take them fifteen minutes to reach the falls. So, she decided not to wake Nicole just yet. She'd take the time for a quick bath and enjoy a few more minutes of solitude. This was always her favorite part, listening . . . waiting for the sounds of morning. The first bird, the first chipmunk. So much more relaxing than meaningless conversation with a complete stranger. Cheyenne nudged her, and Jake automatically reached out a hand, rubbing her ear. Yeah, nothing like a near-death experience to make you appreciate the little things that nature offered. It was a cliché, but it was also true.

Finally, when the water was boiling and the darkness just starting to leave the sky, Jake got to her feet, limping only slightly as she walked to Nicole's tent. She grabbed hold of one pole and tugged.

"Hey. Coffee's ready."

Jake smiled as she was greeted with a groan. She heard the rustling of the sleeping bag and imagined the other woman sitting up.

"Are you sure it's morning?"

"Pretty sure. But if you're not up to a hike, don't worry about it."

"No, no. I want to go."

Nicole heard Jake walk away, and she lay back down, wondering why she'd agreed to this. She wasn't a morning person and if she missed a sunrise or three, well, so be it. But Jake had promised this would be a feast for the eyes, so Nicole tossed off the warm sleeping bag and got up. She tried to tame her hair with her fingers and gave up, settling on tying it back and slipping on a fashionable ball cap instead.

Jake was already sipping coffee, and Nicole squatted down next to her, adding a spoonful of instant coffee to her cup before pouring the hot water in. She raised her eyes, wondering how this woman could look so fresh and clean after just crawling from a tent. Nicole looked at her own clothes, noting the dirty jeans that should have been retired days ago. But she only had one other clean pair. She planned on donning them when she resumed her trip. Jake, on the other hand, sported clean jeans. Faded, baggy and comfortable looking. Even the long-sleeved T-shirt was immaculate.

Don't I feel quite the trail bum?

"Why do you look like you've just emerged from a shower, clean clothes and all," Nicole said, waving her hand at Jake's wardrobe, "And I look like I've been on the trail for a week?"

Jake flashed a smile. "Because I packed one set of clean clothes, these being them, and you *have* been on the trail for nearly a week."

"And the shower part?"

"Hot springs."

"Brushed your teeth?"

"Of course."

Nicole groaned. "God, I feel like a slob."

"Well, after our hike, feel free to bathe. I'll give you some privacy."

"That would be great. Although, these are *your* springs. I really hate that I'm intruding."

Jake shook her head. "I really don't mind the company," she said, surprised that it was the truth. "I'm just going to hang out here today and rest. Tomorrow I'll pack up and head back to my cabin. You're welcome to stay here as long as you like."

Part of her, the polite part, knew that she should be on her way and leave this woman in peace. But the other part, the part that won, wanted nothing more than to hang out here another day and soak in the hot springs. The fact that an attractive woman, an attractive, *naked* woman, would be sharing those springs didn't hurt. And, the fact that Nicole was even considering that as a reason for staying, startled her. This was so out of character for her. Perhaps, she thought, Catherine was right. She just needed to let her hair down and . . . and what? She met the dark eyes looking back at her, and she wondered what Jake's reaction would be if she simply leaned closer and kissed her. God, those full lips were practically begging her to do just that. She finally came to her senses, pulling her eyes away before she made a complete ass of herself.

Jake was surprised at what she saw in the other woman's eyes.

Although brief, she hadn't missed the blatant desire that flashed across Nicole's face. She smiled. It could be an interesting day. So, she leaned forward, her voice low.

"You want to stay with me today . . . and play?"

Without warning, all of Nicole's blood rushed to a long dormant part of her anatomy, causing her breath to catch. The nearly whispered question hung between them, and Nicole again found her eyes captured. She felt herself nodding, unable to speak.

"Good." Jake finally released the blue eyes, surprised at the quickened pace of her pulse. Yes, it could be a very interesting day. She tossed out the rest of her coffee and stood, holding out a hand to Nicole. "Let me show you a beautiful sunrise."

Nicole stared at that hand, noting, in a matter of seconds, the clean, neat nails, the smooth skin, the tiny scar on her thumb. Then she slid her own into it, letting herself be pulled up. She wasn't quite sure what was happening. A few minutes ago, they had been calmly discussing bathing. And now, without a single word spoken, there was an electricity between them, an underlying sense of physical attraction that seemed suddenly to have exploded around them. Her skin felt alive, her senses heightened. Every breath she took, every sound she heard seemed exaggerated. She found herself falling into those eyes, wondering what the day would bring. Then, with a quick squeeze, her hand was released and it fell nimbly to her side. Jake bent and retrieved her cane, then walked away, leaving Nicole to follow. And follow, she did, her eyes never leaving the enticing figure in front of her. Out of character? Most certainly. But, she figured she was entitled to a little craziness once in a while.

Cheyenne led the way to the falls, turning around often to make sure she was being followed. Jake walked along the shore, using her cane as needed but pleased that her leg was holding up as well as it was. Nicole followed, walking silently behind the two, her eyes darting between the dog, the water, and the intimidating woman.

Rolling her eyes, she halfway convinced herself that she'd imagined the whole thing. Jake was simply being polite when she'd invited her to stay the day. There was nothing more to it. But then *why* was every nerve ending standing at attention?

"You're being awfully quiet," Jake stated without turning around.

The voice startled Nicole, and she nearly tripped on a rock. She gathered her thoughts before speaking, her eyes never wavering from the lean body before her. "I'm just enjoying the scenery," she said.

"I guess it's different than what you saw yesterday, eh?"

Nicole blushed crimson, thankful that the other woman had not turned around. "I was so concerned with being lost yesterday, I hardly remember this at all." And it was true. Yesterday was positively a blur. She remembered the hike down the canyon. She remembered the falls. And she certainly remembered seeing Jake for the first time. But here, now, with dawn just breaking around them, nothing looked familiar, nothing felt familiar. And perhaps it was fitting, seeing as how she didn't *feel* familiar, either. Her thoughts were still running in a decidedly intimate direction. And that was something she could not shake.

"You hear them?"

"Yes."

"We'll be just in time," Jake said. "See how the mountains are shining? The sun will peek over in a minute."

Nicole stared where she pointed, seeing the glow between the two mountains, the gap that Jake had spoken of. She suddenly became aware of the birds singing, the gentle rustle of the trees, the water as it flowed past them. Sounds that had been there all along but sounds that she had not allowed to penetrate. She'd been too concerned with what was happening between them that she'd lost the peace around her. She paused, noting that Jake had stopped and was looking into the trees, eyes closed. No, Jake had not lost it. She was still focused, still absorbing. And Nicole envied her. Apparently, whatever was happening between them had not affected Jake in the same way. She still seemed to be normal. She still seemed to be . . . intact.

"You love it here, don't you," Nicole whispered, not even aware that she'd been thinking the words, much less uttering them.

"Yeah, I do. This is paradise." Jake turned around and faced Nicole. "At least, paradise to me."

Nicole didn't even try to fight as Jake captured her eyes. She went willingly. Then Jake moved, pointing, and Nicole's eyes followed.

"Watch," Jake whispered.

They were standing within ten feet of the falls, close enough to feel the spray of the water as it hit and scattered along the boulders. Nicole stood shoulder to shoulder with Jake, following her direction as she stared into the falls, waiting for the sun to strike.

"Almost there," Jake whispered.

Nicole felt her breath catch, and she wasn't sure if it was from the anticipation of the sunrise or from the warm hand that had captured hers. Regardless, both took her breath away.

The falls positively shimmered in colors as the sun hit—reds, oranges, pinks and even a deep purple shot through the water, all exploding as the falls crashed on the rocks, sending the various hues down the stream. For a second, Nicole felt like dropping to her knees with the beauty of it. She stared, her hand squeezing tight with Jake's, almost embarrassed by the tears that had formed in her eyes.

"Oh my God," she whispered.

"I know," Jake murmured. It was the first time she'd shared this sight with anyone. She was pleased Nicole found the same beauty that she did. But in a matter of seconds, as the sun rose higher, the colors changed, dimming and then fading until you questioned whether you'd seen them at all.

"Jake, that was incredible." Nicole turned, finding Jake watching. "It was one of the most beautiful things I've ever witnessed."

Jake nodded then looked back to the falls. "It's almost . . . spiritual, if you believe in that sort of thing."

"And do you?"

"At times like this, yeah." Then she dropped Nicole's hand and looked away. "Of course, real life tends to throw a kink into that sometimes, makes you question it all."

Nicole left her questions unasked as Jake tapped her cane a few times on a rock before turning back. Cheyenne circled both women, then headed back downstream, tail held high as they followed in silence.

Just as their tents came into view, Jake stopped. "Why don't you go on and enjoy that bath you were talking about," Jake offered. "Cheyenne and I will collect some firewood for tonight."

Nicole looked at Jake, then down to the springs, which beckoned. "You don't mind?"

The slow smile that formed on Jake's lips caused Nicole's pulse to race, and she cursed herself for acting like a total fool.

"I don't mind at all. In fact, I'll join you in a bit, if that's okay?"

Nicole held her gaze, knowing that her words meant she'd be *joining* her. And that was okay. Nicole was more than ready. So, she nodded, dragging her eyes away from the other woman, knowing she was coming close to acting like the teenager she felt! She walked purposefully to the tents, refusing to turn back, knowing that Jake was watching her. Then she frowned. Perhaps the other woman was looking for some sign, some acknowledgment that her message had been received. *God, do I feel stupid. What if I'm just way off base? Don't be silly.* She finally turned, finding Jake's eyes still on her. No, she wasn't off base.

Jake bent down, collecting firewood, pleased that her leg was holding up. Still sore from the long hike yesterday, but the recovery time after each excursion was getting shorter and shorter. She was convinced that in another week or so, she'd be back to normal.

And despite her best resolve not to look, she found her eyes searching the springs, waiting for Nicole to bathe. She knew their exchange of earlier was not imagined, but still, intuition told her that Nicole would never initiate anything physical between them.

But she wouldn't have to. Jake could read a woman's eyes, and what she saw in Nicole's was nearly smoldering.

They were both adults, both apparently willing. There was absolutely no reason they couldn't share an afternoon of sex. And, truthfully, this was the first time sex had even crossed Jake's mind in well over a month. Oh, last week before she'd come up here, Heather had come by with the excuse of making sure Jake was managing since her surgery. But Heather, although totally fun in bed, was ten years younger and, quite frankly, more than Jake could handle with a bum leg. So, she'd sent Heather away with a promise to call her when she was back on her feet.

But Nicole was sexy as hell with wet hair and had a body that was nearly sculpted. Jake wasn't afraid to admit that she was attracted to her even though she normally shied away from athletic-looking women. She preferred the more feminine bodies. But, damn, Nicole's body, although muscular, was nearly perfect. And she was attracted to her. So, up here in the mountains, alone, there was no reason she couldn't explore that attraction. It made perfect sense to Jake. Of course, provided Nicole was willing. And that look in her eyes told Jake she was willing.

So, as she bent to pick up another limb, her eyes scanned the stream, stopping when she spotted the blond-haired woman rinsing out her hair.

"Oh, Cheyenne, that woman stirs something, you know?" At the dog's questioning look, Jake ruffled her fur and walked on.

Nicole dipped below the water, rinsing her biodegradable soap from her hair. She always felt guilty when bathing in the streams. Numerous people had told her over the years that biodegradable soap was no better for the environment than regular soap. But, Jesus, a girl had to bathe. And especially today.

She had a moment of panic, of her nerves trying to get the better of her, but she pushed it aside. She was an adult, for God's sake. If she wanted to partake of some afternoon delight—*God, that's pathetic*—then why should she feel ashamed or embarrassed by it? It wasn't like scores of women didn't do it. And this was with a stranger. She'd never have to see her again. One day of wild sex, as Catherine would say, then they'd go their separate ways. And she wouldn't have to even tell anyone. But she grinned as she dipped once again under the water. Oh, she'd tell Catherine. Catherine would be proud of her.

But when she finished bathing, Jake was nowhere in sight. Perhaps she had misread the other woman. And she was oddly disappointed. She stood, putting her toiletries back in her case and leaving them on a rock. She walked back upstream to where the main pool was, careful not to slip on the rocks. The warmer water felt good on her skin after her bath. She submerged, letting the water envelope her for a second before rising to the surface. Slicking the hair back from her face, she moved to a rock to catch the sun. A small part of her acknowledged that she should feel self-conscious, sitting there totally naked. But she felt free and uninhibited. For one of the few times in her adult life, she wasn't concerned with what someone might think of her or say about her. She simply was. She was out here in the mountains, she was sitting in the middle of some hot springs, she was . . . wishing that the gorgeous woman she was camping with would come and ravish her.

She opened her eyes, staring, as if her thoughts had conjured up this vision. But Jake was walking slowly to the springs, eyes locked tight on Nicole's. Nicole swallowed nervously, watching as Jake reached down and pulled the long-sleeved T-shirt over her head in one motion, revealing those perfect breasts. Nicole felt her heart clutch, her breath catching in her throat as faded jeans were removed and lowered, sliding slowly down firm, tanned legs, only the scar there to mar perfection. Nicole realized she wasn't breathing as Jake stepped into the springs and walked closer.

Jake's heart was pounding as she waded through the water, eyes still locked on Nicole's. She saw no surprise or shock in those blue eyes, only desire. Desire for her. She didn't stop, she simply walked closer, pausing only when they were nearly touching. Without speaking, she took Nicole's hand and pulled her into the water. They stood facing, water only to their waists. Jake stared at the pulse pounding in Nicole's throat and realized that her own was beating a similar rhythm.

She slowly reached out, nearly embarrassed by her trembling hand, and laid gentle fingertips against one of Nicole's breasts. The other woman flinched slightly, then relaxed. Jake's eyes followed the path of her fingers, watching in fascination as Nicole's nipples hardened at Jake's touch. She finally raised her eyes, past slightly opened lips to stare into deep blue, a blue that was both calm and anxious. She visibly saw Nicole let out her breath, saw her eyes soften. Jake gave a tiny smile before moving closer, finally capturing those tempting lips.

It was as if a torch had been lit. Nicole's arms circled her shoulders and pulled her closer at the same moment Jake's hands slid to Nicole's hips. Their bodies fused as mouths mated, and Jake felt herself melting in this woman's arms.

Nicole moaned as Jake's tongue moved against her lips, slowly slipping inside her mouth. She welcomed it, surprised that her legs still supported her. She felt nearly wanton as she clutched the woman to her breasts, but she hardly cared. Her entire body was on fire and the fact that it was a complete stranger making her feel the heat mattered not. She simply craved it. Her head fell back in surrender as Jake's mouth left hers and traveled lower, capturing a nipple in her mouth as Nicole pressed her closer.

"Yes," she murmured as her eyes slid shut.

Jake moaned as her lips and tongue surrounded the aroused nipple, licking and touching before sucking it into her waiting mouth. She felt Nicole's hand on her neck, urging her to take more and she did, sucking hard as Nicole pressed into her mouth. For so long, Jake had felt empty, drained, the weight of a little boy's murder slowly sapping the very life from her. But right here, right now, with a stranger's hands on her body, she felt alive.

She heard the whimper as her mouth left Nicole's breast, and she silenced her with a hard kiss, both hands threading through the blond strands of wet hair. Pulling away, their eyes locked, both swimming in desire. Then she lifted Nicole, urging her back on the rock.

Nicole's breath left her as Jake spread her thighs. She offered no protest as warm hands moved slowly up her legs, thumbs rubbing along the inside of her thighs, dangerously close to the fire that was burning. With eyes still locked, she moaned at the first touch as Jake's fingers found her, wet and ready. She watched as Jake's eyes turned nearly black, and she felt herself being pulled forward, watching as Jake's head lowered to her.

Nicole's eyes slammed shut, head bent back as she struggled to hold on to her sanity at the touch of Jake's tongue. Incoherent sounds came from her mouth, mumblings she could not stop. Dear God, she was naked, sitting on a rock, and another woman, a stranger, was feasting on her . . . literally. None of it mattered. She had long ago lost control, and she simply could not fight to regain it. Not when a warm mouth was covering her intimately, not when a tongue was reaching deep inside her. She clenched her hands into fists, giving in to the feelings that this woman, this stranger was bringing out in her. She felt her thighs being pushed farther apart, felt the rapid movement of Jake's tongue, and she became aware of her own hips as they moved urgently against Jake's face. Then Jake's lips were there, sucking her swollen clit into her mouth, teasing with her tongue, and Nicole positively exploded, unable to hold the primal scream that escaped from her mouth.

Jake was so lost in this woman that she very nearly had her own orgasm as Nicole erupted beneath her mouth. It was with difficulty that she released her, resting her head for a second on Nicole's thighs before looking up. What she saw took her breath away.

Nicole still had her head tilted back, mouth slightly opened, eyes squeezed shut. And the pulse in her throat was pounding wildly. Jake stood in the water, her hands reaching out to capture both of Nicole's breasts.

Nicole covered Jake's hands with her own, still trying to focus.

She couldn't *believe* that she had just screamed out like that. She *never* did that. *Never.*

"Kiss me," she murmured. Jake obliged, and Nicole tasted herself on Jake's lips, igniting her desire all over again. *Wanton?* She no longer cared. Her hands moved between them and she cupped Jake's breasts, pleased when the other woman moaned. Pulling away slightly, she looked into those dark eyes. "I need to touch you."

The only response she got was a slightly raised eyebrow. Then she was being pulled into the warm water, sinking below the surface as Jake found her mouth once again. Without warning, Jake's fingers were inside her, filling her, and she bit down on Jake's lip as she opened wider for her.

With the buoyancy of the water, Nicole nearly floated as Jake plunged in and out of her, and Nicole held on, her breath coming fast as she tried to match Jake's rhythm. Jake held her cradled to her chest and Nicole slipped one hand between them, fondling Jake's nipple just as Jake found her lips again. She rocked, hard, taking all of Jake inside. Opening her mouth, Jake's tongue slipped past her lips, and Nicole closed around it, sucking, as Jake's fingers continued their mastery, bringing her to the brink . . . almost, almost . . . until . . . *oh my God* . . . spasms shook her and she again flung her head back, this time able to contain the scream that threatened to spew forth.

"Dear God," she whispered.

"No, it's just me," Jake whispered back into her ear.

Nicole opened her eyes and smiled. "Funny, aren't you?"

"I try."

Nicole took a deep breath as she reached out both hands and cupped Jake's face. Their eyes locked as Nicole brought her closer, touching Jake's lips in a gentle, quiet kiss. Then she pulled away and smiled. "My turn."

Jake raised an eyebrow, then backed up, raising both arms teasingly. "I'm all yours."

CHAPTER FOURTEEN

The boy's too close, she thought. Too close. I'll hit him for sure.

"You've got to take the shot, McCoy," Perkins whispered. "You're the goddamn sharpshooter."

"He's too close," she said. "I can't."

The man pulled the boy with him, the gun pressed firmly against his head, the boy crying in terror, screaming for his mother.

"Let . . . him . . . go!" Jake yelled. "He's just a boy, for Christ's sake!"

"Fuck you!" the man spat. "I ain't dying today!"

"The hell you're not!"

He laughed and jerked the boy by the neck, making him scream. "You gonna shoot me, bitch?"

The sirens got closer, just a block away now and Jake felt some relief. There was nowhere for the man to run, nowhere to go. He had to give it up. Jake walked with them, barely twenty yards away, Perkins just behind her. The man pulled the boy behind the garbage cans, kicking at them with his foot, nearing the corner. They heard the screech of tires, heard voices yelling, and Jake met the angry eyes of the man. He nodded at her and smiled, then she saw his finger go to the trigger, saw the gun press into the boy's soft forehead.

"No!" she yelled.

"No! No . . . I can't," she cried, her arms flailing at her sides. "I'll shoot the boy!" she yelled.

Nicole sat up, watching Jake's movements, the jerking of her arms, the twitching of her legs. *A dream.*

"I'll fucking *kill* you."

Oh dear God. What does that mean?

Nicole moved farther away, wishing she had a flashlight, something, to see Jake's face. *She'll shoot? She'll fucking kill? Who?*

"Oh my God," she whispered. "She's a killer. She's an . . . assassin." *Just my luck.*

Jake sat up too, rubbing her eyes. "Shit."

"You . . . okay?" Nicole asked hesitantly.

"Yeah. I'm sorry. Damn dream."

"Yeah."

Jake lay back down, silently cursing herself. She'd probably scared the poor woman to death. She reached out a hand, pulling Nicole down beside her and wrapping her arms around her again.

Nicole tried to relax. *Just a dream, for God's sake.* But something about the way Jake had said the words made Nicole realize that she'd said them before, perhaps many times. But still, the arm around her shoulders was warm, secure. Jesus, it was the same woman who'd made love to her for most of the day, the same woman that Nicole had touched, had brought to orgasm more times than she could count. She let her breath out. The same woman who had made her delirious with desire, made her scream out with pleasure time and again, made her sink to her knees from the satisfaction of it all.

A stranger.

A woman she knew absolutely nothing about. A woman who could be a killer, for God's sake! She knew she wouldn't get another minute's sleep. Her eyes were wide open as she stared at the dark figure of the woman next to her, a woman who had fallen fast asleep again, a woman whose arms were still holding her.

67

Great, Nicole. Let your hair down for once. Why don't you pick an assassin? That'd make things interesting.

She closed her eyes, trying to relax, trying to find the same contentment she'd had when they'd finally crawled into the tent at dusk, totally exhausted, but still not able to stop touching. Even in her most vivid dreams, she never imagined she could spend an entire day having sex. Jesus, having sex with a stranger. But she had. And, damn, she'd enjoyed every second of it.

But now, now that reality was creeping in, now that she realized this stranger could be a hired killer or something, now she wanted to escape. And escape gracefully. After all, this woman had taken her places she'd never been before. *Now that's an understatement.*

Hours later, as she still fought a fitful sleep, dawn thankfully was creeping into the canyon. She pulled out of Jake's arms, careful not to wake her. As she unzipped the tent, she found herself face to face with Cheyenne, who had obediently slept outside.

"Hi, girl," she whispered and was rewarded with a quick wag of the tail. She reached out and rubbed the dog's ear, then pulled herself from the tent and zipped it up again. Sore muscles protested as she stood, and she was surprised she was even able to walk.

After a quick trip to the woods, Nicole gathered firewood and got a fire going, warming herself as she held both hands over it. It was probably the coldest morning yet, and she contemplated a dip in the hot springs. But, if Jake should wake up and find her out there, Nicole knew she'd not be able to resist, hired killer or not. So, she settled for the fire and hot coffee.

The sun was already up by the time Jake stirred. Nicole had taken her tent down and packed. The only thing she needed to add to her backpack was her coffee cup.

Jake crawled out of the tent, every muscle in her body sore. God, who would have thought? Cheyenne was lying close to the tent, front legs crossed and Nicole was sitting by the fire, twirling her coffee cup. At first glance, Jake knew something was wrong.

"Morning," she murmured as she got to her feet.

"Ah . . . yeah, morning."

Jake hesitated, then motioned to the woods. "Be right back."

Something about Nicole's demeanor indicated that, well, something was wrong. And maybe it was just embarrassment or something. After all, they'd spent the better part of yesterday having sex. Jake scratched her head with both hands as she went into the woods to relieve herself. She absently noted that she was only slightly limping and had not even thought to take her cane.

When she got back to camp, Nicole was standing by her backpack, nervously kicking at a rock.

"You okay this morning?"

Nicole turned, having a difficult time meeting Jake's eyes. Jake just stared, waiting for Nicole to speak.

"I think I should probably head out. I mean, I'm really behind schedule."

Jake nodded slowly, wondering at Nicole's nervousness. Had she done something wrong? She walked to the fire, still watching the other woman. "Sure. I understand. But, you seem a little upset. You want to talk about it?"

"No, no. I'm not upset. It's just . . . well," Nicole paused, shifting the ball cap over her hair. "I don't make a habit of doing this," she said quietly. "In fact, I've never done this."

Jake nodded. "I understand. But," she shrugged. "We're two consenting adults who had a little fun. At least I did. I hope you did." She watched as Nicole turned nearly scarlet, and she couldn't hide her smile.

"You don't really have to ask, do you?"

"But you're going to run away?"

Nicole nodded. "Yes. I'm going to run away. Provided, of course, that you'll give me directions."

Jake stared at her, again noticing the nervousness as Nicole's hands clenched together. Jesus, she'd apparently freaked the woman out. So, she sat down near the fire and held out her hand. "Show me your map."

Nicole produced it from the back pocket of her jeans and handed it over. Jake pointed to the rock next to her, motioning for Nicole to sit.

"Do you have a pen?"

Nicole found one in her backpack, and she sat quietly as Jake studied the map.

"Here we are," Jake said, making a circle on the map. "See the indication for the falls?"

Nicole nodded as she leaned forward, watching as Jake's fingers moved over the map.

"Follow Grizzly Gulch downstream. It'll feed into Cottonwood Creek. You'll know you're there because Cottonwood is twice as wide as Grizzly. Continue downstream, that'll be to your left, and you'll come upon Cottonwood Lake." Jake drew a mark on the map. "The Colorado Trail is on the opposite side of the lake. Once you hook up with that, you're about a day and a half from St. Elmo."

Nicole found herself staring at Jake instead of the map and when brown eyes captured her own, she finally looked away.

"I think I can find my way now."

"Good." Jake leaned forward, brushing her lips against Nicole's. "Because I'd hate to think of you lost somewhere."

Nicole had to restrain herself from taking those lips and begging for more. *Jesus Christ! Surely twenty orgasms with the woman was enough!* She closed her eyes for a second, gathering herself, then stood.

"Thank you for . . . for rescuing me, I guess."

"Rescuing?" Jake grinned. "I should be thanking *you*."

Nicole blushed again as she shouldered her pack, taking a step backward, away from Jake. She walked around the fire, reaching down to pet Cheyenne.

"It was . . . it was nice meeting you," Nicole said awkwardly as she walked away.

Jake watched her leave, feeling a sense of regret. "You, too," she murmured. As Nicole disappeared into the forest, Jake became aware of Cheyenne as the dog leaned against her. "Hungry?"

Jake took one last look into the woods, then turned around, pulling out her pot and stove from her pack. She still had not had coffee.

"Well, it's just us again, girl." She scratched Cheyenne's head, then lit the stove. Once water was heating, Jake walked toward the springs, stripping off her sweatpants as she went. She sunk under the warm water, her mind on nothing but Nicole.

Nicole methodically set up her tent, moving away from Cottonwood Creek and into the forest. She had hiked well past sunset, not relishing the prospect of an evening alone. Not after the last two days.

You're pathetic.

She ignored the little voice in her head and instead set up her stove to heat water for her dinner. She sat, staring into the darkening forest, trying to recall her hike today. It was but a blur. Her mind had been totally on Jake. So she had a shady background? Was that any reason to jump to conclusions that she was a killer?

"There was the dream," she reminded herself out loud.

She rolled her eyes, convinced that she'd overreacted. Jake's touch was too gentle, too loving to be that of a killer. *Loving?* No, Jake probably did that sort of thing all the time. Probably preyed upon stranded women and used her skills to tame them.

It didn't matter. It was time for her to leave anyway. She would simply look back on this trip with fond memories and that was all. Jake was still a stranger.

She let out a heavy sigh, trying to work up the energy for a campfire, wishing she could forget about the hot springs. Wishing she could forget about Jake.

CHAPTER FIFTEEN

"Well, I'll be damned," Rick drawled. "It's Jake McCoy, in the flesh!"

Jake flashed a smile at her partner. Hell, she'd missed him. "Give me a hug."

He shook his head. "No. Everyone's watching," he said quietly.

"Give me a hug or I'll beat your ass right now."

"As if."

But he stood, reaching out and enveloping her in long arms, squeezing tightly. "Damn, McCoy, I missed you."

"Me, too, Rick." She pulled out of his arms, looking around at the others. She met their eyes, nodding. "How's the lieutenant?"

"Anxious. Worried about you."

Jake looked at her desk, wondering where all her stuff was. She pulled out the chair and sat down, folding her arms on the empty desk and watched Rick Chase. Damn, but he was a handsome man—sandy blond hair, dark eyebrows, dark stubble. And not just handsome, but nice. A truly nice guy. A rare find these days. Michele was lucky. Jake had told her that many times.

"Why are you looking at me?"

"Where the hell's my stuff?"

"What stuff?"

"My . . . *stuff*," she said. "I know my desk wasn't this clean when I left."

"I tidied up. You're a slob."

"You stole my favorite pen, didn't you? I knew you would."

"Jake, I know how you love that pen. I would never take your pen."

"You're so full of shit."

"Well, well. You're back less than a minute and already the two of you are bickering? Damn, I've missed this."

Jake and Rick both turned, watching as their lieutenant hurried over with a file in his hand, wearing the same faded suspenders he always wore. His smile was genuine when he touched Jake's shoulder.

"Damn glad you're back, McCoy."

"Thanks, Lieutenant. It feels really good to be back."

"So? Good as new?"

Jake nodded. "Almost. Leg's still a little sore if I overdo it. I'm not likely to run a marathon anytime soon."

"Well, the doc cleared you, so that's good enough for me." He tossed the file on her desk. "Might as well get your feet wet."

"What's up, boss?" Rick said as he snatched the file off of Jake's desk before she could open it.

"They found a body over by the airport yesterday. Been there a few days. The ME's report is nearly identical to the one you had the other week. So, the airport police are graciously letting us investigate it."

"What did you have the other week?" Jake asked, ripping the file from Rick's hand.

"Housewife. Middle-aged. Found over near Chatfield Lake."

"And?"

"Raped. Strangled. Totally nude. Been there a few days."

Jake looked up from the file, meeting his eyes. "Lovely."

"Welcome back."

CHAPTER SIXTEEN

"Okay, Anna. Good," Nicole said, reaching over and lightly squeezing the young woman's arm. It was their third session, but it was the only time Anna had been able to make it all the way through her story without breaking down.

"I wanted to kill him."

Nicole nodded. *Who wouldn't want to kill the bastard?* "That's understandable, Anna. He hurt you."

"What if he gets out? He could come back. I have two other children."

"No. He won't get out. He's not going to hurt anyone else. What you've got to do is try to rebuild your life and go on. Your children need you to do that, Anna. That's why we're here."

"It's hard to look at them," she whispered. "I know they think it's my fault."

"No. How can it be your fault?"

"Maybe if I had done what he asked, he wouldn't have hurt Joseph," she said, tears again forming.

Nicole hated this part. The part where they placed all the blame on their shoulders, and it would take weeks for Nicole to make them see that it wasn't their fault. That was one reason she liked the group sessions. The women could listen to others, hear other stories and see that it was not any of their fault. It made accepting it so much easier. But alone, it was hard for them with only Nicole to tell them they were not to blame.

"Anna, he was wrong, not you. *He* did this. Not you."

"My Joseph was just three," she sobbed.

Nicole pushed the box of tissue closer, waiting patiently for Anna to recover. The woman had suffered a severe beating, then was tied to a chair and forced to watch as her boyfriend murdered her three-year-old child with a knife from her own kitchen. Recover? It would be a miracle.

Nicole sat with her back to the door, staring out the office window, absently watching as dusk enveloped the city, and a sprinkling of lights began appearing in the buildings surrounding her own. Back only three weeks and already her depression was returning.

She had taken Dorothy's advice and cancelled the group session, instead setting up individual meetings with some of them, squeezing them into her normal time slots during the day. Her schedule was full. Too full. But she couldn't turn them away, even if it meant working late most evenings.

At the quiet knock on her door, she turned around, forcing a smile to her face as Catherine stuck her head in.

"Heading out?" she asked her secretary.

"Actually, we're both heading out. You're taking me to dinner."

"I am?"

"Yes. Let's call it a day."

"Catherine, I can't. I've got notes to make yet, and I haven't even started on that article for the journal."

Catherine ignored her and began tidying her desk.

"I'm serious," Nicole said.

75

"So am I. And during dinner, we're going to discuss combining all these appointments you've tried to schedule into your day."

"Combining?"

"Yes. Nicole, you're meeting with the same number of people you would be if you were still doing groups. But there aren't enough hours in the day to meet with them all individually. So, we've got to do something."

Nicole knew she was right. When Dorothy suggested that she forego the group session, she hadn't meant for Nicole to absorb them within her already busy schedule.

"Okay."

"Okay?"

"What? Did you expect me to put up more of a fight?"

"Yes, I did." Catherine stepped back, waiting. "Well, come on. I want Mexican food."

"Don't you have a husband to go home to?" Nicole asked as she shoved away from her desk.

"I'm allowed a night out once in awhile."

Nicole looked back once at her cluttered desk, knowing she should really put in a couple more hours. But, she was tired. And hungry. So, she closed her office door and followed Catherine.

CHAPTER SEVENTEEN

Jake sat on the barstool next to Michele, twirling her wineglass as they watched Rick season the steaks.

"You look really good, Jake. I love your hair that way."

Jake rubbed her hand over her hair self-consciously. When she first cut it, she assumed she would let it grow back, but she'd gotten used to it. So, when she got back to Denver, one of the first things she did was have it cut again.

"Thanks, Michele. I threw a little fit in the hospital when I cut it, but I like it now. I'll probably leave it like this for awhile."

"You call that a little fit?" Rick asked. "You scared the nurse half to death."

"Well, if you had just given me the damn scissors," she said.

"No, no. You weren't allowed to play with sharp objects, remember?"

"I remember," she said dryly. It had been nearly three months, but yes, she remembered every detail. *Suicide watch*? Good Lord.

"You're hardly limping at all, Jake," Michele said as she poured more wine into Jake's glass before refilling her own. "I can't believe how quickly you recovered."

"Me, either, actually. But spending a month at the cabin did wonders."

"I bet you hated coming back to the city."

"Not as much as Cheyenne. She hates being in the backyard during the day."

"You should have brought her over tonight," Rick said.

"She's fine. She was on the sofa when I left."

"You still should have brought her," he said as he picked up the platter of steaks. "Let me get these on. Be right back."

Jake watched him through the window, glad to be back but missing the cabin. And the quiet. She smiled. And the hot springs. And certainly the woman she'd shared them with. For some reason, she couldn't get Nicole out of her mind, and she found herself thinking about the other woman often. Jake wasn't ashamed to admit that she'd had her share of sexual partners over the years but none had taken her like Nicole. Nicole was ardent and nearly unquenchable. If they hadn't both passed out from sheer exhaustion, Jake was convinced that their passion would have lasted until morning.

"I know Rick probably hasn't told you, but he missed you like crazy. I've heard more Jake stories in the last ten weeks," she said with a laugh.

Jake brought her thoughts back to the present, pushing Nicole from her mind. "I missed him, too. It was good to be back at the station today."

"So you're cleared?"

"Yeah. Doc checked me out yesterday." Jake stared at Michele, wondering what was up. She was acting weird. She knew Michele was somewhat jealous of the bond that she and Rick had formed. When they first got married, Michele hadn't wanted anything to do with Jake. But occasionally, like now, Rick would ask her over for steaks, and she and Michele had gotten to know one another better. They weren't what Jake would call good friends, but they got along well enough. "So," she asked, "what's wrong?"

"What do you mean?"

"What's on your mind, Michele?"

Michele looked out the window then quickly back at Jake. "I'm just worried. I want to make sure you're well enough to be back."

Jake nodded. "You're worried I won't be able to back up Rick, is that it?"

"Or that you'll be . . . afraid."

Jake narrowed her eyes. "Afraid? Afraid to pull my weapon?"

Michele touched Jake's arm. "Rick has not said anything. But some of the other guys have brought it up, and I know it's crossed his mind."

"Well don't worry. I talked to the shrink yesterday, too."

"I'm sorry, Jake. But . . ."

"But he's your husband. I understand."

Rick came back in smiling. "God, I love grilling steaks. It's such a manly job."

Jake rolled her eyes.

"It is, and you know it."

Jake reached over and squeezed Rick's arm. "It's good to be back, buddy. But remember, I'm the one that taught you how to grill steaks."

Rick laughed. "Yeah. Like I said. It's a manly job!"

"Very funny."

"A margarita, please," Nicole said to the waiter. "On the rocks."

"I want frozen," Catherine said. "No salt."

Nicole reached in the basket of chips and slid the salsa bowl closer. This was a good idea. She hadn't been out for dinner with a friend in ages. Usually, she had to make inane conversation with a blind date at a formal restaurant.

"Thanks for making me do this," she said.

"You're welcome. I knew it was time. The spark that was in

your eyes when you came back from the mountains disappeared the second day."

"Oh really? A spark, huh."

"Yes. In fact, if I didn't know you as well as I do, I'd say you took my advice and got laid."

Nicole nearly spit out her chip, and she was thankful the waiter chose that moment to bring their drinks. At first, she had planned to tell Catherine about Jake. She knew Catherine would find it quite amusing. But, as the days passed and she finished her trip, alone, she realized that she would never tell Catherine. What started out as a day—and night—of wild sex had turned into an intimate tryst with a stranger. And it was something Nicole wanted to keep private. Not have Catherine tease her about it.

But she wasn't to be spared. Catherine drummed her fingers on the table, staring.

"Out with it." She leaned closer. "I can't believe you had sex and didn't tell me!"

"What makes you think I had sex?" Nicole asked weakly.

"Well, you're blushing. That's a dead giveaway."

Nicole let out a heavy sigh. "Okay. I didn't want to tell you because I didn't want you to make fun of me," Nicole admitted.

"Make fun? I want to applaud you! I didn't think you had it in you."

Nicole sipped from her drink, then sat up straight. "Oh, Catherine, it was the weirdest thing. I got lost and just stumbled upon her. She and Cheyenne were camping at some hot springs."

"Cheyenne?"

"Her dog."

"And does she have a name?"

Nicole swallowed. "Her name was . . . Jake." It was the first time she'd said the name out loud, and she was surprised at the way her heart skipped.

"Jake? A woman?"

"It's a nickname she was given as a kid."

"Oh, *God*. I can see it now. Some big butch woman."

"She was not. She was quite attractive."

"I bet." Catherine leaned closer. "Let me guess. Short, short hair? Not a stitch of makeup? Wore men's clothes?"

"First of all, *I* didn't wear a stitch of makeup either. We were camping. And secondly, are jeans considered men's clothing? If so, *I* was in men's clothes."

"So I was right. Short, short hair."

"Well, it may have been a little short," Nicole admitted. "But she wasn't . . . she wasn't butch. She was . . . handsome."

"*Handsome?*"

"Yes. You know how some women are handsome?"

"She's a dyke. You *slept* with a *dyke*? What were you thinking?"

"You told me to let my hair down," Nicole reminded her.

"Yeah. But, I was thinking more along the lines of your usual dates. Feminine, pretty, someone you can take home to meet mom. Not someone who looks like a man."

"She did not look like a man, trust me."

"You called her handsome."

Nicole leaned forward, speaking quietly. "Catherine, I met her around five o'clock one afternoon and within thirty minutes, we were naked together in the hot springs. By ten the next morning, we were making love in those same hot springs."

"Damn," Catherine whispered.

Nicole blushed. "Even in my wildest dreams, I never would have suspected I was capable of doing what I did. We spent literally hours together, and I was insatiable."

"Who started it? Did you come on to her?"

"I don't really know what happened. It was like I was under a spell or something. And you're right, she's certainly not my type, but I was so attracted to her, I couldn't even think straight."

"Well, what happened?"

"She got me up to see the sunrise. It was beautiful. Then I went into the springs to bathe, knowing that she would come. I could see it in her eyes. And I wanted her to come to me."

"And she did?" Catherine whispered.

"She walked to the springs, taking her clothes off as she watched me. Our eyes were locked together. It was like in the movies. She didn't say a word. Neither did I. She walked right up to me, and the next thing I know, we're kissing and touching and . . . God, I've never had so many toe-curling orgasms in my life," Nicole whispered. "I was actually screaming, Catherine. *Screaming*."

"Jesus Christ," Catherine murmured. She took a swallow from her drink and fanned herself. "Is it getting hot in here or what?"

Nicole blushed.

"So? Where does she live? What does she do?"

Nicole shook her head. "I have no idea. We never really talked. And then, I guess I freaked out the next morning and left."

"Well, it is so out of character for you, I'm not surprised. I'm sure you were embarrassed."

"That and . . . well, the dream."

"You had a dream?"

"No. She did. That night. She was talking about shooting and killing someone. I'd convinced myself I'd just had sex with a hired killer."

Catherine laughed. "And you left? Why didn't you just ask what she did for a living?"

"What good would that have done? And it didn't matter, anyway. I needed to be on my way."

"Wow. I can't believe that happened to you. I'm so proud of you," she teased. "You let your hair down, all right!"

"Please stop. This is exactly why I didn't want to tell you."

"I'm sorry. I don't mean to tease. But Nicole, that is just so not you."

"I know that. Once I came to my senses, I realized how foolish I'd been. I mean, she was a stranger. She could have been a serial killer, for all I knew. Not to mention, we weren't exactly having safe sex. The thought never crossed my mind. I just wanted her hands on me."

"Okay. Enough. I don't really want details."

Nicole closed her eyes for a second, remembering. And realizing that Jake had most likely ruined her for life. She doubted she'd ever have a sexual partner that could compare. She pushed thoughts of Jake aside, tucking them deep down where they belonged.

Nicole cleared her throat. "So, you think we should go back to group sessions?"

Catherine smiled. "Safer subject?"

"Much."

CHAPTER EIGHTEEN

"I'm Detective Chase. This is Detective McCoy," Rick said, introducing them to the chief of the airport police. "My lieutenant spoke with you yesterday."

The older man looked up, peering at them over his glasses. "Oh, yeah. Gregory. Come in."

Jake looked around, impressed. Their offices were top-notch. New, flat-panel monitors sat on every desk, unlike her own squad room. They must have a hell of a budget. She shoved her hands in the pockets of her slacks and waited while he shuffled through files on his desk. Rick was impatiently tapping his index fingers together.

"Here you go." He handed the file to Rick without even a glance at Jake. "That's our field work and investigation. I sent the initial ME's report over to your lieutenant. I'm sure it'll be a few days before they get it all worked up."

"Yes, we have the initial report. Thank you."

Jake cleared her throat. "I'd like to see the crime scene."

"Oh, we've gone over it, detective. It's clean. She was just dropped there."

"I'd still like to see it." She gave what she hoped was a genuine smile. "It gives us more of a . . . a feel for the case."

"If you don't mind, of course," Rick added quickly.

"No, I don't mind. I think it's just a waste of time, is all. I'll have one of my officers take you out there."

"Thanks very much," Jake said, extending her hand. He took it briefly, not bothering to meet her eyes. *Asshole.* Probably a retired sheriff from some small town in the plains, she guessed.

They followed Officer Whitten outside, and Rick nudged Jake with his elbow. "Play nice," he whispered.

"I hate men."

"I know that."

Officer Whitten politely held open the back door for Jake, and she scowled at Rick, who hopped into the front seat.

"Were you out at the scene when they found her?" Rick asked.

"Oh, yeah. We all were."

"Lovely," Jake murmured. She imagined the entire airport police force traipsing over the scene.

She and Rick looked at each other when he stopped. They were a good distance from the main runways, following the outer loop road. But still, they appeared to be nowhere special.

"This is it," he finally said when neither she nor Rick moved.

"Where's the crime scene tape?" Jake asked.

"Oh, we took it down."

"But, you had the crime lab out here, right?" Rick asked.

"No. The ME's office took pictures. We did, too. But there was nothing here. She was just dumped here. She was totally nude. There wasn't even a hairclip."

Jake got out, slamming her door with as much force as she could muster. *Idiots.* "You looked for tire prints, right?"

"Tire prints?"

"So you're saying the scene's been contaminated?" Rick asked.

"You didn't take tire prints? Footprints? You didn't have the crime lab out? People have been walking all over the place?"

"Hey man, she was just dumped here. There wasn't even any blood. I don't believe there were any tire prints or footprints. My captain said to take the tape down as soon as they moved her body."

Jake walked away from the road, seeing the matted grass, the numerous footprints. *Jesus.* She shook her head. Any evidence that had been here was long gone.

"How could someone get out here?" she asked.

"What do you mean?"

Jake flicked her eyes at Rick. "I mean, how could someone, a civilian, get out here to dump the body? This area is secured, right?"

"Oh, yeah. Airport personnel only."

"So, if we're to believe that, an airport employee dumped the body. Right?"

"Well, I suppose."

"Any video surveillance out here?" Rick asked.

"No. Not out here. There's nothing this far out."

"You've checked the fence line, made sure there wasn't a breach there?"

"Well, yeah. Right around here."

"How about we check the entire perimeter?" Jake suggested.

"Now?"

She shrugged. "We've got time. You got time?"

"I guess. Let me call the chief."

"Yeah, you do that," she murmured.

"Play nice," Rick said again as they got back in the car.

Jake's leg was aching when they returned to the station, and she struggled not to limp. The chief had approved their request to search the perimeter fence. On foot. So she, Rick, and Officer Whitten walked the entire goddamn length of fence, finding two gaps. Only one was close enough to have dragged a body. The other was on the opposite side of the airport.

They called the crime lab out before airport security could trample the scene.

"You look beat," Rick said.

"I'm okay."

"If you're in pain, you need to tell me. There's no sense in . . ."

"Rick, I'm okay," she insisted.

Their lieutenant walked over, file in hand. "Got a name on your vic. Sandra Poole. It's not very pretty," he said, handing Jake the file. "Find anything at the airport?"

"Broken fence, if you can believe that. Two spots. The FAA is going to have a field day," Rick said.

"This woman was battered," Jake said, reading the file. "Raped and beaten by her husband."

"Three years ago. And we already checked. He's still locked up tight."

"We're hoping the crime lab might find something at the fence. Where they found the body, the scene's been contaminated. No way we can get anything there," Rick told him.

"She's got a grown daughter. Lives in Littleton." Jake looked up from the file. "Maybe Sandra Poole had a new boyfriend. Battered women tend to pick the same losers."

"Check her out. I'll let you know if they turn up anything at the airport."

She could feel Rick watching her, and she glared at him. "Rick, I'm fine. The leg's a little sore, that's all."

"Too much walking?"

"Yeah. It's been a long day."

"Well, it's already three. You want to hit Littleton tomorrow?"

"Let's run a check on the daughter, see where she works. I doubt she's going to be home at three in the afternoon."

"Okay. I'll do it."

"Where's the file on the first vic? You got it in the computer yet?"

Rick snorted. "Yeah, right. That was always your job."

She held her hand out. "Give it to me."

Jake spent the next half hour going over the file and the short version of the ME's report while Rick was on the phone. Three years ago, Helen Thornton was hospitalized for over a week. She pulled up medical records on the computer, frowning as she read.

"What?"

"The first victim, same thing."

"What are you talking about?"

Jake showed him the report. "Three years ago, she was in the hospital. I pulled up medical, she'd been raped and beaten by her husband."

"Got to be a coincidence. I mean, come on. Unless these women knew each other."

"Doubtful. Helen Thornton lived in an apartment east of downtown. Sandra Poole was suburbs. Don't see a connection." Jake scanned the file. "And different hospitals."

"Okay. The daughter works for a real estate agency in Littleton. We'll check her out in the morning."

Jake stared at the file. "Both raped and strangled," she murmured, shaking her head. "Can't be a coincidence. And where's the complete ME's report?" she asked, shuffling through the papers.

"I guess I haven't gotten it yet."

"Have you asked?"

"That was normally your job, too." Rick leaned back in his chair and smiled. "Glad you're back, McCoy. I'd hate to have this case, just me and the lieutenant."

"Has he been your backup?"

"Hell, yeah. I mean, I like him fine, but . . ."

"He's not me?"

"He's so fucking by the book, it's scary."

Jake laughed. "Guess that's why he's made lieutenant."

"You want to go get a beer?"

"Are you trying to piss Michele off or what?"

"No, I just missed hanging out with you. You've been gone nearly three months, Jake."

"Well, thanks. But I'm going to head home. Cheyenne will be waiting."

"I swear. You treat that dog like she's your kid."

Jake raised an eyebrow. "What's your point?"

"My point is, she's a dog. She's not going to know if you're late. I don't think they can tell time, Jake."

"Of course they can tell time."

"Come on. One beer."

Jake leaned forward and smiled. "Ricky, we both know that Michele only tolerates me. Why do you want to piss her off by going out for a beer with me?"

"Jake, maybe I need . . . to talk."

Jake sighed. "What's going on?"

Rick shrugged. "Divorce rate on the force is seventy-five percent. That's what's going on."

"Are you kidding me? You and Michele?"

"Can we get out of here, please?"

She nodded. "Okay. Sure."

CHAPTER NINETEEN

"I swear, Nicole. It's after six. You can't keep doing this every night."

Nicole looked from her computer to Catherine, frowning as Catherine walked into her room. "I'm not working. I'm reading the paper." She sat back, cocking her head. "Catherine, one of our group sessions about three years ago, wasn't there a woman named Sandra Poole?"

"Three years ago? I can barely remember one session ago, much less three years," she said, as she shook her head. "Why?"

"They found a body at the airport. Raped and strangled," Nicole said. "Sandra Poole. The name is so familiar."

"Get up."

"What?"

"Let me check the accounts."

"I know how to check the accounts, Catherine," Nicole said as she moved her chair out of the way, releasing the mouse to the other woman.

"Right. I've seen you muddle through it, and I'd like to get home within the hour."

"Funny." But she watched as Catherine quickly pulled up their accounts.

"I'll just do a search. It'll be easier than guessing what year."

"I didn't know I could search all the years at once," Nicole said. "I thought you had it broken down."

"It is, and I've shown this to you before. Just click 'combine' and it re-sorts them into one file." Which it did. "How do you spell it? E on the end or not?"

"Yes."

It only took a second before a file for Poole, Sandra was pulled up.

"Damn," Nicole murmured.

"You think it's the same person?"

Nicole stared at the picture of Sandra Poole, a woman in her forties with bleached blond hair. Then she read the brief notes. Raped by her husband, beaten. Two weeks in the hospital. One suicide attempt. She looked at Catherine. "Let's hope not. Nobody deserves that twice in one lifetime."

Jake twirled the beer bottle in her hand, watching as Rick peeled the label off of his.

"It just hit me, you know." He finally looked up. "We have nothing in common."

"You must have something in common. You got married," Jake reminded him.

"I know you told me it was too soon. Please don't bring that up again."

Jake motioned for the waitress to bring them two more, then turned her full attention on Rick. "When did this suddenly *hit* you, Rick?"

He shrugged. "I'm sitting at home one night, listening to her go on and on about the latest house they're decorating, and I realized . . . I didn't really like her," he said quietly.

"Are you shitting me, man?"

"And I don't think she likes me, either," he added.

"What the hell is going on?"

"I talk police stuff, she freaks out, thinks I'm going to get killed. She talks decorating shit, and I want to throw up."

Jake smiled. "Rick, she's a woman. They're going to talk decorating shit."

"You don't."

Jake arched an eyebrow. "You want to date a lesbian?"

He let out a deep breath. "No. But you were right two years ago when you said I should wait. I mean, here she was, this beautiful girl, all the guys loved her . . . and she wanted me."

"Damn ego," Jake murmured. "I told you."

"Yeah. I remember your words, Jake. No need to go over it again."

"Have you talked to her about it?"

He shook his head, pausing as the waitress brought them fresh beers. "No. Hell, we don't talk. We tell about our day, that's it. Then we sit in front of the TV, me thinking about you, wondering when the hell you're coming back, and she's looking at decorating magazines."

Jake reached across the table and took his hand. "I missed you, too."

He looked up, and Jake was surprised at the tears in his eyes.

"I just didn't have anyone to talk to, you know. And you're like . . . my best friend, Jake."

"I swear, Rick, if I were straight, I'd be all over your ass."

He grinned. "Don't sweet-talk me."

Jake squeezed his hand, then pulled away. "You could have called me anytime, you know. I get service up there."

"I know. But I knew you wanted some alone-time, away from all this. I didn't want to lay my shit on you, too."

"You're right. I needed some time alone. Had to get my head straight."

"And did you?"

Jake shrugged. "Enough. I still have . . . well, I still have dreams."

"About the kid?"

Jake nodded.

"But the shrink cleared you."

"I didn't tell her."

"Oh, Jake. Shit, I know you. You're not talking this out with anyone, are you? You're dealing with it all inside that little head of yours, and the only outlet is your dreams."

"Why, Dr. Chase, how very astute of you," Jake said dryly.

Rick leaned forward. "Why didn't you tell her about the dreams?"

"Well, for one thing, she wouldn't have cleared me to come back, and I needed to come back. And you're right. Maybe the dreams are an outlet so maybe it's not such a bad thing."

It was Rick's turn to take her hand. "It wasn't your fault, Jake."

"We don't really know that, Rick. We'll never know that."

"Jake . . ."

"No. It's okay. I've accepted that. The dirt bag is dead, the kid is dead, and Officer Perkins is dead. Hell, I should be dead, too. It was one big shooting fest."

"You almost were," Rick reminded her.

"Yeah. But thanks to my partner's famous tourniquet, I survived."

"Jake . . . wasn't your bullet. You've got to let it go."

Jake's eyes held his. "Ricky, for the rest of my life, I'll never be able to let it go."

Rick shook his head. "You can't carry that weight with you, Jake. It'll just make you crazy. And don't think it hasn't crossed my mind that the next time, you might be afraid to pull your weapon, to use it. Enough of the guys have talked about it. But I told them I'd rather have you watching my back than any of their sorry asses." He drained the last of his beer and twirled the bottle in his hands. "You love me just like I love you. We're not going to let anything happen to the other. No matter what."

Jake couldn't help but smile. God, could she have a better partner?

CHAPTER TWENTY

Cheyenne gave her such a forlorn look as Jake put her outside the next morning that she very nearly let her have run of the duplex. But, hell, she never knew what time she'd get home. So, she leaned down and looked the dog in the eye.

"I promise. This weekend, we'll head out of town and do some hiking. Deal?"

She nearly laughed as Cheyenne cocked her head to the side, ears raised.

"Yeah, I know. You understand every word." She affectionately rubbed the dog's ear. "I'll see you tonight, sweetheart."

She caught her reflection in the window as she walked through her small duplex, pausing to look around. She'd lived here the entire time she'd been in Denver, and it still didn't feel like home. It was sparsely furnished, just enough to get by. And most of her personal things, mementoes and such, were at the cabin. No, it wasn't really home, it was just a place to be. She flipped her keys in her hand absently, suddenly missing the cabin, wondering when she could find a long weekend to drive up there.

It was barely after seven o'clock and traffic was nonexistent as she made her way to the station. She stopped long enough to get coffee and a muffin and still made it in by seven-thirty. Her squad room was quiet, and she used the time to read over the ME's report on Sandra Poole. As she read, she tossed her muffin in the trash, having lost her appetite. The woman hadn't just been raped. She'd been sodomized and nearly ripped open from the force.

"Goddamn bastard," she whispered, as she closed the file. Then she pulled up Helen Thornton's ME report, comparing the two. Raped, strangled. Not sodomized. Might be different perps. But she didn't think so. She didn't really believe in coincidence.

"Hey, McCoy."

Jake looked up from the file, smiling as Belcher walked in. "Good morning."

"Glad you're back," he said as he walked over to get coffee.

"Thanks."

She'd always gotten along fine with Belcher. In fact, she'd been partnered with him the first couple of weeks. But, he'd taken a leave when his wife had their first child, and the lieutenant had paired her with Rick instead. And that was all it took. She and Rick had hit it off, and when Belcher returned, the lieutenant reshuffled, leaving her and Rick together.

"We all found out Rick was a whiney ass," he said as he walked over. "Never heard a grown man pine so much for his partner."

"Probably because no one else would work with him."

"You're okay, right?"

She nodded. "Thanks Belcher. I'm fine."

"Good."

Belcher was a good cop, although she often wondered why he chose Special Victims. He was the only one of them who had kids, the only one married, other than Rick. She raised her eyebrows. Of course, that might change. But Belcher was all about his family. She wondered how hard it was for him to work the cases that came their way. Especially the ones involving kids.

95

The rest of the group came in, one by one. Gina Salazar, the only other female, nodded at her, her long, black hair tied in her familiar ponytail. They weren't what Jake would call good friends, but they got along well, well enough for an occasional beer after work. Gina's partner, Mark Simpson, walked by a second later. He was as fair-skinned as Gina was dark.

"Where's Chase?"

"Late I guess."

"Well, I think you guys should take a look at a case we had several months ago." He perched on the corner of her desk, stirring his coffee slowly. "Dead end. It happened about a month before your . . . ordeal," he said. "Middle-aged woman found in her apartment, raped and strangled."

Jake nodded. "Yeah, I remember. But she was at home. Our victims have been dumped."

He shrugged. "You still might want to check it out. We had zero leads. No prints, no threats, nobody saw a thing. We've tabled it. There's not shit to go on."

"Okay. I'll take a look." She glanced up. "You've got it in the system, right?"

"Yeah. It's updated. What little there is. Shelly Burke was her name."

She scribbled down the name, then turned back to her own files, looking for more similarities between them. Rick finally called. He was stuck in traffic. She cradled the phone against her shoulder as she shuffled the two files.

"Well, I'll spend this time getting the files in the system. Jesus, Rick, I hate paper files."

"Quit your bitching."

"Hey, listen, Simpson told me about a case of theirs that they had several months ago." She looked at the file. "June fifth. You might remember. Middle-aged woman found in her apartment."

"Oh, yeah. Raped."

"Strangled, too."

"They got suspects?"

"No. It was clean. I'm going to check her background, see how close it is to ours."

"Okay. We're starting to crawl, so I guess the accident is cleared."

"Be careful. See you in a bit."

"Roger that. I'm out."

Jake laughed as she hung up. God, she'd missed Rick's radio talk that he generally saved for the phone. Her smile faded when she pulled up the old case and saw that Shelly Burke was also a previous victim of rape. She was found in her bathtub, half-filled with water, nude.

"What the hell is going on?" she murmured as she searched Medical. No semen found on any of the victims. No prints. No rope fibers. No nothing. It was as if they'd been . . . washed. "Is that possible?" She picked up the phone, calling the ME's office.

"Monica? It's McCoy with Special Victims. I need you to pull a couple of posts."

"Sure, Jake. Names?"

"Sandra Poole and Helen Thornton."

"Okay. But Thornton, that was awhile ago. Didn't we send that over?"

"Yeah, I've got the brief version. But I wanted the full report, need to add it to her file here."

"I see. And what are we looking for?"

Jake smiled. "Soap."

"What?"

"Soap, Monica."

"Jake, the ME's report will not just say 'soap'."

"Then do me a favor and grab Dr. Benson and ask her if there was goddamn soap on the victims."

"You don't have to yell at me."

Jake leaned her head back, staring at the ceiling. What the hell is soap made out of? "Not yelling. Monica, the victims were clean. No prints, no fibers. No clothes. My little brain thought maybe they'd been washed. So I called you, the queen of secretaries over

97

there, hoping you could tell me. If you can't, do you mind e-mailing me the entire ME report on our two vics?"

"Much better, Jake. You're learning to ask nicely. And I will e-mail you the reports so that you can Google all the big words."

"Very funny. It's a wonder you still have a job."

"Same to you!"

Jake had half a mind to slam the receiver down when she heard Monica's quiet laughter. She smiled instead.

"I missed you, too, Monica."

"Ah, Jake. It's been so boring without you to torment."

"Well, I'm back. And you're still in fine form."

"That's all I wanted to hear. Write this down. Triclosan. They both had traces of it on their skin."

"What the hell is triclosan?"

"Why don't you Google it?"

"I swear, Monica, one of these days . . ."

"You keep promising me that, sweetheart, but so far, you're all talk and no action."

"You couldn't handle me."

"Try me."

Jake couldn't hold her laughter any longer and Monica joined in. "God, I've missed this."

"Me, too, you old fart. I'm glad you're back, Jake. We need to get lunch sometime."

"Yeah, I know. I owe you several."

"You owe me thirteen."

"Why doesn't it surprise me that you've been keeping count?" Jake asked, as she did a search for triclosan.

"Okay. I've sent you the reports. What else can I do for you?"

"Well, fuck me," Jake murmured. "Triclosan. Active ingredient in antibacterial soap," Jake said.

"Glad I could help."

"Thanks, Monica," Jake said absently as she hung up, her eyes scanning the article. Triclosan was found not only in antibacterial soaps, but also in some mouthwash and toothpaste. She opened her e-mail and printed out the two ME reports on their victims, then pulled up the case file on Shelly Burke. It was neat, Gina's doing, most likely. She clicked on the ME's report and scanned it, her eyes widening when she read that traces of triclosan were found on the victim's skin.

Lieutenant Gregory tapped her on the shoulder, startling her. She looked up from the file long enough to nod.

"Where's your partner?"

"He was caught in traffic, there was some accident."

"What you got, McCoy? Anything good?"

She leaned back and nodded. "Triclosan."

He frowned. "What the hell is triclosan?"

"It's used in soap. Specifically, antibacterial soap."

"And?"

"And all three victims had traces of it on their skin."

"Three? Last count, we had two."

"Simpson and Salazar had a case a few months ago. He told me to take a look at it."

"Oh, yeah. That was right before your . . . shooting. They had nothing."

"All three victims had been previously raped. Thornton and Poole, by their husbands, and Burke, by a boyfriend. All were in their forties."

"And what you're saying, with this triclosan, that they've all been . . . cleaned?"

Jake shrugged. "Even if that's the case, it doesn't really help us much, other than link the three. Still no suspect."

"Okay. If they're linked, we pull Simpson and Salazar in and the four of you work this. The last thing we need is a goddamn serial killer picking off middle-aged housewives." The lieutenant turned, nearly bumping into Rick as he hurried to his desk. "And we don't have time for you to be late, Chase."

"Yes, sir. Sorry. I-70 was backed way the hell up."

"I warned you not to move to the suburbs."

Jake and Rick watched his retreating back then looked at each other. "What the hell's wrong with him?"

Jake shrugged. "Serial killer."

"Serial killer? Two vics don't make a serial killer."

"We got three. Simpson and Salazar's is a match."

Rick leaned back in his chair, looking at the paper Jake had handed him. He raised an eyebrow at the word circled in red. "What the hell is triclosan?"

"Soap."

"So they were clean people. What's your point?"

Jake leaned back, too, twirling a pen in her hand. "I may not have a point. Maybe you're right, and they were just clean people. But triclosan is the active ingredient in antibacterial soap. Most commonly found in hand soap. Which would lead you to think that their hands would show traces of it, not their bodies, although it is also found in some bath soaps."

"Uh-huh. And how do you know all this?"

Jake grinned. "Google."

Rick shook his head. "You can't believe everything you read on the Internet, Jake."

She sat up again, leaning on her desk. "Listen, they were all too clean. No prints, no smudges, no fibers. Hell, no clothes. They were raped, but there were no fluids."

"And you think our guy *washed* them?"

"Why not?"

Rick shrugged. "Okay. I'll go with it. Now what? We look for really clean guys?"

Jake laughed. "I know. It means shit. Anyway, the lieutenant wants Simpson and Salazar in with us."

"Okay, good. And we need to go check out Sandra Poole's daughter. Lydia Stanford. She works for Mountain West Real Estate."

"Let's send Gina out there. She's better at that than we are. I'd really like to go over the Shelly Burke case."

"Fine with me." Rick pushed his chair back. "Let me get them. Might as well all be on the same page."

CHAPTER TWENTY-ONE

Nicole glanced to the west, staring at the mountains as they were silhouetted against the setting sun. She was leaving work much earlier than normal, but Catherine had practically pushed her out of the office. Which was fine. Tomorrow, group sessions would start, and her days would again become shorter. *But is that necessarily good?* Since her return from the mountains, she'd welcomed the extended hours. It left little time to think.

Like now.

She pulled her eyes from the sunset, focusing instead on the highway. She hated times like this, when images of Jake crept in.

"Forget her," she said out loud, meeting her eyes in the mirror. She wished she could forget the whole episode, but it stayed with her, vivid images coming to her time and again. Images of her and a stranger doing incredibly intimate things to one another.

Well, she had to get over it, and perhaps dinner tonight was just what she needed. Debra Fisher was someone she'd known and admired for several years. The fact that she was now single added a new dimension to their friendship. But really, Debra was only a friend. Nicole had never entertained her being anything other than that. Attractive? Sure. In fact, she was glamorous. She'd never been out in public with Debra and had known her to never be less than impeccably dressed. Which caused Nicole to glance at her own clothing. She hadn't been up to hose and pumps this morning and had settled on slacks and loafers. And no doubt Debra would be in one of her power suits.

"I really hate attorneys," she murmured. *Then why go out with her?* Well, because she couldn't very well turn down a dinner date from one of the most powerful lesbians in the city. Catherine had nearly fainted when she told her. Debra Fisher was rumored to be running for mayor. The fact was, no matter how attractive Debra was or how powerful, she still was just a friend who stirred zero romantic interest in Nicole.

She didn't know what was wrong with her. Debra was not unlike the women she normally went out with. Business women, doctors, lawyers—Nicole knew them all. She felt like she'd dated half of them. All just like her, semi-closeted professional women, putting on a straight face in public. And Nicole frankly was sick of it. She envied those women who had the courage to announce to the world that they were gay. And a handful of women in their own circle had done just that, despite protests from their friends. Nicole knew that the protests were mostly based on fear. Fear that they would out them all.

Nicole pushed her thoughts aside when she saw the black Mercedes, and she pulled her more modest Lexus next to it and parked. Debra flashed a charming smile, and Nicole matched it.

"Good to see you again, Nicole. It's been ages."

Nicole leaned forward, accepting the quick hug from the other woman, noting her perfect makeup and hair, and just the barest scent of a very expensive perfume.

"Hello, Debra. You look as beautiful as ever."

"Thank you." She looked at Nicole's slacks. "Did you have casual day at the office?"

Nicole laughed, ignoring the little voice in her head that urged her to tell Debra the truth. That she *hated* dressing the part, day after day. But instead, "Sort of. It was a slow day and I thought I'd take advantage of it."

"I wish I could have slow days. Especially now, I doubt I'll have a moment to myself. That's why I chose this restaurant. Quiet, out of the way. I'm sure we won't be recognized."

"Recognized? Who are we hiding from?"

Debra stared. "Haven't you heard? I'm announcing my candidacy tomorrow."

"No. Just rumors, really." Nicole squeezed her arm. "Congratulations. You must be very excited."

"Yes, of course I am. I think I have a legitimate shot. That's what my team tells me, anyway." She held the door open for Nicole, then ushered her in with a warm hand at her back. Nicole rolled her eyes. Sometimes it just didn't work when lesbians tried to play it straight. "Two, please," Debra said. "Booth in the back, if you have it."

"Yes ma'am, of course. Follow me."

"Have you been here before?" Debra asked.

"No, I haven't."

"Best authentic Italian in the city. You'll love it."

"Ladies, will you need a wine list?"

Nicole took her seat opposite Debra, deferring the question to her. "I think we would like a bottle of pinot grigio. Give us your best."

"Of course. I will bring it right out."

Debra leaned back, smiling. "They make a wonderful pesto. I'll have him bring some out with the bread."

"Sure. That would be lovely."

"You're probably wondering why I invited you to dinner."

"Well, I know you and Ashley . . ."

"Yes, it was messy. But, I knew I had to do it. I couldn't very well have a roommate, now could I? How would that look to voters?"

Nicole leaned forward. "You broke up with Ashley because you're running for mayor?"

"Yes, of course. It cost me a small fortune, but I did it." At Nicole's blank stare, Debra shook her head. "And don't turn into Dr. Westbrook, please. I've already discussed it with Dorothy. She agreed with my decision."

"I didn't realize that your relationship with Ashley was simply one of convenience, I guess. I thought you genuinely cared for one another."

"Of course I cared about her. But she knew of my political aspirations. It was just a matter of time."

"I see." Nicole paused as their bottle of wine was delivered, allowing Debra to taste and nod her approval. When they were alone again, Nicole continued. "If you're concerned about your political future, why are you here with me?"

"There's nothing suspicious about you, Nicole. We're just old friends. You have a thriving practice, you're well respected in your field. There's no reason we can't have dinner."

"And Ashley was what? A liability?"

"I hate that word, but yes."

"She's a teacher."

"She's a high school *coach*. How much more stereotypical could you get?"

At one time, Nicole had the utmost respect for Debra Fisher. She was one of the best young assistant DAs in the city. She could mold the jury with just a smile and make witnesses crumble with the arch of an eyebrow. Yes, she was going places. And now Nicole wanted no part of it.

"She was in love with you," Nicole said quietly. "Debra, you can't just discard people to suit you. You knew she was a coach at the beginning. Why did you let it go so far?"

Debra flashed her trademark smile. "Because she was young and fabulous in bed, of course. But I didn't come here to talk about Ashley. I wanted to talk about you." She poured more wine into Nicole's glass. "You seem to be perpetually single. I need to be single, as well. At least for the time being. Of course, there will be occasions where I'll need a male escort, but I'm sure I can find someone to fill that role. But, since you're not seeing anyone . . ."

"Wait a minute," Nicole said, interrupting her. "You're not suggesting that I . . . that we," Nicole said, motioning between them.

"It'll just be sex, Nicole. I don't expect anything else. But I can't very well date, now can I?"

"With me?" Nicole asked, eyes wide.

"Of course with you. As I said, you're single. It's perfect. It would just be a physical relationship for both of us. No strings attached."

Nicole was absolutely speechless.

"Is that a yes?"

"Are you out of your mind?" she hissed.

Debra seemed taken aback, and Nicole realized that she didn't really know this woman at all. All these years that they had known each other, it was simply an act. A show. She felt like she was sitting with a stranger.

"Nicole, I thought you'd be receptive to this."

"Why in the world would you think that?" Nicole moved her wineglass out of the way and folded her hands together. "First of all, I'm not the least bit attracted to you." At Debra's startled look, Nicole shrugged. "Sorry, but I'm not. And secondly, I'm not really into sex for the sake of sex." She shrugged again. "Call me old-fashioned."

It was Debra's turn to stare. "You're not attracted to me?"

Nicole shook her head. "No. What gave you the idea that I was?"

"Well, nothing. I just assumed . . ."

Ah. Of course. Debra wasn't used to being turned down. Well, Nicole could muster up a little sympathy. She would stay and at least finish their dinner, even though what she really wanted was to run. And fast. And part of her wanted to run from herself. *Not into sex for the sake of sex? Old-fashioned?* Jesus, had it even been two months since . . . Jake?

CHAPTER TWENTY-TWO

Jake nodded, the phone cradled to her ear as she threw a pencil at Rick. "I understand it's confidential. We'd still like to come by. It's very important."

"What?" Rick said as he rubbed his cheek where the pencil had hit.

"We can be there within the hour." Jake nodded. "Thanks." She hung up the phone, grinning. "Found our link. All three spent time at the Women's Crisis Center. She's got files on all of them."

"Okay. Good job. Maybe we've got a rogue counselor or something," Rick said.

"I'm pretty sure the counselors are all women, Rick," she said, standing and shoving her chair away. "I'll let the lieutenant know."

"Meet you outside."

Jake nodded, walking quickly to the lieutenant's door. It was opened, and she knocked on the frame once before entering.

He looked up, his graying hair shining under the fluorescents. Lieutenant Gregory was barely fifty, long ago divorced and never remarried. He seldom spoke of a private life, and Jake guessed that he had none. Yes, he was by the book, as Rick had said, but he wasn't afraid to give his detectives some slack. Working Special Victims was not an easy assignment, and Jake had seen more horror than she cared to remember. But, never fail, Lieutenant Gregory was right there, backing them up. He was the consummate professional and very seldom bent the rules. It had taken him and Jake awhile to get used to each other. Jake bent the rules as far as they would go.

"McCoy. What you got?"

"Women's Crisis Center. All three of our victims had contact with them."

"And you're checking it out?"

"Yes, sir."

"Simpson? Salazar?"

"They're checking out Sandra Poole's last boyfriend. They got some information from the daughter."

"Okay. Keep me posted. I've got a meeting with Captain Zeller at three o'clock. He'll want an update."

"Yes, sir."

"Jake?"

Jake turned back. "Yeah?"

"You know I hate that 'yes sir' shit."

Jake grinned. "Yes, sir. I know."

She walked quickly through the squad room, barely acknowledging the smiles and nods that were flashed her way. For once, her leg felt strong, and she practically jogged down the hall. Rick was waiting in their drab Ford, revving the engine just a bit as she slammed the door.

"Damn glad you're back, Jake."

"Why's that? The lieutenant wouldn't let you drive?"

"He's a control freak, what can I say?"

Jake nodded. "Yeah, yeah. Jefferson Street."

"I know where it is," Rick said as he sped away, squealing the tires just a bit.

"I swear, you're like a kid sometimes."

"But you missed me, right?"

"Yeah, I missed you." Jake settled back in the seat, watching her partner's profile. His day-old stubble was dark on his skin, a nice contrast to his blond hair. Handsome. Damn, but he was. And he knew it.

"What?"

"Nothing. Can't I look at you?"

"You're wondering about me and Michelle, aren't you?"

Jake shrugged. "Yeah." Actually, she'd forgotten.

"Well, we still haven't talked, so don't worry about it."

"I'm not worrying about it. As long as you're okay, I'm okay." She shoved both hands against the dash as he slammed on the brakes at a light, barely avoiding a rear-end collision. "And I'm driving on the way back. *Jesus!*"

He was quiet for a moment, then looked at Jake. "I actually tried to talk to her, you know. But it was like she knew what was coming and changed the subject, so I let it drop."

Jake didn't have any advice for him. She certainly wasn't an expert on relationships, stable or failed.

"Do you want your marriage to last, Rick?"

The light turned green and he drove on, a serious look on his face. Jake wondered what thoughts he was sorting through.

"This sounds awful, Jake, but no. We're like two strangers when we're alone. When other people are around, it's better because we put on this show, you know. But when it's just us, I think, what the hell am I doing here?"

"Then the next time you try to talk to her, don't let it drop. It's not fair to her, Ricky. She may think your marriage is great."

"No. No, she doesn't. I can see it in her eyes when we talk. Neither one of us is the least bit interested in what the other has to say."

"Then do it and get it over with before she ends up pregnant or something."

"That would involve sex, wouldn't it?"

"Oh, Rick. Jesus, you're not even having sex?"

He shrugged. "It's been awhile."

She pointed ahead. "Jefferson's the next block."

"Got it."

"Marriage counselor?"

"What for? That'd mean I'd want it to work out."

"Made up your mind, huh?"

"Yeah. When I'm living with a beautiful woman, and I don't want to make love to her, it's time to get out."

He pulled into the parking lot of the crisis center, looking for a spot to park. "Damn. You think it's always this busy?"

"Over there. A visitor's spot. And I wonder if these are employees or victims? I know they have a shelter, but I doubt it's here." She got out of the car, her leg a little stiff. It was always stiff when she sat for long periods.

"You weren't limping this morning," Rick noted.

"No. It's much better. It's just from riding. It'll loosen up."

"You think it's going to be permanent?"

"I don't know, Rick. If it is, I'll have a hell of a time passing the physical."

He nodded, then held the door open for her. "I'll let you do the talking. They're probably not real fond of men around here," he whispered.

Jake smiled and nudged him with her elbow, hearing his quiet chuckle. At the front desk, they both showed their badges. "I'm Detective McCoy. This is Detective Chase. I spoke on the phone earlier with Patrice Kane."

"Yes. She said you'd be stopping by." The young woman stood and motioned for them to follow. "I'll show you to her office."

They followed her down a long corridor, passing a room with twenty cubicles, Jake guessed. "Excuse me."

The woman stopped and turned around. "Yes?"

"The room there. Is that the crisis line?"

"Yes. We have counselors working the phones twenty-four hours a day."

"On average, how many calls do you get a day?"

The woman smiled but shook her head. "Perhaps Ms. Kane should answer your questions."

Jake and Rick looked at each other, then continued on. The office they stopped in front of was small, barely room for the two visitors' chairs. Most of the available space was taken up with file cabinets.

"Ms. Kane? The detectives are here."

A woman, probably Jake's age, looked up and nodded, motioning for them to come in. "Please close the door, Connie."

Jake reached out and shook the woman's hand, noting her firm handshake and the quiet acknowledgment in her eyes. Jake nodded. "I'm Jake McCoy. We spoke earlier."

"Yes."

"This is Detective Chase." The woman's handshake with Rick was much briefer.

"Thanks for taking the time to see us, Ms. Kane. Your parking lot was overflowing. You must be extremely busy," he said.

"Unfortunately, yes."

Jake sat down and pulled out her pad and pen. "What services do you offer on site?"

"We offer counseling sessions here. Legal advice. Referrals to federal and state agencies for monetary assistance. Of course, the crisis line."

"Is the shelter located here?"

"No. But it's close. Only three blocks down."

"Your counselors? Are they all female or do you have any male counselors?"

"Here, all female. Although we do have a few psychologists who we refer clients to."

"Any of them male?"

"One, yes. There is the rare occasion where an abused woman feels more comfortable talking to a man about it. But it is rare."

"If you have counselors here on staff, why do you refer out?" Rick asked.

Patrice Kane smiled and motioned around her office. "We are a nonprofit organization. The counselors we have here are volunteers, mostly medical students and the occasional practicing therapist who donates their time. Some of our clients need more professional help than we can provide. However, therapy is expensive and most of the women we see here cannot afford it. So, we have arrangements with a few psychologists in the area who will work with us, charging much less than normal. We help pay the fee."

Jake nodded. "Okay. We're just trying to understand how it works here. The three women I asked you about, can you tell me how they came here? Did they call the crisis line or what?"

Patrice leaned forward. "You're very close to that line, Detective."

"They're dead, Ms. Kane. What confidence would you be breaking?"

She picked up three folders on her desks and straightened the papers inside. "I pulled their files, Detective. I don't really remember them. I see hundreds of women come through here."

"I understand."

"Two of them, Helen Thornton and Sandra Poole, called our crisis line. We were not able to convince them to get out of their situations. You'd be surprised at how many women think it's their fault that they are being battered. But after the attacks that sent them both to hospitals, they came for counseling. We referred them both to Dr. Westbrook. That was nearly three years ago."

"Westbrook? Male or female?" Rick asked.

"She's an expert on family violence. We're very lucky that she's willing to accept our clients."

"What about Shelly Burke?" Jake asked.

"There's no record of her calling the crisis line. She was referred to us by a doctor in the emergency room. Her boyfriend decided she was being argumentative when she refused to have sex with him and his son. This was eighteen months ago. Shelly was also referred to Dr. Westbrook."

Jake and Rick looked at each other, eyebrows raised.

"How many women do you refer to this Dr. Westbrook?" Jake asked.

Patrice shrugged. "It's hard to say. We may go months without referring anyone, then in a span of a few weeks, we may send five."

"I'm just assuming here, but you refer women who have been more brutally beaten to her? Since you said she's an expert on family violence."

"Basically, yes. The resources that we have here are sometimes limited. Victims of extreme domestic violence require more than we can offer. Dr. Westbrook has had great success with these women."

Jake nodded. "I don't suppose we could get a copy of their files?"

Patrice laughed. "No, Detective, you can't."

Jake grinned and met the other woman's eyes. "Can't blame a girl for trying." She was rewarded with a slight blush from Patrice Kane. She stood, again offering her hand. Patrice's grip was much softer than before. "We really appreciate you taking the time to see us. You've been a big help."

"My pleasure."

Jake raised an eyebrow teasingly, ashamed at herself for flirting, but she couldn't resist.

"Thank you, Ms. Kane," Rick said politely. Patrice only nodded, her eyes were still on Jake.

At the door, Jake turned back around. "By the way, this Dr. Westbrook, where could we find her?"

"Her office is downtown. Ask Connie to give you the number."

"Thanks."

"Anytime, Detective."

"Well, I'll try not to be a nuisance," Jake promised. Rick gave an exaggerated cough as they walked away.

"Good Lord, could you be any more obvious?"

"What are you talking about?"

"You were flirting with her to get information," Rick accused. "That's disgusting."

"Like I haven't seen you do it."

"She's not even gay," he whispered.

"Of course she is." Jake stopped at the front desk and smiled. "Hello again, Connie. Ms. Kane said that you would give us the address and phone number for Dr. Westbrook."

CHAPTER TWENTY-THREE

Catherine glanced up as the door opened, expecting to see Carol Hulsey, for once early for her appointment. Instead, a handsome blond man entered and smiled at her, and a tall, dark-haired woman met her eyes. For some reason, she wasn't able to look away from those dark eyes.

"May . . . may I help you?" she asked.

The dark-haired woman smiled and walked closer, nodding. "We'd like to see Dr. Westbrook," she said, holding up her police badge. "I'm Detective McCoy."

"I'm sorry, but she's with a patient." Catherine watched as the woman flicked her wrist, glancing at her watch.

"Five more minutes?"

Catherine glanced at the clock on her desk and nodded. "Yes. About."

"We'll wait."

"But . . . she has another appointment. I can try to schedule you in sometime later this afternoon or perhaps tomorrow," Catherine suggested.

"It won't take but a second," she said. "Just a couple of questions."

The door to an inner office opened, and a young woman walked out, smiling at Catherine.

"See you next week, dear," Catherine said as she passed.

Jake stood. "Do you mind?" she said, pointing at the phone. "Or should we just go in?"

"No, no," Catherine said quickly, picking up the phone. A few seconds later she nodded. "Dr. Westbrook? There are a couple of police . . . people here. They'd like a word."

A slight smile touched Jake's face as the woman frowned.

"No, I don't. They didn't say," Catherine said, looking quickly at Jake. "Very well."

Jake pointed to the door. "In there?"

"Yes. You have five minutes."

Jake looked at Rick. "Five minutes, buddy."

"Just my speed."

"I know it is," Jake said as she knocked once and opened the door.

Nicole sighed, trying not to be irritated by the interruption. She glanced up, first seeing a nice-looking young man with blond hair who flashed her a charming smile. Behind him, a tall, slender woman with short dark hair. Disbelief crossed Nicole's face as her eyes collided with Jake's.

"Dr. Westbrook, I'm Detective Chase, this is Detective McCoy. Patrice Kane at the Women's Crisis Center directed us your way. We just have a few questions."

Nicole knew she was staring, but she couldn't help it. Those dark eyes held her captive. She felt her hands clutch the top of her desk, and she wondered foolishly if her mouth was hanging open.

"Dr. Westbrook?" Rick looked from one woman to the other, eyebrows raised. "Jake? You okay?"

"Yeah," she murmured, her eyes never leaving Nicole's.

Rick stared. "You two know each other?"

Jake slowly shook her head. "No, no. We don't know each other."

Nicole came to her senses, finally pulling her eyes away. Surely to God Jake hadn't forgotten her? Not when she could barely get through a night without remembering every touch of the other woman, every kiss.

"I'm sorry," Nicole finally said, rising. "You looked like someone I . . . know." She extended her hand to Detective Chase, then to Jake, managing a light squeeze before pulling it away. Jake's hands were as soft, as strong as she remembered. "Please, sit down. What can I do for you?"

Rick looked at Jake, expecting her to take the lead, but Jake remained silent, her eyes darting around the room, landing time and again on the therapist. Maybe she's just nervous, he guessed. Jake had never been comfortable seeing a therapist. He turned his full attention to Dr. Westbrook.

"We're investigating three murders. Three women who were referred to you by the Women's Crisis Center." He flipped open his notes. "Helen Thornton, Sandra Poole, and Shelly Burke."

Nicole sat back in her chair, shocked. She knew about Sandra Poole, of course. But the others?

"I read about Sandra Poole in the paper. I had no idea about the others."

"They were all patients of yours?" Jake asked.

"Yes, the names are familiar, although it's been years. Shelly Burke, I saw her up until a few months ago. Six at the most."

"Dr. Westbrook, we really need to take a look at their files," Rick said.

Nicole shook her head. "You know I can't do that."

Jake leaned forward. "Why not? Three of your patients are dead."

Nicole rested her elbows on her desk. "I'm sure you've heard of doctor-patient confidentiality, Detective McCoy."

Jake smiled, holding Nicole's eyes captive. "Of course. I read up

116

on it today, in fact. If you have cause to believe that your patient . . . or the general public, is in danger, you're free to reveal aspects of your sessions without violating your patient's privileges."

Nicole smiled, too. "And what medical journal did you read that in?"

Jake looked away. "I forget."

Nicole laughed. "I never would have pictured you as an Internet surfer."

Rick coughed, wondering at the conversation that was taking place without him. "Excuse me, but Dr. Westbrook, three of your former patients have been murdered. It's not a coincidence."

"And you'd like me to turn over my files to you? Privileged, private information about my patients?"

Jake stood up suddenly, pacing across the room. "Rick, give us a second, would you?"

"What?"

She motioned to the door. He raised his eyebrows. She shrugged.

"Okay." He stood. "I'll go . . . interrogate the secretary."

As soon as the door closed behind him, Jake turned and faced Nicole, a slow smile forming on her face.

"Guess you didn't get lost on the way out of the mountains, eh?"

Nicole took a deep breath, trying not to let that smile affect her. "I managed, thank you."

Jake walked closer again, finally sitting down across from Nicole. "So, *Dr.* Nicole Westbrook. Small world."

Nicole nearly laughed. Jake was a . . . cop. Not a hired killer, but a goddamn cop. *Jesus.* Nicole met her eyes. "You're still not getting my files," she said quietly.

"I could get a court order."

"You could try."

"Their lives may be in danger."

Nicole leaned forward. "Why would someone want to kill old patients of mine? It's got to be coincidence."

Jake grinned. "I don't like that word. Nothing is ever a coincidence."

117

"I won't violate their privacy."

Jake stood up, leaning over the desk. "Nicole, how are you going to feel if another one gets killed?"

"And how will it help you if you have the files of all my patients? There are hundreds, Detective. Are you going to watch them all?"

Jake shoved her hands into the pockets of her slacks, knowing she couldn't make Nicole give up the files. She shook her head. "Can you at least give us some background on the three women who've been murdered?"

Part of Nicole wanted to tell this . . . this *detective* to get the hell out of her office. But, Jake's voice was not threatening, only pleading. So, against her better judgment, she decided to help. "I'll give you their files if you promise me the information will never be made public, as in a trial, and that it will only be used in the investigation of this case."

Jake nodded. "I promise," she said softly. "You have my word."

Their eyes locked for a moment, and Nicole felt herself drifting back, reliving once again the hours spent in this woman's arms. Her glance dropped to Jake's mouth, and, she would swear, she could still taste those lips. She swallowed with difficulty, finally pulling her eyes away.

"I'll . . . I'll have Catherine print out the files for you."

Jake nodded, then looked around the room. "Never would have guessed this is what you did for a living." She stared at Nicole, taking in the neat suit and skirt. She smiled. "You looked more comfortable in jeans."

Nicole straightened up. "And I never would have guessed you were a cop. Why didn't you tell me?"

"I don't recall you asking."

No, Nicole hadn't bothered to ask a thing. She was too busy . . . drowning in this woman. Jesus, a small world indeed.

"I have another appointment, Detective." Nicole motioned to the door. "If you don't mind."

Jake nodded. "Thanks for seeing us. And for the files," she added.

Nicole nodded and walked Jake to the door. The other detective and Catherine looked at them as they walked out.

"Catherine, please print out the files that they want." She looked around. "Is Carol not here?"

"Yes. She went to the ladies room."

"Just send her in when she's ready."

"Yes, ma'am."

Nicole turned to go back into her office, but hesitated. She felt Jake's eyes on her, God, just like she'd felt them in the mountains. She looked back, eyes colliding with Jake's for a brief moment, then she made herself walk into her office and close the door firmly behind her. She leaned against it, noting her racing pulse. Wouldn't you know it? The one time she gets wild and does something totally out of character, it comes back to haunt her. What were the chances that she would run into Jake again?

And try as she may, she could not force herself to concentrate on Carol Hulsey's monologue. She nodded when the other women paused, but her thoughts were completely on a dark-haired woman . . . who was a cop, for God's sake!

"How did you talk the files out of her?"

Jake shrugged.

"Come on. Don't tell me she's gay, too, and you sweet-talked her?"

"I didn't say she was gay, but maybe I did sweet-talk her."

"I don't know how you do it. Damn, Jake, you have better luck with the ladies than I do."

"You think so?"

"Well, you have your moments. But the way she was looking at you . . . you sure you didn't know her?"

Jake shook her head. "No. But we got the files. Let's see where they take us."

CHAPTER TWENTY-FOUR

As soon as Carol Hulsey left her office, Catherine was there to replace her, standing in front of her desk with hands on hips.

"What?" Nicole asked.

"I have been with you more years than I can count, and you have never, ever given out copies of files before."

"It's a murder investigation, Catherine." Nicole leaned back and raised her eyes to the ceiling. "And it was . . . her."

"Her? Her who?"

Nicole sighed. "Jake."

"Jake? *That* was your Jake?" Catherine sat down heavily in one of the visitors' chairs. "Oh my God! That *cutie* was your Jake?"

Nicole smiled. "She's not *my* Jake."

"She's cute as hell. Not butch, really. A dyke, yeah."

Nicole sat up. "Will you stop?"

Catherine laughed. "Not your type, that's for sure."

Nicole bristled. "And what is my type, Catherine?"

"Debra Fisher, for one."

"Please don't bring that up again. I'm sorry I ever told you about her . . . proposition."

"I'm sorry. But isn't it ironic? You let your hair down for once and have sex with a stranger, and she ends up being a cop that needs your help."

Nicole gave a sarcastic smile. "Ironic, yes. But still, Catherine, three of my patients are dead. I passed it off as coincidence, but could it really be?"

"Well, what did your cop say?"

"She doesn't think it's a coincidence."

Catherine shrugged. "Shelly Burke. I remember her. It makes it more real. I don't remember the other two."

"Sadly, I really don't either. There have been so many women come through here."

"You think there's really a connection?"

"God, I hope not."

Jake walked quickly behind Cheyenne, giving the dog as much leash as she could. She knew Cheyenne hated the leash, but she couldn't take a chance in the park. As much as she trusted Cheyenne to obey her, she couldn't account for another dog running up to them. But her leg felt good. It was getting stronger every day. It was just the moments of inactivity that stiffened it. Once she worked the kinks out, she was fine. Sort of.

As Cheyenne sniffed around a juniper, Jake let her thoughts drift back to Nicole. Damn, but she'd been shocked speechless when she'd seen her. Never would she have suspected that the Nicole she'd spent time with in the hot springs was a goddamn therapist. First of all, she never thought she'd run into her again. Not that it was unwelcome. She had nothing but fond memories of that day . . . and night. But she suspected that Nicole would just as soon forget the whole thing. She looked as shocked as Jake.

"Pumps and a business suit," she murmured disgustedly, shaking her head. The Nicole she remembered was too comfortable in jeans and hiking boots to bother with dress clothes. But, apparently not. She'd seen it with her own eyes, and she was having a hard time reconciling the two Nicoles. One who seemed to be completely at home in the mountains and this one. This professional one that looked stiff, confined, sad nearly.

And now that she knew who Nicole was and where she was, would she attempt to see her again? She doubted the Nicole she saw today would be eager to see her. The eyes were the same but the rest . . . no. It wasn't the same woman.

Jake sighed. It didn't matter. Nicole was a part of a murder investigation. And that was a line Jake never crossed.

Nicole paced across her living room, wineglass held lightly in one hand. The robe she'd donned after her shower hung loosely around her, and she tightened the belt again.

I can't believe it was her.

"Well, believe it."

And she didn't even act like she knew me. A cop, for God's sake! Wouldn't Dorothy have a field day with this?

Nicole stopped. She didn't know why she was so upset by it. She should be glad Jake was a cop. My God, she'd thought she was a hired killer or something.

Then she frowned. But the dream was so . . . so real, so painful. She wondered what that was all about? And the professional side of her wondered if Jake had sought counseling.

Doesn't matter. It wasn't likely they'd run into each other again, unless Jake had some other police business. They traveled in different circles. But still, Nicole wondered why she hadn't run into Jake before, at court, if nothing else. She shrugged. Maybe they had. And maybe she just hadn't noticed her because Jake wasn't her type.

She rolled her eyes. How could she not notice her? Jake had a presence about her, an energy. And Nicole was drawn to it.

"She's definitely not your type."

CHAPTER TWENTY-FIVE

Jake's eyes opened at the first ring and she rolled over, shoving Cheyenne out of the way.

"McCoy," she said, when she snatched the phone.

"Jake. Found another body."

"Shit. Where?" she asked as she tossed off the covers.

"It's at a goddamn cemetery," Rick said. "I'm on my way in but, you can get there quicker. It's out by Sloan's Lake. You know where that is?"

"Out near Edgewater, right?"

"Yeah. Dispatch said take twenty-sixth."

"How do we know this is one of ours? ME out there already?"

"No. But it's a woman, she appears to have been raped. ME's been dispatched."

"Okay. Who's on the scene?"

"Got a unit and a cemetery security guard, as far as I know."

"Great, a security guard." She struggled into jeans, her right leg not quite cooperating. "I'll meet you there."

"Go easy on them, McCoy."

"Yeah, yeah."

She pulled a sweatshirt over her head, then looked at Cheyenne. "You need to go outside? I don't know when I'll be back."

Cheyenne tucked her head back between her front legs, watching Jake.

"Okay. So, you want to go with me?"

Cheyenne jumped off the bed, tail wagging excitedly. Jake ruffled the dog's fur then grabbed her keys and jacket, walking out into the dark morning. Hell, she didn't even know what time it was. She glanced at her watch and groaned. Two o'clock. It would be at least a couple of hours before she got back. Too late to attempt to go back to bed and snatch some sleep. She opened the back door and Cheyenne jumped in, immediately sticking her head between the front seats and swiping Jake with a wet tongue.

"Don't get so excited. We're just going for a drive."

She sped through the dark streets, the traffic unusually light despite it being Friday night. Well, Saturday morning now. She hoped this body was not going to match the others. Working three victims was hard enough. But four? Then the press would be all over it, and everyone got nervous, and then copycats came out. With three, they could still keep it quiet. Maybe.

She found the cemetery without a problem, the cruiser's flashing lights were seen from blocks away. She noted the Triple A security car parked against the gate and a large, bearded man standing beside it. His uniform looked about ready to pop at the seams.

Jake rolled the windows down halfway, then slammed the door, giving Cheyenne a quick pat. She held up her badge as she walked over to the two uniformed officers.

"Detective McCoy, Special Victims. Where is she?"

"Just inside the gate."

She looked at the security guard. "You found her?"

"Yeah. Just doing a routine sweep, a drive by. Headlights picked up her white . . . her white underwear."

"Okay. You stay here." She pointed at the two officers. "Come with me, let's take a look. ME should be here any minute."

All three shown their flashlights, careful where they walked. "Drag marks," Jake said.

"There's a shoe."

"She was alive when she was being dragged. See this," she pointed. "Heels were digging in."

Jake stopped within five feet of the victim and looked around. She was naked from the waist down. White panties were snagged on a bush, as if someone had thrown them after leaving the body. The area was grassy, no chance for shoe prints.

"Lot of blood," Jake said quietly. "Definitely not a dump."

They all looked up as headlights approached. The ME's van. Right behind it was Rick's black truck.

"Let's get this area roped off," Jake said. "We may want to wait until daybreak to get the crime lab out here."

"I'll radio dispatch."

Jake nodded, then walked over to meet Rick.

"Not ours," she said. "Young woman, twenties, killed here. Probably raped here, too."

"Crazies out, huh?"

"Two days before the full moon." Jake flipped open her cell and called their lieutenant. It rang four times before he picked up. "It's Jake. Rick and I got called to a scene, but it doesn't match ours. You want us to work this, too, or call in Belcher?"

"No, you guys have your hands full. Go ahead and work the scene tonight. We'll hand it over to Belcher in the morning. I'll call him. He's going to love getting his butt up there on a Saturday."

"Okay. Sorry to bother you at this hour."

"Jake?"

"Yes, sir?"

"Back a week, you kinda got thrown into the fray. You holding up okay?"

"Yes, sir. It's good to be back."

"Right. We'll hook up in the morning."

She slipped her phone back into her pocket, then went to find Rick. He was watching the ME.

"Going to be Belcher's case." She nodded at David Gamble, the assistant ME. "How's it going, Dave?"

"Hey Jake. Good to have you back."

"Thanks." She shoved her hands in the pockets of her jeans. "Killed here, right? Not dumped?"

"Definitely killed here. And I'd say only a couple of hours ago. She's got a lot of vaginal trauma. I'd guess more than one had a go with her."

"No ID? No purse laying around?"

"No."

Jake took her flashlight and walked around the area, careful where she stepped. Everything looked clean. The grass was mashed down in places, that was it. Then she cocked her head, staring.

"Rick?"

"Yeah?"

"To your right, about four feet."

He looked, following the beam of her light. "Paper?" He pulled on gloves, then bent down, picking it up by one corner. "Matchbook," he said. "The Oasis. Right here in Edgewood."

"Then we'll assume that's where the party started."

"Maybe we should take this one, Jake. Might have it closed in a couple of days."

Jake laughed. "Don't tell me you're concerned with our conviction rate?"

"Too easy to hand off to Belcher, and it'll probably beat the hell out of our serial killer."

"Sorry, Ricky. It's Belcher's." She turned to the ME. "Dave, make sure her clothes get sent to the crime lab. They're going to come out at first light. Belcher and Moreno will be in touch."

He only nodded, then pulled out his camera, snapping pictures from several angles.

They walked to the gate where the security guard and the two uniforms waited. "Sorry guys," Rick said. "But you're going to have to secure the area until the crime lab gets here."

"Great. Just what I wanted to do. Hang out in a cemetery."

"Yeah, well, if anyone in there starts talking to you, ask if they saw what happened."

"Very funny, Detective."

Rick laughed as he and Jake walked away. "God, I remember the days of being on patrol."

Jake nodded. "My patrol days took place in Gunnison. Most excitement we had was during hunting season when everyone drove around with a gun and a case of beer."

"No murder sprees, huh?"

"We had one homicide during the time I was there. Eighteen-year-old kid found dead up at the college. Stabbed twenty-four times."

"Let me guess. Argument over some girl?"

"That's right. Took us about a week to figure it out."

Rick paused at Jake's Land Cruiser, affectionately rubbing Cheyenne's neck. "I swear, Jake. You take this dog everywhere?"

"I asked if she wanted to go. She said yes."

"You don't even have the back seats up."

"What for? Nobody ever sits back there but her."

Rick patted Cheyenne one more time, then stepped back. "Okay. I guess I'll meet you in the morning."

"If you don't feel like driving in, Rick, I can handle it. I don't mind. It shouldn't take long to brief Belcher."

"I'd just as soon be there than at home, Jake. Maybe we can go grab a burger for lunch or something."

Jake nodded. "Sure. See you . . . what? About eight?"

Rick looked at his watch. "It's three-thirty. I might get in a few hours sleep. Make it nine."

"Okay, buddy."

Jake watched him saunter off, head held low, and she felt sorry for him. Rick had always been one of the most positive persons she'd ever been around. A smile on his face, no matter what. Now, it was hit-and-miss with his smile. And she hated it.

But, really, none of her business. He had to work through his own pain.

She made the drive back to her duplex in silence, shutting off the CD and opening the back windows for Cheyenne. The air was cool, hinting at winter, but she didn't mind. Cheyenne enjoyed it.

Without warning, Nicole's face flashed through her mind. They were back in the mountains, the breeze rustling through the pines, and Nicole . . . opened to her, welcoming her.

"Damn," she murmured, shaking her head. It was a one-time thing, she told herself. Forget about it.

And she tried. But, without warning, visions of that day crowded in, and Jake let them, remembering Nicole's touch, Nicole's response, and . . . God, those screams that sent chill bumps across Jake's skin.

Jake glanced in the mirror, seeing Cheyenne's happy face. "Wouldn't it be ironic, Cheyenne, if Nicole was the one? Ironic because she's here in the city, wearing business suits and heels and . . . too much makeup." She shook her head again. Not the same woman.

CHAPTER TWENTY-SIX

"The matchbook was sent to the lab for prints." Jake handed Belcher a piece of paper. "That's the name of the club. It's in Edgewood."

"You know, you could have called me last night. I'd have driven out."

Jake shrugged. "What was the point? We were already out there."

Belcher nodded, and they both looked up as Rick walked in looking like he hadn't slept at all.

"Hey guys. Coffee?"

"It's made," Jake said. He only grunted.

"Well, guess I'll go visit the crime lab, see what turned up. Thanks, Jake."

"No problem. See you later."

Rick walked over, blowing into his coffee cup. "It's cold out. Wouldn't be surprised if it snowed later."

Jake stared at him. "You look like hell."

"Couldn't go back to sleep. My tossing and turning apparently woke Michele, which caused a fight."

"You talk?"

"Yeah. When I left, she was packing a bag and going to her mother's."

"Oh, no. Her mother hates you."

"Yeah. Can't wait for *that* phone call."

"So, you want to talk about it?"

Rick shook his head. "No. I just want to forget about it." He sat down. "Belcher okay with this case?"

"Yeah. He's so okay with it, he's not even asking Moreno to come in today."

Rick smiled. "You wouldn't do that for me, though."

"Hell, no. If I've got to be here on a Saturday, so do you."

Rick sipped from his coffee, then motioned to her desk. "I see you've got Dr. Westbrook's files out. What are you looking for?"

"Don't really know. Most of this is just notes from their sessions. The doc's take on things. Sandra Poole seemed to be the least receptive to therapy. At least at the beginning." Jake flipped through the pages. "But at the end, Dr. Westbrook lists her as 'extremely positive attitude'." Jake sat back. "I don't think we're going to find anything here. There is no link other than the crisis center and Dr. Westbrook."

"So we can assume someone is killing women who have been referred from the crisis center to Dr. Westbrook."

"But who could get their hands on that information? And why?"

"Someone at the crisis center? Surely they have records. What about Dr. Westbrook's secretary? She would have access."

Jake shook her head. "Did you see her face when she was printing out these files? She was very protective of the information. My guess is that was the first time Dr. Westbrook authorized the release of anything."

"So let's go talk to Patrice Kane again." Rick stood up. "You think she's there on a Saturday?"

"I'd bet she probably lives there. She seemed very dedicated."

The traffic was light, and Jake drove them through the city quickly. Again, the parking lot at the Women's Crisis Center was overflowing. Even the visitors' spots were full.

"Must have been a busy night."

Jake parked on the street nearly a block away, and they walked back side-by-side, Rick occasionally bumping Jake's shoulder.

"Such a kid," she murmured.

"How's the leg today?"

"It's fine. Will you quit worrying about it?"

"You're limping again."

"I told you, it's from sitting in the goddamn car. That, and the cold doesn't exactly help."

Rick stopped. "Are you PMSing? I've gotten off track with you being gone and all."

Jake rolled her eyes. "Trust me, you don't only irritate me when I'm PMSing." She walked on. "And I don't PMS."

"The hell you don't."

The small lobby was crowded. Jake looked around and noticed young mothers with crying children, older women with red, puffy eyes. Yes, must have been a busy night. Connie was again at the reception desk.

"Good morning, Connie."

"Detectives. Back so soon?"

"We wanted to bother Ms. Kane again. If she's got a second."

"She's with someone right now, Detective. If you care to wait," she said, motioning to the lobby, "I'll let her know you're here."

Jake smiled and nodded. "Thanks very much."

There was only one seat available and Rick gallantly offered it to her, but she shook her head.

"I'll stand here with you, thanks."

"Good. Because it kinda makes me nervous with all these women, you know," he whispered.

"I'll protect you, don't worry."

"What do you think happened, anyway?"

"What do you mean?"

"Look at her," he said, with a quick toss of his head. "Black eye, busted lip."

"Well what the fuck do you think happened?"

"But, why didn't she call the cops?"

"Because he beats her and threatens her and she's afraid to call the cops, why do you think?" she said, her voice rising.

"Don't yell."

"I'm not yelling. But Jesus, I can't understand how some women allow this to happen," she said quietly. "I'd beat the shit out of anybody that did that to me."

"Yeah, well, you *could* beat the shit out of someone. Look at her. She's tiny. Her husband's probably a six-foot-tall asshole with a beer gut."

Jake's reply was cut short by Patrice Kane's voice.

"Detective McCoy?"

"I guess she doesn't see me here," Rick muttered.

Jake poked him in the ribs and walked forward, nodding politely at Patrice. "Ms. Kane, sorry to bother you again. But we just have a couple of things."

"Of course. Anyway I can help." She turned back down the hallway. "Come back to my office."

The office was just as cluttered as the first time they were there, and Jake moved files off of one of the visitors' chairs before sitting down.

"Sorry about that, but it's been crazy today."

"Are the weekends usually like this?"

"Yes. More so around a full moon."

"Do you work seven days a week?"

Patrice smiled. "I could ask you the same thing, detective?"

"Yeah. Kinda work when you're needed, I guess."

"Exactly." She leaned back. "Now, what can I do for you?"

"Well, we visited with Dr. Westbrook. She was kind enough to talk with us about the three murders we're investigating." Jake met her eyes. "We've concluded that the only connection between them is your crisis center and Dr. Westbrook. What we'd like is a list of people you've referred to Dr. Westbrook in the last three years."

Patrice shook her head. "That's impossible."

Jake sighed. "We don't want information on them, you'd be breaching no confidences. We'd just like a list of names."

"I'm sorry, Detective."

"They might be in danger," Jake said, her voice rising.

"It's not that I wouldn't like to help you. I would. But look around. We're not exactly automated."

"What are you saying? You don't have a list of referrals?"

"No. If we refer someone and they are accepted, it's noted in their file . . . their paper file . . . and put up. There's not a computer record."

"You've got to be kidding?"

"I wish I were. But our budget is extremely limited. Not to mention staffing. There hasn't been time to put everything in a database. Don't think we've not talked about it. It comes up every year. And every year, the money is best used elsewhere."

Jake leaned forward, resting her elbows on her knees and holding her head. "Okay. So what are the chances that Dr. Westbrook keeps a running list of your referrals?"

"Probably much better than ours. Her secretary, Catherine, is very efficient. However, Nicole Westbrook is a stickler for doctor-patient privilege. I'm surprised she even spoke with you about her patients."

Jake smiled. "Well, it took a little prodding."

Patrice nodded and winked at Jake. "I'm sure it did."

Jake grinned, then followed a hunch. "Are you and Dr. Westbrook . . . friends as well as colleagues?"

Patrice glanced quickly at Rick then back to Jake. "I've been around her socially, yes."

"Good. So what do you think the chances are of her giving up her files?"

Patrice laughed. "Cold day in hell. Like I said, she's a stickler."

"Well, I'd like to think that if it meant stopping any more murders, she'd be inclined to help."

"Good luck, McCoy. You'll have your work cut out for you."

Jake stood and Rick did the same. "Okay, then. Sorry to have taken up more of your time. Judging by the lobby out there, you're going to have a long day."

"Yes. Saturdays are usually busy."

Rick left with only a nod, but Jake turned around and smiled. "Thanks, Patrice. I appreciate you seeing us."

"Of course. Come by or call if you need something."

"Thank you."

Jake found Rick waiting in the hallway. He rolled his eyes as soon as she walked out.

"Please tell me you're not going to ask her out?"

Jake shrugged. "Why?"

"I don't like her for you."

"Ricky, you don't like anyone for me."

"No, she's too . . . manly."

"Manly? She's not manly. You didn't even think she was gay." Jake nodded to Connie. "Thanks."

"Sure, Detective McCoy."

Rick shook his head. "Like putty in your hands."

"Shut up."

"Now we get to see if you can mold Dr. Westbrook."

Jake arched an eyebrow, but kept her comment to herself. For the time being, she still did not want Rick to know that she and Nicole were familiar with each other. For some reason, she didn't think Nicole would appreciate that.

"Let's hook up with her on Monday. Right now, I'd like to enjoy what's left of our Saturday," she said, as they walked back to her Land Cruiser.

"The sun is shining, and you don't care how cold it is. You're going to sneak out of town, aren't you?"

Jake nodded. "Promised Cheyenne we'd do some hiking."

"It's cold as hell, Jake."

"It's not cold. You're a wimp."

"Yeah, city boy. But don't overdo it Jake. Your leg still bums you, you know."

Jake cocked her head. "You want to come with me? Or maybe that burger you talked about?"

He shook his head. "Might as well face the music. I'm sure her mother has called all the sisters by now. They are either waiting at the house for a lynching or have taken her into protective custody."

"I'll have my cell. Call me if you need me."

"I know I can count on you to come to the rescue, Jake. Thanks."

They both got in and slammed the doors, Jake reaching over to squeeze Rick's arm affectionately before driving away.

CHAPTER TWENTY-SEVEN

Early November was a funny time of year in Colorado. Jake left the city, still shrouded in clouds. As Rick had said, it was cold as the wind whistled across the concrete and between the high rises. But as she climbed into the mountains a half hour outside Denver, the sun was bright, warming the landscape. She lowered the back window, and Cheyenne immediately took advantage of it. The colors were gone from the mountains, the aspens having long ago shed their brilliant golden leaves. The days had definitely been hinting at winter, and she had a sudden longing for her cabin.

In the old days, she'd drive up during a blizzard just to be able to sit by the fire, gaze out the giant windows overlooking the Collegiate Peaks and watch the snow fall. She really missed the cabin. And after spending more than a month there, it reminded her of why she bought the place to begin with. Jake felt stifled in the city, and she could feel the tension leave the farther they drove into the mountains.

She looked in her side mirror, smiling at the nearly laughing face of Cheyenne as she stuck her face into the wind. Yeah, this is what she liked. Quiet time, alone time with her dog. They would drive out to Idaho Springs instead of venturing to the much-used Mt. Evans Wilderness. She'd go west to the tunnels and hike some of the old mining trails.

There were only two other cars at the trailhead. No one was about so she let Cheyenne out without the leash. After clipping her water bottle to her waist and hooking Cheyenne's leash to a belt loop, she started out. Cheyenne ran ahead of her, turning around frequently to make sure she was coming.

"I'm still here," she said, motioning to the dog to go ahead. She knew Cheyenne would not get too far ahead, and she kept a look-out for other hikers. Some hikers weren't too keen to have a dog running wild up to them.

Clouds were gathering far to the west, over the Continental Divide and Jake suspected the mountains would have snow by morning. Denver would see perhaps a little rain, if that.

The trail climbed higher, moving through the ponderosas and into the spruce, affording Jake a beautiful view of Mt. Evans to the south and the ski area to the west. She paused at a switchback, looking to the south. Cheyenne walked back to her, finally nudging her leg. She walked on, her leg feeling strong, only an occasional twinge on a very steep portion of the trail. This hike should be fine for her. They'd go up about an hour, then head back down, well before dark.

They only encountered one hiker coming back down the trail, and he simply patted Cheyenne on the head and kept going. They were still a good hour from reaching the tunnels and Jake looked to the sky, noting the dark clouds. Best to head back down now.

"Cheyenne? Come on, girl," she called. The dog immediately came dashing down the trail, brushing Jake as she passed by. She made the trip down easily, although Jake's leg was aching by the time they finished the last switchback. She was visibly limping as they walked to her truck. She offered Cheyenne some water from her bottle, and the dog drank, lapping up the liquid from Jake's palm.

By the time they headed back, dusk was upon them, and the temperature had dipped into the forties. Jake pulled on the sweatshirt she kept in her backpack, then settled in, driving them slowly back to Denver. Cheyenne was lying in the back, head resting on the console. Jake absently rubbed her head as she drove.

"You're spoiled rotten, you know," she murmured.

She got no response except a thump of the tail.

CHAPTER TWENTY-EIGHT

Catherine looked up as the door opened, expecting their next client. She was surprised to be locking glances with Nicole's Jake.

"Hi again, Catherine," Jake said.

"Detective," she greeted.

"The doc busy?"

Catherine nodded, watching silently as Jake perched a hip on the side of her desk. She barely noticed the other detective take a seat in the lobby.

"Can you squeeze me in between appointments?"

The door opened again and Lori Simmons walked in, head held low, as usual. She barely met Catherine's eyes, and she took a seat at the opposite end as Detective Chase.

"She's nervous," Catherine whispered. "Do you think he could leave?"

Jake frowned, then looked at the woman fidgeting, eyes darting between Rick and the door.

"Rick," she said quietly. When he looked up, she motioned to the door. He nodded and followed her outside. "The lady in there is . . . kinda freaked with you being in the room."

"What'd I do?"

"Nothing. She's probably abused. Why else is she here?"

"Okay. What do you want me to do?"

Jake cocked her head. "Wait in the car?"

"Oh, Jesus. Wait in the fucking car?"

"If we freak out her patients, do you think Dr. Westbrook is going to give us anything?" Jake reasoned.

"No, you're right. Hell, I hate waiting in the fucking car."

"Big baby." Jake pulled the keys from her pocket and tossed them at him. "This doesn't mean you're driving on the way back."

"Yeah, yeah," he murmured as he walked down the hall and dejectedly punched the elevator button.

"I won't be long," Jake called.

When Jake walked back in, another woman was walking out. She stepped aside, holding the door open for the woman. When she closed the door, she glanced at Catherine with raised eyebrows.

"Five minutes," Catherine said firmly as she picked up the phone. "Detective McCoy is here."

Jake listened, watching Catherine frown.

"Yes, she's here, too."

Jake shifted. She'd hate to have to throw a fit. But she would. She needed to speak with Nicole.

"Okay. I'll tell her." Catherine hung up the phone. "You have two minutes."

"Two? You said five."

"You have a minute and a half."

Jake pointed a finger at Catherine. "You're cruel." But she hurried to Nicole's door, not bothering to knock.

"Two minutes?" she asked, as soon as the door was closed.

Nicole looked up, catching her breath as her eyes met Jake's. "I have a patient waiting. And trust me, Lori does not need to be kept waiting."

"I noticed she was a little nervous."

"Yes." Nicole leaned back, her eyes traveling the length of Jake despite her resolve not to. "What can I do for you?"

"I need some names from you."

"Names?"

"Of all the clients that were referred to you from the crisis center."

Nicole leaned forward. "Are you out of your mind?"

"I don't think so. Is that a problem?"

"Of course it's a problem. Jake, I can't just give you this information."

"Why not? I'm not asking for anything other than names. And maybe addresses."

Nicole sighed. "Detective, I don't have time to argue with you. I have a patient waiting. Maybe we could discuss this another time?"

"Time is short, Dr. Westbrook," Jake said. "And I need your help on this."

Nicole's eyes locked on Jake's and, for the life of her, she couldn't look away. She found herself being pulled, once again, to this woman.

"Make a real appointment, Jake. Then we'll discuss this."

"How about over dinner?" Jake asked, the question startling her as much as Nicole.

"No." *Dinner?* Nicole pulled her chair closer to her desk. "Have Catherine set you up with a time."

Jake shrugged. "Sure. Sure, I'll do that." She leaned her hands on the desk, and again caught Nicole's eyes. "I need your help, Nicole. Women are being murdered, and they are linked to you." She stood up straight. "So we'll talk soon. One way or the other."

Nicole watched her walk out, her eyes locked on the retreating back. *One way or the other? What the hell did that mean?* But she pushed Jake from her mind, smiling as Lori entered her office. It was only the third visit for Lori and she was still way, way out there. Nicole had yet to reach her.

"Hi, Lori. Did you have a good week?"

Lori barely lifter her head. "No, not really."

Nicole nodded. It was a standard reply.

Jake tapped on the window, smiling as Rick jerked his head up. "Didn't sleep much?"

"Hell, no." Rick stretched. "Between the threatening calls from the sisters, and my own paranoia, no, I didn't get much sleep last night."

"Afraid the lynch mob was going to come get you?"

"Yeah. Maybe you could let me borrow Cheyenne for a few nights."

"No way. But if you want to bunk at my place, you can."

"Hell, no. I'm not scared of a bunch of women."

Jake laughed. "Of course not." She pulled into traffic, then glanced at Rick. "You have to talk to her, you know."

"I know. I just want to wait a few days and let her settle down."

"What exactly did you tell her?"

"I told her I wasn't in love with her, and I really didn't even like her much."

"Good Lord, Rick. Real subtle."

"Well, you said I should tell her."

"Ever heard of sugarcoating it?"

He shrugged. "It just kinda came out. And when it started, it wouldn't stop."

It was her turn to shrug. "Well, I guess you got it all out at once. At least that's over with."

"Yeah. But she acted all shocked and everything, like I'd just imagined all these problems."

"It's just a defense mechanism."

"I know. But still, I felt like a total asshole."

Jake laughed. "Well, I can't help you there." Jake again reached over and squeezed his arm.

"So, did the doc give up names or what?"

"Hell, no. She let me have my say, then had me make an appointment to see her."

"An appointment?"

Jake shrugged. "Apparently, she's very busy. So, I sweet-talked Catherine a bit, and she said her last appointment leaves at four-thirty."

"So we'll show up then?"

"I'll show up then."

"Come on, Jake. For some reason, I get the feeling that Dr. Westbrook doesn't exactly like you. Maybe *I* should go in solo," Rick suggested.

But Jake shook her head. "Nothing against you, buddy, but all day long, she listens to women who've been abused by their husbands. I don't think a man asking her for a favor is going to go over well."

"You're probably right. But what if she won't give it up? Do you think the lieutenant could pull off a court order?"

"No." But Jake smiled. "She'll give it up."

"Now, Jake. Dr. Westbrook didn't look like your type. In fact, I'd bet money that she doesn't play for your team."

"Why does everything revolve around sex with you?"

" 'Cause I'm a guy. That's what we do."

Jake shook her head. "She'll give it up because I'll talk her into it. Don't worry."

"Okay. I won't worry. Because we've got shit for leads in this, anything the doc will give up can only help."

143

CHAPTER TWENTY-NINE

Nicole kicked off her shoes, glad the last appointment of the day was finally over. Catherine was right. She needed to space things out more. She'd been at it nonstop since nine that morning. Tomorrow would be slower. Much slower. The group session would last a couple of hours. After that, she had the afternoon to herself.

"Right," she murmured. The afternoon would most likely be spent making notes. She was *so* behind. The scribbled notes she made while in session would hardly be legible in a few more days.

A knock on her door brought her head up and she frowned, wondering why Catherine was knocking.

"Come on in, Catherine," she called.

But it was not Catherine who entered. Jake stood in the doorway, a smile lifting up one corner of her mouth.

"You said to make an appointment."

"So I did."

Jake shrugged. "This is it."

Catherine stood behind her, an apologetic look on her face. "I didn't get a chance to tell you, Dr. Westbrook."

"Uh-huh." Nicole noticed the slight blush of Catherine's cheeks, no doubt the result of Jake's presence. Even a happily married woman like Catherine was not immune to her charms, Nicole noted.

"Really. But I think . . . you're in good hands."

"Thanks a lot, Catherine," Nicole said, as Jake walked into the room and perched in one of the visitors' chairs. Nicole took a deep breath, then looked up and met Jake's eyes. "Detective . . . *McCoy,*" she said. "You have something new to tell me?"

"No. We still just have three murders linked to you. I'm sure there'll be more," Jake said easily.

Nicole leaned forward. "Jake, what do you want from me?"

"I want the names of everyone referred to you by the crisis center in the last three years."

"And that'll do what for you?"

"Well, we can try to monitor them . . ."

"Jake, there is not just a handful. In three years, there have probably been forty or fifty women referred to me by Patrice."

Jake raised an eyebrow. "Are you and Patrice Kane . . . close?"

"Close? We're friends. Not good friends. Why?"

Jake shrugged and looked away. "So, you have a list?"

"And you're going to watch them all?"

"We've got to start somewhere." Jake stood and walked to the desk, leaning a hip on the corner. "Have you had any unusual phone calls? Anyone hanging around?"

"No. But Catherine would know about the phones. What are you getting at?"

"There's a possibility that whoever is killing these women is not after them, but you."

"Me?" Nicole sat up. "Why would you think that?"

"You're the link. You and the crisis center."

"If you're trying to scare me, you're not succeeding. I've had more threats from my patients' husbands than I can possibly tell you."

Jake stiffened. "What kinds of threats?"

Nicole let out a deep breath. "Jake, they're just threats. Their wife goes to court to testify, I get a threatening phone call, maybe a letter. They get sentenced to prison, I get another threatening letter. It's old hat."

Jake shook her head. "This is different, Nicole."

"Jake, if someone wanted to kill me, it wouldn't be hard to do. I work in a public place, I drive home alone, I live alone. It wouldn't be difficult."

"You're not the target right now, Nicole. But you will be. He wants to make sure he has your attention first. No doubt, he's watching you. He probably knows that I've been to see you more than once."

Their eyes met across the desk and Nicole smiled. "You really want me to give up names, don't you?"

"Nicole, he's killed three women," Jake said quietly. "And he won't stop with three women."

Nicole nodded. "Okay, Jake. You win. I'll have Catherine pull you a list of names."

"Thank you."

Nicole twirled her pen nervously between her hands. "You realize that if I didn't know you, I wouldn't agree to this, don't you?"

Jake smiled. "And you realize, if I didn't know *you*, I wouldn't care so much." She stood up, shoving hands into pockets. "We can discuss this more over dinner, you know," she suggested.

Nicole nearly accepted. God knows she wanted to. But she looked at the endless assortment of paperwork on her desk and shook her head. "Can't. I have at least two hours of work still."

Jake nodded. "Maybe another time, then."

Their eyes met, and Nicole went back, back two months ago, high up in the mountains. Those eyes had pulled her in, had consumed her. They were threatening to do that again. With difficulty, she looked away, making a show of straightening the papers on her desk.

"Can I ask you something?"

Nicole nodded.

"Are you . . . afraid of me?"

"Afraid? Of course not."

"Maybe embarrassed?"

Nicole opened her mouth to speak, then closed it again. What could she say? Yes, she was embarrassed. That wanton, insatiable woman who had begged Jake to take her one last time, then one more . . . was simply not her. She didn't *do* that. So, yes, she was embarrassed.

"Jake, I wish I could forget what happened. Obviously, the chances of us meeting again were very, very slim. But what happened between us, that's just not me. I don't do things like that." Nicole finally dared to meet Jake's eyes. "So I would appreciate it if we could just pretend that it never happened. I certainly don't want to talk about it."

Jake smiled. "I see. Embarrassed *and* ashamed." Jake walked closer, her eyes never leaving Nicole's. "But you know what? The time we spent together was far too incredible for me to want to forget it. Because I can still hear you scream," Jake finished in a whisper.

Nicole's breath caught and, with difficulty, she swallowed, finally pulling her eyes away. She sat up straighter, determined to forget. "I have a lot of work to do, Detective McCoy. If you don't mind."

Jake smiled at Nicole's obvious discomfort and decided she'd play along with her and pretend that just being in her presence didn't conjure up all kinds of delicious memories. "Okay, *Doctor* Westbrook. If you could just ask Catherine to get me the list?"

"Of course. Good night, Detective," she said, as she reached for the phone, instructing Catherine.

Jake noticed the frown on Catherine's face as she hung up the phone. No, this woman was not used to giving out information.

"I promise, it won't get into the wrong hands," Jake said, as she perched on the familiar corner of Catherine's desk. "But three of the people on the list you're about to give me have been murdered. I've got to find a connection before it happens again."

"I don't know what kind of influence you have over her, but she has *never*, ever given out information before," Catherine said disapprovingly.

"I don't have any influence over her. Perhaps she recognizes the importance of these names."

Catherine only shrugged, her mouse clicking away. Finally, she sat back, waiting as the printer began churning out pages.

"How many?"

"Forty-seven women."

"Damn." Jake waited patiently, watching the printer. Then she glanced at Catherine, smiling when the woman met her eyes. "How long have you worked for Dr. Westbrook?"

"A long time," she said evasively.

Ah. Protective, Jake guessed. But, what the hell? "Is she . . . seeing anyone?" Jake asked quietly.

Catherine smiled. "Nicole sees a lot of people."

Jake shrugged. "Okay. Is she . . . romantically involved with anyone? How's that?"

"Why do you want to know?"

Jake lost her patience, grabbing at the papers on the printer. "Forget it. Thanks for the list, Catherine." Jake walked quickly to the door, but stopped when Catherine called to her.

"Dr. Westbrook is single, Detective." She grinned slightly. "But you didn't hear it from me."

Jake winked. "Thanks."

Nicole tried to work. She really did. But transcribing her notes was proving to be a chore tonight, especially since she couldn't get Jake out of her mind. *"I can still hear you scream."*

"Good Lord," she murmured. She tossed her pen down and leaned her head back, eyes squeezed shut. Yes, she could still recall her screams, too.

A quick knock on her door, and Catherine stuck her head in. "Heading out." Then Catherine moved into the room. "Are you okay?"

"I'm fine. Tired," Nicole said.

"Why don't you call it a night? It's nearly six."

"I am *so* behind on these notes, that's why. If I don't get them in while they're still fairly fresh, I never will."

"Okay. But don't stay all night. We've got group tomorrow. That makes you cranky enough."

"I won't." As Catherine turned to leave, Nicole called her back. "Did Detective McCoy get the list okay?"

"Yes, she did. There were forty-seven names on it, though. I think that threw her."

"She has this crazy idea that someone's killing women who have been referred from the crisis center to us."

"Is it crazy?"

"Of course it is. Why would anyone want to kill these woman? They are victims several times over. There is no rhyme or reason for them to be targeted."

"Awful lot of coincidence though, Nicole."

Nicole sighed. "Yes. I suppose so." Jake's words came back to her. Was she a target?

Jake sat on one corner of her sofa, absently rubbing Cheyenne's head as she read through the list of women and their addresses. They were mostly scattered across the city. No way they could watch them all. Hell, no way they could even interview them all.

She tossed the list down and picked up her drink, taking a sip, enjoying the fire of the Scotch as she swallowed.

Well, one thing was certain. They still had shit to go on. But ultimately, if the crisis center wasn't the target, then Nicole was.

CHAPTER THIRTY

"Patrice Kane, please," Nicole said. "It's Dr. Westbrook."

"Of course, Dr. Westbrook. One moment."

Nicole tried to convince herself not to worry about this, that the police could handle it. After all, she'd had numerous threats over the years. But still, three murders. Three murders close to home. Jake's words were still running through her mind.

"Hello, Nicole. I thought I'd be hearing from you," Patrice said.

"So the police have been bothering you, too?"

"Not bothering. Detective McCoy and some . . . guy."

"Yes. They've been here. What do you think?"

"Well, it's troubling, of course. But what can we really do about it? I'd thought about handing over all the threatening mail that we get, but it would take them weeks to go through it."

"Still get that much?"

"Daily, I'm afraid."

Nicole sighed. "Yes, I get my share."

"Of course, I wouldn't mind calling that detective for a little protection," Patrice said with a laugh. "It's been awhile since someone's gotten my juices flowing just by standing next to me. Good Lord, but she's cute."

Nicole was shocked by the stab of jealously that shot through her. She nearly bristled, then reminded herself that she didn't care one way or the other. Jake was but an acquaintance, Patrice a colleague and social friend. If Patrice wanted to snag her claws into Jake, so be it. And with that said, she simply ignored her statement and pretended that her heart wasn't beating just a little too fast.

"I'm going to have Catherine go through the handful of letters we get each week from disgruntled husbands. Just in case. I gave Detective McCoy a list of your referrals, by the way."

"You did? I told her she'd have a hard time getting information from you, Nicole. I know you're a stickler for the confidentiality rules."

"Yes. Normally I am."

Patrice laughed. "I know what you mean. That woman had me ready to hand over all my files."

Nicole couldn't help it. "She got to you, I see."

"God, yes. I just wanted to sit and stare at her."

"Well, I didn't give her information because she's a pretty face. She has legitimate arguments. And she promised the information would not leave her hands."

Patrice laughed again. "And you just took her word? Nicole, I remember the time you forced them to get a court order for one of your files when they were trying to nail the husband for rape of your patient's sister."

Nicole sighed. Yes. And she had just handed everything over to Jake without a fight. "Well, thank you for pointing that out, Patrice. Perhaps I'm becoming more flexible in my old age."

"Feel like dinner one night? We haven't been out in ages."

"I'd like to, but I'm usually up here until seven most evenings. It would have to be late."

"That's okay with me. I'm dying to get the gossip on Deb Fisher."

"What do you mean?"

"I heard you asked her out, and she turned you down. It's not like Deb to turn anyone down."

"Where in the world did you hear that?" Nicole demanded, as she grabbed the bridge of her nose. Damn Debra Fisher! Deb couldn't stand to be turned down, so she had to get the word out before Nicole announced it. Jesus, as if she'd go around telling people that Debra Fisher had propositioned her!

"A group of us had drinks the other night," Patrice said. "I forget who brought it up."

It was on the tip of her tongue, but Nicole decided not to stoop to Deb's level. Well, that, and the fact that no one would believe her. So, she tried the graceful way out.

"Well, it wasn't exactly like that, Patrice. Call me in a few weeks if you want to get dinner," Nicole said.

"I will. And let me know if there's anything I can do with this police investigation."

Nicole's reply was cut short as she heard the dial tone. *Police investigation?* She wasn't being investigated. *Was she?*

CHAPTER THIRTY-ONE

"There are forty-seven," Jake said. "Well, forty-four that are still alive. But even then, it's not like we can watch them all."

"Some have maybe moved away," Gina suggested.

"I'm sure they have. But we still can't do surveillance. How about this? Of these forty-four women, let's break it down to whose husband, boyfriend, whatever, is still on the inside. Or was incarcerated and is now out. And find out if Dr. Westbrook was involved in any of their trials."

"That still won't tell us how someone got his hands on this list," Lieutenant Gregory said.

"The connection has to be the crisis center," Rick said.

"But they don't keep records. Not on a computer, anyway. There's no way they could have gotten a list," Jake reminded him.

"Maybe they didn't need a list. Maybe they work there and just . . . knew."

Jake shook her head. "That makes no sense. Two of our victims were referred three years ago."

"So maybe it's a former employee," Gregory said. "Simpson, let's check that out. See if you can get employee records, going back at least three years."

"I think that Dr. Westbrook is the target," Jake said.

"If she was the target, she'd have been popped by now," Rick said.

"Why? He's in control this way. Picking off her patients, one by one. Making her watch her back, making her think that maybe it's her fault this is happening. Eventually, it'll affect her practice. I mean, who's going to want to see a shrink whose patients are getting whacked? And then, when he's had his fun, he takes her out."

Gregory shrugged. "Okay. I'll buy it. How cooperative is Dr. Westbrook?"

"Well, she's given us what we want so far," Jake said.

"See if she's up for a detail. We can spare a unit to follow her home at night, hang out. But let's find our guy. Gina, you do background on our list."

"Yes, sir."

"Simpson?"

"Crisis center. I'm on it."

"Take Chase with you. Jake, can you handle Dr. Westbrook?"

Jake let a ghost of a smile touch her face and nodded. "I'm on it."

Nicole held the door open, smiling reassuringly to the women as they walked past. The group session had been good, beneficial even, for only their second meeting.

"Dr. Westbrook?"

"Yes, Joni?"

"I wasn't real enthused about this group session, you know."

Nicole smiled. "Yes, I know."

"But, I feel better today. It was good to listen to others."

"Good." Nicole affectionately squeezed her arm. "It helps, sometimes, to know that you're not alone in situations like this."

"Yeah, it does." The other woman smiled for what Nicole thought was the first time since she'd met her. "I'll see you next Tuesday, Dr. Westbrook."

"Have a wonderful weekend, Joni."

Nicole waited until the elevator doors opened for Joni before going back inside, but she stopped as a familiar figure got off just as Joni got on. Jake caught her eyes, a slow smile forming on her face, a smile that Nicole returned.

"Hanging out in the hallway?"

"I just had a group session. Joni was the last to leave."

"Group, huh? Any of them on my list?"

Nicole sighed and nodded. "A couple." She walked back into the small lobby with Jake following. "Has it helped at all?"

Jake shrugged. "Just getting started on it."

"I see. And what can I help you with today?"

Jake arched an eyebrow. "Actually, I came to talk to Catherine."

"Oh." Nicole hoped the surprise and perhaps disappointment didn't show on her face. She stepped aside and pointed at Catherine. "She's all yours. I have some paperwork to catch up on."

"Thanks."

Nicole met Catherine's eyes briefly, then walked into her own office and shut the door. She leaned against it for a second, eyes closed. *Jealous of your secretary! God, you're pathetic.*

"How are you doing today, Catherine," Jake asked easily, walking to sit on her usual corner of the desk.

Catherine smiled, wondering why she wasn't immune to this woman's charm. No wonder Nicole had melted. "I'm fine, Detective."

"Jake, please. I hate all that detective stuff."

"Okay." Catherine leaned back to look up at the other woman. "You really came to see me?"

Jake smiled. "Well, you and the doc." Jake turned serious.

"Listen, have you been getting any strange phone calls, hang-ups, heavy breathing, anything like that?"

Catherine laughed. "All the time."

Jake pulled out her notebook and pen. "Oh, yeah? Tell me about it."

"Jake, I've worked here for years. We've always gotten calls like that."

"Oh. What about the mail? What about threatening letters and such."

"That, too."

"Great," Jake said dryly. "Have you gotten anything recently?"

"Had a pretty good one last week. Normally, they just threaten Dr. Westbrook, but this one included me."

Jake's eyes narrowed. "Do you still have it?"

Catherine shook her head. "No. I don't keep those things. They make me nervous."

Jake leaned forward. "Tell me what you remember about it."

"Well, it was pretty typical. They mostly blame Dr. Westbrook for them losing their wives and families, and they vow revenge. This one was no different. It said something about taking away her life, little by little, including your loyal secretary. Something like that."

Jake scribbled quickly on her notepad, eyebrows drawn together. "Do you think this particular guy has written before?"

"I couldn't say. Usually, I get letters like that, I just throw them away without reading them."

"And you never thought to contact the police about these letters?"

"Jake, when I first started working here and got the first one, I freaked out. But Nicole said I'd get used to it. And I have. We get letters weekly."

Jake nodded. "Okay. Do me a favor? If you get another one, hang on to it. I'd like to see it." She pulled her card out and handed it to Catherine. "My cell is on there. You can reach me anytime." She stood up. "Now I'm going to bug your boss."

Catherine smiled. "Well, good luck. She's been in a mood the last few days."

"A mood?"

Catherine shrugged. "She won't tell me what's bothering her."

"I see. Well, hopefully, she won't bite my head off."

Nicole looked up as her door opened, and Jake walked inside, closing the door behind her.

"Busy?"

Nicole sighed. "Yes. Does that matter?"

Jake smiled. "No."

"I didn't think so," she murmured. "I thought you wanted to talk to Catherine."

"I did. I also wanted to talk to you."

"Well, Detective, I can spare a few—"

"Let's stop this, Nicole," Jake interrupted.

"Stop what?"

"Stop this bullshit. Stop pretending we don't know each other. Stop pretending that we . . . we haven't seen each other naked. Stop pretending that we're damn strangers."

Nicole stared at Jake's flashing eyes, trying to ignore that she was aroused by her words. "What brought that on?"

"This formality between us, Nicole. That's what brought it on. If you want to pretend that it didn't happen, you can. But don't pretend in front of me. Because I know it *did* happen." Jake walked closer. "And because it did happen, and because I know you, that's why I'm fucking concerned about this goddamn case," Jake said, her voice rising.

Nicole swallowed, her eyes never leaving Jake's. "I'm sorry. I'm only pretending it didn't happen because I . . . I wish it hadn't. That's not me. *You're* not me."

Jake frowned. "*I'm* not you? What does that mean?"

Nicole sighed and leaned her head back. "You're not my type, Jake. I've never been . . . with anyone like you."

157

Jake raised an eyebrow. "And who is your type?"

Nicole stared. Why was she bothering with this discussion? "I normally go out with other professional women. It's very discreet."

"You're in the *closet*?" Jake asked incredulously.

"Sort of."

"You're kidding me."

"Why do I have to explain this to you?"

"But why?" Jake asked. "You are who you are," she said simply.

"Exactly. And this is who I am."

Jake shook her head. "No. I don't think so. I think who you are is out there," Jake pointed. "In the mountains."

"Look, do you have any . . . *police* questions? I really have work to do."

Jake nodded. "I want to discuss this case with you, yes. But not here."

"Not here?"

"No."

"Where do you suggest?"

Jake arched an eyebrow. "Your place or mine?"

"Very funny."

"I'm serious. Or, we could get dinner out."

"And why can't we discuss it here?"

"I'm hungry."

Nicole took a deep breath. They could go out somewhere or pick up a pizza and eat in. Out and they risked being seen. She frowned. Seen by whom? And should she care? But if they ate in, it would be far too intimate. Jesus, why did it have to be so difficult?

"Nicole, you look almost frightened. What's wrong?"

"Do I?"

Jake put her hands on her hips and stared. "Are you scared of me?"

"No, no. Of course not," Nicole said quickly. "Look, can we maybe grab a pizza and . . . I don't know, go somewhere? I live out near Golden."

"I'm a lot closer. Besides, Cheyenne is waiting for me."

Nicole couldn't help but smile at the mention of the dog's name. "Okay. How about I follow you?"

Jake nodded. "I'll call one in. Anything you don't like?"

"No. Get whatever you want."

Nicole parked behind Jake in the tiny driveway. The entire street as far as she could tell seemed to be nothing but duplexes. Identical duplexes. It was depressing. She got out and locked her car, then followed Jake. She silently took the pizza from her as Jake struggled to unlock the door.

Jake pushed it open and flipped on a light, motioning Nicole inside. A high-pitched bark and a thud on the back door signaled Cheyenne wanted in.

"Let me get her before she knocks the door down. Make yourself at home."

Nicole put the pizza on the small table just off the kitchen and looked around. This is not how she pictured Jake's home. There was nothing here to indicate the woman loved the mountains, as Nicole knew she did. Then she spotted something familiar. Jake's cane. It was leaning against the wall, not far from the recliner.

"Heads up," Jake called, as Cheyenne burst into the room.

Cheyenne wagged her tail excitedly as she sniffed Nicole, finally nudging Nicole's hand with a wet nose.

"Hi girl," Nicole said, bending down to pet the dog.

"She remembers you," Jake said.

"You think so?"

"Yeah. She never greets anyone."

Nicole straightened up and smoothed her skirt, one hand still rubbing Cheyenne's ear. "How long have you lived here?"

Jake shrugged. "Since I've been in Denver. Five years or so." She pulled out two plates and handed them to Nicole. "What would you like to drink?"

"It doesn't matter."

"Wine? Beer? Coke?"

"What will you have?"

Jake grinned. "Pizza and beer."

Nicole nodded. "Okay. I'll have the same." Nicole put the plates on the table and sat down, still looking around the duplex. No pictures. No . . . *stuff*. It was odd. She wondered if Jake's bedroom was any more personal. She looked up as Jake sat a beer bottle in front of her and a pile of napkins.

"Would you like a glass for the beer?"

Nicole smiled. "No, this is fine," she said, reaching for the bottle and taking a drink. It was cold. And good. She didn't often drink beer. Most of the dinner dates she went on were at expensive, upscale restaurants, and wine was the norm.

"How long did it take you to reach St. Elmo?" Jake asked unexpectedly.

Nicole paused as she was opening the pizza box. "Three days."

"You made good time," Jake said. "Must not have stopped at many hot springs."

Nicole smiled. "The ones I came across were crowded." She took a large piece of pizza and placed it on Jake's plate. "You're not limping at all," she stated.

"Not much, no. If I overdo it, it still aches a bit."

"Going to tell me what really happened?"

"What do you mean?"

"All you said was, you had an accident."

Jake took a bite and nodded. "I forget sometimes, that you're a professional at this." She took a swallow of beer before continuing. "There was a shooting. Three ended up dead. I survived."

Nicole leaned forward. "You're leaving out an awful lot of detail, Jake."

"Yeah? Well, maybe I'll tell you about it sometime." She motioned to the pizza. "You're not eating."

Nicole picked up the piece of pizza on her plate and took a bite, her eyes never venturing far from Jake. It was so familiar, sitting here eating with her, that it was almost eerie. Cheyenne leaned against her leg, her eyes darting between the two of them, hoping for a treat.

"So, Catherine tells me you're single," Jake said.

Nicole stopped chewing and stared. "Catherine talks too much."

Jake shrugged. "Beautiful woman like yourself . . . successful, why are you single?"

Nicole reached for a second piece of pizza. "And you?"

Jake took another piece, too. She smiled. "Haven't yet met that one person who wants to give up this life and retreat to the mountains with me." Jake raised an eyebrow. "Might not ever meet her. Might have to live in my cabin all by myself."

"Your cabin's home, isn't it?" Nicole motioned to the living room. "This place is just . . . what? A place to sleep?"

Jake nodded. "Is it that obvious?"

"Yes, Jake. It's as stark as a motel room."

Jake put her pizza down and took a swallow of beer. "Catherine tells me she gets threatening mail weekly."

"Is that what she tells you?"

"And phone calls, too."

"Like I said, she talks too much."

"And you just dismiss it?"

"Jake, I've been getting threatening mail for years. I told you that."

"It's different now, Nicole. This is for real."

"You're saying that someone is so pissed at me that they are willing to kill my former patients? For what, Jake?"

"Revenge. It's always about revenge, Nicole."

"But why? I've only testified in a handful of cases over the years. Usually, by the time I get them, the court cases are set. I encourage them to go through with it, of course. But I rarely have to testify."

"We're going over every person on the list, looking at old cases, seeing who is still in prison and who is not. That sort of thing," Jake said.

"And you're convinced it's not just coincidence?"

"It's not coincidence, Nicole. Don't even think that."

"It makes no sense, Jake."

"Killing rarely makes sense."

161

Nicole shoved her plate away and picked up the beer bottle, draining the last of it. "So, do you think I'm at risk?"

"Yes. Maybe not right now, but . . . soon."

"Because he's targeting women to get back at me but eventually, that won't be enough."

"Exactly."

"And he'll come after me."

"Yes."

Nicole twirled the empty beer bottle in her hands. "I had a stalker once," she said. "About five years ago. Maybe six now."

Jake stood up, going to the fridge and grabbing them each a fresh beer. "Oh yeah?"

"Scared the hell out of me when he showed up at my house."

"And Denver's finest came and rescued you?"

"Something like that."

Jake frowned. "What happened?"

"They shot him. Killed him on my front lawn."

Jake slid the beer bottle toward Nicole. "Why?"

Nicole met her eyes. "I'm not really sure. He wasn't armed."

Jake reached across the table and captured Nicole's hand, squeezing gently. "I'm sorry."

Nicole stared at their hands, surprised that she felt comforted by such an innocent gesture. She looked up, again falling into dark eyes and wanting to stay there. It was odd, the familiarity between them. They had only spent a day and a half together in the mountains, yet Nicole felt more comfortable in Jake's presence than almost anyone else in her life. Yes, it was scary. So, she pulled her hand away. It was the only sensible thing to do.

Jake leaned forward and smiled. "Don't be afraid of me. Whatever happened between us is in the past. I'm on a case, and you're a part of it. And I don't ever mix business . . . with pleasure," she said quietly. Her eyes locked on Nicole's again. "Okay?"

Nicole nodded. "Okay."

Jake smiled. "Good. And because we do know each other, sort

of, I'd like to think that you'd trust me with your files, if I need them."

"Jake . . ."

"I know. Confidential. But maybe, off the record, we could have an understanding?" Jake reached across the table again and captured Nicole's hand. "I'm serious. This could get very personal."

"I'm worried about my integrity."

"And I'm worried about your life," Jake said.

Nicole sighed. "You think it's that serious?"

"Of course I do," Jake said, her voice rising. "He's killed three women."

Nicole lowered her head. "The profession I'm in, Jake, there are threats. I know taking clients from the crisis center is risky, but they have no place else to go, and they need help." Nicole shrugged. "So, you live with the risks."

"Not this time."

"Jake, I have a job to do. I have obligations. I can't just run because there might be complications."

"Complications? Nicole, trust me, if it points to you, you're in protective custody so fast you won't have time to protest."

"Like hell! Jake, I won't have my life disrupted. I won't have my *practice* disrupted. No!"

"And you know what? I don't care," Jake said easily. "My job is to protect you. And if that means disrupting your life and your practice—so be it."

"You can't do that. Not without my cooperation."

Jake smiled. "Watch me."

CHAPTER THIRTY-TWO

"Of the forty-four women, thirty-two still live in the area. Of those thirty-two, eighteen of their accusers are still behind bars. Of the remaining fourteen, six never saw jail time. Four of those six live in Denver. The eight that did time, three have been released, all within the last year. The latest, out six months ago. I don't have current employment for the three. If there even is any. I didn't have time."

Gina handed out copies of her report, and Jake reached for hers, scanning it for names. "Good job, Gina."

"Let's get some background on these three," Lieutenant Gregory said. "We'll start there. Bring them in if there is *any* question. I don't want them slipping away. They're all recent. Their parole officers have to have current info. I'll bring the DA up to speed," he said walking away.

"We'll take Nichols," Jake said.

"Perez lives out by the airport," Chase said.

"So? We had one body dumped at the lake and one at an apartment."

Chase shrugged. "Just a thought."

"Okay, we'll take Perez first," Simpson said. "Since Chase has a hunch."

"And we're sure on these numbers, Gina?"

"Yeah. Of course, we're going on most current address. Who knows if they even have a job."

"Simpson? Anything check out at the crisis center?"

"No, not really. For one thing, you were right, their record-keeping sucks. And in the last five years, they've had two male employees. One was maintenance and the other worked in the office. Ms. Kane said he was just out of college and worked as her assistant for one summer. That's it."

"Well, let's focus on these three then. Maybe something will shake out," Jake said, standing.

"Hold on, people," Gregory called from his office door. "Got a body. Botanic Gardens. Matches the others."

"Botanic Gardens?"

"In the Rock Alpine Garden, to be exact," Gregory said. "Probably dumped last night. ME's on the way, crime lab's been called. McCoy, Chase, you take it. Simpson and Salazar, check out our three suspects."

Jake grabbed the keys off of Rick's desk. "I'm driving," she said.

"So you had pizza? Then what?" Catherine asked.

"Then what? Then nothing. I went home," Nicole said. "And she's threatening protective custody. Can you believe that?" She grabbed her gym bag from behind the door and slung it over her shoulder.

"Well, you know, I got that letter last week."

"We get letters every week."

"Yeah. But this one was different. It wasn't just the normal ranting. It was deliberate, almost."

165

Nicole smiled. "Because he threatened you?"

"Maybe."

"Well, I'm going down the street to the gym. And I promise to be back on time. Lock the door," she called after her.

The ME beat them to the scene, and they both leaned over his shoulder, looking at the victim.

"Detectives."

"Hey, Dave. You got days now?"

"Still on nights. But Benson's in court."

"That's a bitch," Jake murmured.

"Tell me. I got three hours sleep last night."

"Rape?" Rick asked.

"Looks like it. There's bruising."

"You got a time of death?" Jake asked.

"Not yet. But guessing, forty-eight hours at least."

Jake straightened up and looked around, searching for the security guard who'd called it in. She found him talking to the two patrol officers who answered the call. She elbowed Rick. "Come on."

Holding up her badge, she nodded at the two uniforms, dismissing them. "I'm Detective McCoy. This is Detective Chase. You found the body?"

"Not exactly. A kid spotted her first, then the mother started screaming, and everyone came running."

"Okay. Where are they now? Did they touch anything?"

"I don't think so. But I'm sure they split. The mother was freaked out."

Rick looked around. "How locked up is this place at night?"

The security guard shrugged. "It's twenty-three acres, and we have two guys working the night shift."

"But the gates are locked at night?"

"Yeah. And in the main areas we have security cameras."

"So you have a security camera here?" Jake asked.

He pointed to one of the light fixtures over the sidewalk. "It films the walkway, not the exhibits."

"We'd like to take a look at it."

"Sure. Come by the administrative offices. I'll have it pulled for you."

"Thanks." Jake turned to Rick with raised eyebrows. "Maybe he slipped up. Maybe we'll get him on tape."

"Keep dreaming, McCoy."

"Hey, Dave?"

The ME stood and peeled off his gloves. "Strangled. But there's a knife wound, too. I won't know which killed her until I open her up."

"Knife? That's new. Before the post, Dave, run her prints. We need to know who she is."

"Will do. I'll have Monica let you know."

Nicole hurried out of the elevator and to her office door, cursing because she was five minutes late, and Catherine would fuss. You're the boss, she reminded herself as she opened the door and peeked inside. Hazel eyes looked back at her disapprovingly.

"Sorry," Nicole whispered. "Where is she?"

Catherine turned back to her computer. "She cancelled."

Nicole walked in and slammed the door. "Cancelled? Why?"

"She wouldn't say."

"Goddammit," she murmured. "We're going to lose her, aren't we?"

"Lori needs round-the-clock help, Nicole. You said that yourself after the first session."

"I know. But I thought I could help her. She's not going to make it, Catherine. The next time she'll succeed."

"I already called her mother."

"Good. Because I don't want a suicide on my head," she said, as she moved toward her office door. "I've got three murders to deal with."

"Nicole, you don't blame yourself, surely?"

"If what Jake says is true, then yes. He's after me and using them."

"But he's doing it, not you. You have no control over this."

Nicole stared, her head tilted sideways. "Have you been listening in on my sessions, *Doctor* Catherine?"

"I knew that was bothering you. That's why I called Dorothy."

Nicole frowned. "You called Dorothy? Catherine, I'm fine. We don't need to bother Dorothy with this. Geez, she's got her own patients." Nicole paused with her hand on the doorknob to her office. "You call her right now and tell her not to come up."

Catherine smiled. "Okay. Sure."

"I mean it."

"Yes, ma'am."

Nicole walked blindly into her office, gasping in surprise as Dorothy sat quietly on her sofa, flipping through a magazine.

"Jesus! Dorothy, you scared the hell out of me."

"Catherine didn't tell you I was here?"

Nicole shook her head. "I need to have a talk with Catherine," she muttered, tossing her gym bag on the floor beside her desk and joining Dorothy on the sofa. "I think she forgets who the boss is. I'm sorry she dragged you up here."

"It's two floors. I used the elevator."

"You know what I mean. I'm sure you're as busy as I am."

"Well, Catherine's call alone might not have sent me running, but Patrice Kane called me yesterday. Nicole, why haven't you told me what's been going on?"

"And what would I say? Three of my former patients have turned up murdered. It could be a coincidence," Nicole said.

"What do the police say?"

Nicole lowered her head. "Not a coincidence."

"Well, what are they doing about it? Just sitting around waiting for the next victim?"

Nicole bristled, wanting to defend Jake. "They want old files, they want protective custody for me."

Dorothy stared. "They had the nerve to ask for your files? I swear, can they not do their own work?"

"You just asked what they were doing, as if they weren't doing anything. Of course they're doing something, and of course they wanted my files."

"They have no concept of doctor-patient privilege. They never have. But protective custody? Why?"

"Detective McCoy seems to think that I'm the eventual target."

"Oh my God," Dorothy said, reaching over to take Nicole's hand. "But why?"

"They don't know."

"You can always stay with us. You know I wouldn't mind."

Nicole smiled. "No, but Ellen may."

The older woman smiled affectionately at the mention of her lover's name. "Ellen would be disappointed in me if I didn't offer our home."

"I know. And thank you. But if I'm in danger, I certainly don't want to involve my friends. Besides, I have no doubt that the police will let me know if I'm targeted."

Dorothy scoffed. "Please, Nicole, don't be naive. Do you know how many cases they work? You're just a number."

Nicole shook her head. "No. Not this time."

"What do you mean?"

"I know one of the detectives on this case. I'm not just a number."

"Well, good. That makes me feel a little better." Then Dorothy smiled. "It's not that same detective that Patrice has been going on and on about, is it?"

"Probably. Jake McCoy."

"Yes. I knew she had a man's name, I just couldn't place it. How do you know her?"

Nicole felt the blush travel up her face, and she prayed Dorothy didn't notice. "Actually, it was quite a coincidence, but I ran into her on a hiking trail. You know, on my trip."

"I see. That is a coincidence." Dorothy leaned closer. "Why are you blushing?"

"Am I?"

Dorothy's eyes widened. "You had a . . . a thing with her?"

"I wouldn't really call it a *thing*. I camped with her a couple of nights." Nicole smiled. "Actually I was lost when I found her soaking in hot springs."

"Naked?"

Nicole nodded.

"And? You're still blushing."

"Okay, Dorothy, let's quit beating around the bush. Yes, we had a *thing*, as you call it."

"With a cop?"

"I didn't know she was a cop at the time. And she didn't know who I was. We exchanged first names only."

"Oh my God! You devil. That's so out of character for you," Dorothy laughed.

"Don't you think I know that?"

"So what does she look like? Patrice is almost beside herself over the woman."

"She's . . . attractive. She's . . . oh hell, Dorothy, she's gay. She looks gay, she acts gay. She's gay."

"She's a cop, and she's out?"

"Yes."

Dorothy frowned. "Is she like . . . a dyke or what?"

Nicole frowned. "God, I hate that word. She's just . . . Jake." Nicole stared across the room. "I'm attracted to her, Dorothy."

"Attracted? Well, I would hope so. You slept with her."

Nicole shook her head. "It's more than that."

"Attracted like you want to go out with her? *Date* her?"

"She's not my type, right?"

"Of course not! Nicole, she's a policewoman. No, she's definitely not in your league. And I've told you before, Deb Fisher is your type."

"I don't like Debra. I told you what happened."

"Well, I mean someone like Deb. Even most of her colleagues don't know she's gay."

"But what does it matter, Dorothy? What are we gaining by hiding who we are?"

It was Dorothy's turn to stare. "What you're gaining is a thriving practice. What Deb Fisher hopes to gain is the mayoral election. What do you mean, what are we gaining?"

Nicole shrugged. "It's just such a waste of energy."

"Just remember, Nicole, you wouldn't be where you are today if not for our circle of friends. We're a close-knit community, and we take care of our own. It's always been that way."

"Times change, Dorothy. We're a close-knit community, but shouldn't we broaden out? Shouldn't we take a chance now and then?"

Dorothy stood, her nearly white hair glowing under the fluorescent lights. "Take a chance? Nicole, a discreet affair with a cop might be tolerated, but don't bring her around and don't mention names to her. Lord, it was bad enough when Deb insisted on bringing Ashley to dinners with the group."

"Dorothy, what's wrong with Ashley?"

"She's a coach, Nicole. She just screams *gay*. I can't believe Deb was with her for as long as she was."

"All these years, Dorothy, I never realized you were so prejudiced. And so judgmental."

"I'm sixty-two years old Nicole. And my consultation has been requested by the mayor of this city and the governor of this state. You don't get to that position by being *out*."

Nicole held her tongue, wanting to tell Dorothy that *everyone* knew she was gay. For God's sake, she and Ellen had been together since the sixties. And yes, everyone knew they were together as a couple, but no one talked about it. So therefore, they had to continue to hide and pretend that no one knew. Jesus, it was an endless cycle.

"I'm just saying, Dorothy, that maybe there comes a time when we need to just be ourselves."

"You know the rules, Nicole." Dorothy walked to the door and stopped. "If you need a place to stay, you're always welcome."

"Thank you. But I'll be okay."

The older woman nodded, then opened the door. "Let me know if you need to talk."

Nicole watched her leave, wondering at the isolation she suddenly felt. Had she simply been pretending all these years to be friends with these people? She was a psychologist, for God's sake! Dorothy was a psychiatrist! Surely she could see how unhealthy it was, this closeted community they'd formed over the years.

Nicole walked to her desk and sat down, spinning around in her chair and facing the window, looking out over downtown Denver. She admitted that, yes, it was unhealthy. But she'd just fallen into the crowd like the rest, believing that it was best for their professional endeavors to be secretive about it. She only had herself to blame. And it suddenly occurred to her why she'd been so unhappy for the last several years.

"Because you're living a lie," she murmured. She hated what she'd become. The business suits and makeup, high heels and hose, the phantom boyfriend who was *always* out of town, anything to suggest she was a straight woman. Except on the few occasions that the group got together, or a date with someone new, someone just like all the others. A single, professional woman pretending she wasn't a lesbian.

Jake grabbed her phone with one hand and tucked it against her shoulder, continuing to type the report into the computer.

"McCoy."

"Jake, it's Monica."

Jake paused and picked up the list. "Got a name?"

"Jena Nichols."

"Fuck," Jake murmured, circling the name on the list.

"I'll take that as a thank you."

"I'm sorry, Monica. Yeah, thanks." Jake slammed the phone down. "Son of a bitch." She looked up, motioning to Rick. He was locked in a conversation with Belcher.

"What's up?"

"Got an ID. Jena Nichols."

"And her husband is . . ."

"Frankie Nichols. Let's pick up his ass," Jake said, pushing her chair back.

"Address was a dead end, Jake."

"Are you shitting me?"

"Gina's going over employment records, trying to get a hit on his SSN."

"Fuck!" She grabbed the list and marched into the lieutenant's office, knocking on the door frame before walking in.

Gregory looked up, his glasses sliding down his nose. "McCoy? What you got?"

"ID on our victim. Jena Nichols. Her husband is Frankie Nichols, one of the three Gina picked out."

"So why are you still here?"

"Bogus address."

"Call his parole officer. Someone's got to know where he is."

"Gina's doing a search on his SSN, trying to get a hit on employment."

"That's assuming he's working. Check with his PO. Let's get Simpson and Salazar on her last whereabouts."

Jake nodded. "On it."

Nicole looked up from her notes at the quiet knock on her door. She'd seen her last appointment she was sure. And it was unlike Catherine to knock and wait.

"Come in."

But indeed, it was Catherine who stuck her head in.

"You said to remind you."

Nicole frowned.

"You have a date."

Nicole sighed. "Shit." She tossed her pen on her desk and took a deep breath. "Tell me again why I'm going out with her?"

"Because she's a physician with a thriving practice, and she's Irene's good friend."

"Oh, yeah. And Irene thinks we'd be perfect together."

Catherine shrugged. "You said to remind you."

"I know, I know. It's just . . . I'm so tired of this."

"So say no once in a while," Catherine suggested.

"It's not that easy."

"Well, I hope you're not wearing that. Did you bring clothes to change into?"

Nicole narrowed her eyes at Catherine, wondering what was wrong with the skirt she had on. "No, I did not bring clothes. I guess I'll have to run home first, won't I?"

"Well, that depends. Where are you meeting?"

"Sullivan's."

"Oh, yes. You definitely need to change."

"Why? What's wrong with this?"

Catherine shook her head. "I swear, sometimes I wonder at your fashion sense. You're in a business suit. Perfect for *lunch* at Sullivan's. Not dinner."

"Oh, Catherine. I don't feel like going home and getting more dressed up than I already am. It makes no sense to me."

Catherine leaned forward. "You're going to Sullivan's, one of the finest restaurants in Denver. Don't skimp on your wardrobe."

Nicole's shoulders sagged. "I guess that little black dinner dress would work."

Catherine smiled. "That would be perfect."

"And it would also help if it were twenty degrees warmer outside tonight," Nicole said sarcastically.

"Price we pay."

"Yeah, yeah." Nicole moved to shut down her computer. "Why don't you cut out early, too?"

"Oh, I've got a few more files to update. Besides, traffic is already a bitch."

"Thanks. You're just full of good news."

"I'm sorry. He's already gone for the day."

Jake stared at the young girl. "Great." Jake pointed at her watch. "Five till five. What are his hours?"

"Well, normally eight to five."

Jake drew her brows together, and the girl took a step back.

Rick stepped forward and smiled charmingly as he pushed Jake out of the way. "What time will he be in tomorrow?"

"He'll be in at eight, like always."

"So? If we needed information from one of his files, could you get that for us?"

The girl shook her head. "Oh, I'm sorry. No. I can't do that."

Jake leaned forward again. "This is very important. We're just looking for employment records for one of his clients. Can't you just look it up on the computer?"

"I can't access the files."

"Aren't you his secretary?"

"Yes, of course. But I've only been here two weeks."

Jake looked at Rick and rolled her eyes. "Jesus Christ," she muttered.

Rick pulled out his card and handed it to the girl. "Make sure he gets that first thing in the morning. Okay? We'll be here at eight sharp."

"Yes, of course. Detective Chase, was it?"

Jake grabbed Rick's arm and pulled him away. "Christ, Rick," she murmured. "She's twelve years old."

"She's at least eighteen."

"And you're still married."

Rick laughed. "Jake, it ain't no different than when you were sweet-talking Patrice Kane."

"Patrice Kane wasn't jailbait, and at least I got some information from Patrice Kane."

Rick stopped at the car and checked his watch. "So, it's five. Call it a day?"

Jake frowned. "We got shit, Ricky. We got another dead woman, and we got shit."

"We got Frankie Nichols."

"Oh, yeah? Where the hell is he?"

"We'll be here at eight sharp. By eight-thirty, we'll have him."

Jake nodded. "Okay. But I think I'll look up Dr. Westbrook and let her know the latest."

Rick cocked his head. "You got the hots for her or what?"

"Of course not. She's part of this case, and you know my rule."

"Oh yeah. Forgot. And I've never seen you break it."

"And you won't. You could learn from this."

"You mean now that I'm soon to be single again?"

Jake slammed the door shut and waited until Rick did the same. "Are you? Have you talked to her?"

"No. But I've listened to voice mail from her sisters and her mother. And trust me, we won't be living together again."

Jake shook her head. "It's funny how that plays out, isn't it?"

"What do you mean?"

Jake pulled into traffic and slowed. It would take them at least a half hour to get back downtown. "I mean, one day you're sleeping in the same bed, then the next, because of words spoken, you're like total strangers. Or worse, you hate each other."

"I think we could talk this out and both agree that it wasn't working, if her family wasn't involved. They're like a swarm of piranhas, you know?"

"Then call her and talk it out." Jake pulled out her cell phone, dialing a number with her thumb, surprised that she remembered it. "Catherine? Glad I caught you. It's Jake McCoy. Is the doc still in?"

"Yeah, you got the hots for her," Rick whispered.

"A date, huh? Well, I need to talk to her, Catherine. Where's she going?"

"Are you serious?" Rick asked.

"Sullivan's? Shit. No, no, I won't tell her you told me. But I owe you." Jake disconnected and tucked the phone in her jacket.

"Sullivan's? Jake, you can't crash a dinner date at Sullivan's."

"Watch me."

"Just call her in the morning."

Jake shook her head. "She needs to know. And I think it's time to bring her in. We all know she's the target."

"And if we bring her in, how are we going to nail the guy?"

Jake raised her eyebrows. "She won't be bait."

"I'm not saying bait. Hell, Jake, she's a civilian. I'm just saying, round the clock, maybe, but not bring her in. If he's after her and she's protected, then we got shit."

"We already got shit."

"Oh, Christ! I hate having these conversations with you. We always go in circles."

Jake pounded the steering wheel. "Goddamn traffic!"

"It's five o'clock. What'd you expect?"

Jake leaned back, resigned to waiting out the traffic. "It's times like this, Ricky, when I miss the quiet of the mountains. You've got to come up to my cabin sometime. It's incredible, the peace there."

"I believe you. But you know, I'm a city boy. I wouldn't know what to do with all that . . . that space with no people around."

Jake shook her head. She never understood some people's fear of being alone in the vastness of the wilderness. For her, there was nothing better.

CHAPTER THIRTY-THREE

Nicole locked her car and hurried to the entrance, knowing she was late. Her feet felt cramped in the heels she'd chosen to wear, not to mention that the skimpy dinner dress was not suitable for a cool fall evening. Once inside, she relaxed a bit, pausing to let the chill seep out before she looked for her dinner date. She'd only met Cheryl one time before, and she hoped she remembered what she looked like. How embarrassing would that be if she didn't? But she needn't have worried.

"Nicole?"

Nicole turned, finding herself face to face with a petite redhead. She smiled, swearing that the Cheryl she'd met before had blond hair.

"Cheryl?"

"Good to see you again. I'm running late, and I was so afraid I'd kept you waiting."

"No, I just got here myself. How are you?"

"I'm doing great. And I apologize for being late. Had complications in surgery."

"Everything okay?"

"He's still alive," Cheryl said with a grin.

Nicole smiled, too, not sure if that was a joke or not.

"Shall we?"

Nicole nodded and walked beside Cheryl through the lobby, waiting only a moment before they were greeted by a gentleman in a tuxedo.

"We have reservations for two. Dr. Logan."

"Of course, Dr. Logan. This way."

The restaurant was dimly lit and the tables spaced far enough apart for privacy, but still Nicole glanced around, her eyes lighting on the enclaves and corner tables where couples sat talking quietly in candlelight. Elegant, yes. Romantic, too. She nodded politely as their host held out a chair for her. Romantic, yes indeed. It was a shame she wasn't with someone who conjured up those feelings in her.

"I've only been here a handful of times," Cheryl admitted. "But, discreet and private, you can't beat it."

"I suppose."

"What types of wine do you like, Nicole? They have the very best here."

Nicole smiled. "I'm not all that particular. You choose."

"You sure? I'm partial to red."

Nicole nodded. "I'll be sure to have one of their famous steaks then."

Cheryl reached across the table unexpectedly and captured Nicole's hand. "I'm really looking forward to getting to know you better. Irene has told me so much about you. I admire you for what you're doing with your practice. You can't possibly be making much money giving away time slots to the crisis center."

Nicole bristled. "I didn't actually get into the profession to make tons of money. I had this crazy idea that I could help people."

"We all do at first, Nicole. Then reality hits."

Nicole stared, her reply stuck in her throat when she realized that Cheryl was serious. And that scared her. Cheryl was far too young to be disillusioned already.

Jake stood back, waiting for the party of four to disappear before she walked to the desk. She waited patiently as she was perused, head to toe, by an impeccably dressed man in a tuxedo.

He cleared his throat before speaking. "May I . . . help you?"

Jake smiled. "Yes, you can, actually." Jake held up her badge. "I'm Detective McCoy. I need to speak with one of your patrons."

His eyes widened. "Please, we cannot have a scene here, madam. If you'll tell me who you wish to speak with, I'll get them for you."

Jake tucked her badge on her belt and shook her head. "Actually, I'd like it to be a surprise." Jake moved to walk past when he moved and intercepted her.

"Madam, you really shouldn't go in there. You're not exactly dressed for dining."

Jake looked at her slacks, which, surprisingly, still held a crease. "Well, that's okay, 'cause I'm not going to be dining." She walked on, moving quietly into the restaurant, her eyes scanning the tables, looking for a familiar figure. An involuntary smile touched her face when she saw her. Jake stopped and waited, her eyes moving once over Nicole's date before settling on her. It only took a few seconds for Nicole to feel her presence. Then her head turned slowly, her eyes finding and meeting Jake's.

Jake smiled. "Hey."

Nicole felt her seconds before she saw her. It was eerie almost, but she knew when she turned her head, Jake would be there. And she was. A lazy smile on her face, totally unself-conscious in her slacks and dark blazer that covered a slightly rumpled shirt, her hands shoved casually into pockets.

Hey? The professional Nicole, the Nicole that was out on a date, knew she should be upset by Jake's presence. So . . . she tried to be.

"Excuse me?"

Jake tilted her head. "Excuse you what?"

Nicole leaned back. "I hope there's a very good reason for this."

"Well, I thought it was at the time. Now, I'm not so sure."

Cheryl finally spoke up. "Excuse me, but . . . do you know each other?"

Jake took that opportunity to walk closer, and she discreetly showed her badge to Cheryl. "Police business, ma'am. I just need to have a word with Dr. Westbrook."

"Nicole? Are you in some kind of trouble?"

Nicole rolled her eyes. "No, Cheryl, I'm not." She slid her chair back and stood, her eyes glaring at Jake. "This better be good."

"Just take a second of your time, Dr. Westbrook."

Nicole walked away, leaving Jake to follow.

Good Lord. The sleek black dress that Nicole wore left little to the imagination, and Jake's eyes were glued to her backside, watching each sway of her hips, finally lowering to stare at two perfect legs—legs walking away from her.

"Excuse me."

Jake turned and flashed Cheryl a grin. "Right. Nice to meet you." Then she frowned. "Did we meet?"

"Cheryl Logan. *Doctor.*"

Jake lifted an eyebrow. "Jake McCoy. *Detective.*" Jake looked up just as Nicole turned, blue eyes searching for her own. She walked toward those eyes, then stopped short when she saw the flicker of anger in them.

"What the *hell* are you doing here?" Nicole demanded quietly.

Jake took her arm and led her farther into the lobby. "I just need to talk to you."

181

"And it couldn't wait until morning?"

"No, it couldn't."

Jake was intercepted again by the tall man in the tuxedo. "Madam, please. If you're going to arrest someone, could you please do it discreetly. We do not wish to make the morning paper."

"*Arrest?*" Nicole asked.

"No one's getting arrested. But if you have an office or something, it'll just take a second."

"Of course, madam. Right this way."

He opened a door and motioned them into a small office. "Will this do?"

"Perfect. Thanks, chief."

The man cleared his throat. "Actually, madam, it's Charles."

"Uh-huh. Good-bye, Charles," Jake said and closed the door. She faced Nicole, a slow smile forming as she looked at her. "So, how are you?"

"I *was* on a date," Nicole said.

"A date? With *her?*"

"Yes, with her."

Jake shook her head. "She's all wrong for you."

"Wrong for me? She's a surgeon. She's very attractive, and she's single. There's nothing wrong about her."

"She's wrong for you, and do you really think she's attractive?"

"Does it matter what I think? Jake, you said you pulled me out of there because you had something urgent to talk about. What is it?"

"How about, after you ditch your date, we go get coffee or something?"

Nicole walked closer, her voice low. "And perhaps I had a very long evening planned with her."

Jake shook her head. "No, I don't think so. Not with her."

"What's that supposed to mean."

"That woman," Jake said, her eyes traveling down Nicole's body, "will not touch you tonight."

Nicole's skin burned where Jake's eyes touched it, and she fought to keep her breathing normal. She had a date waiting for her outside, an attractive woman who would fit nicely into her life. Yet it was this . . . this *cop* who turned her bones to jelly with only a look. Nicole crossed her arms, trying to cover herself.

"How did you find me?"

Jake shrugged. "I'm a cop. It's what we do."

"So you're telling me *Detective*, Catherine had nothing to do with it?"

Jake laughed outright, causing Nicole to smile and relax. God, but she loved Jake's laugh.

"So, coffee?"

Nicole shook her head. "Can't." Jake raised an eyebrow and Nicole smiled. "I'm tired, Jake. And after dinner, I'm going home, alone, and crawling into bed. So, talk now or save it until morning."

"Jena Nichols."

Nicole frowned, recognizing the name, but she couldn't place her. "One of mine?"

"Yeah."

"And?"

"She was found this morning, dumped like the others."

Nicole's shoulders sagged. "The body that was found at the Botanical Gardens?"

Jake nodded. "I'm sorry, Nicole. But I didn't want to wait until morning. The murders are escalating, getting closer together. I think maybe it's time we get you some sort of surveillance."

"Jake, no. We've been over this. I'll not have my practice disrupted like that."

"Just a precaution for now. He's not threatened you directly. Not yet. Believe me, he'll want you to sweat a little. But just in case, we can have an unmarked car follow you home, follow you to work, that sort of thing." Jake's voice softened. "Humor me, please."

Their eyes met, the few feet separating them not enough to

prevent the heat from seeping into Nicole's body. She couldn't pull her eyes away, and once again, she was back in the mountains, her naked body being pulled from the water, a warm mouth settling over her breast the instant long fingers plunged deep inside her. She very nearly moaned out loud from the memory.

She felt the rise and fall of her chest and became aware that her breathing was labored. But it was Jake who pulled away first, making a show of straightening papers on the desk. Nicole hadn't missed the throbbing pulse in Jake's neck or the eyes that had turned nearly black.

"So, is that a yes?" Jake finally asked, after clearing her throat.

Nicole sighed but nodded. "Okay."

"Thank you."

Nicole pushed off the desk, putting even more distance between them. She paused at the door. "I better get back."

"Oh, yeah. Your date."

Their eyes met again, and Nicole wanted to tell Jake that Cheryl was but another in a long list of blind dates arranged by well-meaning friends. But it didn't really matter one way or the other. What she and Jake had was in the past. And even if she were inclined to pick it up again—which she wasn't—Jake had already made it clear that it was only business between them.

It wasn't until Jake was on her way home that she allowed visions of that day in the mountains to pour over her. She'd been keeping them at bay, telling herself it was just another one-time affair. Nothing she couldn't handle. But damn, sitting on that desk with Nicole, it was all she could do to remind herself that she was on a damn case. And the only reason she and Nicole had any dealings with each other now was because of that case.

But, she admitted, there was something there, something between them, and she knew that Nicole felt it, too. Or maybe it was just the sexual attraction that dominated in the mountains showing itself again.

Regardless, it didn't matter. Nicole made it clear she didn't date women like Jake. And hell, she was on a fucking case, and she refused to cross that line. It would be *dangerous* to cross that line. It didn't matter that she still remembered the sounds of Nicole's screams as if it had been just last night that they'd touched.

Jake drove home, oblivious to her surroundings, her mind seeing nothing but Nicole's wet skin.

"Jesus," she whispered.

CHAPTER THIRTY-FOUR

"She's a cop. She's not your type. She's a cop, *she's a cop*," Nicole murmured over and over. But she couldn't get Jake out of her mind. And each time she saw her, each time she was around her, the pull was harder and harder to resist. And tonight, if Jake had made even the slightest effort to kiss her, Nicole knew she could not, would not, have resisted.

And then there was Cheryl. It was all Nicole could do to make it through dinner with the woman. When she wasn't thinking about Jake, she was silently cursing Irene for thinking that she and Cheryl would hit it off. They had absolutely nothing in common, and if not for the fact that Cheryl enjoyed talking about herself so much, Nicole would have been hard pressed to come up with a topic of conversation. She declined Cheryl's offer of after-dinner drinks, but reluctantly accepted Cheryl's business card with her home number scribbled on the back. She had no intention of ever calling her.

As she pulled into her driveway, hand just inches away from the remote for the garage door, she paused, frowning. Had she left lights on in the house? Maybe in the kitchen, but certainly not in the living room. She stared, the brightly lit window almost mocking her. Well, obviously, she had left the lights on.

She touched the remote and waited while the garage door opened, a frown still marring her features. Something wasn't right. She felt the hairs on the back of her neck stand out, and her heart raced. Without thinking, she threw the car into reverse and backed onto the street. The motion lights over the garage had not come on. They *always* come on.

"Calm down," she murmured, as she gripped the steering wheel hard. Jake's words were haunting her, and she was letting her imagination get the better of her. But even so, she'd seen enough movies to know that she shouldn't go into the house. *Can't sit here in the street, Nicole.*

She revved the engine a bit, trying to decide what to do. *Call Jake.*

"Of course, I could call Jake."

She reached blindly into the back seat and grabbed her briefcase. She'd shoved Jake's card in there last week. She checked her watch, wondering if Jake was home already. She dialed the number for her cell, impatiently tapping the steering wheel as the phone continued to ring. After four, she was about to disconnect when Jake's breathless voice sounded in her ear.

"McCoy."

"It's . . . it's me."

"Nicole? What's wrong?"

"Well, I'm not sure."

"Where are you?" Jake asked urgently.

"I'm sitting in my car, on the street in front of my house."

There was a pause. "Okay. And why?" Jake asked slowly.

"Because there's a light on inside and the motion lights didn't come on when I drove up."

"Fuck!"

"Do you think I should go check it out?"

"Are you crazy? Get out of there! Now!" Jake yelled into the phone.

"Jake, I could have left the light on myself. I'm probably over-reacting."

"Listen to me, Nicole. Get the fuck out of there. Just drive away."

"Jake, really, I think it's okay."

"The hell it is! I'm on my way."

"But you don't know where I live."

"Of course I do."

As Jake disconnected, Nicole was sure she saw a shadow cross the windows of her house. Her throat closed completely as she shifted into drive and sped away.

Jake ignored the traffic laws as she sped down the interstate, hands gripped tightly on the steering wheel. Nicole could be right. Maybe they were overreacting. She could have accidentally left lights on, the motion lights could be out. But, better safe than sorry.

"Right?" Jake looked in the mirror, smiling slightly at the sight of Cheyenne as she hung out the window.

Nicole parked two blocks from her house, wishing she'd thought to lower her garage door again. She jumped when her phone rang.

"Hello?"

"Where are you?"

Nicole let out a sigh of relief. "A couple of blocks from my house."

"Good."

"How do you know my phone number?"

"I'm a cop. We know these things."

"I see. And where are you?"

"Speeding down the interstate, trying not to attract attention."

"How much longer, Jake?"

"Ten minutes."

"Okay. I can do ten minutes."

"What's wrong? Are you scared?"

"Cold."

"Cold?"

Nicole rubbed her bare arm and smiled. "You saw what I was wearing tonight."

"Oh, yeah. I saw. I'll be there before you know it."

Nicole started her car again and put the heater back on. The residential area was quiet, even though it was barely after nine o'clock. Nicole glanced into her rearview mirror and gasped. Someone was walking quickly toward her car, a dark figure, all in black. Her heart was pounding as she shifted into drive and sped away. When she looked in the mirror again, she expected to see the man running after her but he had stopped.

"The hell with this," she whispered as she continued driving, thinking she would go all the way to South Golden Road before she stopped. But then she saw Jake's Land Cruiser rounding the corner and felt an instant wave of relief. She pulled her car to the side of the road, hoping Jake would recognize her. She did.

Jake pulled up next to her, noting the wild eyes, the pale skin. "What happened?"

"Someone . . . I thought I saw . . . I mean, I *did* see . . . there was someone . . . oh, shit."

"It's okay, Nicole." Jake got out and quickly walked over. "Just park on the street here. Ride with me."

"Okay. Good. Because I don't mind saying, I'm plenty scared."

"Don't be scared. I won't let anything happen to you."

When Nicole was safely seated in Jake's vehicle, she relaxed a little, accepting the wet kiss from Cheyenne.

"Thank you," she murmured, as she wiped slobber off her cheek.

"Want to tell me why you're as white as a ghost?" Jake asked, as she drove off.

"When I was parked, I looked in the mirror and there was a man walking toward the car. Not exactly strolling, but not quite running. I panicked."

Jake reached over and took her hand, squeezing once before releasing it. "You did the right thing. It could be nothing, but Nicole, you've got to take this seriously."

"I know. And I'm thinking that your surveillance idea is a really good one."

Jake smiled, but her eyes were scanning the dark street, looking for movement. She slowed when she approached Nicole's house. It was dark. Except for the lights over the garage door.

"It's closed," Nicole whispered.

"What?"

"The garage. I left it open. And the light is off in the house now."

Jake pulled into the driveway and stopped. She took a deep breath before asking the question she knew she had to ask. "Nicole, are you . . . are you *sure* there was a light on inside?"

Nicole glared at her. "Jesus Christ! Of course I'm sure there was a light on. You think I imagined the living room lit up? Just imagined that these lights weren't on out here? Or I imagined the shadow that walked across the window? Or the damn man running behind the car?" she asked loudly, her voice rising with each word.

Jake turned in her seat and grabbed Nicole's arm and shook her lightly. "Calm down. I'm sorry, but . . ."

"I know. You probably get a lot of crazies in your line of work. But I'm not one of them."

"Okay. Sit tight. I'm going to check it out."

"What? The *house*? No, you're not."

"You'll be fine. Lock the door after I leave." Jake handed her keys to Nicole. "Push the panic button if anything happens."

"No, I mean, I don't think you should go in there. Shouldn't you call your partner or . . . or backup?"

"And tell them what?"

Nicole nodded. "I see." Her eyes locked on Jake's. "We could just leave," she suggested.

Jake smiled. "You're worried about me?"

"Yes. Don't take it personally."

"I'll be fine. Whoever was here is gone. But I need to make sure. Then you'll have to come in and look around, see if anything is disturbed. Can you do that?"

Nicole nodded. "Just be careful."

Jake raised an eyebrow.

"What?"

"Key to the front door?"

"Oh. Right." Nicole opened the tiny, black handbag she carried and pulled out her keys. Then she looked at Jake, brows drawn together. "The alarm. Why didn't the alarm go off?"

Jake sighed. "He must know the code. What is it?"

"Pound key, then one, zero, five, two, eight."

She took the keys from Nicole's hand and opened the door, then ruffled Cheyenne's fur. "Look after her."

Nicole watched as Jake lifted her sweatshirt and pulled out a gun, holding it in front of her as she walked. Nicole swallowed with nervousness, her eyes glued to the woman. She was . . . magnificent. Long legs covered by loose-fitting jeans, dark sweatshirt that hugged her upper body, she moved with the grace of a panther stalking its prey.

Jake's eyes never stopped moving, and Nicole waited anxiously as she disappeared inside.

"Why doesn't she put a light on, Cheyenne?"

Finally, long minutes later, lights came on, and Nicole relaxed. Then Jake came jogging back, gun again tucked away. Nicole unlocked the door and waited.

"All clear. I need you to come inside now."

"Okay. Cheyenne, too?"

Jake shook her head. "No. She'll be fine."

"Did you find anything?" Nicole asked as she followed Jake to her house.

"There's . . . there's something in your bedroom."

191

Once inside the house, Nicole stayed close to Jake. She'd lived in the house over six years and only one time previously had she been afraid. But she was nearly terrified now. She was grateful when Jake took her hand.

Looking around the living room, nothing seemed disturbed, but Jake didn't stop long enough for Nicole to be sure. Jake led her down the hallway to her bedroom at the back of the house. There on the bed lay dozens and dozens of wilted roses, some of their shriveled red petals tossed about haphazardly on the pale carpet.

"There's a note," Jake said.

"What . . . what did it say?"

"Be careful. I'm watching you," Jake quoted.

Nicole met Jake's eyes, frowning.

"He's just fucking with you," Jake said. "I've called Rick and the crime lab. We might get lucky on some prints, although I doubt it. If he's savvy enough to know your alarm code, then most likely, he left without a trace."

"And the lights?"

"I think he knows you. Knows you wouldn't come inside if something was out of order. Again, he's playing you."

"So what do I do now?"

"You're coming home with me tonight. Tomorrow we'll decide about surveillance."

"Well, don't think I'm going to argue with you. There's no way I'm staying here tonight."

"Why don't you pack a bag? Get enough clothes for a couple of days."

Nicole nodded and moved past Jake, pausing to squeeze her arm. "Is this normal?"

"Normal?"

"You taking a scared lady home with you?"

Jake grinned. "No. Normally Rick does that."

"Thank you, Jake. I know this isn't exactly procedure. If you'd rather, I could call someone."

"No. I'd feel better if you were with me. That way, I won't spend the whole night worrying about you."

Nicole went into her closet to get an overnight bag, ignoring as best she could the decaying roses. They seemed to be everywhere. She heard voices and recognized Rick's. Jake walked back in with three guys. They immediately went to work, and Jake motioned for Nicole to follow her.

"Let's get out of their hair, huh?" Jake took the bag from Nicole and led her into the living room where Rick waited.

"Dr. Westbrook, glad you're okay."

"Thank you, Detective."

"Jake's left me in charge of locking up the place after we're done. I also have your alarm code. I'll be sure to set it when we leave."

Nicole looked at Jake. "My car?"

"Someone will bring it by my place tonight. Is that okay?"

"Yes. I'm suddenly very tired."

"I know. Come on." Jake looked at Rick and nodded. "Thanks, buddy."

"Wasn't like I had anything else to do tonight."

"Don't forget. We're checking with Nichols's PO in the morning."

"Right. You want to just meet at his office?"

Jake nodded. "See you then."

CHAPTER THIRTY-FIVE

The ride to Jake's duplex was made in silence. Nicole sat staring straight ahead, and Jake looked at her often, wondering if she should say something, anything. But, before she could decide, she exited off the interstate and headed to her small duplex. It occurred to her then that one of them would have to sleep on the sofa. Jake would offer her bed. Nicole was probably in more need of rest.

"Who do you think it is, Jake?"

"We're thinking it's a husband of one of your patients. Frankie Nichols was released just six months ago. We're meeting with his PO—his probation officer—first thing in the morning."

"But I don't know him. And I wasn't involved in his trial," Nicole said quietly.

"I'm sorry, but it's all we've got."

"And if it's not him?"

Jake glanced at her quickly. "We wait."

"Until he does it again?"

Jake nodded. "He dumps his victims. Usually a day or two after he kills them. My theory is he washes them before he dumps them. None of them have had any trace evidence. They are totally clean."

Nicole slowly moved her hand across the console and touched Jake's arm. "I'm really glad I know you. If not, I have this fear I'd be at my house alone tonight."

"I hate to say it, but yeah, you'd be pretty much on your own. Because, Nicole, really, we got shit on this case."

"And it's just your gut feeling that I'm in danger?"

"Yeah. Up until tonight, of course."

Nicole took a deep breath. "I was parked in the street, watching my house, wondering if I should wait for you there or drive off, when I saw this . . . this shadow cross the window from the inside of my house. It was just like before," she said quietly.

"Before?"

"The stalker I told you about. The night he was at my house, it was just the opposite. I was inside, and I saw his shadow in the window as he walked in front."

"That's the night you called the cops?"

"Yes."

Jake pulled into her driveway and cut the engine. She opened the back, letting Cheyenne jump out before grabbing Nicole's overnight bag. The chill hit her immediately, and she watched as Nicole wrapped her arms around herself trying to keep warm.

"Why in the world would you wear something like that this time of year?"

"Don't ask."

Jake shook her head. "I never understood that . . . that fashion thing," she said. "If high heels and pointed toes make your feet hurt, why do women wear them?"

"Why do women do most things? To please a man."

"And your reason would be?"

Nicole sighed. "I'll blame Catherine. She wouldn't let me wear the suit I had on."

Jake walked quickly to the front door, Nicole right beside her. Cheyenne waited patiently for the door to open, then preceded them both inside. Jake went around and turned on lights, then made sure the door was locked. Nicole stood at the edge of the living room, watching her.

"Jake? Can I change?"

"I'm sorry. Of course. The bedroom's in there," she pointed.

Nicole picked up her bag from the sofa where Jake had tossed it and walked quietly into the room. It wasn't much different from the rest of the house although there was a lovely print hanging on one wall, a mountain scene, and Nicole stared at it for the longest. It brought a sense of peace, and she could almost smell the forest. She took a deep breath, then sat her overnight bag on the neatly made bed. Kicking off her shoes, she looked around, looking for anything personal of Jake's, something to shed a little light on her personality. But there was nothing. The dresser was clean, except for a wristwatch and two framed pictures. Before changing, she walked closer, bending over to peer at the pictures. One was of a cabin, tucked into the forest. Nicole smiled fondly. Cheyenne was on the porch, staring at the camera.

"Jake's cabin," Nicole murmured. *Beautiful*. The other, the falls at sunrise. One of Jake's attempts to capture the colors, no doubt. It was beautiful, yes. But Nicole knew, having seen it in person, the picture just didn't do the falls justice, as Jake had said.

After changing into sweat pants, Nicole went into the bathroom. It, too, was neat, clean. She splashed water on her face, then took out her facial soap and washed off what was left of her makeup.

She found Jake and Cheyenne on the sofa. Jake's feet were resting on the coffee table, and Cheyenne was lying half on her lap, eyes closed as Jake rubbed her ear.

"She looks comfortable," Nicole said.

Jake smiled. "There's room for you, too."

Nicole sat on the other side of Cheyenne and mimicked Jake's posture. She let out a contented sigh.

"Long day?"

"Yes." Nicole turned her head to look at Jake. "Thank you. I feel . . . safe here. With you."

Jake only nodded. She was thankful Cheyenne was there to separate them, because right now, Nicole looked too enticing to resist. Her face looked clean, soft, her hair still damp. She finally pulled her eyes away. "We need to get out of here early in the morning. You'll go straight to your office, right?"

"Yes, provided I have a car."

"Rick is having someone bring it by tonight. I'll talk to my lieutenant about having a patrol assigned to you."

"The thought of going to my house and staying there alone is frightening. I'm not sure I can do that."

Jake nodded. "We'll work something out. Let me talk to my lieutenant first." She gently lifted Cheyenne's head off her lap and stood, her leg cramping just a little as she put weight on it. "You look beat." Jake held out her hand to Nicole, who took it and let herself be pulled to her feet.

They stood together, hands still clasped. Nicole had this nearly overwhelming desire to nestle in Jake's arms and burrow herself against the other woman, where it was safe.

"Just let me grab a blanket and pillow, then it's all yours," Jake said, pulling her hand away and leaving Nicole standing alone.

"Your bed? Jake, I can take the sofa," Nicole offered.

"You'll be more comfortable in a bed. The sheets are clean. Well, two days clean. I can change them if you want."

"No, that's fine." She watched as Jake came out, limping slightly, and tossed the pillow and blanket on the sofa next to Cheyenne, who hadn't budged. "Is your leg bothering you?"

"It stiffens up on me when I sit."

Nicole nodded. "Well, thanks for your bed. I . . ."

"It's okay. I seldom sleep through the night anyway."

Nicole was about to ask why, then remembered Jake's aversion to personal questions and answers. But she asked anyway. "Why don't you sleep through the night?"

Jake just shrugged. "Dreams."

Nicole remembered another time when Jake had woken them both. And all Jake had said was "damn dream." But she wouldn't pry. Not now. So, she moved to walk past Jake, then she stopped and leaned over, lightly kissing Jake's cheek. "Thank you for coming to my rescue."

Jake took a step away from Nicole and simply nodded. "Good night."

As soon as Nicole was settled, Jake stretched out on the sofa and pulled the blanket over her, eyes wide open. Cheyenne lay on the floor next to her, and she let her hand drop, fingers curling into soft fur. No doubt her resolve was about to be tested by Nicole's nearness. *A kiss on the cheek and you're getting all gooey-eyed? Geez.*

Nicole snuggled under the covers, eyes closed contentedly. Jake's scent nearly overwhelmed her. It was a scent she remembered distinctly from another time . . . and another place. And despite her assertion that Jake was not her type—*at all*—she still couldn't fight the attraction she had for the other woman.

A cop. You're attracted to a cop. Could it be any worse?

CHAPTER THIRTY-SIX

Jake glared at the young blond, tapping her fingers impatiently on her slacks. Rick finally nudged her.

"Relax, will you?"

"It's five after eight."

"So he's not a clock watcher."

Jake stood and walked to the desk, towering over the young girl. "When do you expect him?"

"Any minute."

"Can you call his cell phone?"

"Well, I can, but really, I'm sure . . . oh, there he is. *Thank God,*" she murmured.

Jake turned, her eyes narrowing as a middle-aged man maneuvered his ample weight through the door. He was breathing heavily as he walked to the desk and held out his hand.

"Messages?"

"Well, no, but these police officers have been waiting to see you, Mr. Taggert."

He looked at both Jake and Rick, nodding. "I got a few minutes. What you need?"

"I'm Detective McCoy, this is Detective Chase. We need some info on one of your clients."

"Sure, sure. Come on inside."

Jake and Rick exchanged glances, then followed the huge man into an office.

"Susie? Coffee?" the man bellowed.

"Yes, sir."

"You two want any?"

"No thanks. We want to know about Frankie Nichols," Jake said. "Employment and residence."

"Nichols? Why?"

"We just want to question him," Rick said.

"Whatever it is, he didn't do it. I've been at this job a lot of years, and Frankie ranks right up there with the best. He's never missed an appointment."

Jake leaned on his desk and met his eyes. "His wife was found raped and murdered. As I'm sure you know, he was convicted of raping and assaulting his wife." She stood up. "Now, employment?"

"No problem. But I'm telling you, he's not your guy."

Jake watched as his pudgy fingers moved over the keyboard, waiting until Frankie Nichols's file appeared on the screen. "Can you print that?"

"Sure."

"Where does he work?" Rick asked.

"He is a janitor for Rocky Mountain Solutions."

"Janitor?"

"Custodian. They clean office buildings in the downtown area at night."

Jake and Rick exchanged glances.

"What?"

"Nothing." Jake reached across the desk and grabbed the

papers off the printer, scanning them quickly. "This home address good?"

"Yeah."

Jake again glanced at Rick. "Thanks, Mr. Taggert. Appreciate it."

"Oh my God! No wonder you freaked. And you spent the night at Jake's?"

"Yes, Catherine. And even though she's denied it, I know you told her that I was at Sullivan's."

"It's hard to keep things from her."

"Well, I suppose I'm thankful that you did. But I don't know exactly what this all means. I only know that I don't want to stay at my house alone."

Catherine followed Nicole into her office and hung Nicole's gym bag behind the door for her.

"So what happens now?"

Nicole stood at the window and looked out over downtown Denver. "I don't really know. Jake said she'd be in touch today and let me know what's going on." She turned and faced Catherine. "I know one thing. I'm not up for a group session today."

Catherine looked at her watch. "Thirty minutes."

"I know. I'll muddle through." She pulled out her chair and sat down, flipping on her computer at the same time. "You might want to call Dorothy. See if she'd be up to covering for me this week if it's necessary. I'd rather do that than have to cancel sessions."

"Cancel? Is it that serious?"

Nicole shrugged. "I only know that last night, it all seemed very real. So if Jake insists I stay away, I guess I'll stay away. We'll see."

"It's not like you to run, Nicole. Like you said, we get threats all the time."

"The man running behind my car last night was not just a threat."

Jake and Rick stood on either side of the door. Jake had her badge out and Rick's hand was touching his weapon. She nodded, and he banged on the door.

"Frankie Nichols? Open up. Police." He waited a few seconds before knocking again. "Open up."

They heard shuffling inside, then the sound of the dead bolt being unlocked. The door opened and a sleepy Frankie Nichols looked at them as he rubbed his eyes.

"What the hell you want?"

"Bad time?" Jake asked, as she pushed her way into the room.

"I got off work at six, so yeah, bad time. What do you want?"

"We've got some questions. In fact, we've got lots of questions. Let's take a ride."

"No way. I'm clean. You call Michael Taggert. I ain't missed a meeting, I've done everything I'm supposed to do. I ain't going."

"This isn't exactly about a parole violation," Rick said. "Not exactly."

"Your ex-wife was found murdered, her body dumped."

His eyes widened. "Jena? And you think I did it?"

Jake raised an eyebrow. "Now what do you think we think?"

Rick took his arm. "Come on. Let's go."

"No. I'm not going. I didn't do it."

"Come with us, or I'll arrest your ass right here," Jake threatened. "We'll see how that affects your parole."

"Goddamn bitch."

"Thought you'd see it our way."

CHAPTER THIRTY-SEVEN

"Sit down."

"I want to call Mr. Taggert."

"I already took care of that for you." Jake pulled out a chair and sat across from him. Rick stood by the door. Frankie Nichols leaned back in his chair, silent for the first time since they'd picked him up.

"Where were you night before last?"

"Working."

"All night?"

"Go in at eight, get off at six."

"Night before that?"

"Look, I work every night, eight to six, Monday through Friday."

"Where do you work?"

"Now, I know you already know where I work."

"What buildings, specifically, do you clean?"

"Downtown. Hell, I don't know the names. They just drop us off and pick us up."

Jake sighed. "When was the last time you saw Jena?"

He rubbed the stubble on his face, then looked up and shrugged. "She was at the trial. However long ago that was."

"And you never once saw her since you've been out? Six months now?"

"No."

"Didn't go sneaking around, maybe trying to catch a glimpse of her when she left her apartment?"

"No. I didn't. That's in the past. Besides, I'm not allowed to."

"Parole violation. Yes, I know." A knock on the door interrupted Jake, and Rick moved to open it.

"I need a word with you two," Lieutenant Gregory said.

Jake shoved her chair away. "Stay put," she told him. When she closed the door, Gregory handed her a file.

"He's not our guy, McCoy. Cut him loose."

"What the hell?"

"He's been a model employee. Never missed a shift."

"That means shit. They drop them off at a building at eight and pick them up at six the next morning. Plenty of time."

"Four people to a shift. Just so happens, one of the four in Frankie's group is a supervisor. Talked to him myself, and he says Frankie is his best employee and has never missed. So cut him loose. Salazar and Simpson are checking out the other two leads."

"Goddamn it! He's a janitor! He *cleans!*"

"Jesus Christ, McCoy! Will you let the soap thing go?"

"Not soap. Triclosan," she murmured as he walked away. She turned to Rick. "Can you fucking believe this?"

"We got shit, Jake."

"Well it goddamn sucks," she snapped as she walked away, leaving Rick to cut Frankie Nichols loose. She followed after the lieutenant, knocking once on his doorframe before walking in.

"McCoy?"

"It's about Dr. Westbrook. You got the report from last night?"

"Yeah. You want a detail?"

"At the very least, yes."

He shook his head. "That's all I can offer. We can't bring her in. We don't have the budget for that. Besides, we got no case."

Jake met his eyes. "She stayed at my place last night. I don't mind doing it again."

"Well, that's admirable, Detective. Not exactly orthodox."

"She was scared out of her mind. I couldn't very well leave her at her house."

He took his reading glasses off and stared at Jake. "There is nothing personal here, right?"

"Of course not. But I'm convinced that she's the target. If we can spare a unit to watch her office during the day, I don't mind taking the night shift. Of course, I haven't mentioned any of this to her. She may balk. But last night, she was plenty shook up."

"Until we get a suspect and something concrete, the DA won't touch it. And they're the ones with the budget for this sort of thing."

"Well, I'll run it by her."

He nodded. "I'll get a unit sent over to her office. You might want to brief them, let them know what we're looking for."

"Thanks, Lieutenant."

Nicole looked up at the light tapping on her door, then bent her head and continued writing.

"Come in, Catherine."

"Jake called. She wanted to let you know that there's going to be a police car in front of the building. And she said she would come by later. She needed to talk to you."

Despite everything that was going on, Nicole felt a smile tugging at her mouth. But she simply nodded without looking up. "Thanks."

Jake sat at her desk, twirling her pen. Gina and Simpson weren't back yet, and they hadn't heard from them. She reached out and fingered the mouse, lightly tapping on it as thoughts flew through her mind, bouncing off one another, not pausing long enough for her to follow up on them.

Nicole had a stalker before. No wonder she was freaked out.

Jake moved the mouse, wanting to search the database. But when she entered Nicole's name, there was no match. She then entered Nicole's address. Again, no match.

"That makes no sense," she murmured.

"What?"

She looked at Rick and shook her head. "Nothing." She reached for the phone, dialing Nicole's office. Catherine answered on the second ring, her voice as professional as ever.

"It's me again," Jake said. "Do you remember when she had the stalker?"

"Nicole? Yes. It wasn't very long after I started working for her. It must have been six years ago. Why?"

"Was she living at the house she's at now?"

"Yes. That's where it happened."

"What happened?"

"Well, the police shot him. Right in her yard."

"She told you or you went out there?"

"She told me. She was so upset, she stayed out of the office for a week. Of course, I wanted her to stay out before that because the guy was showing up here."

"In your office?"

"No. Outside. He'd follow her when she walked to the gym. He'd call, do the heavy breathing thing."

"Do you remember the guy's name?"

"Oh, no. I don't have a clue."

Jake sighed. "Okay. She's free after three, right?"

"Yes. And I told her you were coming by."

"Thanks, Catherine."

Jake went back to her search, wishing she had the exact date of the shooting. But it shouldn't matter. If she didn't get a hit on

Nicole's name, at least her address should match. But it didn't. And if the guy had been stalking her, calling her, why hadn't Nicole reported it then? And why hadn't Nicole told her the whole story?

"What the hell are you doing?" Rick finally asked.

Jake looked up, frowning. "Dr. Westbrook said she had a stalker about six years ago. He showed up at her house and she called the cops, and they ended up shooting him, killing him, right there in her yard."

"No shit? Damn."

"Except there's nothing in the system. There's no match on her name or address."

"Well, that can't be. If there was a shooting, there's got to be a record of it."

Jake shrugged. "I'll ask her about it later." She leaned back and tried to stretch her leg. "Heard from Salazar or Simpson?"

"Yeah. They checked out Charles Ramsey. He's now in a wheelchair, lives with his mother. He's found God or something."

Jake lifted an eyebrow.

"I know, but that's what Simpson said. The other guy, Steve Brousard, works as a mechanic. They were on their way to interview him."

Jake stared at him. "We got shit."

"I'd say."

"Maybe our angle is wrong. Maybe it's not a disgruntled former husband. Maybe it simply has to do with Dr. Westbrook."

"Maybe it's random."

"Nothing is random. Just like nothing is a coincidence."

"Four dead women. There'll be a task force before we know it."

Jake shook her head. "I don't think so. If we had some leads, maybe. But we don't, and a task force will just send him underground."

"How long do you think the lieutenant can keep the word 'serial killer' out of the papers?"

"Not much longer, that's for sure. One more body and I'd say the thing blows up."

CHAPTER THIRTY-EIGHT

Jake stopped to brief the two officers who were parked across the street from Nicole's building. She realized it was more for show than anything. If their guy decided to make a move in Nicole's office, eight floors up, there was little these two could do about it.

Catherine motioned her inside when she stuck her head in. "She's still with her last appointment."

Jake nodded. "I'm a little early."

Catherine glanced once at Nicole's door, then back at Jake. "She was shook up last night, huh?"

"Yeah. I don't blame her. You should have seen her bedroom."

"Dead roses?"

Jake nodded. "Any letters today?"

"Not a one."

Jake cocked her head, watching Catherine. "How do you go home?"

"What do you mean?"

"Do you take the same route every day?"

"Well, yes."

"Park in the same place?"

"Yes."

Jake raised an eyebrow. "Well, stop it."

"You think I might be in danger?"

"I don't want to scare you, Catherine, but you've got to think about the possibility."

Catherine shook her head. "I can't believe that someone would want to get back at Dr. Westbrook that badly that they'd resort to all this."

"I've seen so much shit out there, nothing surprises me anymore. So, take a different route home tonight, and park someplace else tomorrow. Deal?"

"Okay. But, I've told my husband about all this, you know. He actually wants me to quit. And I've had this job longer than I've had him."

"I take it you haven't told Nicole this?"

"No. I'm not going to quit. Besides, not that I'm blowing my own horn or anything, but Nicole would be lost without me."

Jake walked closer, perching on the edge of Catherine's desk. "So, what do you know about this woman she was out with last night?" Jake asked quietly.

Catherine smiled. "Cheryl Logan, some hotshot surgeon. She's a friend of Irene, who is a friend of Nicole's."

"Blind date?"

"Yeah."

"Well, trust me, they weren't right for each other."

"No?"

"Not at all."

"And you know this how?"

Jake smiled and leaned forward, causing Catherine to lean back. "Now Catherine, we both know that Nicole told you about our encounter in the mountains."

Catherine nodded. "She told me."

Jake wiggled her eyebrows. "What all did she tell you?"

"Enough to make me blush, thank you."

Jake laughed then tried to stifle it as Nicole's door opened, and Nicole walked out with a young woman. She wasn't quite able to wipe the smile from her face as her eyes met Nicole's. She nodded once. "Doctor."

"Detective," Nicole greeted, as she moved past her. "Rachel, see you next week." When the outer office door closed, Nicole turned back to stare at first Catherine, then Jake. "Up to no good?"

"Just chatting," Jake said, shoving off Catherine's desk. "Got a minute for me?"

"Of course."

Jake turned and winked at Catherine before following Nicole into her office and closing the door behind her. Nicole leaned casually against her desk, and they watched one another. Jake much preferred Nicole's look today. Black slacks and a burgundy blouse beat the hell out of the power suits she usually wore.

Nicole waited patiently as Jake's eyes traveled over her body. She felt the involuntary reaction she always felt when Jake looked at her that way—difficulty breathing and the constant rapid pulse that seemed to mock her. Jake must think it was safe here, with Catherine just outside. But last night, when Nicole had innocently kissed her on the cheek, she'd not missed Jake's quick intake of breath, or her sudden withdrawal.

"You look nice," Jake finally said.

Nicole swallowed before speaking. "Thank you."

Jake took a step closer. "The husband checked out. He's not our guy."

Nicole only nodded.

"So, I want you to stay with me again tonight," Jake said quietly as she took another step closer.

Nicole nodded, but was unable to speak. Jake's eyes held her, and she labored to breathe normally.

Jake told herself she was playing with fire, but her body

wouldn't listen. Something about being in Nicole's presence did that to her, made her forget all about that line she vowed she'd not cross. Even then, she was still confident she could control this desire she had to take Nicole in her arms and taste her lips again. But she hadn't counted on Nicole giving in as well. The rise and fall of Nicole's chest, the rapid pulse in her throat, and the blue, blue eyes that bored into Jake completely shattered her resolve.

Nicole wasn't certain how it happened. In the next instant, her mouth was claimed by Jake, and she opened willingly to her, her arms sliding over Jake's shoulders to pull her closer. There was nothing gentle about their kisses, and Nicole groaned loudly when Jake's tongue found its way into her mouth. She felt her body trying to mold itself to Jake's hard frame, and she let it. Their hips pressed together intimately, and Nicole just barely resisted opening her thighs to straddle Jake's leg. She could not, however, control her hands as they cupped Jake's breasts.

Jake came to her senses, pulling away from Nicole and holding her at arm's length while she tried to catch her breath. She had been only seconds away from ripping open Nicole's blouse. *You're on a case. You're on a goddamn case!*

"I'm sorry. But I've wanted to do that since I saw you again," Jake whispered.

"I know," Nicole murmured. "Me, too." *She's a cop. Not your type, not your type.* She moved behind her desk, putting some space between them as she tried to get herself under control again. "So, you want me to just come by your place after I'm done here?" Nicole asked, her voice still husky with desire.

Jake shoved her hands in her pockets, angry with herself for losing control, still able to feel Nicole's hands on her breasts. So, she cleared her throat and took a deep breath, finally able to meet Nicole's eyes again. "I'd really feel better if you'd let me pick you up."

"That would mean you'd have to bring me back here in the morning."

"I don't mind."

Nicole leaned her elbows on her desk, watching Jake. "We can't do this indefinitely, Jake. I have to eventually go back to my house."

Jake shook her head. "Not until this is over with." She walked closer to Nicole's desk again, feeling the need to apologize. "Look, about that . . ."

"It's not like I tried to stop you, Jake." Jake may not be her type, but Lord, the woman could kiss. "It's not like I didn't . . . touch you," Nicole whispered.

So, it was like that, was it? They could be in really big trouble, Jake knew. Tonight, alone . . . who would stop?

"What time should I pick you up?"

Nicole looked at her cluttered desk, knowing on a normal day she'd be here until well after seven. She knew Jake would never go for that. "Whenever you're done for the day, just come by."

"Rick and I have an appointment with the ME in"—Jake looked at her watch—"fifteen minutes. It'll be after five before I get back here."

"When Catherine leaves, I'll be sure and lock up."

Jake nodded, then stopped at the door. "Nicole, about the stalker?"

"Yes?"

"Do you remember when it was?"

"It was summer. Late July, but I don't remember the exact date."

"Six years ago?"

Nicole nodded. "It was six years this summer."

"And you called 911?"

"What's this about?"

"Nothing. I just wanted to follow up on it. It's no big deal."

Nicole picked up a pen and twirled it in her hands. "Yes, I called 911. They sent two police cars out."

"Two units responded?"

"Jake, why all the questions?"

Jake sighed, wondering what it all meant. "I can't find anything in the system."

"What do you mean?"

"There was no hit on your name, no hit on your address."

"But . . ."

"We'll talk about it tonight. I've got to meet Rick."

Jake left quietly, leaving Nicole staring at the closed door, wondering how her life suddenly became so complicated.

CHAPTER THIRTY-NINE

"About damn time, Jake." Rick stood up, waiting as Jake rushed over. "You know Benson hates it when we're late."

"I know, but traffic was a bitch." Jake checked her watch again. Only ten minutes late. "Did you get Dave? Will he be able to join us?"

"He's finishing up the post on Jena Nichols. He'll come in as soon as he's done."

"Good." Jake stopped at the reception desk, smiling at Liz. "Hey, Liz. How are you?"

"McCoy? I heard you were back. Feeling better?"

"Good as new." Jake motioned to the closed door. "Dragon Lady waiting on us?"

"Afraid so." Liz picked up the phone and waited only a second. "The detectives are here." Liz held the phone away as Dr. Benson spoke loud enough for Jake to catch the "about goddamn time." Liz smiled apologetically. "Go on in."

"Thanks." Jake gallantly stepped aside, offering Rick the chance to walk in first, but he shook his head.

"No way. You get to hear it for being late, not me."

"Wimp," she murmured, as she opened the door to Dr. Benson's office. She conjured up one of her most charming smiles, hoping to deflate some of Dr. Benson's anger.

"Do you have any idea how busy I am, detectives?"

"Of course, Dr. Benson. It's totally my fault that we're late. I can assure you it will never happen again," Jake said.

Dr. Benson took off her glasses and impaled Jake with a stare that actually caused her to take a step backward. "You don't have to assure me, Detective McCoy. This is the last appointment I will ever make with you. If you need information from a post I did, you'll have to get Dr. Gamble or one of the assistant MEs to help you. I will not waste my time with you."

"We're ten minutes late, Dr. Benson. Ten minutes because I was downtown following up on a lead in our investigation of these murders. But I do know how valuable your time is, and if you can't spare a half-hour to assist us with four murdered women, I understand." Jake turned to go, ignoring Rick's wide-eyed stare. "Perhaps Dr. Gamble has the time." Jake heard the chair bang against the wall as Dr. Benson stood up quickly.

"Who do you think you are, speaking to me that way?"

Jake smiled. "I'm just a lowly detective trying to solve four murders. I don't have time to play games with you, Dr. Benson."

"Detective McCoy, you have just made an enemy."

"Yeah? Well, get in line. I've got plenty." Jake left, leaving Rick to stay or follow. As expected, he hurried out the door after Jake.

"Have you lost your goddamn mind?" he hissed.

"Apparently so. But she's pissed me off for the last time." Jake stopped again in front of Liz. "Gamble still doing the post?"

"Yes."

"Jake, please tell me we're not going in there. You know I hate that."

"Best to grab him now before Benson talks to him."

215

"Christ, I hate when you go off like that," Rick said, as he walked quickly to keep up with her. "And what lead were you following up on that you're late?"

"None. I was with Dr. Westbrook."

"I swear, Jake. What is it about that woman?"

Jake stopped suddenly and met Rick's eyes unflinchingly. "What it is, Chase, is that she's going to get her ass killed unless we find this bastard."

"So you're . . . protecting her?"

"You got a better idea?"

Rick shook his head. "You're in a mood today," he said quietly.

"Because we got fucking shit on this case and goddamn Dr. Benson thinks it's a fucking game!" she yelled.

"Will you calm down?"

"I am calm," Jake said. She knocked once on the glass and waited for Dave to motion them inside. "Hey, Dave."

"Tired of waiting on me?"

"No. But I pissed off the Dragon Lady again, and she's refused to help us. So you're it."

"No problem. I'm done here anyway." He pulled the sheet over their victim and nodded to Carl, his assistant. Carl wheeled the body away, and Rick finally let out his breath. "I know you hate autopsies, Chase."

"With a passion. The last time I sat through a full one, I had nightmares for a week."

"How similar is she to the other one you did?" Jake asked.

"The one at the lake? Thornton?"

"Yes."

"Identical. Except for the knife wound. And it was done postmortem." He picked up his notes. "Cause of death is strangulation. Vaginal trauma, but no fluids present."

"She was cleaned up?"

"She was cleaned up inside and out."

"Helen Thornton, Sandra Poole, and Shelly Burke all had traces of triclosan. It's listed in every post."

"Triclosan is the active ingredient in antibacterial soap," Dr. Gamble said. "It's not unusual to find traces on victims."

"But our victims are all . . . really clean," Jake said. "No fluids, no fibers. Nothing. So, my theory is, they've been cleaned. They've been washed."

"And you're most likely correct, Jake. I assisted on the post of Sandra Poole, too. She'd been sodomized. And raped. But she was clean. Almost as if he'd . . . douched her. Which I wouldn't rule out. But other than the tissue tears, there was no outside evidence. So yes, he cleaned her up."

"So, he cleaned her up as if he had a background in forensics . . . or he just cleaned her up?" Jake asked.

"I'd say he knew what he was doing," Dave said. "My guess is he left them soaking in a tub of water and soap for a day, then perhaps sprayed them down. All four victims were found at least forty-eight hours after death."

Jake nodded. "Dave, do me a favor? If we get another one, can you do the post?"

"Dr. Benson is still my boss."

"Yeah, but if she finds out it's our case, she might pass it to you anyway."

"Well, let's hope we don't have any more."

"Seeing as how we've got shit for leads, I'd say that's not possible."

"I'll do what you need me to do, Jake."

"Thanks, Dave. Can you make sure Monica sends us the full report?"

"Of course."

It was well after five when Jake and Rick walked into the squad room, but their lieutenant was waiting for them.

"Goddamn McCoy. Dr. Benson?"

Jake squared her shoulders. "She pissed me off."

"So I take it."

"She called you?"

"Oh, no. Not that simple. She called the chief."

"Damn. The chief called you?"

"Chief called the captain."

Jake grinned. "Well, that's good. You only heard it like . . . third hand."

The lieutenant let a quick smile cross his face before he hid it. "Consider yourself reprimanded."

"That's it? You don't want to know what went down?"

"I heard her version. I can only imagine yours."

Jake nodded. "Sorry, Lieutenant, but she plays these fucking games."

"I know. Everyone knows how she is. We can only hope she'll retire soon, McCoy." He glanced at Rick. "What you got?"

"Nothing," he said.

"Four dead women and nothing. Great. We'll get killed on this one."

"The only consistency in these cases is that they are all clean." When the lieutenant rolled his eyes, Jake went on. "I know you don't like my soap theory, but Dr. Gamble backs it up."

Lieutenant Gregory looked at Chase.

"Yes, sir. Gamble said most likely that they'd been washed before being dumped."

"Great. And that helps us how?"

Jake shrugged. "Well, I don't know."

"And this Westbrook woman? Where are we with her?"

"Her secretary is monitoring their mail and phone calls. Dr. Westbrook has given us access to her files. Well, some of them. She's agreed for me to watch her again tonight. She's not exactly crazy about this, though."

"Well, I talked to the DA. Debra Fisher is not assigned to us on this one. Apparently, she's running for mayor and working with us will apparently cut into her time."

"Imagine that," Jake murmured. She'd never liked Debra Fisher. On the surface, Fisher appeared to loathe Jake, barely speaking to her. But privately, she'd made it no secret she wanted to sleep with Jake. Jake wasn't interested.

"Marcus Thompson has been assigned. As soon as we get a suspect, he'll bring Dr. Westbrook in if need be."

"There's something else, Lieutenant. About six years ago, Dr. Westbrook had a stalker. She says that she called 911 and two units responded. She says that they shot the suspect in her front yard."

"And? You think this is related?"

"I don't know. The system has jack on her."

"*What?*"

"No hit on her name or address."

"Not possible, McCoy."

Jake met his eyes. "She's not lying to me."

"If it happened, it's in the system. If she called 911, it's in the log."

"And if it's not?"

He let out a breath, eyes closed for a second before speaking. "See if you can verify it. Neighbors, somebody. We'll go from there."

"Yes, sir."

CHAPTER FORTY

"Are you sure takeout is okay?"

Nicole smiled. "It's fine, Jake. I've been here before. Their lasagna is wonderful." Jake just nodded, and Nicole watched her profile as they waited in line. Her face was etched with worry, and Nicole wondered if she was the cause of it. "Bad day?" she finally asked.

"Understatement," Jake murmured. The car in front of her moved up and Jake did the same. "You know Dr. Benson, the ME?"

"I've met her, yes."

"Well, she hates me. Unfortunately, she did the post on two of our victims. And I was ten minutes late for our meeting this afternoon. Apparently, her time is much more valuable than anyone else's. She let me have it. For once, I didn't just stand there and take it. So, she called the chief who called my captain, who called my lieutenant."

"I'm sorry. She's always been . . . well, difficult."

"Difficult?" Jake laughed. "I was going to say a bitch."

Nicole laughed, too. "Well, there's that."

Jake turned in the seat and met Nicole's eyes. "I also have a problem with your stalker."

"What do you mean?"

"I can't find a match anywhere, Nicole. Not on our system, not on the log."

Nicole folded her arms across her waist, remembering. "When they showed up, I was in the house, of course. I saw their lights, I heard their sirens. I was in the living room, watching. The guy, the stalker, he ran toward the cars, hands held up. And then there were shots fired, and he just dropped, right there on the lawn."

"What time did all this happen?"

"I don't know. It wasn't really late. Ten maybe."

"Okay. What happened after the shooting? The cops came and talked to you?"

Nicole nodded. "One of the officers did, yes. He said that the guy wouldn't be bothering me anymore. That was about it."

"What about investigators coming to talk to you about the shooting? Internal Affairs?"

"No. No one did."

"Reporters?"

"No."

Jake moved forward again, opening her window and handing the girl some money. "Nicole, if a patrol unit is involved in a shooting, there'll be an investigation. There's an internal investigation anytime there's a shooting, regardless."

"Well, no one talked to me about it."

Jake took the bag through the window and handed it to Nicole, then took her change. "Did anyone else witness this? A neighbor?"

Nicole stared. "Are you questioning whether this really happened? Do you think I'm making this up?"

Jake drove off, getting back on the highway. "No, I don't think you're making this up. And that's what scares me. Because there's no record of it."

"My neighbor came over that night, after it happened. Mr. Reynolds is sort of a busybody in the neighborhood."

Jake turned down her street, slowing as she glanced at Nicole. "I'll talk to him. There's probably no connection whatsoever to your stalker and the murders, but it's just odd that I can't find a record of it."

Nicole watched the street as Jake drove, seeing the identical duplexes flash by until Jake turned into a driveway and cut the engine. Once again, Nicole wondered why Jake lived where she did. It was so out of character from the woman she knew.

A short time later, after Cheyenne had run inside and inspected the visitor, Nicole served portions of lasagna on the two plates Jake had produced. A bottle of wine appeared, and Nicole watched as Jake reached into a cabinet and took down two wineglasses. Nicole unfolded the garlic bread, pleased that it was still warm.

"Smells great," Jake said. She handed Nicole a paper napkin and a fork, then sat down opposite her.

"Yes. And I'm starving," Nicole said, taking a bite. "Delicious," she murmured.

Jake watched her, still dressed for the office but with her sleeves unbuttoned and rolled over at the cuffs. Nicole's wrists were slender, the left one sporting a loose-fitting silver watch, the other bare.

"What?"

Jake looked up. "Hmm?"

Nicole smiled and pointed her fork at Jake's plate. "Eat before I start stealing off your plate."

"You're probably not used to such informal dinners as you've had here, huh?"

"It's not like I eat at Sullivan's every night."

"But when you go out on a date, you go someplace nice? Formal?"

Nicole nodded. "Usually."

Jake leaned forward, smiling. "So, you're really in the closet?"

Nicole nearly blushed. "Professionally, yes. Privately, not really. I mean, my family knows. Catherine obviously knows."

"Where is your family?" Jake asked after sipping from her wine.

"Grand Junction."

"Is that where you grew up?"

"Yes. I got a rather nice scholarship offer from CU and moved to Boulder the summer after graduation." Nicole added more wine to both their glasses. "I don't get back there much, but my mother and I talk often." She looked at Jake, wondering about her own family. "What about you?"

"Family? My folks retired, sold everything they owned and bought a travel trailer."

"You're kidding?"

"They love it. Don't see them much, though. They usually make it up this way in the summer."

"Siblings?"

"No, there was just me."

Nicole took another bite of lasagna, then asked the one question that had been bothering her the most. "Tell me about your dream."

Jake looked up, startled. "My dream?"

Nicole leaned her elbows on the table, resting her chin in her palms. "Up in the mountains, that night or early in the morning, I guess, you had this dream. You were talking about shooting someone, killing someone." Nicole smiled. "It freaked me out. And I'd convinced myself that you were a hired killer or something. A cop never once crossed my mind."

Jake laughed. "So that's why you cut out in such a hurry?"

Nicole felt a slight blush creep up her face and nodded. "But now . . . now that I know you, the dream means something else entirely. And it troubles you," she said quietly.

Jake swallowed. "And professionally, you want to hear about it?"

Nicole met her eyes. "Professionally—and personally."

Jake was about to refuse, but the look in Nicole's eyes was purely sincere and nothing but caring. Jake decided it might actually do her good to say the words out loud, instead of the lie she'd told the police psychologist. So, she filled her wineglass again and closed her eyes, and remembered.

"Rick and I, we were at this apartment complex, looking for an informant. He wasn't home, so we were checking with neighbors, you know. I think we were on the third floor when we heard shots." Jake shrugged. "Could have been anything, but we decided to check them out. By the time we ran down three flights of stairs, we heard sirens and figured something had been called in. Then we heard shots again, behind the building, in the alley. We ran." She looked up and met Nicole's eyes. "This guy had a little kid around the neck and had a gun pressed against his head. Another guy was running away so Rick chased after him, leaving me with this guy and this kid. I held my weapon at him, told him to release the boy, but he just laughed at me." Jake shrugged again. "A unit pulled up. One officer went after Rick, the other one, Perkins, he came with me, pulling his weapon, too."

Nicole reached across the table and took Jake's hand. "What happened?"

"We didn't have a clue as to what went down, we only knew this guy had a gun to this kid's head. He was pulling him down the alley and we followed, telling him to drop his weapon, to let the kid go. But he wouldn't. And Perkins was telling me to take a shot, but I couldn't. The boy was right there, he was too exposed. I remember thinking, if he would only do something, bite the guy's hand, kick him . . . anything . . . anything to cause a distraction, then I'd nail the guy. But this kid, he can't be more than eight, and he's scared to death."

Jake's hand trembled as she picked up her wineglass and took a sip. She took a deep breath, forcing herself to continue. "The guy came to a fence. He had his back against it. We had him. I told him to let the boy go, that there was no way out. And he started laughing at me. The next thing I know, shots are going off everywhere. I see the boy fall, I see Perkins fall . . . I'm firing my weapon, and I feel this fire in my leg, and I go down. And he's still standing. I shoot again and finally, he goes down, too." Jake squeezed the fingers that were still entwined with her own. "I thought that was it. I was bleeding, I couldn't stop it. That's all I remember."

"What happened?"

"Rick came back, found me. Put a tourniquet around my leg. I made it. Perkins and the boy, they were both dead. I spent two weeks in the hospital and then another week in bed. The fourth week, I was doing therapy. And the fifth week, I went to my cabin."

"Which is when we met?"

"Yes."

"And you still have dreams about it?"

Jake nodded. "Not so much anymore. It was pretty much nightly there for awhile."

Nicole raised an eyebrow. "How did you get cleared?"

"You think I've told this story before?"

"No. You told them you were fine, that you had no adverse effects, and that you were good to go back on duty."

"Just because I had a recurring dream didn't mean I wasn't ready to go back," Jake said.

"You were having a dream, Jake, because you hadn't gotten it out, you hadn't talked it out with anyone. There's a clinical reason they make you see a doctor, you know. It's not just for kicks."

"Well, if I'd known you then, I'd have gladly bared my soul to you," Jake said quietly.

With their fingers still entwined, Nicole pulled Jake's hand closer. "And I'd have given anything to be there for you."

Jake tucked her head and sighed. "Well, there you go," she said.

"I know you've heard this before, but . . ."

"I shouldn't blame myself?"

"Well, I think that's futile to tell you not to blame yourself. It's human nature to blame yourself, Jake. It's your profession. But you have to reconcile that you did what you could do. If you'd taken other action, like trying to take the guy out, you might have hit the boy. And I don't think you could have survived that," Nicole said quietly.

Jake nodded. "At first, I thought maybe it was me who took him down. There was so much shooting," she whispered. "A day after my surgery, Rick told me that it wasn't my bullet." Jake tried to smile but failed. "It didn't really matter at that point."

Nicole had tons of clinical statements she could make, but the look in Jake's eyes told her that none were needed. So, instead, she squeezed Jake's hand tightly and offered what comfort she could. She was finally rewarded with a genuine smile from Jake.

"Thanks for listening."

"Anytime," Nicole whispered.

Jake pulled her hand away from Nicole and stood, taking their plates to the sink. "If you want to shower, go ahead. I'll clean up dinner."

"Are you sure? You can go first."

"No, it's fine. Go ahead."

Jake watched Nicole walk away, wondering why she'd been compelled to talk about that day. Three months had passed, going on four, but still, the memory was vivid. But she had to admit, her feelings weren't quite as raw as they had been. She couldn't help but smile. It was a cliché, but damn, it was true. Time heals. Her emotional wound wasn't quite healed, but it was getting there. The guilt she'd shouldered at first had dissipated somewhat, but it wasn't gone entirely. She wondered if it'd ever disappear completely.

Cheyenne finally grew impatient as she leaned heavily against Jake's leg. Jake reached down and ruffled her head, knowing that Cheyenne thought it was time for her nightly snack.

"Ready for your bone?"

Cheyenne danced excitedly and followed Jake to the pantry where she kept the bucket of dog treats.

CHAPTER FORTY-ONE

Nicole stood under the hot water with eyes closed. Jake's story had touched her deeply. She couldn't say that she knew Jake well, but she knew her well enough to know that the guilt Jake carried most likely ran deep. She could hear it in her voice, see it in her eyes. And the dream was simply her subconscious attempt to alter the outcome of the shooting. And unfortunately, the outcome never changed.

Nicole turned off the water and stepped out, wrapping a towel around her before moving to the sink to brush her teeth. She felt lucky, actually, to know Jake. Or to know her as well as she did. If their little tryst this summer hadn't occurred, she and Jake would be nothing but strangers, and Nicole would most likely be staying with a friend. Or worse, trying to tough it out at home alone.

But she was here, in the safe company of a cop. A cop who . . . *God*, made Nicole question her entire lesbian life. If it was Jake who turned her bones to liquid, no wonder she couldn't work up an appetite for sex with one of the countless blind dates she'd been out on. Not a one of them was anything like Jake. And now here they were, alone, both of them clearly avoiding the subject of what happened in Nicole's office earlier that day.

Avoiding it, yes. But nonetheless, it was still there. She wondered if Jake regretted her momentary lack of control. Most likely.

Jake was sitting quietly on the sofa when she heard the water turn off in the shower. Before she could stop them, images of a wet and naked Nicole flashed through her mind, and she closed her eyes, remembering. Sometimes, it felt like it was only yesterday that they touched. Nicole had been so . . . responsive, so *ready*.

It had been more than a couple of months, but still, Jake couldn't get it out of her mind, couldn't get *Nicole* out of her mind. Perhaps that was why she hadn't bothered going out, hadn't bothered returning Heather's phone calls. She didn't want her memories—her very vivid memories—to be replaced just yet. And the little kissing episode in Nicole's office hadn't helped.

"I lost it, Cheyenne," she said quietly. "Couldn't help myself."

And lost it was an understatement. When Nicole had responded, had moved against her, when Jake felt Nicole's hands cup her breasts, all she wanted to do was touch flesh. And she knew without a doubt what she'd find. She knew Nicole would be wet for her. *Sweet Jesus*.

She stood up quickly and walked into the kitchen, pausing long enough to splash her face with cold water. How in the world was she going to get through the night?

"Hey."

Jake turned, her voice sticking in her throat as she looked at Nicole. Damp hair tucked behind ears, smooth skin, and a robe that barely reached to mid-thigh. Jake didn't have to stare long to realize that Nicole was naked beneath the robe.

"Shower's all yours."

Jake nodded, then cleared her throat. "Thanks," she managed

as she hurried from the room, not stopping until she had the bathroom door closed firmly behind her.

"You're on a case, you're on a case, you're on a case," she murmured over and over as she shed her clothes and stepped into the shower that only moments ago Nicole had been standing in—naked.

Christ, you're pathetic.

But nonetheless, Jake turned on only the cold water, forcing herself to stand there until she regained some control over her body.

Nicole watched as Jake nearly ran from the room, then looked at Cheyenne with raised eyebrows.

"What was that all about?"

Cheyenne simply cocked her head, as if to shrug.

The bottle of wine they'd started still sat on the table, along with both their glasses. Nicole added some to hers and took it into the living room. Looking around, once more she thought how stark the room was. It was as if Jake was afraid to make it a home. Again she was curious as to what Jake's cabin looked like. She could imagine it being warm, cozy. Not so sterile, like this duplex. She finally moved closer to the built-in bookcases, casually inspecting the handful of titles there. Most were travel books from Colorado and New Mexico, including hiking trails and mountain bike trails. A few books of fiction, their titles suggesting a mystery, and an old, worn dictionary. That was it.

"Where's your . . . *stuff?*" she whispered.

When she heard the shower turn off, she glanced into the bedroom, smiling at Cheyenne who lay next to the bed, her eyes watching the closed door of the bathroom. Nicole moved to her, perching on the edge of the bed and casually reaching down to pet Cheyenne. She was rewarded with a cold nose that nuzzled her palm.

When the bathroom door opened, she glanced up, and her

heart tumbled in her chest. Jake walked out, totally naked except for a towel wrapped loosely at her hips. Nicole's eyes traveled up her body, stopping only when she locked glances with Jake.

"I'm sorry," Jake murmured. "I didn't think you'd be in here."

Nicole stood slowly, barely able to breathe as her heart hammered in her chest. Jake's eyes were wide, and Nicole knew she was about to bolt back into the bathroom.

"Don't go," Nicole whispered.

"Nicole . . ."

Nicole walked closer, blindly setting her wineglass on the dresser as her eyes held Jake's. They were but a foot apart, and Nicole could almost hear Jake's heart as it pounded against her chest. Her eyes finally dropped, staring at the breasts, the perfect breasts that had been haunting her for so long now. The small breasts were firm, taut—the nipples hard—practically begging for Nicole's touch. And she couldn't fight the urge to feel warm flesh.

Jake watched as Nicole reached out a hand, seeing it tremble but unable to stop its movement. She didn't want to stop it. She couldn't. Her breathing was labored as she waited for Nicole's touch. Finally, her eyes slammed shut as a warm hand covered one breast.

"Jake . . . I can't stand this anymore," Nicole whispered. Her other hand reached lower, gently tugging at the towel, letting it fall helplessly to the floor.

No, Jake couldn't stand it, either. Common sense flew out the window, along with her resolve, and was immediately replaced with a blinding desire she didn't even attempt to control. She could actually feel the electricity as it surged between them. And for the first time in her life, she literally ached for someone's touch. She forgot about the case, forgot the reason Nicole was even here in the first place.

Jake's hand reached out slowly, tugging on the belt of Nicole's robe. The robe fell open, revealing the body that Jake had been dreaming of for weeks, months. She raised her eyes, falling into the blue depths that looked back at her.

"I'm on a case. And right now, I don't care. I just want to make love to you," Jake whispered.

The words were spoken almost painfully, and Nicole suddenly realized that before, back in the mountains, they'd had sex. But now, now they knew each other, now they cared for each other. It was no longer just sex.

Nicole took the one step that moved her into Jake's arms. Flesh met flesh and they both moaned as gentle mouths found each other, tasting, remembering.

But the fire that had consumed them in the mountains took over and hands moved against warm skin, touching, stroking, reacquainting. Jake finally let her desire take over, and she pulled Nicole flush against her, her tongue moving past Nicole's lips, moaning as Nicole sucked it into her mouth.

Nicole's hands wouldn't be still, and she slipped them lower, cupping Jake's lean hips, molding their lower bodies together. Then her hands were captured and forced behind her own back. She leaned her head back, relinquishing control as Jake's mouth moved across her throat, sucking lightly below her earlobe.

"Jake . . . *please.*" Nicole freed her hands, then cupped Jake's face and moved it lower. She groaned as a warm mouth finally found her breast. She felt the robe slip from her body, felt Jake's hands as they danced across her skin, touching everywhere except the one place Nicole needed her the most. She whimpered when Jake's mouth left her breast, then moaned when that same mouth took hers again.

Suddenly, the bed was there beneath her, and Nicole's thighs parted, welcoming Jake's weight upon her. Her lower body rose up, aching to feel Jake's touch.

Jake could hardly breathe as her body lowered, inch by inch, coming closer and closer to the body she'd been craving. When Nicole's thighs opened, Jake wanted to dive inside her, wanted to take her right then. Nicole's soft hairs glistened with her wetness and Jake wanted nothing more than to have her mouth there, tasting, bringing Nicole to orgasm. But she let Nicole's arms pull her close, sighing contently when her weight finally settled upon Nicole. She pressed her hips hard against Nicole, her own clit throbbing, aching. With her knees, she pushed Nicole's thighs farther apart and her hips undulated, moving in rhythm with Nicole, hearing the gasps that Nicole breathed each time they came together, harder and harder, faster until Jake felt Nicole's hands squeezing her arms, their breathing ragged. Jake slowed, smiling as Nicole urged her to continue.

"Don't stop," Nicole whispered.

"I've got to feel you."

Jake's hand slid between them, finding the wetness that she knew would be there. Her fingers slipped past slick folds, entering Nicole as Nicole's hips thrust higher.

"*Oh* . . . yes."

With her hand between them, Jake's hips again began to dance with Nicole. Nicole's mouth opened, each breath matching the rhythm of their bodies, and Jake stared at Nicole's face as it was transformed, pleasure evident with each thrust of her hips. Jake opened her thighs more, her clit hitting her own hand as she pounded into Nicole. She felt her orgasm build, afraid she would explode before Nicole was ready, but Nicole opened wider, her hips moving faster, meeting Jake again and again, until finally, her breath held and Jake watched the familiar convulsions that shook Nicole's body, heard the glorious sounds that came from Nicole. She let go, her own orgasm matching Nicole's as she let her breath out, sounds of pleasure echoing Nicole.

Nicole lay still, her hands still clutched around Jake's forearms. She finally released her hold, and Jake lowered herself to Nicole's body, sliding her weight to the side as her lips gently touched Nicole's.

"We shouldn't have done that," Jake whispered as her fingers slipped out of Nicole.

"You're kidding, right?"

Jake smiled against Nicole's mouth, then laid down, resting her head against her palm as she leaned up. The other hand stroked

Nicole's breast, moving lower, making lazy circles on Nicole's smooth belly.

"Well, you know, I'm not your type and . . . *damn*, Nicole, you're a part of a case of mine."

Nicole stopped Jake's hand, then moved it higher, placing it on her breast, sighing when Jake's fingers closed around it.

"Despite my declaration that you're not my type, and you saying that you don't *ever* mix business with pleasure . . . Jake, we both knew this would happen. Didn't we?"

Jake dipped her head and lightly raked Nicole's nipple with her tongue. "I haven't been able to get you out of my mind," Jake admitted. "I haven't . . . I haven't been with anyone since you. I haven't wanted to."

Nicole touched Jake's face, bringing her to her mouth. Their kisses were gentle, unhurried now, and Nicole relished the feel of Jake's lips moving softly against her own. She didn't protest when she felt Jake stir, felt Jake move between her legs. Two warm hands spread her thighs apart, and she drew a quick breath as Jake trailed kisses down her stomach. She wanted to urge her to hurry, she wanted to beg her to take her time. Nicole leaned her head back onto the pillow, eyes closed, anticipation causing her to nearly tremble as she felt Jake's mouth move lower.

"*Jake* . . ."

Jake held Nicole by the hips, feeling the tremors that ran through Nicole's body, all before Jake's mouth even reached her. She nearly groaned as her mouth lowered. She knew exactly how Nicole would taste, knew exactly how Nicole's hips would move against her face. Her tongue moved through her wetness, and she groaned as Nicole lifted her hips, urging Jake to take her. Jake's mouth opened, and she covered Nicole, finding her clit and closing around it, sucking hard as Nicole moved against her.

"*Christ, Jake,*" Nicole hissed as her fists clutched at the sheets. Jake's hands moved over her hips to her stomach, holding her down as her mouth and tongue took her, took her to places no one had ever came near before. Nicole couldn't stop the sounds of pleasure that came from her, and she knew she was panting, practically delirious as Jake sucked her clit into her mouth. It hit her so suddenly, she had no time to prepare, and she screamed out, her hips bucking against Jake's face as she rose off the bed. "Jake . . . *damn*," she murmured as Jake's tongue left her. "I swear to God, I'm not a screamer," Nicole whispered, still unable to open her eyes.

"Oh, yeah?" Jake rolled on her back, pulling Nicole with her, opening her thighs to allow Nicole to settle between them. "That's not what I remember."

Nicole laughed. "I seem to . . . lose control with you."

Jake's hands traveled across Nicole's back, cupping her hips and drawing her closer. "You don't know how often I've thought about the hot springs."

Nicole leaned closer, touching Jake's mouth with her own. "I've thought about it daily," she whispered. Then she captured Jake's hands and held them down on the bed. "And now it's my turn," she murmured, as she moved down Jake's body, her mouth and tongue wetting a path, pausing only briefly at her breasts before moving lower.

Jake closed her eyes. *I'm in so much trouble.*

CHAPTER FORTY-TWO

Jake was showered and dressed, pacing quietly in the living room, wondering if she should wake Nicole or just let her sleep. She glanced at her watch again, letting out another heavy sigh. It was nearly nine o'clock. Any minute now, Rick would be calling, asking where the hell she was. And frankly, she was surprised that Catherine hadn't called, worried about her boss.

But hell, they hadn't slept. Not really. Once they'd . . . well, once they started, they couldn't stop. Just like at the hot springs. It didn't matter that Jake knew it was a mistake. She was powerless to stop it. But she had to stop it now. *Nicole was part of a goddamn case.* What the hell had she been thinking?

"Hey."

Jake turned quickly, crumbling at the sight of Nicole. The robe they'd discarded last night was again covering her body, but her hair, her lips . . . evidence of their lovemaking.

"Good morning," Jake managed. "It's nearly nine."

"I'm sorry. I couldn't wake up . . . last night . . ."

"I know. It's okay. But, we should probably get going."

Nicole frowned, crossing her arms around her waist. "What's wrong, Jake?"

"Nothing. Just . . . late for work."

Nicole took a step forward, then stopped. "Jake, what's on your mind? Talk to me."

Jake let her shoulders fall. *Shit.* "Last night . . . last night was a mistake."

"A mistake?"

"Nicole, you're a huge part of this case. We can't be . . . *involved.*"

"I trust you more than anyone, Jake. I don't want you off this case. Is that what you mean?"

"That's exactly what will happen. And if we do get a suspect, and if their defense has a clue, then any evidence I bring forward is going to be subject to review. We can't take that chance, Nicole."

Nicole met Jake's eyes. "And the fact that I can't be in the same room with you without wanting to . . ."

"Don't you think I feel the same way?" Jake whispered. "Christ, Nicole, last night, I wanted to . . . bury myself inside you and never come out."

"This is crazy."

Jake squared her shoulders. "No, it's not. I'm a cop. And I'm not your type, remember? It's just sex, Nicole. It's not anything we can't do without. Right?"

Nicole felt her heart squeeze painfully and she took a step back. *Just sex?* God, is that what Jake really thought?

"I see," she murmured. "Well, let me get showered. Won't take but a second."

"Nicole . . ."

"No, it's fine, Jake. I understand completely." She shrugged. "Just sex."

She hurried from the room, nearly slamming the bathroom door behind her. *Just sex?* No, not for her. It hadn't been just sex.

She'd made love to Jake. And God, she'd swear that Jake had made love to her.

"Stupid, *stupid*," she whispered to her reflection in the mirror.

Jake stood still, watching Nicole run from her. She felt like an ass. Last night had been fabulous, more wonderful even than the hot springs, something she'd not thought possible. But they couldn't keep this up. She would be yanked from the case and would have no say at all. And she couldn't take that chance. She didn't trust anyone else to keep Nicole safe.

"I think I hurt her, Cheyenne," Jake whispered. "And I think she's plenty pissed."

Nicole stared out her office window, feeling guilty. But not guilty enough to change her mind. She'd had Catherine call and cancel her appointments for the day. She knew she couldn't get through them, and she wasn't about to ask Dorothy for assistance. Catherine had disapproved, of course. And why wouldn't she? There was no reasonable explanation for canceling.

It's just sex.

God, she wished she could forget Jake's words. But she couldn't. And she also wished she could agree with that statement. It would make it all so much easier. When they were at the hot springs, yes, it was just sex. She'd be the first to admit it. Fabulous sex, but still . . . just sex.

Last night was not. And that's what bothered her. It was the same as at the hot springs, but so different. The same in that they were insatiable for each other. Different in their actions, their touch . . . the whispered words.

And that's why she couldn't understand Jake this morning. She was so distant. Almost like a stranger. She'd dropped her off in front of the building and waited until Nicole was inside before driving away. And she'd not heard from her since.

CHAPTER FORTY-THREE

Jake rang the doorbell and waited patiently. When no one came, she stepped back, trying to look through the window for movement. She rang the bell again, this time pounding her fist on the door.

"Police. Anybody home?" Jake waited again, then shook her head. "Fuck." She rang the doorbell one more time. Finally, she saw movement through the windows.

"Hold your horses out there."

Jake let a smile touch her face, then she pushed it away. She pulled her badge off her belt and held it in her palm, waiting.

"Who is it?"

"Police."

The door opened and suspicious eyes looked out at her. "Police who?"

Jake held up her badge. "Detective McCoy. Special Victims."

A rather thin man with steel gray hair stuck his head around the door, inspecting her before opening the door fully. He tightened the belt of his robe and tried to straighten his thinning hair. "What can I do for you, ma'am?"

"I just have a few questions."

"For me?"

Jake nodded. "May I come in?"

"Well, the missus is still in bed," he said, glancing over his shoulder.

Jake casually looked at her watch, then raised her eyebrows.

The man smiled sheepishly. "We're night owls."

"I see. Then I won't take much of your time, Mr. Reynolds." Jake pulled open her notepad and glanced at the questions she'd jotted down. "How long have you lived here?"

"Well, let's see. We bought the house when I was still working. In fact, it was the year before the missus retired. So, that'd be . . ."

Jake waited patiently as he counted back the years, watching as he frowned, struggling over the number of years. Jake finally cleared her throat. "Ten years?"

"Oh, more than that. I was going to say fifteen, but it's maybe only fourteen."

"That's fine. What about Dr. Westbrook? Do you know approximately how long she's lived here?"

"Nicole? Oh, she moved in five or six years after us, I suppose. It's hard to keep track, it's been so long ago."

"I'm interested in a night about six years ago," Jake said. "Police were called to a disturbance at her house. Do you recall the night?"

His eyes widened. "Oh, yes. The stalker. I'm surprised that young lady didn't move after it was all said and done."

"Can you tell me what happened?"

"Oh, I talked to her out in the yard one evening, and she seemed very upset. She told me a man had been coming by her work, had been calling, threatening. I told her to call the police. She said she had. Then, just a night or two later, the cops showed up, two cars, and they went running into Nicole's yard. We heard shots and looked, and there he lay, right by a police car."

"The stalker?"

"Yeah. And the way they left, I thought it was kinda strange, but it wasn't any of my business."

"What do you mean?"

"Two of the cops, they just picked this guy up by his arms and legs, and put him in the backseat of one of the cars and drove off. Like they were in too big of a hurry to wait for an ambulance. I guess they took him on to the hospital themselves."

Jake frowned, quickly scribbling down notes. "And the other unit?"

"The other car?"

"Yes, the other car."

"One of the officers went on in and talked to Nicole. They left about ten minutes after the first. I went over right away to make sure she was okay."

"And was she?"

"Shook up, that's for sure."

"Did anyone ever question you? Did a crime scene unit come out, tape off the area where the suspect was shot?"

Mr. Reynolds shook his head. "No. That was it. Wasn't in the paper, either. But what with so much crime these days, I guess it wasn't big enough to make it."

Jake folded her notebook and politely thanked Mr. Reynolds for his time. Unfortunately, she now had more questions than answers.

"You want to talk about it?"

Nicole turned from the window, surprised to find Catherine standing beside her. She hadn't heard her come in.

"Not really."

"You don't ever cancel sessions, Nicole."

Nicole sighed and let her shoulders drop. "Am I not allowed a personal crisis, or is that privilege reserved for my patients only?"

Catherine's eyebrows shot up. "Continue with that kind of talk, and I'll call Dorothy," Catherine threatened.

"You will not call Dorothy." Nicole moved away from the window and sat down on the leather couch, patting the area next to her. "Come on. We'll talk." Nicole would much rather bare her soul to Catherine than Dorothy. Catherine was less likely to judge her.

"I'm assuming it has something to do with Jake," Catherine said, as she sat down.

Nicole gave a half-smile. "It has everything to do with Jake."

"Something happened last night?"

Nicole nodded. "Jake insisted that our relationship, whatever that may be, would remain strictly on a business level. She's investigating a case that apparently revolves around me. And that was fine with me, because Catherine, Jake is *not* my type. You've said it. Dorothy has said it. And I *know* she's not my type."

"But you're attracted to her?"

"Insanely attracted to her," Nicole admitted.

"And Jake?"

"The attraction is . . . mutual."

"And last night?"

"And last night we couldn't fight it."

Catherine smiled. "So what's the problem?"

"The problem is, last night we didn't have sex. We made love," Nicole whispered.

"Oh my God, you're *falling* for her?"

"I don't know if it's that or just this . . . this lust between us that we can't control. And it doesn't bother me that she's a cop, that she's a gay cop, an *out* gay cop. None of that bothers me. It bothers Dorothy because Jake would threaten this little group of ours, you know? But it doesn't bother me. And it should bother me, right? I mean, technically, I'm in the closet."

"Have you and Jake talked about this?"

"Of course not. In fact, this morning, she said that last night was a mistake. I know it's because of her investigation. I know that, but still, she tried to make light of it, saying it was just sex, no big deal. Her words hurt me, Catherine, because I know it wasn't just sex. At least for me." She shook her head. "For her, too. I know she's trying to protect this case, trying to protect me."

241

"Well, if you want my opinion, Jake's the best thing that's ever happened to you. You probably don't know it, but your eyes light up every time she comes around. And you said so yourself, you have no interest in the women you date. You get depressed every time you go out."

"I know. And with Jake, God, I feel so *alive* when I'm around her."

"Then just go with it, Nicole. Who cares what Dorothy or your little closeted group of women think? It's your life. Go with what makes you happy."

"That's easy to say, Catherine. Unfortunately, there are two people involved here. And the other one has indicated that there won't be a repeat of last night. She's afraid she'll get pulled off the case. And I don't want that anymore than she does."

"Well, then I guess you'll just have to wait until this case is over."

"Wait? I don't know that that's possible, considering I want to rip her clothes off every time I'm around her."

Catherine laughed. "That could be a problem."

Nicole leaned her head back, eyes closed. "But Catherine, realistically, Jake could never fit into my life. Can you see her at one of our group dinners? She'd be like a fish out of water."

"You underestimate her."

Nicole shook her head. "I didn't mean she couldn't handle herself. She wouldn't be comfortable. It's not her thing."

"Are you so sure it's *your* thing?"

Nicole sighed. "It must be. I've been doing it for ten years."

CHAPTER FORTY-FOUR

Jake knocked on her lieutenant's door, not waiting for him to look up. She walked to his desk, meeting the questioning look in his eyes.

"I need to talk something out with you," she said.

"Okay. Sit."

She did, flipping open her notes. "Dr. Westbrook's stalker that we talked about?"

"Where there was nothing in the system?"

"Right. So I talked to one of her neighbors." She looked up from her notes. "He remembers the night. Two units showed up. There were shots fired. He saw a body laying in Dr. Westbrook's yard. He saw two of the officers pick the suspect up and toss him into their squad car and drive off. The other unit, he says one of the officers went into Dr. Westbrook's house to talk to her. They left approximately ten minutes later."

Lieutenant Gregory pulled his glasses off. "Yet there's nothing in the system to verify this?"

"No."

"And you believe Dr. Westbrook and this neighbor?"

"Absolutely."

Lieutenant Gregory nodded, then leaned forward. "McCoy, you're working a murder investigation. Why are you bothering with something that happened six years ago when we've got four dead women right now?"

"Because I feel like the two events could be related," she said.

"How? An alleged stalker was supposedly killed by cops at Dr. Westbrook's house, yet, policewise, we have nothing to substantiate that. What we do have are the bodies of four murdered women. So I'm not interested in a goddamn stalker from six years ago. Let it go, McCoy. That's an order." He leaned back again. "Now, tell me what's up with this case. What are you doing for *this* case?"

"Salazar is putting together profiles on all four of our victims, trying to trace back the last two or three days that they were alive. Simpson is interviewing friends, relatives. Chase is doing employment."

"And you?"

"I'm . . . concentrating on Dr. Westbrook."

He nodded. "Are we monitoring her phone, mail?"

"I'm going to talk to her today about the phone. Her secretary is monitoring the mail. Other than the one threatening letter they got a couple of weeks ago, there's been nothing out of the ordinary."

"The captain's questioning the unit we've got at her building. Do you feel like it's beneficial?"

"It's beneficial only because it gives peace of mind."

"Then I'm pulling it. We've got enough going on in the city without having two officers camped out doing nothing."

Jake stared, wondering at the lieutenant's motives. It was unlike him to be this negative about a case. In fact, just the hint of a police cover-up on the stalker would have normally had him up in arms. He was a stickler for detail and doing things by the book.

"I know you feel like Westbrook is in danger, but I haven't been

244

given the okay to bring her in. Are you still doing babysitting duty on nights?"

She nodded. "Actually, I think Chase is going to take tonight."

"Oh yeah? How's that going to set with his wife?"

"Haven't worked it out yet," she said. In fact, she'd not talked to Rick about it at all. "But, yeah, I think Dr. Westbrook is in danger. It would be foolish to leave her unprotected."

"Well, just remember, you're a detective, not a babysitter."

Jake stood, feeling their conversation was going nowhere. "Well, let me get on it, Lieutenant."

"Keep me informed."

"Yes, sir." She walked out, frowning. "To protect and to serve," she murmured sarcastically. "Right."

Despite her lieutenant's directive to leave the stalker alone, Jake couldn't. It didn't make sense. So, she called dispatch. Susan Rice, a woman who had asked Jake out countless times before, picked up.

"Susan? It's Jake McCoy."

"Hello, Detective. I heard you were back."

"Yeah. About a month now. Listen, I'm wondering if you're free for lunch?"

"Lunch?"

"I need to pick your brain."

"I see." There was only a short pause. "Sure, why not."

"Great. What time can you swing it?"

"How about one?"

"Okay. I'll pick you up out front by the flagpole. And thanks, Susan."

When she hung up, Jake called Rick's cell. He was just leaving the offices where Shelly Burke used to work.

"The last person here to see her was her officemate. The woman left shortly after five, and Shelly was still here, finishing up a report that was due the next day. She logged off her computer at five forty-four. Surveillance tapes in the parking garage show she never made it to her car."

"Yet she ended up at her apartment."

"Yeah. Simpson is going back to the apartment complex, but hell, that's been months already. And the original report they filed turned up nothing, as far as neighbors."

"Yeah, I know. Listen, buddy, are you still home alone?"

"Yeah. Why? I talked to Michelle yesterday. We're supposed to get together this weekend and hash it out."

"Good. I was wondering if maybe you could stay with Dr. Westbrook tonight? At her place? She hasn't been there since the other night. I'm sure she needs . . . things."

"Now, Jake, how's that going to look? The lieutenant will never go for it."

"Then how about you take the early shift, and I'll relieve you?"

"What's going on? You got a date or something?"

"No, I don't have a date. I just have something to check out. I'll explain later. It's just, she hasn't been to her house in a couple of days, and I'm sure she's tired of bunking at my place."

"Okay, okay. We'll work it out later. Right now, I'm heading to a lumber yard."

"For?"

"Jena Nichols's place of employment."

"Okay. I'll be around."

The normally busy cafe was relatively quiet at this hour and Jake stood politely until Susan took her seat. She slid into the booth opposite Susan and folded her arms on the table. Even though she'd told herself to make casual conversation, she was too keyed up to do so.

"How long have you worked dispatch, Susan?"

"Eleven years, if you can believe that."

Jake smiled. "Time flies." She leaned forward, pushing the menu to the side. "Six years ago, who was over dispatch?"

"Six years? That's probably when your Lieutenant Gregory was there. He was sergeant at that time, of course. Captain Harris was over the unit."

"No shit? Gregory was in dispatch?"

"He moved to Special Victims right before you came on board," Susan said.

Jake looked up as the waitress ambled over to their booth. She moved back as a glass of water was placed in front of her.

"Ready to order?"

Jake hadn't bothered looking at the menu so she ordered her standard. "Burger, no pickles," she said.

"Mustard? Mayo?"

Jake sighed impatiently. "Both."

"And for you?"

Susan looked carefully over the menu, ignoring Jake's impatiently tapping fingers. "Club sandwich, with fries. Swiss cheese. Mayo only."

"Excellent. I'll have your lunch out before long."

Jake hesitated only briefly after the waitress walked away. "Okay. Walk me through it. Call comes to 911, they notify you, you dispatch units. Is that it?"

"That's the short of it, yes."

"So, once a 911 call is logged, and then dispatched through you, there should be a record in the system, right?"

"Of course. Every transaction is logged. On a normal 911 emergency call, you'll have three logs. One from the 911 call, one from the dispatcher, and one from the unit responding."

Jake leaned forward. "And if anyone wanted to, say, delete these transactions, what would be involved?"

Susan shook her head. "That's nearly impossible. You're talking about three separate entities."

"Who could authorize something like that?"

"To delete information?" Susan shrugged. "If you're a subordinate? Anyone outranking you, I guess. But again, you're talking about three different databases. They're all linked together, but they're still separate."

"So, even if a captain or a lieutenant wanted something deleted from one system, it doesn't necessarily mean it could be deleted from another?"

"Exactly."

Jake again tapped the table with her fingers, thinking. "So how *could* something be deleted from all three?"

Susan smiled. "I take it you mean how could something *illegally* be deleted?"

"Yes."

Susan shrugged. "Hacker?"

"Surely these databases are secure," Jake said.

"If someone can hack into the FBI's database, don't you think they could get into ours? And I mean, six years ago? What do you think firewalls were like back then?"

"Okay, so unless three different supervisors ordered files deleted, we can assume a hacker, for whatever reason, did it?"

"Works for me."

Jake shook her head. "Makes no sense. Still doesn't help me with the why of it."

"You want to tell me the case you're talking about?"

Jake hesitated. If there was a coverup, the less people knew she was snooping around, the better. "I'd rather not get you involved," she said carefully.

They both sat back as their lunch was delivered. When the waitress left, Susan leaned forward again.

"You can trust me, you know."

Jake stared. No, she had no reason to believe that she could trust Susan Rice. They knew each other only in passing and the few times they went out socially with others. They were friendly, but they weren't exactly friends. But she nodded politely. "Well, I'm just playing a hunch, anyway. There's not a whole lot I can tell you."

CHAPTER FORTY-FIVE

Catherine smiled when the door opened. She was expecting Jake, but it was the other detective that walked in. And now that Catherine thought about it, Jake hadn't called all day.

"Detective," she greeted.

"Hello. I'm here to pick up the doc," Rick said.

"Oh? Where's Jake?"

Rick shrugged. "She's got something going on." He motioned to the door. "You think she's ready?"

Catherine picked up the phone, waiting only a ring before Nicole answered. She smiled at Rick and shook her head. "No, it's Detective Chase." She put the phone down again. "You may go in."

Rick smiled sheepishly. "Everyone's expecting Jake, huh?"

"Well . . ."

"It's okay. I get that a lot from women. Not exactly sure why."

Catherine smiled as he walked to Nicole's door. He was an

attractive man for sure. But Jake, Jake had a unique charm about her that even Catherine, married and straight, could not ignore. No wonder Nicole had melted.

Nicole was gathering her things when Rick knocked and walked inside. Nicole greeted him with what she hoped was a genuine smile.

"Detective Chase, how are you today?"

"Been a busy day, Dr. Westbrook, don't mind saying. How are you holding up?"

"I'm okay." She hesitated, but couldn't hold back the question. "Where's . . . Detective McCoy?"

"I haven't seen her today. She's checking out a hunch, she said. But she thought you'd like to stay at your own house tonight. She volunteered me to take you."

Nicole raised her eyebrows. "Volunteered? So this protective custody that I'm getting is not sanctioned by the department?"

"No. I mean, technically, you haven't had any threats, and we don't have a motive, much less a suspect."

"I see."

"The DA's office would be the one to bring you in, put you up at a hotel, if the case was farther along. But Jake, well, after the night at your house . . . you know, with the roses, well, she didn't want to take a chance."

Nicole nodded. "And is this common practice for her?"

"Well, I can honestly say that no, you're the first person she's taken in like this." He grinned. "If I didn't know Jake so well, I might get the wrong impression here."

Nicole squared her shoulders. "What do you mean, Detective?"

"Nothing. I'm sorry. I didn't mean to imply anything, Dr. Westbrook. It's just been a hell of a long day."

"I understand." Nicole flicked her eyes to the clock, then back to Rick. "And technically, your shift is over, and you should be on your way home."

"Yeah."

"Then I hate to be the reason you're not on your way home, Detective. I can probably manage on my own tonight. I can call a friend and stay at their place."

"Are you kidding? Jake would kill me." He walked to the door. "Come on."

Nicole wanted to protest, but truthfully, she was afraid to go alone. She followed Detective Chase out her office door, wishing that it was Jake instead.

CHAPTER FORTY-SIX

Jake raised her eyebrows. "So?"

Steven shook his head. "No. No way anyone fucked with our databases."

"Six years ago, man. You weren't even here then."

"Jake, I've been here almost four years, and I know the security on the servers. So unless this guy was some hacker geek, no way he gets in."

"And what if he was?"

Steven shoved his glasses back on his nose and leaned forward. "You think your guy hacked our system and deleted just *one* entry? What's the point?"

To Jake, it was so simple, so obvious. She couldn't understand why it didn't just jump out at Steven. "He deleted just one entry because just *one* pertained to him."

"What do you mean?"

Jake let out a deep breath, trying to hold on to her patience. "I think that whoever deleted the entries was directly involved in the case."

"That's crazy."

"Why?"

"It just so happens your perp is a hacker? No way."

"Okay. So the hacker is a close friend of the perp," Jake said, her patience running thin. "It's fucking connected. It has to be."

Steven drummed his fingers on the keyboard, then finally nodded. "Okay. Tell me what you want."

Jake grinned. "Thanks, Stevie."

Steven blushed and began typing. "I hate it when you call me that."

"I know."

Nicole pulled into her driveway, pleased that the motion lights came on. She hit the remote to the garage, glancing in her rearview mirror once to make sure Rick was behind her.

She was so stunned at the sight, she very nearly hit the body hanging from the ceiling of her garage. She gasped, stifling the scream that threatened. Throwing the car into reverse, Nicole hit the gas, then slammed on the brakes again when she realized Rick had parked right behind her. Her heart was pounding and she still held the steering wheel in a death grip. *God, I wish Jake was here.*

"Stay there," Rick yelled.

Nicole nodded, her eyes wild with fright.

Rick pulled his weapon and walked slowly into the garage, ignoring the body for a moment as he made sure the garage was empty. Nothing else looked disturbed. He pulled out his cell phone, dialing quickly.

Nicole slid her eyes to the naked woman hanging in her garage, feeling her heart tighten as she recognized the face.

"Lori, oh, no." Nicole's heart broke for the young girl, and she couldn't stop the tears that formed and fell. Lori had survived two suicide attempts, but Nicole could never quite reach her. When she'd skipped her session the other day, Nicole knew she'd lost her. But not like this.

Rick opened her door, then saw the tears.

"You know her?"

Nicole nodded. "Lori Simmons. A current patient."

Rick nodded. "I called it in. Crime lab and ME will be here in a minute."

"Jake?"

"I'll call her next. Let's go inside, make sure everything's okay."

Nicole got out, looking quickly at Lori, then away. "Can't we get her down?"

"No. Not until the crime lab goes over everything."

It was suddenly . . . so real. Having someone tell you that four women were murdered and you are somehow the link is frightening, but still unbelievable. Why would she be the cause of someone going on a murder spree? But this . . . opening your garage door and seeing a body hanging, a body of a patient—Nicole could ignore it no longer. Her hands were trembling so badly she could hardly punch out the code on the alarm. She felt somewhat comforted by Rick's presence, although she knew she was on the verge of becoming hysterical. She was trembling head to toe when they walked through the garage into her kitchen. There, on her breakfast table, sat a dozen roses. Unlike the wilted roses in her bedroom, these were fresh, fragrant.

"Don't touch anything," Rick said.

Nicole nodded, standing quietly as tears ran down her cheeks.

"Shit," Rick murmured. "Come on." He took Nicole's arm, wishing Jake were here. He wasn't good with crying women. "Bedroom. Pack a bag. Can you do that?"

Nicole nodded, following Rick into her bedroom. It was as they'd left it the other night, the wilted roses still visible.

"Pack casual clothes," Rick said. "I doubt Jake will let you go back to your normal routine."

Nicole hardly cared. She wanted to run, run far away. She pulled jeans and sweaters out of her closet, then tossed a couple of sweatshirts onto her bed.

"Take it easy, Dr. Westbrook."

Nicole met his eyes. "Easy? Are you kidding me?"

He held his hands out. "Just . . . calm down. I'm going to call Detective McCoy."

Nicole took a deep breath, trying to calm her nerves somewhat. "Okay. Good," she murmured.

Jake had just unlocked her front door when her cell phone rang. She wanted to ignore it. She was late, and Cheyenne was letting her know it.

She slipped the phone off her waist as she walked to the back door. "McCoy," she said, tucking the phone against her shoulder. She heard Cheyenne jump up, placing her front paws on the door. As soon as she unlocked the door, Cheyenne burst in, dancing excitedly around Jake.

"It's me. Got a . . . situation."

Jake stopped, her hand tightening on the phone. "Where's Nicole?"

"She's here."

"Here where?" Jake demanded.

"I'm at her house. There was a . . . hell, there was a fucking body hanging in her garage, Jake."

"Jesus Christ!" Jake hissed. "Okay, okay. I'm on my way. Have you called it in?"

"Yeah."

"Good." Jake moved through her duplex, grabbing a bottle of water from her fridge and motioning for Cheyenne to follow her. "How's she holding up?"

"Not good. The victim is a current patient."

Jake slammed the front door, quickly locking it and nearly running to her truck. "I'm on my way, Rick."

Cheyenne hopped into the back and perched her front feet on the console, looking importantly out the windshield as Jake backed up and sped away.

Rick slipped his phone into his front pocket, glancing at the pale face of Dr. Westbrook. "Jake will be here soon," he said. His words were met with only a slight nod. "I'm going out to meet the crime lab. You'll be okay in here, right?"

"I'll be . . . fine."

Rick shrugged. "Just stay put. I'll come get you in a minute."

Nicole nodded, sinking onto her bed, jeans clutched in her hands protectively.

"Jesus Christ!"

Nicole's quiet street was transformed as blinking lights from squad cars and an ambulance broke up the night. Jake parked on the street, lowering the windows just a bit for Cheyenne. The night was cold and her breath frosted out around her as she hurried to the opened garage.

"Hold on there," someone said to her.

She held up her badge. "Detective McCoy. This is my case."

"Sorry, ma'am. Chase is inside."

Jake stopped, watching as they lowered the woman. She stared, frowning. She recognized her. She'd seen her at Nicole's office the other week. Lori something or other.

"Got a name?"

"Lori Simmons."

Jake nodded. She walked into the house from the garage, seeing the flowers on the kitchen table. They were dusting for prints and she sidestepped them. "Was there a note?"

"Not this time."

"Okay. Where's Chase?"

"He went to check on the lady. He's having her pack some things."

Jake walked quickly through the house, stopping in the doorway to Nicole's bedroom. Nicole sat quietly on the bed, nodding occasionally as Rick tried to pack some clothes for her. Nicole sensed her presence, and blue eyes finally looked up, blue eyes that flooded with relief.

"Jake, good, you're here," Rick said. He motioned to the silent woman sitting on the bed. "Getting a little worried."

Jake nodded, her eyes never leaving Nicole's. "Why don't you give us a minute, Ricky."

"Sure, sure. I'll go see if they found any prints."

Jake closed the door as soon as Rick left, then turned. Nicole was trembling and tears fell from her eyes.

"Come here, sweetheart," Jake whispered.

That was all it took. Nicole flew into her arms, burying her face at Jake's neck. The tears she'd been holding back flowed freely, and she clung to Jake.

"Shhh," Jake whispered.

"It's . . . it's Lori. Oh, Jake, it's all my fault," she sobbed.

"No, it's not," Jake said quietly.

"Yes, it is," Nicole sobbed.

Jake just held her, rocking her slightly until her tears subsided. She forgot all about that line she was trying to back across. Nicole's tears simply tore at her heart, and Jake wanted nothing more than to take away her pain. She rubbed Nicole's back with gentle hands, letting the other woman have her cry.

Finally, Nicole took a deep breath and lifted her head, finding Jake's steady eyes. "I'm sorry."

"For what? Showing emotion? Don't ever be sorry for that."

Nicole rubbed her face, knowing she must look a sight. "It just hit me, I guess. It's real now."

"Yes. It's very real."

"He's invaded my home twice." Nicole straightened up, separating herself from Jake. "And Lori, God, poor Lori." Nicole paced across the room. "I have that same feeling I had with the stalker, you know? Where I didn't feel safe anywhere."

"You're safe with me. I promise that."

Nicole nodded. "I know. And that's why I wished you'd been here with me. The way you left this morning, I was afraid you were jumping ship."

Jake walked closer, taking Nicole by the hands. "I'm afraid . . . if we're too close, I'll lose my objectivity. I'm afraid I won't be able to protect you."

"Jake, I don't care what we have to do, but I want you around. I felt . . . exposed with Rick. With you, I feel like you're more concerned with my well-being than anything else."

"Exactly. And that's not always a good thing."

"It's a good thing for me."

Jake smiled, unable to argue with Nicole's logic. "Okay. Pack casual clothes. You won't be going back to the office until this is over."

"Jake, no way. I can't do that."

"You don't have a choice anymore. Tonight was a message, I think. You're next. And he'll have to go through me."

"I can't just close up my practice," Nicole said.

"Find someone to cover. That's your only choice. We'll call Catherine tonight."

Nicole crossed her arms, knowing Jake was right. She finally nodded.

"Good. We're going to be just a little while. You want to take a shower or something?"

"Do I look that bad?"

"You look beautiful," Jake whispered. Then she ducked her head. "But I thought it might make you feel better. We're going to be just a little while yet."

Nicole tried to smile. Her eyes felt puffy, red. No doubt her nose was, too. "I'll shower."

Their eyes held for a second longer, then Jake left, closing the door behind her. The kitchen was still crowded, and she found Rick leaning against the counter.

"What we got?"

"We got shit, just like always. Not a print one."

"What about the victim?"

"Dave's already taken her. Been dead two days, he thinks."

"Like the others."

"Yeah. The hanging was definitely postmortem. He says he'll do the post first thing in the morning."

"Why do you think this bastard can come and go like this and not leave one goddamn print or fiber?"

"I think it's like you said. He knows something about forensics."

"Yeah. And we still got shit." Jake pulled him aside. "Come by my place when we're done here. I've got some things I need to talk out with you."

CHAPTER FORTY-SEVEN

Jake lifted the lid on the pizza box, her eyes darting between Nicole and Rick. Proper police procedure would dictate that they not discuss anything in front of Nicole. However, Jake felt like Nicole had a right to know what was going on. And, because things were personal between them, she would no doubt tell Nicole everything anyway. But Rick would think it very unusual for them to discuss things out here in the open.

Fuck it.

"Beer?"

"Sure," Rick said.

Nicole nodded, her chin still resting on her palms. Cheyenne was leaning against Nicole's leg. Most likely because she remembered the handouts from previous dinners. Nicole buried her hand in Cheyenne's fur, lightly stroking.

"You holding up okay?" Jake asked for the third time.

Nicole nodded. "It doesn't seem real yet. I'm sure tomorrow, it'll hit."

Jake met her eyes briefly, then nodded at her as she placed three beers on the table. "I want to talk about the stalker."

"Why?" Nicole asked.

"Because it doesn't add up. Whatever happened that night has been wiped from our system," she said.

Rick cleared his throat, and Jake slid her eyes to him. Both his eyebrows shot up. She ignored him and took a piece of pizza instead.

"I had lunch today with Susan Rice. From dispatch."

"Yeah?" Rick asked, before shoving pizza in his mouth.

"The only way records disappear is if a superior orders them wiped. And that is highly unusual." Jake leaned closer to Rick. "And get this, Lieutenant Gregory was with dispatch six years ago."

"What the hell does that have to do with anything, Jake?" He motioned with his head to Nicole, who'd been silent. "And is this something we need to discuss here?"

"Yes, it is. Saves me having to tell her about it later," Jake said easily.

Rick looked first at Nicole, then Jake. "Something I should know about?" Rick asked quietly.

Jake and Nicole exchanged glances, their eyes holding. Finally, Jake shook her head. "No. I just feel like, Nicole's at the center of this; she has a right to know what's going on."

"And I'm assuming you trust her to keep all this to herself?"

"I trust her completely."

There was silence around the table as the three of them shifted gazes. Rick broke the silence by taking another piece of pizza.

"Okay. Your call, McCoy. So what about Gregory?"

Jake tipped her beer bottle at Rick before continuing. "He's acting very weird. Yesterday, and the day before, he was all for having a car follow Nicole around. Hell, he wanted to bring her in. And he was curious about the stalker not existing in the system. Today when I talked to him, he said he was going to pull the car off Nicole, that it was a waste."

"*What?*"

"Yeah. And when I brought up the stalker, he told me to leave it alone, that it had nothing to do with this case. He ordered me to ditch the stalker."

"But why?"

"I had no idea at the time. Then at lunch, Susan tells me that Gregory was the sergeant over dispatch."

"And you think he knows about my stalker?" Nicole asked.

"Either he's remembered it, or he knows about the coverup."

"Oh, Jake," Rick warned. "You start talking coverup, and you're opening up a whole can of worms."

"I talked to her neighbor this morning, a Mr. Reynolds," Jake said.

"You did?" Nicole asked.

"Yes. And he had exactly the same story you did. Two units responded. He and his wife heard the shooting, saw the body on the lawn. Saw them toss the suspect into the patrol unit without waiting for an ambulance."

"But there's no record of it?"

"None." Jake turned to Rick. "I talked to Steven over in IT about it."

"Steven?"

"You know, tall, skinny guy . . . wears glasses. Typical computer geek."

"I don't know him. How do you know him?"

"Oh, hell, Rick, we met him a couple of years ago," Jake said impatiently. "He hacked into a computer for us . . . the teenager who was having sex with her teacher."

"Oh, yeah. That guy." Rick grinned. "He had such a crush on you."

Jake blushed and glanced quickly at Nicole who smiled warmly at her. "He did not have a crush," she murmured. "Anyway, Steven is going back over the logs in dispatch, to see if he can find . . . dead time, he called it. If he finds some, then he's going to hack into the 911 log and do the same thing."

"If he finds something in 911, you know we can't use it."

"If he finds something period, we can't use it. But we'll at least have grounds to push for a subpoena for their tapes."

"That's assuming the lieutenant will go along with it."

"Well, yeah, there's that."

"We're forgetting about the four officers that responded. Four potential witnesses."

"Or four potential murderers. Remember, they drove up and shot this guy. He had no weapon that Nicole saw." Jake turned to her. "Right?"

"Right. He was on the lawn, watching me through the window. He was standing there, hands in his front pockets. When the police came, he walked toward them, hands held up in the air. There were two or three shots maybe. That's the last I saw. I ducked down on the floor. Then one of the officers came to talk to me, to tell me that it was all over."

"Makes no damn sense," Rick said.

"Nicole, did anything stand out? The guy that came to talk to you, was he in a standard issue uniform?"

"How would I know if it was standard issue?"

"Okay, was anything out of place? Shoes? Cap? What about the cars?"

Nicole shook her head. "Jake, this was six years ago. I can close my eyes and see the scene unfold, but it's just shapes, shadows. And the stalker, I never saw his face. He wore a stocking over his head that night. I have this distorted image of him is all."

"Didn't you think it odd that there wasn't a follow-up investigation?" Rick asked.

"Yes, now I do. But at the time, I was just so thankful it was over. I was able to resume my life, my practice, and it just became a bad dream. A bad dream I didn't want to think about."

Jake put her elbows on the table, staring at Rick. "You think I'm reaching at straws here?"

Rick shrugged. "Well, considering we got shit as it is, it makes sense to follow up on the stalker."

Jake turned to Nicole. "The only link we have between the victims is the crisis center, but that's getting us nowhere."

Nicole frowned and shook her head. "Lori was never at the crisis center."

Jake's eyes widened. "*What?*"

"No, Lori wasn't sexually abused. She was borderline schizophrenic. She'd been seeing Dorothy—Dr. Peterson—since she was a teenager. She'd had a couple of suicide attempts when Dr. Peterson recommended that she see me, thinking I could reach her."

"Well, fuck," Jake said, locking glances with Rick. "The first four victims being from the crisis center was a goddamn *coincidence?*" She shoved her chair away from the table, pacing across the kitchen. "Great. Now we got less than shit!" she said loudly.

Nicole and Rick both stared at her, and Cheyenne pressed closer to Nicole as Jake pounded her fists on the counter.

"Jake, stop," Nicole said quietly.

Jake shook her head. "No! How can I even begin to protect you when this guy is like a fucking ghost?"

"I won't go back to the office. I'll have Catherine shuffle the appointments. I won't go to my house. I'll . . . do whatever you say."

Jake met her eyes, oblivious to Rick. "Nicole, what if I can't protect you?" she whispered. "What if I . . . can't?"

"That's not going to happen, Jake. We'll be fine."

"Excuse me, but . . . *hello*, I'm still here," Rick said. He pointed at Jake. "And don't tell me there's nothing going on with you two."

"What are you talking about?"

"You know what the *fuck* I'm talking about." Rick glanced at Nicole, then back at Jake.

"Goddamn, Rick, just let it go."

Rick pounded his fist on the table. "I want to know what the hell is going on!"

Jake shoved her hands in the pockets of her jeans, facing Rick. She shrugged. "There's nothing going on."

"I'm not blind," he said. He glanced at Nicole again. "I've known you five years, Jake." He motioned between the two of them. "And this is a first."

Jake sat down again. "Look, Nicole and I have developed a . . .

friendship. And yeah, I know it's not procedure, but the fact remains that she's not simply a witness or a piece of the puzzle."

"Jake, you know you can't—"

"No. I can, Rick." Jake reached across the table and grabbed Rick's hand. "Nicole means something to me, Rick." She glanced quickly at Nicole, then back at Rick. "Do you know how long it's been since someone's . . . meant something to me?" she whispered.

Rick stared at Jake, then looked at Nicole. He shook his head. "Walk me out, Jake." He stood, touching Nicole's shoulder briefly before walking away.

Jake nodded, then leaned over and squeezed Nicole's hand. "If you're tired, go on to bed," Jake said.

Their eyes locked.

"Will you join me?"

Jake wanted to shake her head, saying she would take the couch, but Nicole's eyes were holding her, and she slowly nodded.

"We should . . . talk," Jake said.

Nicole gave a half smile. "At the very least."

"I'll be right back."

Rick was waiting at the door, and they both walked out into the cold night air. The wind was blowing the young spruce tree on the corner, and Jake caught the scent of the tree and inhaled. At night, like this, when the city was obscured, the scent of this lone spruce could almost make her feel like she was in the mountains. Almost. But then a car, a horn, a door slamming, would bring her back to the present. Like now.

"How long has this been going on?"

Jake tucked her hands under her armpits and tilted her head. "I met her in late August, up in the mountains."

"*What?* You knew her before this? And you still didn't say anything?"

"Say *what?* We spent one night together in a tent. We didn't even exchange names when she left. I was already working this case when she came into it. It was too late for me to back out."

"But you're involved with her, Jake. Jesus Christ!"

"Ricky, I'm trying hard to separate this. I know the risks, I know the protocol. And I know Lieutenant Gregory would pull my ass from this case if he knew." She stepped closer. "But this is *our* case. I'm not letting my feelings for Nicole overshadow that. Rick, that's why I wanted you to stay with her tonight. I wanted to separate a bit."

Rick ran a hand through his hair. "Now what the hell am I supposed to do?"

"Does it matter any if I say that I might be in love with her?"

"Jesus Christ! Are you serious?"

Jake tilted her head, her eyes avoiding Rick. "I'm not sure what it's supposed to feel like, Rick. So I might be way off base here."

"Well fuck me," Rick muttered. "We don't have time for this, Jake! You can't feel something for this woman now, okay?"

"I'm sorry. But I do." Jake grasped Rick's arms. "For the first time in my life, I feel something, Ricky. She's like . . . gotten inside me. I can't walk away from it."

"Christ Jake! *Now?*"

Jake dropped her hands. "It's not like it matters, Rick."

"What do you mean?"

Jake shrugged. "She's a *doctor* for Christ's sake. You've seen her in her power suits. I'm a lowly cop. I don't exactly fit."

"So then what the hell is going on?"

"We have this . . . attraction. It doesn't mean it's going anywhere."

"But you said you were in love with her."

Jake gave a sad smile. "Takes two, Ricky. And I know my place. But she's important to me. Okay?"

Rick pointed his finger. "Don't get yourself hurt over this, Jake."

"No." Jake took his arm and walked him to his truck. "But we're okay, right? Lieutenant doesn't need to know, nobody needs to know."

"Are you sure you can do this?"

"Of course, Ricky. I know what my job is."

"Okay, I'm going to trust you on this."

"Thanks."

Jake surprised Rick by the tight hug she gave him, and the quick kiss on the lips.

"Jesus, you want to start rumors, or what?" Rick said, wiping at his mouth.

"Be careful going home."

"Yeah, yeah."

Jake waited until his lights faded before going back inside. She was actually a little nervous. Like she'd told Rick, she and Nicole had not talked about their relationship. Nicole may be feeling none of the emotions that Jake did. It may simply be sex to her. Jake paused before opening the door, her mind flashing back to last night. Nicole's touch had been soft, sure. Her eyes did not lie, and it hadn't been just sex. Last night, Nicole had made love to her. And she had loved Nicole. The thought of that caused an odd sensation in her stomach. It didn't matter that she knew they had no future. And it was so ironic. All these years of random dating, random sex, never really meeting someone who stirred her. Never finding that one person who made her ache with wanting.

Nicole made her ache.

And Nicole was someone she couldn't have.

Nicole went into Jake's bedroom. She was exhausted, both mentally and physically. They had not slept much last night, not really. She felt a slight blush creep up her face as she recalled their night of lovemaking. Nicole had always been rather shy in bed, a lingering remnant from her chubby high school days, no doubt. But with Jake, there was nothing shy about her touch. Nicole transformed into a sensual, insatiable woman in Jake's presence.

And they had spent hours loving each other last night.

Nicole stood in the bathroom, looking at her reflection in the mirror. Jake's words to Rick echoed in her mind. *Nicole means something to me.* Did she really mean something to Jake? She met her eyes in the mirror, nodding. Yes, Jake's touch was too intimate, too . . . loving. Nicole nearly shivered, remembering. And tonight? What would happen tonight? Would they continue to pretend that this was just sex?

Jake moved quietly through the house, putting the pizza box into the fridge and turning off lights. Cheyenne followed her every move, although her eyes darted into the bedroom.

"Yes, she's in there," Jake said quietly. "Waiting for us." She paused in the living room, hearing Nicole leave the bathroom. She could imagine Nicole sliding under the covers, waiting. Would she be naked? *Jesus, they needed to talk.*

"Jake?"

Jake stood still, listening to the question hanging in the air. She closed her eyes for a second, then made herself move. "Yeah. Coming."

She stopped in the doorway, the dark bedroom lit only by the light from the bathroom. Nicole was leaning up against the pillows, thankfully covered by a T-shirt. Jake stared, nonetheless.

"You wanted to talk?"

Jake nodded, still unable to move. She saw Nicole smile.

"Going to talk from way over there?"

Jake chuckled, then walked into the room. "Let me grab a shower first. Okay?"

"Sure."

Nicole watched her disappear into the bathroom, wondering at Jake's hesitancy. But she knew, didn't she? Here in bed, like this, they would get little talking done. And again, there was Jake's admission to Rick that Nicole *meant* something. That frightened her a little. It was one thing to be physically, sexually attracted to the woman. Quite another should she feel something for Jake . . . in her heart. And Nicole knew she was dangerously close to falling in love with Jake, something she never would have thought possible. Certainly not in late summer when they'd had their tryst in the mountains, and certainly not when Jake had walked back into her life so unexpectedly. As she'd told herself—and had been told by others—Jake was just not her type.

Well, that hardly mattered now. She heard the water turn off, and she only had to close her eyes to imagine Jake standing there naked, water still glistening on her skin. She took a deep breath. No, they would get little talking done.

Jake stared at herself in the mirror, trying to shake her nervousness, wondering why it had such a grip on her. Maybe because last night had been so unexpected, that she hadn't had a chance for thought. Tonight, however, if she walked out of this bathroom and into bed with Nicole, it was a totally conscious decision. Because she knew, once she crawled in beside Nicole, they would not talk. They would touch, they would make love. And the case would fade away, if only for a few hours.

Was that so bad?

Jake closed her eyes briefly. It wasn't like she had a choice. Not really. For some reason, her body overrode her good sense when it came to Nicole.

With one last look in the mirror, she moved away, dutifully having donned a T-shirt to cover her nakedness. She would at least pretend they were going to talk.

She opened the bathroom door and flipped off the light at the same time. The tiny nightlight against the far wall softened the shadows in the room. But still, Jake hesitated.

"Come to bed," Nicole instructed quietly.

Those softly spoken words caused Jake's heart to pound just a little faster, and she again wondered what it was about Nicole that could turn her into a big *mush ball*.

But her feet moved, carrying her closer to the bed, closer to Nicole. She noticed that Cheyenne had chosen Nicole's side of the bed to guard, lying quietly on the floor, not even begging to jump up. She paused again, wondering what to say. Wondering if she should say anything at all.

Then Nicole sat up.

"Jake, we're not going to talk just yet." Nicole pulled the T-shirt over her head and tossed it on the floor. "Come to bed."

Jake was speechless. She felt like a fumbling teenager, not a woman in her late thirties. Jesus, she was a cop, for God's sake! But she had no resistance. She pulled her own T-shirt over her head, standing there clad only in a pair of navy panties. Without another thought, she slid them down her thighs, conscious of Nicole's eyes following their path.

Jake lifted the covers and slid next to Nicole, pulling her close. Nicole immediately snuggled against her, wrapping her arms around Jake. They just held each other, flesh on flesh, breathing the same air.

"I was scared tonight Jake," Nicole whispered. "And I needed you."

"I'm right here."

"Yes. Right here." Nicole lifted her head, soft lips gently kissing Jake's neck, moving slowly across her jaw, finally finding her lips. "I just want you to make love to me . . . make me feel alive, Jake."

Jake's arms tightened, trying to ignore the ache between her legs. She rolled them over, settling between Nicole's thighs. Without another word, her mouth found Nicole's breast and she lost the little resolve she still clung to.

CHAPTER FORTY-EIGHT

Jake opened her eyes, instantly aware of the woman curled beside her. She lay flat on her back, Nicole snuggled at her side, arm wrapped around Jake's midsection. She let her breath out slowly, mentally reliving the night. They had talked some, yes, talked about the case. But hands wouldn't stop touching, lips wouldn't stop seeking. She closed her eyes, her arms tightening around Nicole.

How had it come to this? At her age, how did she become so . . . insatiable? It wasn't like other partners hadn't wanted sex all night long. Heather, in fact, ten years her junior, had begged for it. Jake had tried to keep up, really she had. But it was a halfhearted attempt. Nicole however, could take Jake places she had never been. And a rather pleased part of her knew that she did the same to Nicole.

But what did that mean? They were good in bed? That much was obvious. But the ties ran deeper for Jake and she suspected they did for Nicole, too. But, Nicole was damn near closeted. Where in the world would Jake fit into her life? What they shared in bed was most likely all they could ever share. As Nicole had said numerous times, Jake was not her normal date.

Lost in thought, she was startled when warm lips covered a nipple. With her eyes closed, she felt Nicole's hand slide across her skin, and Jake's hips involuntarily rose to meet that hand. *Insatiable?* Yes.

But Nicole simply touched her, that lazy hand moving over her thighs, pausing briefly at the now healed scar, and back up again, finally resting on Jake's breast.

"Are you teasing me?"

Jake felt Nicole smile against her breast. "No. Just . . . touching you."

Nicole sat up, resting her head in the palm of her hand as she watched Jake, her other hand still drawing lazy circles around Jake's nipple.

"You're not sorry, are you?"

Jake raised her eyebrows. "Sorry?"

"That we . . . made love. I know, the night before, you thought it was a mistake."

Jake smiled. "It's a mistake if my lieutenant finds out."

"Rick was okay with this?"

"No, not really." Jake sat up, too, leaning against the head-board. "I told him that I could keep this separate. And I think that I can. It's just that I've not ever had to try before."

"Yes. But this case might be over in a day, a week," Nicole shrugged.

"Yeah. It could be over soon." And then what? Would Nicole just walk out of her life again? Most likely. "We hope it's over soon, anyway. Five murders to pin on this guy are enough, and I know you're ready to get your life back to normal."

Nicole attempted to smile. Back to normal? Back to her lonely house, and the never-ending stream of blind dates? Back to her life . . . where there was no place for Jake. Strangely, that thought made her heart ache.

CHAPTER FORTY-NINE

Jake pointed at the gray metal chair next to her desk. Nicole obediently took a seat, nodding once at Rick. Jake logged into her computer, wanting to check e-mail before the lieutenant was around. She hoped Steven had found something.

"Did you have a good night?" Rick asked quietly, unable to keep the smirk off his face.

"I'm guessing it was better than yours." Jake looked up and met Nicole's eyes. She felt a sudden sense of loss, of regret. Yeah, as they'd said, it would be over soon. Nicole would go back to wearing her power suits and too much makeup, and Jake would simply fade from her life. Jake knew it was true, but it was hard to reconcile that with the Nicole she saw now. The woman sitting at her desk in blue jeans, sweatshirt, and hiking boots—hair still rumpled and wind-blown—was not the Dr. Westbrook Jake knew she would transform into. No, the woman sitting here now was the one that Jake wanted to haul back to her cabin and snuggle with in front of the fire. She was the one that Jake wanted to make love to as the snow fell in the mountains, the one that Jake wanted to sink into the hot springs with. Jake's heart ached as she realized that Nicole was the one she'd been searching for, waiting for. The one she wanted to share her life with. And she was also the one person she knew who could never share her life. *Damn, but God and his jokes.*

"Maybe. But at least I got some sleep." He lowered his voice. "You two look like you didn't sleep at all."

Jake ignored him and scanned her e-mail for something from Steven. There were two. The first at midnight. The second at two-thirty a.m. Damn. Stevie was like a dog after a bone.

"Got a couple of e-mails from Steven," she said, opening up the first one.

Found your dead time, Jake. July 23, 1999. 9:47 p.m., there are 93 seconds missing. This was hard as hell to find. I'm going to find a back-door into 911 now and crossmatch the date/time and see what shakes. I'll be in touch.

"He found it," she said, looking at Rick. "Nine forty-seven. July 23, 1999." She glanced at Nicole. "Sound right?"

Nicole nodded. "Yes."

Jake opened up the second e-mail, her eyes widened as she scanned it.

The 911 log was deleted on July 25, 1999. You were right. It was from the outside. There was no trail to follow. Dispatch log was deleted from the inside. Your Lieutenant Gregory deleted it at 10:21 that same night. I dug a little deeper and found two units, four officers unaccounted for between 9:40 and 11:00 that night. They were on duty. There is activity earlier in the evening and then again later. Their shift ended at 6 the next morning. I've got names, but let's do it in person. Inside job, Jake. Be careful. Delete the e-mails. I've already covered up my tracks.

"Well fuck me," Jake murmured. She looked around, making sure Gregory was out of sight before printing out the e-mails. Then she dutifully deleted them both from her file. "We can't talk here," she said quietly.

274

"What the hell is going on?" Rick demanded.

Jake stood, grabbing both papers from the printer and folding them, shoving the paper into the back pocket of her jeans. "We're in big trouble, Ricky. Come on, let's get out of here." She grabbed her coat from her chair and started walking, motioning for Nicole to follow.

"Jake?"

"Not here."

Then she stopped suddenly, Rick and Nicole nearly bumping into her. Lieutenant Gregory had just walked into the squad room.

"Where you off to?" he asked, brushing the snow from his coat.

Jake cleared her throat. "Started to snow?"

"Just flurries." He looked at Nicole. "What do you have?"

Jake stepped back. "This is Dr. Westbrook. We're heading over to her office now. She's going to allow us to dig a little into her files. I want to see if we can find a pattern with the crisis center. With five victims now, we'll have more to go on." She stared at her lieutenant, hoping Rick and Nicole would simply go along with her ramblings.

"Five?"

"Last night," Rick said. "I thought the sergeant called you. I was taking Dr. Westbrook home. There was a body dumped there. Hanging in her garage."

"Another patient?"

Rick nodded.

"Salazar and Simpson?"

Jake looked around. "I haven't spoken with them this morning. Salazar was working on the profiles of the victims. I'll make sure she gets Dr. Westbrook's file on the latest."

"I don't have to tell you that Captain Zeller will get involved if we don't break this soon. I got a call from the chief's office, too. They have word that the paper is going do a story using the serial killer angle, and I believe they know the link with Dr. Westbrook now."

"Great," Jake murmured. "That'll bring the crazies out."

"Keep me posted."

"Yes, sir."

They watched him walk into his office, and Jake let out a relieved sigh. "Let's go."

"Where?"

"Nicole's office might be safest. For now."

"What the hell is going on?" Rick hissed. "You're making me crazy."

"Good thing Dr. Westbrook is around then, eh?"

"Very funny."

CHAPTER FIFTY

Catherine looked up as the outer door opened, relieved to see familiar faces. She wasn't ashamed to admit that she was a little scared being at the office alone, especially after Nicole's phone call last night. Nicole had told her not to come in today, but Catherine knew she had to make arrangements for the patients and reschedule appointments.

She smiled brightly at them, but Nicole shook her head disapprovingly.

"Catherine? What the hell are you doing here?"

"Someone had to rearrange your schedule."

Jake brushed past Nicole and leaned on her usual corner of Catherine's desk. "Weird phone calls? Anything?"

"I did have a hang-up, actually."

"When?"

"First thing. Right after I got here."

"Okay. Wipe her clean for all of next week."

"Jake, no. That's too long to be away," Nicole complained. "A few days, maybe."

"Sorry. But it's not your call."

"The hell it's not! This is *my* practice. I've already missed too many sessions in the last two weeks. I can't cancel everything for next week. I won't do it."

Jake met her eyes without flinching. "Sorry, Dr. Westbrook, but you will do it."

Nicole started to protest, but Rick grabbed her arm tightly. "She's right, Nicole. You've got to shut it down until this is over. You're not safe, Catherine is not safe. Your patients aren't safe."

Nicole let out a deep breath, her eyes still locked with Jake. "Okay. You win." She glanced at Catherine. "See if Dorothy can squeeze some in. You might need to refer some to Dr. Andrews, too."

"I'll call right now."

Jake's eyes softened as Nicole looked over at her. "I'm sorry, Nicole. But I won't take a chance with this."

"I understand, Jake."

"Good. Now, we need to talk. Come on."

The three of them settled casually on Nicole's sofa, foregoing the desk and chairs. Jake pulled out the folded pieces of paper and handed the second e-mail to Rick.

"The stalker was an inside job, Nicole. I'm going to meet with Steven later today to get more information. He was afraid to reveal too much in the e-mail."

"Holy shit!" Rick waved the paper at Jake. "*Gregory?*"

Jake shrugged.

"We're fucking screwed, Jake."

"No we're not."

"What about Gregory?" Nicole asked.

"He deleted the dispatch records six years ago."

"Oh my God," Nicole said quietly. "Why?"

"And a hacker deleted 911?" Rick said. "Gregory is not a hacker. Hell, he can barely get around the system as it is."

"You're right. He's not the hacker. But we've got to get the names of the four officers who responded that night. They had to have known about the coverup."

Rick leaned back. "Okay, wait. We're working two different cases here. We have five murders, Jake. Don't you think we need to focus on that first?"

"Ricky, do you think the stalker coverup is simply a coincidence?" Jake stood, beginning to pace. "The stalker was murdered, really. Shot down in Nicole's yard by four cops who knew what they were doing. They got rid of the body and Lieutenant Gregory got rid of the dispatch call. The only other evidence was Nicole's original call to 911. So, two days later, you find a hacker who gets in the system and deletes that as well. Then, all you have are four guys who pulled it off in the first place." She stopped, staring at Rick. "We find the four guys."

"And we start asking questions. How long before Gregory gets word of it?"

"And I still don't see how that incident is linked to the murders," Nicole said. "I mean, that was just a random guy. And he's dead."

"Who was he and why was he stalking you?" Jake asked. "What did he want? And what link did he have to Gregory? Was Gregory the one who ordered him killed? Maybe someone higher up," she said. "It was shortly after that he got transferred to Special Victims. Maybe someone owed him a favor."

"Christ, Jake, you're making me nuts with all this. We'll be lucky if we don't both lose our shields over this one."

"You're right. And the less people know about it, the better. Not a word to Salazar or Simpson. We don't know who we can trust." Jake pulled her cell phone out and dialed. "I'm calling Steven. We need to meet."

"How do you know you can trust him?"

"I just know." Jake waited only two rings. "It's McCoy. Where

279

can we meet?" She nodded, then disconnected. "Damn. Never knew Stevie was gay."

"What are you talking about?"

"He wants to meet at Louie's Down Under."

"Are you serious?"

"Afraid so, buddy. Don't worry, I'll protect you."

"What is Louie's?" Nicole asked.

Jake grinned. "It's a bathhouse."

"For gay men?"

"Right."

"Oh." Nicole looked at Rick and laughed. "Sorry."

CHAPTER FIFTY-ONE

Friday afternoon, Louie's was crowded, despite the threat of snow. Rick looked nervously at Jake. "I don't like this one bit."

"Yeah? Well, I'm not exactly crazy about seeing a bunch of naked men either," Jake said, as she pulled into a parking spot.

"Why in the world would he pick this place?"

"My guess is because he doesn't think anyone from the department would be here."

"I feel like we're in a damn spy movie, sneaking around like this."

"I know. I'm plenty nervous myself," Jake admitted. She looked in the rearview mirror and met Nicole's eyes. "You okay?"

Nicole nodded. They had locked up Nicole's office as soon as Catherine had made arrangements for her patients. Nicole hated it, but conceded it had to be done. She reached across the seats and touched Jake's shoulder. "I'm okay as long as you're around."

Jake grinned. "I don't plan on leaving you."

Rick groaned. "Please, you two are making me nauseous."

Jake leaned back in the seat, keeping an eye on the parking lot for Steven's red Volkswagen Bug. "When are you and Michelle getting together?"

"Tomorrow. God, I'm dreading that."

Jake looked in the mirror again. "Michelle is his wife," she explained.

Rick turned around in the seat, facing Nicole. "We're separated."

"I'm sorry," Nicole said automatically.

"No, it's okay. It was my choice."

"Rick decided they had nothing in common," Jake stated.

"Geez, it's not that," Rick said.

"Then what is it?"

"Do we have to talk about this now?"

Jake grinned. "You might be able to get some free counseling, Ricky."

"I'm sure Dr. Westbrook has more to worry about than my marriage problems."

Jake met Nicole's eyes in the mirror. "Rick and Michelle have nothing in common. Never had, never will. I tried to tell him."

"Will you stop with that?" Rick said, as he punched Jake's arm. He turned again, facing Nicole. "Jake thought I was rushing the marriage thing. Michelle was a catch, and most of the guys on the force were eyeing her," he explained.

"She's like . . . a model," Jake said. "Beautiful."

"Well, I can see how the two of you made a perfect couple," Nicole said.

"Are you trying to give him a big head?" Jake asked.

"No, but he's an attractive man. I'm sure that was a lure, to have an equally attractive woman on his arm."

"Yeah, he's cute as hell. But still, you have to have something other than looks between you, right?"

"Hey, guys? You know, I'm still here." He laughed. "And just what I need. A couple of lesbians fawning over me!"

"Sorry," Nicole said. She realized then that this was the first time in her life that a straight man had called her a lesbian—and she hadn't fainted dead away! Well, it would be something to tell Dorothy, at least. She pushed her thoughts aside and reached out, grasping Rick's shoulder. "I just mean, perhaps the physical attraction was so strong that it overpowered your logical thinking. It happens sometimes."

Jake let the words settle, knowing they weren't meant for her, but unable to shake the truth. Yes, she and Nicole had a physical attraction that was . . . well, beyond her comprehension, really. Had it altered her logical thinking? *No. Logically, they still wouldn't fit in each other's lives.*

Rick ducked his head. "It was an ego thing, yeah, I admit. She liked me. And all the guys liked her. But now that we've been together . . ."

"You don't like her?" Nicole guessed.

"Are you like . . . charging me for this session?"

Nicole leaned forward. "Actually, I was thinking this was more of a friendly chat, not professional."

Rick nodded. "Okay, then." He let his shoulders sag. "I don't like her."

"You don't like her . . . what?"

"I don't like her . . . period," Rick said. "I don't like her. She's an interior decorator. Like Jake said, we have nothing in common, and I can't stand to talk to her about another goddamn house project."

"I see," Nicole murmured.

"We pretend to like each other if someone's around, you know. Like we had Jake over for steaks when she first got back. We were fine together because there was a buffer. But as soon as we were alone, it was back to being strangers."

"And she feels the same way?"

"I don't know. She says not. But hell, how could she not feel the same way? We never talk. Never."

"So, the separation idea was not mutual?"

"No."

"Are you going to seek counseling together?"

Rick shook his head. "Like I said, I don't really like her. I don't think counseling is going to save a marriage that I don't want."

Nicole gave a humorless smile. "Well, there you go," she murmured. At least they were ending it. She'd seen far too many clients who continued their marriage, only to see it end in violence.

"It was a mistake, and I just want to be done with it," Rick said. "And move on and let her move on. If she ends up hating me, so be it."

Nicole gave her standard answer. An answer she hated. "Time will tell."

Jake sat up and pointed. "There he is."

"The Bug?" Rick asked.

"That's what he said." Jake flashed her headlights once and the red car returned the sign. "Okay. He's going to go inside. We're to follow."

"I really don't want to go inside, Jake."

"I swear, you're such a baby. It's fucking undercover, Rick. We're going to find a dark corner and talk. That's it." Jake opened her door, bracing against the cold. "That's it, of course, unless you follow some big brute into the hot tub," she teased.

"Such a comedian," he murmured, rolling his eyes as Nicole laughed at their banter. "She cusses like a sailor."

Jake pulled her coat on, glancing up at the sky. The clouds hung low, threatening snow, but so far only a few flurries had fallen. The dark clouds to the west gave testament that the mountains were getting much needed snowfall. She glanced at the two following her. "Just act natural," she said.

"Act natural? How the hell am I supposed to act natural at a gay bathhouse?"

Jake heard Nicole try to suppress a laugh and ended up laughing out loud herself. She wrapped an arm around Rick's shoulders and gave him a quick kiss on the cheek. "You're precious, you know," she murmured in his ear. He tried to shrug her away, but she held him tighter. "Like you don't want me to protect you," she teased.

"As if I'll need it."

Jake gave him one last squeeze, then dropped her arm. She held open the door, letting Rick and Nicole precede her into the building. As soon as the door closed behind them, darkness prevailed, and Jake squinted her eyes, moving toward the glass enclosure where a lone man sat.

Before she could speak, a familiar voice sounded.

"McCoy, over here."

Jake turned toward Steven's voice, seeing him in the shadows. "Hell of a place to meet, Stevie," she said. "Didn't know you frequented these joints."

He laughed. "I don't. My wife would be appalled to know that I'm here now. But I thought it would be safe."

Jake nodded. "Thought so. Good choice." She motioned to Rick and Nicole. "This is Detective Chase. You might remember him from awhile back. And this is Dr. Westbrook."

Steven nodded quickly, then opened the door to the main entrance. "I was able to secure a room where we could meet. The gentleman out there was very helpful."

"Yeah? What did it cost you?" Jake asked.

Steven opened another door, and they found themselves in a dimly lit room with one bed and an assortment of . . . toys.

"A hundred bucks," he said, looking around the room.

"Jesus . . . what is all this *shit*?" Rick asked.

"Just never mind," Jake said. "Let's get to the business at hand. And Steven, I'll reimburse you for the hundred bucks, no problem."

"Do you think they have cameras?" Rick asked, glancing around the room.

"No. Too much liability," Steven said. "Sit everyone."

"Do you think it's clean?"

"Jesus! Rick, give me a break," Jake said, as she pushed him onto the bed. Nicole stood near the door, her eyes darting between them. Jake reached out and grabbed her hand. "It's okay. Relax."

"Easy for you to say," Nicole murmured, as she pulled her hand from Jake and wrapped both arms around herself. She felt like she was in a bad dream. Only the warmth in Jake's eyes made it seem real.

"No, it's okay," Steven said. "This is secure. Trust me, I checked."

Jake perched on the edge of the bed next to Rick. "Okay, what the hell is going on?"

"On the surface, your Lieutenant Gregory covered up a crime. And that's only because he's the one trail I can trace. I did a search on the four officers who responded to the 911 dispatch six years ago. Three are dead. Accidental deaths, all three. The fourth, from what I can tell, is in Canada." Steven met Jake's eyes. "My gut tells me he fled there for safety."

"Please don't tell me you're suggesting that Gregory had the three killed," Jake said.

"Two were killed while on active duty. Brakes failed and their car went over an embankment. It happened only a few months after the stalker."

"Yeah, I remember that one," Rick said. "Out by the lake, wasn't it?"

"Yes. The third one was found up in the mountains. He was an avid hiker. Went on a trip in early fall after this incident. He didn't make it back."

"No sign of foul play?"

"Hard to tell. He fell off a cliff."

Jake leaned forward. "So, three of the four responding officers to a 911 call that doesn't exist are dead."

"That's correct."

"And one is in Canada?"

"I'm fairly certain he fled there. His arrival date is just three weeks after the last death here. He married a Canadian shortly afterward. I don't show any activity outside of Canada since then."

"Jesus Christ," Jake muttered. "You've been busy, Stevie."

He shrugged. "Once I started, I couldn't stop."

"How far are you willing to go?"

"What's on your mind?"

Jake glanced at Rick, then Nicole. "I don't know how involved you want to be in this, Steven. Technically, I'm defying an order of my superior by even investigating this. Who do we trust? Do we go to Captain Zeller? What if Gregory was ordered to delete the log? He was a sergeant at the time. Suddenly he makes lieutenant and is given Special Victims?" She looked at Rick. "Maybe someone owed him a favor."

Steven nodded. "You're right. But Gregory is the only player we know for sure. We dig on Gregory first, see what shakes out."

Jake stood, pacing across the room. It was dangerous. All three of them could lose their jobs if they didn't find anything. Or worse, if it pointed to someone higher up, they could lose their lives. "Can you do it without causing red flags?"

"I'll do it from my home computer and spoof an IP address. I won't be traced. I can sneak around without anyone knowing."

Jake met his eyes. "This isn't really your fight, Stevie. I asked for a favor, and it's turned into more."

"I'm good at this stuff, Jake." Then he grinned. "I work for the police department but I don't really ever get to do anything exciting. I'm enjoying this."

"Okay. We dig on Gregory. Let's go back . . . what? Ten years?"

"I'll get started tonight. You want financials, too?"

"Whatever. Just no red flags."

Steven scoffed. "I do this all the time."

"What? Hacking is a hobby?"

He grinned. "It's an art."

Rick finally stood up and brushed his hands on his pants. "Great. If you guys are through with all this spy stuff, I'd like to get out of this room. It gives me the creeps."

Jake looked back at Nicole, who hadn't said a word throughout the whole conversation. She raised her eyebrows, and Nicole simply nodded.

287

"Okay. You've got my cell number, my home number. You got Rick's number?"

"No." Steven pulled out his PDA, and Rick rolled his eyes as he gave out his cell number.

Jake grabbed Steven's arm as they turned to leave. "Be careful. Don't take any chances."

He grinned back at her. "I'm an expert at this shit, Jake. Relax."

It was dark when they walked out of Louie's, and the cold hit them. Jake tugged the collar of her coat closer around her neck, glancing at Nicole as she did the same.

"Fuck," Rick murmured, "Is it going to snow or what?"

"Actually, no," Steven said. "But the mountains are getting hammered. The weekend is supposed to be nice."

"And he's a meteorologist, too," Rick whispered to Nicole.

Steven headed to his car, then turned. "No, Detective, not a meteorologist. I just happened to catch the weather forecast on the way over here. Enjoy the weekend."

"You never could whisper," Jake murmured.

"Damn computer geek."

Jake turned on Rick. "He's a nice guy, and he's doing us a favor. A big favor. Cut him some slack."

"Yeah, I know. It's just this whole thing is freaking me out, Jake. We're getting in too deep. We're digging up shit we probably shouldn't be digging in."

Jake grabbed his arm. "Six years ago, this woman had a stalker," she said, pointing at Nicole. "And now someone is leaving dead bodies at her house. After all Steven told us tonight, you think we shouldn't be digging?"

"Gregory is our fucking boss, Jake."

"And if he did what Steven suggests he did, he needs to be taken down."

Rick looked at Nicole, noting the frightened look in her eyes. His voice lowered. "We could be in over our heads, Jake."

"I know, buddy. But I won't be a part of a coverup. Especially one that results in the deaths of three cops."

"But we can't do this alone. Maybe we should fill in Salazar and Simpson," he suggested.

"No. No way. I trust you, Rick. But I don't trust anyone else right now. We've got to be careful."

"Excuse me," Nicole said, stepping closer to them. "I'm not an expert at police psychology, but I understand the need to confide in partners, superiors, other team members. But in this case, I have to agree with Jake. I think it's imperative that no one know what you're doing." She met Jake's eyes. "I only hope the two cases are related. I'd hate to think that we're wasting time on a six-year-old case."

Jake shook her head. "My gut tells me they are related."

Nicole gave a half-smile. "Then I'll trust your gut."

"Hey guys? It's freezing. Can we go now?"

"I swear, you're such a city boy," Jake said, as she unlocked the car. "It's Friday. You got any plans, Ricky?"

"No. I thought I'd pick up a pizza on the way home. I've got to tidy up the house. Michelle is coming over in the morning."

"I wonder if she'll be alone."

"We both know she'll have her sisters and mother with her."

"You're going to have to sell the house, you know," Jake said.

"Which is fine. It's been a decorating project of hers. It hardly feels like home to me."

Jake pulled out into the Friday evening traffic, her eyes meeting Nicole's again in the mirror. The woman had been unusually quiet. Jake wondered if this whole situation hadn't finally taken its toll on her.

"Well, call me if you need some support," Jake said. "I don't know what we're going to do." Would they spend the weekend together?

Rick cleared his throat. "You know, I was thinking. Maybe Sunday, if the weather holds, you guys could come out. We could do some steaks maybe, watch football."

Jake heard the loneliness in Rick's voice, and it tugged at her heart. For all his brave words, this separation with Michelle was affecting him.

"Sure, buddy. Count me in." Jake looked again in the mirror. "Nicole might have other plans, though."

"I have no plans." Nicole shrugged. "It's not like I would relish spending the weekend at my home, alone."

Jake bit back the words of apology she was about to utter and instead offered a cheery outlook for the weekend. "I was planning on taking Cheyenne out hiking tomorrow. Steaks and a few beers at Rick's on Sunday. How does that sound?"

Nicole reached across the back seat to the front and squeezed Jake's shoulder. "Thanks."

CHAPTER FIFTY-TWO

Nicole put the bag on the table and waited for Cheyenne's greeting. She wasn't disappointed as the dog danced excitedly around her.

"So either she likes me or she wants me to give her one of our burgers," Nicole said, rubbing both her palms across Cheyenne's face.

"I'd guess both," Jake said. She opened the fridge, staring inside at the nearly empty compartment. "No beer. One Coke." She turned to Nicole and cocked an eyebrow. "There's a bottle of chardonnay," she said almost apologetically.

"Yes, please."

"Wine and burgers." Jake shook her head disgustedly, as she pulled the bottle of wine from the fridge. "Just doesn't go together. And it's certainly not what you're used to."

Nicole walked over and stilled Jake's hands as she fingered the corkscrew. She drew Jake to her, wrapping both arms around her.

291

Nicole moved her lips over Jake's neck to her ear. "Burgers and wine with you beat a blind date at the fanciest restaurant any day," she whispered.

Jake dropped the corkscrew on the counter, pulling Nicole close, letting their bodies meld together. They just held each other, nothing more. She finally loosened her grip, and Nicole slipped slowly away from her.

"So, where are you taking me hiking tomorrow?"

Jake picked up the corkscrew, smiling at Nicole. "Thanks," she said quietly. Damn, but she sometimes felt so inadequate around Nicole. *Out of her league*, her mind screamed. And yes, she knew that. Jesus, they'd had cheap takeout every time Nicole had been here. "You know, I really do like to cook. I just rarely do it." She shrugged. "I didn't want you to think I did takeout every night."

"It's not like we've had time to cook a meal, Jake."

"Well, maybe tomorrow, after our hike, we'll cook in. How's that?"

"That'd be great. But you never said where you were taking me."

"We'll have to see how much snow the mountains got. I like going out around Mount Evans." Jake brought the wine and two glasses to the table, shoving Cheyenne out of the way as she opened the wrap on her burger. "But we may have to stay in the lower elevations. Red Rocks Canyon, maybe."

Nicole bit into her burger, nodding. "Yes, I've hiked Red Rocks before. But if the weather is okay, I'd prefer to go farther up in the mountains. Get away from the city, you know?"

Jake nodded. She knew exactly what Nicole meant. Run away from all this madness for at least a day. But in the end, the case would still be here, hanging over their heads. "I love to hike the old mining roads around Mount Evans. We could maybe try that," she suggested.

"I haven't been on a hiking trail since . . . well, since I met you out there," Nicole said quietly. "Although you and I never actually hiked together."

Jake grinned. "We didn't hike, no."

Nicole put her half-eaten burger down and leaned toward Jake. "Do you do that often?"

Jake raised an eyebrow. "Do what?"

"Seduce stranded hikers?"

Jake reached across the table and lightly fingered Nicole's hand. "Actually, I can honestly say that you were a first."

"Really?"

"Really."

Nicole nodded and picked up her burger again, trying to hide the very pleased smile that threatened. It was a silly question to begin with. How many lesbians could possibly get lost and end up at Jake's hot springs?

Jake was surprised at the hint of jealously in Nicole's question. For all they had been through—back then in the mountains and now here, with this case—they had yet to talk about their personal relationship. It was almost as if that part of things existed only when they were alone and only when they were in bed. And even then, they didn't really talk about what was happening with them, between them. It was just . . . there. And when the case was over, that would be over, too. They both knew it. Perhaps that was why they didn't talk about it.

Jake lost interest in her burger, and a very happy Cheyenne was the beneficiary, finishing it off in two large bites.

"Oh, God, it's beautiful," Nicole said, her breath frosting around her as she turned a circle, surveying the snowcapped mountains around them. "I haven't been up here in the winter in so long, I'd forgotten how breathtaking it could be."

Jake smiled as she watched Nicole trudge through the snow, Cheyenne at her heels. The upper elevations got over a foot of snow, but here, the old mining roads were still visible. Unfortunately, they weren't the only ones to take a chance on the snow. Three other cars were already in the lot.

Nicole turned around, waiting. Then she frowned as Jake grimaced when she took a step. "Is your leg bothering you today?"

Jake shook her head. "Oh, it's just stiff from the long drive and with the cold, it just takes it longer to loosen up." And it was mostly true. However, last night, as Nicole climaxed, her knee hit Jake square on the fading scar, sending shooting pain down her leg. Pain, yes, but nothing so severe that it squelched her own pleasure as Nicole straddled her hips. Just the thought of their lovemaking caused her stomach to clench. She locked glances with Nicole, acknowledging the lingering desire still there. Their shower together this morning had turned into more and Jake wondered, if they were to have a real relationship, would the physical part remain as intense as it was now?

Nicole walked closer, stopping but a breath away from Jake. "Did I hurt you last night?" she asked quietly. She blushed, remembering how she'd wantonly taken Jake last night. She simply couldn't get enough, and she'd straddled Jake's body in her desire to get as close as possible to the woman. It scared her, this physical need she had of Jake. When it ended, how was she going to survive?

Jake shook her head. "No. You didn't hurt me."

Nicole nodded. "We don't have to hike for long, Jake. Just say the word."

"I'm fine. I'm looking forward to this as much as you are."

Nicole flashed a bright smile before turning down the trail. Cheyenne followed her, looking back once to make sure Jake was coming.

"Fickle dog," Jake murmured.

"Perfect weather for stew," Nicole said, as she blew on the spoon to cool it. She smiled after taking her first bite, her eyes meeting Jake's across the table. "Delicious."

Jake passed the homemade bread across the table, secretly pleased that Nicole liked it. She'd wanted to cook today, not settle for takeout. Well, the homemade bread came from the bakery down the street. They were both chilled from their hike in the mountains, and Jake got the stew going, quickly chopping onions and potatoes while Nicole showered. By the time Nicole had emerged from the bathroom, Jake had a fire going in the tiny fireplace, and the smell of their simmering dinner wafted through the small duplex.

"I checked e-mail earlier. There was only a brief note from Steven," Jake said. "He's found something but he wouldn't go into it. He wants to meet in the morning."

Nicole noticed the worried expression on Jake's face. "And you're afraid of what he's going to tell you?"

"It's got to do with Gregory, I'm sure. And you know, he's a good lieutenant. He's always been by the book. That's why this whole thing just blows me away. I can't believe he's involved in something like this."

"If you have evidence, who will you go to?"

"Captain Zeller, if I'm sure he's not involved. From there, Internal Affairs." Jake dipped the bread into the stew, taking her first bite. "Of course, we may be solving a six-year old stalker case. I'm not certain how this is going to help us on this case."

"I read the *Post* online this morning. There wasn't a big write-up about the murders, just a follow-up on Jena Nichols. Nothing about Lori."

"Probably tomorrow. I get the Sunday paper delivered so we'll know soon enough. With our luck, the story will make the front page."

"Wonder why there hasn't been more written about it?" Nicole shrugged. "Four women's bodies dumped over a three-month period should cause suspicions, don't you think?"

"There hasn't been an official announcement from the police department, it would only be speculation by the crime beat reporter. And unless they are absolutely positive, the paper is not going to suggest we have a serial killer on the streets."

"But your lieutenant said they are going to report it as a serial killer so they must have something."

"My guess is Dr. Benson may have let something slip. She's

notorious for that. She doesn't care how it impacts an investigation."

Nicole nodded as she ate more of the stew, wondering if it would be impolite to request a second bowl. "Have you talked to Rick today?"

"No. I'll call him tonight. I want to make sure Michelle is gone."

"You two really get along, don't you?"

"Me and Rick? Yeah, he's the best partner I could ever hope to have." Jake met Nicole's eyes for a second. "That and . . . you know, he saved my life."

"He seems like a really nice guy."

"Yeah. And he understands me, he accepts that I'm gay, he . . . loves me."

What's not to love? But Nicole managed to keep her thoughts to herself. She was again envious of the freedom Jake had by being open about her lifestyle. How much easier would it be to not have to pretend to be straight? And how foolish was it really? How many people knew the truth but played along with the lies, just to save face?

"Steaks and football tomorrow?" she asked instead.

"Yes. Depends, of course, on what Steven has for us."

CHAPTER FIFTY-THREE

"I can't believe he wants to meet at a goddamn park! It's like twenty degrees," Rick complained, as he pulled his coat tighter around him.

"It's thirty-six and sunny. My God, I never realized you were such a wimp."

"It's Sunday morning. I should be watching ESPN pregame, nursing my third cup of coffee. Not out here," he said, motioning to the nearly empty park.

Nicole watched their exchange with amusement. She wasn't the least bit cold, and judging by Jake's opened coat, neither was Jake. There wasn't even a hint of a breeze, and the blue, blue sky was sparkling and cloudless. It was actually a lovely morning.

Out of the corner of her eye, Jake spotted the flash of the red Volkswagen bug through the trees. It came to a stop on the other side of the park. Steven was careful, she'd give him that. Actually, she thought he'd probably watched too many spy movies as a kid. "There he is," she said.

"Good. I'm ready to get this over with. Because I gotta tell you, Jake, I got a bad feeling on this one."

"Me, too, buddy," she murmured.

Steven walked up, barely nodding at them before continuing down the hike and bike trail, leaving them to follow. Jake walked shoulder to shoulder with him, keeping quiet until the trail snaked into the trees, hiding them from the openness of the park.

"I know who the stalker was."

They all stopped. Jake looked at Nicole and Rick, then back to Steven. "Who?"

"Matthew Gregory."

Jake's eyes widened, and Steven nodded.

"Yes, Lieutenant Gregory's son."

"I didn't even know he had a son." Jake nervously ran fingers through her short hair, her eyes locked on Rick's. "He had his own son killed?"

"Not exactly," Steven continued. "You won't believe all the shit I found out. One trail led to another." He motioned to a park bench. "Better sit down. Especially you, Dr. Westbrook."

Nicole was suddenly frightened, and she was thankful for Jake's comforting presence. She looked expectantly at Steven, waiting.

"Ten years ago, a woman named Rebecca Gregory sought therapy. She spent one year with Dr. Dorothy Peterson." At Nicole's shocked expression, Steven continued. "After that one year, she was referred by Dr. Peterson to a young colleague. You, Dr. Westbrook."

"Do you know who he's talking about?" Jake asked.

Nicole shook her head. "No. Nine years ago? No."

"But you still have the files?"

"Of course."

"I'm not sure of the initial reason she went to Dr. Peterson, nor am I certain of what your sessions revealed, Dr. Westbrook. But the medical records for Matthew Gregory indicate that he was sexually abused by his mother."

Jake stood up. "What medical records?"

"As a teenager, he spent eight months at the Trinity Clinic," Steven said. "There was nothing in his early records to indicate abuse." He looked at his notes. "He was admitted again in 1999. One week after Nicole's stalker was allegedly killed. The medical records from that time indicate the abuse."

"Wait a minute. You're saying this kid was the stalker, his father knew about it so he staged a killing and had him locked up in a mental facility?"

"It's even better than that, Jake. Rebecca Gregory was found murdered. She'd been brutally raped, disfigured."

"What do you mean?" Rick asked. "Disfigured how?"

"Her breasts were cut off."

"Jesus Christ."

"No prints, no evidence, no motive—and no suspect. The case was never solved."

"When was this?" Jake asked.

"December, 1998."

"Nicole, when did you first notice a stalker?"

Nicole rubbed her hands together. She was suddenly very cold. She had a brief memory of an early case where she suspected the mother was having sex with her son. But she'd heard such horror stories over the last nine years, and that one hardly stuck out anymore. She could recall nothing about it.

"It was in the spring of ninety-nine. There's a park not too far from my house, in the foothills. I used to go out there to jog. I noticed him for three afternoons in a row. He was just . . . creepy. So I stopped going there. Then I would see him on the streets, on my way to the office, on my way to the gym."

"But you said you didn't know what he looked like," Jake reminded her.

"No. He was always watching from a distance. He had dark hair. That's all I could tell."

"We're positive he was the stalker?" Jake asked Steven.

"Yes. It's documented in his medical file."

"So why stage a killing? By cops, no less? It makes no sense."

"I don't know. Maybe Gregory didn't think Dr. Westbrook would let it go unless she thought he was dead. Maybe he was protecting his son from jail time. Hell, maybe he was protecting his own job."

"So he finds four cops he can trust. Was it a setup? Did he know Matthew would be at Nicole's house that night?"

"We'll probably never know that."

"Was the kid in on it or did they really shoot him?" Jake continued.

"There was no mention of physical injuries."

Jake turned around again, eyebrows raised. "That still doesn't tell us who deleted the 911 call."

"I would say it's probably the same person who discharged Matthew five months ago."

"Discharged? He's out?"

Steven nodded. "Someone hacked into their medical files and put a discharge notice on Matthew's record. It happened at night, during shift change. By the time his doctor showed up the next morning, he was long gone."

"And Lieutenant Gregory?"

"He was notified the next day."

Jake stared. "And what are the chances that Matthew Gregory is a computer geek?"

Steven grinned. "Considering he was suspended twice in high school for hacking into their system to change grades, I'd say pretty good."

It was Rick's turn to pace. "This is all too fucking unbelievable. If he hacked into the 911 system, then that means he knew what the lieutenant was up to."

"Not necessarily," Jake said. "If the plan was for him to appear to have been killed, I doubt they would have let it go so far as to have Nicole even call 911. Just because you're a hacker, doesn't mean that you're going to be able to delete the info that you want to delete." She looked at Steven. "Right?"

"Absolutely. You hack into someone's system and just because you're able to view data, doesn't mean you can always manipulate it."

"I'm guessing the lieutenant did this on his own, then talked the kid into deleting the 911 call."

Steven nodded. "That'd be my guess, too."

"After it was done, Lieutenant Gregory had him shipped back to Trinity Clinic, hoping he could just wash his hands of the whole thing."

"What about the mother?" Nicole asked quietly.

"No prints, no fibers." Jake looked at Rick. "Where have we heard that before?"

"So you think . . . he killed his own mother?"

"Yeah. And so does the lieutenant. Why else would he go to such great lengths to hide the kid?"

Nicole cleared her throat. "And you think he's now killing my patients?"

"For whatever reason, Nicole, you are the catalyst. And yes, I believe he's our murderer."

"Surely to God, Gregory knows what's going on," Rick said. "We've had five murders. He's almost nonchalant about them."

"Steven, any hint as to where Matthew Gregory might be?"

Steven shook his head. "There are no credit cards issued in his name, no bank records. So, unless he's using his computer skills to obtain cash, someone has to be funding him."

"How old is he?" Rick asked.

Steven looked at his notes. "He's twenty-four."

Nicole shook her head. "Still practically a kid," she said quietly.

"A kid who has killed," Jake reminded her. She stood in front of them, hands shoved into her coat pockets. "We have two things to do. One, we have to let Captain Zeller know what's going on. Hopefully, we have enough to convince him about Lieutenant Gregory's involvement. And two, we need Nicole's files on Rebecca Gregory." Jake met Nicole's eyes. "We can get those files, right? You won't hold them back for privacy's sake?"

"You can have the files for your investigation. Other than that—"

"That's fine. We'll deal with that when the time comes. I'd like for you and Rick to go to your office today, now, and get the files.

And I want Steven, if he's willing, to go with me to talk to Captain Zeller. He's going to want to know how you found this shit out."

"I'll go, sure. I just hope I don't get busted for hacking the system."

"Rick? Nicole?"

"Sure. We'll swing by there," Rick said. "Meet you where?"

"My place."

As they walked back along the trail, Jake bumped Nicole's shoulder, causing the quiet woman to look at her.

"You okay?"

Nicole attempted a smile. "I'd feel better if I was staying with you."

"You'll be fine. Rick won't let anything happen to you."

"No. I don't suppose he would." She shrugged. "It's just so unbelievable, you know. Maybe once I read the files, it'll make more sense."

"We might understand it more, but I doubt it will ever make sense to us."

"I know you're upset about your lieutenant. It must be a huge shock to you."

"That's an understatement. He's well-respected, and I'm going to have a hell of a time convincing Captain Zeller of all this."

Nicole moved her hand between them and captured Jake's fingers. "I guess a relaxing day with steaks and football is out," she murmured.

Jake smiled. "Do you even like football?"

"Not really. But I would have liked spending time with you."

"I thought you'd be sick of me by now."

Nicole stopped and quickly stole a kiss from Jake, unmindful of Rick and Steven's presence. "After the way I made love to you this morning, how could you think that?" she whispered.

Jake felt her temperature rise as she fell into Nicole's eyes. Jake was awakened this morning by a warm mouth suckling her breast. Before she was fully awake, that same mouth had moved down her body and Nicole's hands had spread her thighs before Jake's eyes had even opened. By the time she was conscious of what was happening, Nicole's tongue had found its way into her wetness.

"Oh, yeah. Did I thank you for that . . . wake-up call?"

Nicole squeezed her hand and continued walking. "You can thank me later," she whispered.

CHAPTER FIFTY-FOUR

Jake rang the doorbell, waiting nervously for Captain Zeller to open the door. Steven, too, shifted tensely beside her.

"I'm going to get fired, I just know it," Steven whispered. "I'm not even a damn cop. What was I thinking?"

"You're not going to get fired," Jake said. *At least I hope not.*

She straightened her shoulders as she heard the door unlocking. Captain Zeller peered out at them, his steel blue eyes meeting her own.

"Detective McCoy."

"Captain Zeller, thanks for seeing me." She cleared her throat. "This is Steven Turner, he works for us over in Information Technology."

"I see. Well, I must admit, you piqued my curiosity when you called." He stood back, motioning them inside. "Especially when you said it pertained to Lieutenant Gregory."

They followed the sound of a football game on TV and Captain

Zeller settled his large frame into a well-used recliner. "Sit down, please." He touched the remote, silencing the game. "Broncos are getting their ass kicked, anyway." He leaned back, folding his hands across his stomach. "Now, McCoy, what's on your mind."

Jake rested her forearms on her thigh, wondering where to begin. "You're aware of the murders we are investigating."

"Of course. Your lieutenant believes it's a serial killer. In fact, we met on Friday to discuss the possibility of a task force."

"Well, six years ago, a Dr. Nicole Westbrook had a stalker . . ."

Rick was startled when Nicole simply pulled on the front doors of the building and they opened.

"They leave this building unlocked all the time?"

"No. But there are offices inside that do business over the weekends. The doors are locked at seven each night, but there's a security code, if anyone wanted in after hours."

He pointed to the empty reception area. "They don't man this on weekends?"

"Yes. Starting at noon on Sundays." She glanced at her watch. "I guess they're running late today."

The elevators swiftly took them to the eighth floor, and Nicole pulled out her keys as she approached her outer office. The blinds, which Catherine normally kept open, were closed. She shrugged. Perhaps, since they'd be out for at least the next week, Catherine decided to close them.

She flipped on the lights, noting Catherine's neat desk. It was quiet inside and Nicole felt an eerie chill on her body. She pushed it away, instead walking to the file room and unlocking that door as well.

Rick stood in the doorway, surveying the dozen or so file cabinets that were crowded into the tiny room. "I'll help look. How are things filed? Alpha?"

Nicole shrugged. "Some."

"Some?"

"The earliest stuff is filed by date. My first secretary's idea. Catherine changed it to alpha."

"But they are not merged?"

"They are not merged because there has never been idle time to do that. Besides, rarely do I have to go back ten years to look for a file. And anyway, the last six years, most of that is on the computer."

"But you still keep paper files?"

"Yes."

Nicole tossed her purse on the top of one of the file cabinets, reading the labels as she walked past them. The dated ones were at the end of the row, if she remembered. Truth was, she hadn't been in the file room in years. "Rick? Would you do me a favor?"

"Sure."

"Give me some room here? This place isn't big enough for both of us," she said, as she squatted down beside the second to last file cabinet.

"Sorry," Rick said. "Didn't realize I was hovering." He backed out of the tiny room, giving Nicole some space.

"Thanks. Hopefully, this won't take long," she murmured as she pulled out one of the drawers, her eyes scanning the names on the files. *Date order?* Geez. What had she been thinking?

By the time Jake finished her story, Captain Zeller was pacing across his living room, the TV long ago having been turned off. Three glasses of untouched iced tea sat on the coffee table, compliments of his wife.

"First of all, let me say that I don't condone the illegal investigation that you've done," he said, pointing at Steven. "With the encouragement of one of my detectives, no less."

"Captain—"

"With that said, we have a terrible situation. Lieutenant Gregory is a fine man, McCoy."

"Yes, sir."

"I find it hard to believe all of this."

"I know, sir."

"But, facts are facts. And regardless of how you've obtained them, we need to act on them. The DA will have our ass, of course, as most of this is inadmissible. But, the court proceedings are his problem. Ours is to stop a murderer."

Jake let out a sigh of relief. She'd watched Captain Zeller as she'd told him everything they'd found out. At first, she could see the disbelief in his eyes. But when Steven told them how he'd found out about the medical records, how he had proof that Lieutenant Gregory deleted the dispatch log, he had no choice but believe them.

"Question is, what are we going to do?"

"Sir, with all due respect, we need to bring Lieutenant Gregory in. His son has been missing for five months. That's the time the first victim was found. Lieutenant Gregory has to suspect his son in this by now."

"I will not bring Gregory in as if he's a criminal. I've known the man twenty years."

"Yes, sir. That's why I came to you today. I was hoping we could go to his house and speak with him there. Privately."

"And Mr. Turner here?"

"I'd like him to come along, sir. He's the only one privy to all the information."

Captain Zeller nodded and faced Steven. "You ever wanted to be a cop, son?"

Steven visibly swallowed. "Actually, sir, I fancied myself more like . . . James Bond."

Jake saw a ghost of a smile cross the older man's face. As she'd suspected, Stevie had watched too many spy movies.

"Bond? Well, don't pull any fancy gadgets out of your pockets. We're just going to talk to Lieutenant Gregory." Zeller turned to Jake. "And you do know, he won't like this one bit, seeing as how you went over his head and all."

"Yes, sir."

307

Zeller laughed. "I'd heard you were a little fireball, McCoy. But investigating your lieutenant ranks right up there. You got balls, I'll say that."

Jake lifted one corner of her mouth. "Yes, sir."

Rick walked back to Catherine's desk, idly tossing her paperweight between his hands. He stopped, frowning. Nicole's office door was ajar. He blindly laid the paperweight on the desk and walked slowly to the door, head cocked to one side. He would have sworn that it was closed when they'd first gotten there. He moved his coat aside, hand lightly touching his weapon as he used his foot to open the door. It was dark inside, the blinds lowered, preventing the early afternoon sunshine from entering.

The few times he'd been in here, the blinds were always up.

"You must be Detective Chase," a voice said behind him.

Rick visibly jumped, struggling to pull his weapon. He saw the man's face, noted the smug smile that graced his mouth—then pain and blackness overtook him.

"I really think we should have some backup," Jake said again, as they approached the front door.

"Yes, it's duly noted that you've mentioned it three times, Detective McCoy. However, I know Gregory. We're in no danger."

Jake held her tongue. Of course they could be in danger. This man possibly killed three cops. This man was most likely hiding his son. Jake looked at Steven, trying to reassure him. His eyes were wild, and Jake suspected his heart was pounding out of control.

"Stevie," she whispered. When he met her eyes, she grinned. "Chill, man."

"Yeah, okay."

Captain Zeller chuckled as he rang the doorbell. "Yes, chill, Mr. Bond."

Jake grew impatient as the seconds passed, finally reaching around Zeller, pressing the doorbell two more times. As Zeller stared at her, she shrugged. "Sorry."

"Could be a wasted trip, Detective. Apparently, your lieutenant is not home."

"We can't let this go until tomorrow, Captain."

"What should I do? Put out an APB for one of our lieutenants?"

"With the evidence we have—yes, sir."

"Well, that's why you're a detective and I'm a captain. It doesn't work that way."

"You're right. I never learned how to play politics," she said, her voice rising. Steven cleared his throat, but she ignored him. "He very possibly killed three cops six years ago. His son is the only suspect we have in the murders of five women." She pounded her fist against the door. "So I really don't want to play politics right now!"

Captain Zeller only smiled. "Now I know what Dr. Benson was talking about. You kinda go off the deep end, don't you McCoy?" When she would have protested, he held his hand up to stop her. "I know you think I'm taking this lightly, but I'm not. Lieutenant Gregory's position has earned him the benefit of the doubt, not to mention the means at which you've *gathered* this evidence against him. And truth be told, McCoy," he said with a shrug. "A lot of this could be called circumstantial."

Jake took a step closer to Zeller. "A lawyer might call it circumstantial. A cop never would."

He nodded. "And I'm still a cop, which is why I'm even here in the first place." He turned to go. "I'll have a unit come by and wait. As soon as Gregory shows, I'll have them bring him to me."

Jake let out her breath. "Thank you."

Nicole found the file, finally. She pulled it out, then turned toward the door and the muffled sound of something falling.

"Rick?" she called.

She stood, closing the file cabinet behind her with her foot. She briefly flipped through the file, but nothing stood out, and she had no recollection of Rebecca Gregory. She stopped and stared out into the now dark outer office. She distinctly remembered flipping on the light.

"Ricky?" she called again. She actually felt the hairs on the back of her neck stand out seconds before a shadow crossed the door.

"No, no. Not Ricky, darling."

Nicole stifled her scream as the handsome young man in the pressed business suit walked into the light. He flashed her a charming smile before bowing at the waist.

"Dr. Westbrook, a pleasure to finally meet you. Matthew Gregory, at your service."

Nicole dropped the file she'd been holding and pressed back against the file cabinet, her eyes wide with fright.

He spread his arms out. "So this is where you keep the old files. I'd already searched your secretary's computer, thinking surely to God you've got all that imaged by now."

"What . . . what do you want?" Nicole whispered.

Again, that charming smile. "I've missed you, Dr. Westbrook." He took a step closer. "Have you missed me as well?" When Nicole didn't answer, he motioned to the papers scattered on the floor around her. "Mommy's file, no doubt. That should make for interesting reading later tonight. Don't you think?"

"What do you want from me?"

"Oh, Dr. Westbrook, let's don't spoil the fun, shall we. We'll have several days to play." He pointed at the file. "Pick it up."

Nicole's hands were trembling as she gathered the fallen papers and put them back inside the file folder. She was too rattled to even think coherently, but one word kept crowding into her muddled brain. *Jake.*

"You know, I must say, your cop friend is pretty resourceful." Matthew Gregory leaned casually against the doorframe, watching as Nicole straightened the papers. "Imagine my surprise when I noticed in the Trinity logs that someone had been snooping through my medical records. I sniffed him out, followed him back outside but the IP address was located in China." He shrugged. "Doesn't matter. I have what I want, don't I?"

"Why?"

"Why? Why you? Perhaps as we read this file later, it'll all come back to you." He stood straighter and pulled both sleeves of his jacket down around his wrist. With a slight tilt of his head, he motioned for her to move out of the room. "Time to go. We don't want your *Ricky* in there to surprise us, do we?"

"Is he . . . okay?"

"Okay? Well, that depends how you look at it. He's still breathing, if that's what you mean. Or he was." Matthew Gregory laughed. "For some reason, I can't bring myself to hurt another man. Wonder why I don't have that same compassion for women?" He snapped his fingers. "Oh? Could it possibly have something to do with Mommy?"

"Where . . . where are we going?"

"We are going for a very short ride, Dr. Westbrook." With that, he grasped her arm and clasped one end of a handcuff around her wrist. The other end, he snapped securely around his own wrist. "Don't want you bolting, now do we?"

Nicole jerked her arm away, but he pulled it back, his fingers clutching hers. She noticed that his hands were warm, but damp. Damp like her own. The elevator was waiting, and he pulled her inside, quickly punching the button for the ground floor.

"My car is parked right outside," he said. "The receptionist unfortunately called in sick today," he said with a smile. "So, don't try screaming like some hysterical girl."

Nicole nodded, part of her wishing frantically that Jake would show up and save her. The other part, the more realistic part, realized that if she had any chance to survive, she would have to create a psychologist-patient relationship with him. And that, of course, she was trained to do.

"You want to call it a day or do you want to finish this?" Jake asked.

Steven grinned. "My wife will most likely kill me, but I'd like to hang out with you guys."

Jake grabbed his shoulder and squeezed. "Great. Because something tells me we're going to need your expertise again." She pointed at her Land Cruiser. "Follow me to my place. Rick and Nicole might already be there." She looked at her cell again, wondering why they hadn't checked in. It shouldn't have taken this long. She used her thumb to dial Rick's number as she maneuvered through traffic onto the interstate. A quick glance in the rearview mirror found the bright red Bug tailing close behind.

"Come on, Ricky," she murmured impatiently. When voice mail sounded, she disconnected, dialing instead Nicole's number. After two rings, she was notified that her party was unavailable. She frowned. What the hell did that mean?

CHAPTER FIFTY-FIVE

Although still daylight, the sun had long disappeared behind the mountains to the west. They were traveling down a familiar road, and Nicole was surprised that they were heading to Golden. As if reading her thoughts, Matthew shook his head.

"We're not going to your house. But up in the foothills, yes. My father has a cabin there." He grinned. "It's been very useful."

"So that's why it was so easy for you to get to my house," she said quietly. "I am curious as to how you knew my alarm code."

He laughed. "Dr. Westbrook, with a computer, you can find out all sorts of interesting facts. Your alarm company has what I hesitate to even call a firewall. I was in their system in seconds."

"I'll take your word for it. I'm not really . . . into computers."

"And apparently, neither is your secretary. Your records are very vulnerable."

"I don't see how. Only our two computers are linked, but we're not open to the outside. Are we?"

"I sent an e-mail to your Catherine. As soon as she opened the attachment, I was in."

"Catherine's very strict about e-mail. I can't believe she'd open an attachment from someone she didn't know."

Again, that smug laugh. "It was disguised as coming from the Psychiatric Journal wanting updated information on you. It was a Trojan Horse virus that gave me remote access to her computer. So, at night, I could log on and view all your files."

"Which is how you gained access to the names of my former patients."

"See how easy that was?"

"But why?"

He shook his head. "We have plenty of time to talk, Dr. Westbrook." Matthew pulled off the main road and headed farther out into the foothills. "We'll be there soon enough."

By the time Jake got to her duplex and there was still no sign of Rick or Nicole, she was in panic mode. Steven did his best to calm her.

"We'd have heard something."

"From whom?" she nearly yelled, once again dialing Rick's cell. "Let's just go to Nicole's office and see what we find." She whistled for Cheyenne, pausing to grab two water bottles from her fridge, one of which she tossed to Steven. "Come on, Stevie. No time to waste."

Rick opened his eyes, then quickly shut them again. It hurt to blink, it hurt to move his eyes. He tried it again, a loud moan escaping as he struggled to sit up. He reached to the back of his head, feeling the wet stickiness.

"Fuck," he whispered. He rolled to his side, finding his cell. He held it to his face, but his eyes would not focus. He punched caller ID, knowing that Jake's cell was the third number. His head rested against the carpet, and he was aware of his shallow breathing.

Jake snatched up her phone on the first ring. "McCoy," she said tersely.

"It's me."

"Jesus Christ, Rick! Where are you? Are you okay?"

"I'm . . . I'm at Nicole's office . . . and no, not really okay," he murmured.

"Where's Nicole?"

"I don't know. I don't . . . know," he whispered.

"Hang on, buddy. I'm almost there." Jake disconnected, then tossed the phone to Steven. "Call it in. We need an ambulance."

"What about backup?"

"No time for that." She gripped the wheel tightly, speeding through downtown. "No time for Zeller."

Jake refused to speculate what was going on. It would do no good. So, she pushed her personal feelings aside and tried to focus on the situation. If Rick was injured, and he didn't know where Nicole was, chances were, she'd been . . . taken.

By him.

"Goddamn *fucker*," she murmured, as she sped down the streets.

"So? What do you think?"

Nicole stood outside the small cabin, still handcuffed to Matthew Gregory. With dismay, she noted the seclusion of the cabin. She was on her own.

"Nice," she finally said.

"It's cozy, I'll say that." He pulled her up the steps and opened the front door. Not exactly spacious, but the living room was indeed cozy as it was flanked on one side by the opened kitchen and a giant fireplace on the opposite wall. "I know it's cold," he said. "And if you'll behave long enough, I'll get a fire going."

"Were you this courteous to your previous victims?"

He walked closer. "I was as courteous as I needed to be."

Nicole swallowed nervously, reminding herself to hold her

tongue. This young man held her life in his hands. She stood still as he produced a handcuff key and unlocked them. She instinctively rubbed her wrist where the cuff had been.

"Did I hurt you?"

She shook her head. "No, I'm okay."

He nodded. "Please sit there," he said, pointing to the worn sofa. "I'll get a fire going."

She silently watched him, wondering if she should make a run for the door. Common sense told her to stay put. For one thing, she doubted she could outrun a twenty-four-year-old kid. No matter how scared she was.

Jake pulled on one of the doors, surprised that it was unlocked. She'd had visions of having to shatter the glass doors to gain entrance. She walked quickly past the empty reception desk and punched the elevator button impatiently.

"You think this place stays unlocked?"

Jake glanced at Steven, then punched the button again. "Who the hell knows? With our luck, probably." The quiet tone of the elevator signaled its arrival, and Jake squeezed between the doors as soon as they opened.

"Once we get to the floor, stay behind me," she said. "We don't know what we're going to find."

Steven nervously clasped and unclasped his hands as he watched the digital numbers announce each floor. "Ambulance should be right behind us. Right?"

"Right," Jake murmured. The doors opened quietly, and she reached for her weapon, holding it out in front of her as she walked silently toward Dr. Westbrook's office. "The blinds are down," she murmured.

"What?"

"The blinds. They're down. They're always up."

The office door was ajar, and Jake used her foot to ease it open slowly. Her gut told her it was clear, but she wouldn't take the chance. She motioned Steven against the wall, then slid her hand through the door, touching the light switches and illuminating the inner office. Nothing looked out of place.

"Rick?" she called. She moved into the room, weapon pointing out in front her. Her eyes flew to Nicole's office door. It, too, was ajar. She cocked her head, listening. "Ricky?" she called again. Nicole's office door moved, opening slightly.

When Steven moved forward, Jake stopped him. "Wait. Let's make sure," she whispered. She moved silently against the wall, her eyes glued to the opening. But she needn't have worried. Rick's faint voice called to her.

"Jake. You there?"

Jake pushed the door open, hitting Rick's leg in the process. She flipped on the light switch by the door. Her partner lay sprawled, face down, eyes closed. She quickly knelt beside him, gently touching his head.

"Ricky? What happened, buddy?"

"Don't really know," he whispered.

"You've got a knot the size of a baseball," she said. "It's split open."

"I know." He showed her his bloody hand.

Jake bent close to his ear. "Where's Nicole?"

"He has her," Rick murmured. "I'm sorry I . . . failed."

"You shut the fuck up. You didn't fail." Jake looked at Steven. "Where's the goddamn ambulance?"

"I'll . . . I'll go downstairs and wait."

"Call it in again. Tell them we have an officer down," Jake said calmly, knowing that Steven was probably ready to piss in his pants.

"I'm on it," he said and bolted from the room.

"Jesus, Jake . . . what have you done to him? He's a computer nerd," Rick mumbled.

"I think he prefers computer 'geek'." Jake stretched out on the floor beside Rick, meeting his tired eyes. "Tell me what happened."

Rick closed his eyes for a second, then opened them and met Jake's. "She was in the room there. The file room . . . by Catherine's desk," he murmured. He closed his eyes again. "I saw that her office door was open. It had been closed when we got here," he said slowly. "He was in here." When he opened his eyes, Jake was there. "I walked right into it. He was behind the door. Nice looking young man," he whispered.

"Okay." Jake reached out and squeezed his hand. "Just lie still, Ricky. Close your eyes," she said softly. "We'll find her."

CHAPTER FIFTY-SIX

Jake slowly ran her fingers through Cheyenne's fur as she listened to Captain Zeller on the phone. The night air was cold, and she watched Steven's breath frost around him as he waited.

"Yes, sir. I understand. First thing in the morning, yes sir."

As she disconnected the call, she just barely resisted the urge to hurl the phone across the parking lot.

"The son-of-a-bitch wants to wait until goddamn morning to meet on this. Wants to give Lieutenant Gregory time to *surface*," she said. She paced next to her vehicle, between Steven, who had moved farther away from her, and Cheyenne, who was still hanging her head out the window. "Well . . . *fuck* that," she said. "Stevie, I need you now," she said seriously. "We've got to dig and dig fast."

"I can dig."

"Your office? My house? Where?"

"My computer in my office is top-notch. Let's go there."

"What about covering your tracks?"

"Not a problem," he said as he slammed the door. "But what are we digging for?"

"Matthew Gregory has to be somewhere. We've got to find him."

"I've already checked bank records, credit cards," Steven said. He quickly locked his seatbelt as Jake darted into traffic. "He had none. If he's at a motel, he's paid cash and used a fake name."

"Not a motel. Not for what he does. He has to have someplace private."

"The only property that came back to your lieutenant was his house."

"Then we'll have to dig deeper, won't we?"

Steven nodded. "I can dig."

Nicole watched as the flames grew, shooting up the chimney and emitting a tiny bit of warmth into the cabin. She still could not prevent herself from wrapping her arms around herself from the cold. Matthew was still feeding the fire, piling on another log, and Nicole wondered how much time she had left. *Was Jake looking for her?* Of course. But Jake would need time, and Nicole needed to give her time.

"It's already warmer in here," she said quietly. "Thank you."

"You don't have to thank me," he said.

He rubbed his hands together, then took off his jacket and tossed it on a chair, leaving him in his starched white shirt and dress pants. He was a handsome young man, Nicole noted. It had probably been easy for him to gain the trust of her former patients as he seduced them . . . and then killed them.

"I was wondering, maybe we could read your mother's file now," she said. "I'm sorry, but nine years ago, I don't remember it."

He nodded. "No, I'm sure you don't remember her. I've been through your records, remember? You've been very busy, Dr.

Westbrook. Not only do you take hopeless cases from the crisis center, you also have been taking Dr. Peterson's rejects all these years."

Nicole frowned. "What do you mean?"

"Come on, haven't you noticed? Your friend Dorothy only refers patients to you who are about to bolt or who need hospitalization. Those patients that she can milk for years and years, she keeps for herself."

"So you've been checking her files as well?"

He smiled and nodded. "She's been using you, Dr. Westbrook. Dumping all her garbage on you while she keeps the fat accounts."

"That would be unethical, and Dorothy Peterson is anything *but* unethical."

"Why do you think she referred Lori Simmons to you? She'd had a couple of years with her, yet was still getting nowhere. When she realized that Lori was about to quit or do herself in, she shoved her off on you. And then what? Two or three sessions with you and then gone."

Nicole cleared her throat. "She was . . . murdered."

Again the smile. "Murdered or not, she wasn't going to show up at your door again."

Nicole motioned to the file that Matthew had tossed on the table. "Are you ready to read it?"

He looked at it, then slid his eyes back to Nicole. "You're a little anxious about what it contains, aren't you?" He shrugged. "I can't blame you. You feel responsible." He met her eyes. "But you shouldn't."

"But I should," she countered.

He raised his hands. "You can't possibly control other people's actions, Dr. Westbrook. Surely, in your line of work, you've uttered those very words," he said.

She nodded. "Of course."

With that, he pointed to the file. "Feel free. See if it . . . enlightens you."

Nicole stood, casually walking to the table to get the file. Yes, she was eager to read it, to see if it shed any light on this young man who held her captive.

"There's really nothing here to offer you to drink," Matthew said. He opened up a couple of cabinets and Nicole watched a frown form on his handsome face. "Although, apparently, someone's left us some scotch." He held the bottle up. "Would you like a drink?"

Nicole was about to decline, then reconsidered. If he drank with her, perhaps it would loosen him up, perhaps he would confide in her. She nodded. "I'll join you for a drink."

He met her eyes and smiled, as if reading her thoughts. "Straight up?"

She cocked her head. "Do you mind adding a splash of water to mine?"

He laughed. "A lesbian, but still a lady."

Her eyes widened in shock. He knew? Of course he knew. He'd been watching her.

"The closet, it's a lonely place, isn't it?"

"I doubt I'd have a practice if I was out," she said.

"You've listened to the old lady for too long, Dr. Westbrook. She's living in another era."

"Dr. Peterson?"

"Yes. That's quite a group of powerful women she's amassed, isn't it? One even hoping to be mayor? Doctors and lawyers, all tucked safely in the closet." He handed Nicole her drink and sat at the opposite end of the sofa, giving her space.

"You . . . know an awful lot," she said.

"Yes, I do. I also know you're bucking their little system by hanging out with your cop friend."

Nicole visibly swallowed. Of course he would know about Jake.

"She's cute. I like her for you. A lot better than that surgeon you went out with the other week. She has no . . . convictions. No scruples. You, Dr. Westbrook, are honorable. You need someone the same."

She cleared her throat. "You . . . listen in on conversations?"

"No. I've not broken that privacy." He motioned to the file. "Read. I'm afraid time is not exactly on our side, Dr. Westbrook."

She didn't need to ask what he meant by that. She dutifully opened the file, scanning Dorothy's handwritten notes that she'd jotted down upon referral. There was no mention of sexual abuse. She only hinted that perhaps Rebecca Gregory was in a verbally abusive relationship. Nothing about a son.

"You're frowning," he said. "What?"

"Nothing. I was reading Dr. Peterson's notes." She watched as he impatiently tapped his fingers on his leg. She wondered what he hoped to find in the file.

"I only met you one time, you know. It was the second to last appointment she had with you. I was fourteen, almost fifteen, I think. She had picked me up earlier from school. I was being punished and wasn't allowed alone," he said vaguely. "I remember sitting in your office, waiting. You walked out with my mother and when you looked at me, I could see in your eyes that something clicked."

"What do you mean?"

He shook his head. "Nothing. Read the file. Then you tell me."

She studied him for a second. He wanted her to read the file, he wanted her to bring up the sexual abuse. He wanted to talk about it. He spent six years at Trinity Clinic. They knew of the abuse. Had he not ever talked about it? All these years, keeping it inside, until he snapped, snapped so completely that he went on a murder spree.

So, she read, reacquainting herself with Rebecca Gregory. As she read the notes she made after each session, she realized how much she'd grown over the years. Some of her comments were so elementary, right out of the books she'd studied. There was little insight on her behalf, just clinical answers to the responses Rebecca had given her. And at first, she, too, suspected the woman was abused. Not physically, no. There was no evidence of that. She sipped her drink occasionally, aware of the silent man beside her.

323

Her breath caught as she read the entry she'd made on . . . yes, the second to last visit. The first truly insightful observation on her part.

Met her son today. The haunted, defeated look in his eyes spoke volumes. Rebecca is not the victim here. Something she said last week comes to mind. She mentioned how she and her husband were so far away from each other but that she and her son were very close. The boy that I met today did not mirror those feelings. There was no love or admiration in his eyes for Rebecca. There was simply a wariness. I fear he is the victim. Next session, let's talk about the son. Perhaps she would not be opposed to have him sit in with us. Check with Dorothy and get her feelings on this.

Her hand trembled as she turned the page. Bits and pieces came back to her. She remembered now that she'd confronted Rebecca. And Rebecca had run.

Rebecca did not wish to discuss her son. We got nowhere. Frustrated. I finally asked her point blank. Was she having a sexual relationship with her son? The answer was in her eyes, but she denied it. She cut our session short. I fear I won't see her again. The human side of me says to call Child Protective Services. The ethical side of course won. Rebecca is my patient, not the son.

There was only one more entry, dated the next week. *No show.*

And Rebecca and her son had faded from her mind as others came through her door to take their place, their problems and troubles pushing Rebecca Gregory's away.

She cleared her throat. "Was it true?" When she met his eyes, it was the same haunted look that she now remembered.

"Yes, it was true," he murmured.

She took a deep breath, knowing instinctively that he wanted to talk. "When did it begin, Matthew?"

"Seems like it was always that way," he said, his eyes still far away. He finally blinked and shifted on the couch. "When I was a little boy, I remember her touching me and stuff. Touching me . . . there." He shrugged. "I was a kid, but I knew it wasn't right. But she was my mother."

"Was it occasionally? Or all the time?"

"All the time."

"You never thought to tell your father?"

"No. I knew he would beat her. He used to beat her. I remember the horrible fights. Something happened, because he stopped. I asked her once, and she said they had come to an understanding. So I didn't want him to start hitting her again."

Nicole leaned closer, unable to stop herself as she clasped her fingers around his forearm. "When did the touching turn to more?"

She watched as he stared into the fire, unblinking. "I was fourteen."

"And did you know what was happening?"

"I wasn't that naive, Dr. Westbrook. Of course I knew what was happening."

"I'm sorry. I didn't know if maybe you had withdrawn from society and lived in a bubble, where it was only your mother."

"I was withdrawn, yes. I had no friends. I spent every spare moment on a computer."

Despite everything, Nicole's heart broke for the young man. He was very attractive. She could imagine that girls would have been swooning over him in high school.

"Once your relationship became sexual, did you not consider telling your father at that time?"

"No. I was too embarrassed. And by that time, the whole thing was almost normal to me. I had no problem getting an erection. She told me—and in my young mind I believed her—that she was simply teaching me, so that when I got married, I'd know."

"Weren't you afraid your father would catch you?"

He laughed. "Terrified. So was she." He spread his hands out. "Why do you think she bought this?"

"So this is where you'd come?"

He pointed to a closed door. "In there. That was our room. She'd pick me up after school, and we'd come here. Not every day. Most days."

"Did you ever protest?"

"Like I said, it had become routine, normal. There was nothing to protest."

"So you were getting pleasure from it?" She saw him swallow before he answered.

"I was a teenager having sex almost every day. As long as I didn't dwell on the fact that it was my mother I was fucking, yeah, I got pleasure."

The anger that Nicole heard in his voice frightened her, and Nicole was afraid she'd overstepped her boundary. They weren't doctor-patient. He was a murderer, and she was his hostage.

He stood up, and she shrank back against the couch. But his apology startled her.

"I'm sorry. I didn't mean to be so blunt." He was pacing now, and Nicole watched as he moved back and forth in front of the fire. "Yes, it bothered me. When I was at school, when I was at home, it bothered me. It was disgusting to think that I was having sex with my mother. But when we came here, she was no longer my mother. She was just my lover. Here, I was normal. Out there," he said, pointing out the window. "Out there, I was a freak."

"So the only peace you had, you had here at this cabin," she stated quietly.

"Yes."

"And whatever you do here, it's normal," she guessed. "Is that why you brought them here?"

His eyes stared into hers, and she was surprised by the misting of tears she found there.

"Who?"

She looked away. Clearly, he was not ready to talk about the murders. So, she went back to his mother.

"What happened to your mother, Matthew?"

"I'm sure you know the answer to that, Dr. Westbrook." He wiped at his eyes and got himself under control again.

"You killed her?"

He smiled. "Don't you think I had a right to?"

"But you said it felt normal to you. Why would you kill her?"

Again he paced. The once starched shirt was now rumpled, the neat hair in disarray. Yes, he was the victim, Nicole noted. A victim who turned into a vicious killer.

"She told me once that you were the only one who suspected, you know." He walked back to the couch and sat down beside her. "She was wrong."

"What do you mean."

"He suspected."

"Your father?"

Matthew nodded. "It was a Sunday, cold, like today. We had a fire going. She had soup on the stove." He looked at Nicole. "It was nice," he said quietly. "He was supposed to be working."

Nicole's breath held. "He caught you?"

"He wasn't supposed to know about the cabin. It was ours. We were in the room there, I was . . . I was on top of her. She was begging me to . . . to take her harder. I just wanted to please her," he whispered. "Then he was there and he pulled me off her and threw me against the wall so hard I blacked out."

Without thought, Nicole's hand slid into his. "Then what happened?"

CHAPTER FIFTY-SEVEN

Jake paced back and forth behind Steven's chair. The thoughts running through her mind were threatening to drive her insane. All she could see was Nicole and some bastard hitting her, raping her . . . strangling her. Hell, she'd seen the bodies. She'd read the autopsies. She knew what he would do to her. What he may have already done. She also knew she could not live with herself if . . . if she was too late. She glanced again at her watch. Three hours since she'd been taken. Too much time.

"Steven? Anything?"

Steven turned around, his voice tense. "Don't you think I'll tell you if I find anything?"

"I'm sorry. *Fuck.*"

"I can't miraculously produce a hit." Steven leaned back in his chair. "I'm telling you, he doesn't own any property other than his house. We'd have found it by now."

"What if it's not in his name?"

"What do you mean?"

"What if the title is in someone else's name?"

"Jake, how is this going to help us? We still don't know the name."

Jake paced again. There had to be a place where Matthew Gregory went. Someplace private.

"Can you check property taxes?" she asked.

"Yes, of course. They're listed by county."

"Okay, let's check a hundred mile radius around Denver. See if Lieutenant Gregory pays taxes on property other than his home."

"Oh, man. I didn't even think of that," Steven said, as his fingers flew across the keyboard. Jake leaned over his shoulder, waiting while he searched. There were two hits. One was his home. The other, a cabin in Jefferson County owned by Rebecca Gregory. It had a Golden address.

"Golden Gate Canyon? Print us a map, Steven," she said excitedly. "That's where the son of a bitch is."

"Matthew?"

Tears had formed again, and he struggled to get the words out. She sat quietly, her hand held tightly in his.

"He . . . he tied me to a chair and put it by the bed. He had beaten my mother. Her face was just a mess. Blood everywhere. Her eyes, they pleaded with me to help her. But I couldn't. He had hit me so hard, I could hardly hold my head up."

"He made you watch while he raped her?" Nicole guessed.

Matthew nodded. "She couldn't even scream," he whispered. "He raped her over and over. Every time I begged him to stop, he hit me." He wiped at his eyes. "She had passed out. When he . . . when he put his hands around her neck, she was unconscious. She didn't know what happened. He squeezed so hard, he broke her neck. I can still hear the snapping of the bones."

His quiet voice echoed in the cabin and for once, Nicole was at a loss for words. She simply held his hand while he wept.

"I passed out, too. I wanted to die right along with her. But I wasn't so lucky. When I came to, he had her in the bathtub, soaking. The water was so full of blood." Matthew got up again and walked to the fire, tossing on another log. "He was disgusted with me. He said I was a pervert. He said if I told anyone what happened, he would say that I killed her. And it would come out that I'd been . . . having sex with her all those years. And who in the police department would believe me over him?"

Nicole nodded. "What did he do with her?"

"He cleaned her up and then took her away. He locked me in the room by myself," he said and his voice caught. "Not that I could have gone anywhere. I was so beat up, I looked like a truck had hit me." He gave a pitiful laugh. "And that's what he told everyone. That I'd been in a car accident."

"And you didn't tell a soul?"

He shook his head. "I dropped out of school two months before graduation."

Nicole nodded. "And came looking for me?"

"I was scared. I remembered the compassion in your eyes that day, you know. So I thought, maybe I'd look you up."

Nicole lost every ounce of professionalism she had at that point and she let her tears fall down her cheeks.

"I just couldn't bring myself to approach you."

"And you became . . . the stalker."

"The first time you reported it, my father put two and two together right away. He threatened to send me to Trinity if I didn't stop."

"So they didn't really shoot you that night," she said.

"Tranquilizer gun. I dropped like a rock."

"And he sent you away."

"It was probably for the best."

"He told them about you and your mother. You never said a word, did you?"

"No. I didn't . . . talk much. I behaved, and they were kind enough to get me a computer."

"And you were smart enough not to abuse it?"

He smiled. "I could hide myself quite well."

"Six years," she said. "Why now?"

"Why now?"

"The killings. Why did he start now?"

Matthew looked startled. "Everyone thinks I'm the killer."

"Yes. But you're not. Why the game?"

Matthew lowered his eyes. "He told me I would be blamed for them all anyway. I'd almost convinced myself I'd done it."

"He comes here with them, doesn't he?"

"Yes. He takes them to . . . *our* room," he finished in a whisper. "He *kills* them in . . . *our* room."

Nicole stood and went to him. She wrapped both arms around him and held him. "You're not a killer. You've done nothing wrong." She felt him relax, felt the tentative arms that reached around her waist. In that instant, she knew that she was the first person he'd had physical contact with in six long years.

"I know I'm not a cop, but isn't this where we should call for backup?" Steven asked, as he held on to the dash when Jake rounded a corner. "I mean, they do on TV."

"Normally, yes. But we have a captain that isn't sure he believes us, and we're accusing a lieutenant of a major coverup and possibly the murder of three cops."

"So . . . it's just us?"

"Sorry, Stevie. But don't worry. You're staying in the car with Cheyenne. You give me a little bit of a head start, then you call for backup. They'll have to notify Golden PD."

"You can't go in alone. You don't know what you'll find."

"I know what I'll find. He works alone."

But something was nagging at her, and she couldn't put her finger on it. It was something Rick had said about Gregory, about the murders. That he was nearly nonchalant about them. At first, he was gung-ho and riding their ass. But it was almost as if he backed off every time they found another body. Maybe he didn't want his son caught, maybe that was all. But hell, it wasn't like they had any leads that should have caused concern. The only thing was the stalker.

"And he ordered me to drop it," she murmured.

"What?"

She shook her head. "Thinking out loud." She turned off the highway and headed to Golden. "Nicole lives out this way. It would have been easy for him to slip to her house and then back to this cabin."

"We'll take Highway 93 all the way through Golden. Turn left on Tucker Gulch, also known as County Road 70."

"Listen, you got your notes with you?"

"Notes?"

"About the kid and all."

"Oh, yes." He pulled his PDA from his coat pocket.

"When did he get out of Trinity?"

"The exact date?"

"Yeah." Traffic was light on this early Sunday evening, and Jake cruised through Golden and headed out into the foothills of the Rockies. The light had faded from the sky and her headlights picked up patches of snow that had not melted during the day.

"June seventh," he said.

"Something's bothering me, Stevie." She pulled her cell from her pocket and dialed a number from memory. She waited only a few moments. "It's Detective McCoy, Special Victims. I need you to pull up a post for me."

"Who are you calling?" Steven asked quietly.

"ME's office."

"On a Sunday night?"

"Melissa works the night shift," she said. "Yeah, I'm here. Shelly Burke, back in June." She nodded. "Okay." She glanced at Steven. "Are you watching for our road?"

"Yeah. It should be the next one to the left."

"Thanks, Melissa. I'm just looking for dates. When the post was done and time of death." She frowned and nodded. "Thanks,

kid." She slipped her phone back into her jacket. "We got a problem."

"What?"

"They did the post on the sixth. They have her time of death as
the fourth."

"Matthew Gregory got out on the seventh."

"He's not our killer. At least, not Shelly Burke." Jake's hands
tightened on the wheel. "Of course, Shelly Burke was the only one
not dumped. She was found in her apartment. The others were
dumped."

Steven held his head with both hands. "This is making me
crazy. I think we really need some backup, Jake. We don't know
who the hell we're looking for now."

"We're looking for Nicole. And she's at this cabin."

"He threatened to kill you if I said anything. And again, he'd
blame it on me. So, over the years, I kept a watch out for you. I've
been in Catherine's computer for years. I knew who Shelly Burke
was. When I got the report that she'd been raped, strangled, I
knew it was him. And I couldn't take the chance that he'd go after
you."

"Why didn't you come to me then, Matthew?"

"I didn't think you'd believe me. A stranger walks in off the
street and tells you all this? What are you going to do?"

"Send you back to Trinity," she said honestly.

"Exactly." Again, he paced. "So, I watched you. I knew the cops
thought you were the link with these women. I also knew you
didn't really believe them. That's why I broke into your house that
night. I wanted to leave you a warning."

"Be careful," she said quietly, remembering the note.

"Yes."

She walked to him and took both of his hands. "Matthew, if
you're up to it, we need to go to the police. You need to let me call
Jake."

"Yes. I'm ready for it to be over."

"Good," she said, letting out a relieved sigh. "Is there a phone?"

"Not here, no."

"My cell is in your car."

"I'll get it. Stay here by the fire."

Nicole wrapped her arms around herself, trying to remain rational. The whole thing was one big nightmare. But it was about to be over. She watched as Matthew opened the door . . . and stopped dead in his tracks.

"Oh, *no*," Matthew hissed. He quickly shut the door and hurried back to Nicole.

"What is it?"

"My father. He *never* comes here on the weekends. We've got to get out!"

"Oh, God, no. He's *here*?"

The words had barely left her mouth when the front door burst opened and Lieutenant Gregory stood there, gun in hand. His other hand held a rope, of which he gave a forceful tug and a bound and gagged young woman was pulled into the room. Nicole's eyes widened. It was Joni Connell from her group session. Joni fell to her knees, then was kicked to the ground by Gregory.

"My, my. Thank you, son. You got the good doctor for me. Saved me the trouble. I was going to give her until Wednesday."

Matthew stood in front of Nicole, shielding her. "No. I won't let you hurt her."

He laughed. "Don't think I won't shoot you, Matthew."

Gregory walked closer and for the first time in her life, Nicole looked into the eyes of pure evil. And she was scared.

CHAPTER FIFTY-EIGHT

"It should be the next driveway," Steven said.

Jake killed the lights, thankful for the half-moon that hung high above them. The lot was wooded, and Jake pulled her Land Cruiser among the trees and stopped. They could see lights through the branches.

"I hope this is the right fucking cabin, Steven." She opened the door quickly. "Be right back. I just want to take a look."

She moved through the shadows, small twigs and pine cones cracking loudly beneath her boots. Her breath frosted around her as she squatted behind a large spruce. She moved the lower branches out of the way, seeing figures move across the windows. Smoke trailed out of the chimney, and she wondered if they had the wrong place. Surely their killer wouldn't take the time to build a fire. Then she spied the two vehicles in the drive and her eyes widened.

"Fuck," she whispered. She backed up, moving as quietly as possible to her vehicle. Once inside, she reached into the console and took out a gun. She inspected it, then loaded the chamber before handing it to Steve. "Here."

"No, Jake. I don't do guns. I'm a computer geek, remember."

"Take it, Steven. There are two cars. One belongs to my lieutenant. I'm going to assume the other is his son's."

"We need to call for backup," he said quickly.

"Yes. You do that. I'm going in."

"Jake, no, you wait for backup."

She met his eyes. "I just realized why police procedure forbids fraternization between partners. You lose your objectivity. Hell, you lose your common sense," she said.

"What the hell are you talking about?"

"I'm in love with her. And I'm going to get her out."

"Oh, fuck, Jake."

"You take care of my dog, Mr. Bond." Jake ruffled Cheyenne's head, then was gone.

"I said I would shoot *you*, Matthew. I'm not going to shoot the doctor. That would be far too quick and painless."

Joni struggled to sit up, and Gregory kicked her down again. Nicole could stand no more. She moved from behind Matthew, her voice pleading.

"Let her go. She's done nothing."

"Nothing? Why, Dr. Westbrook, surely you know the crime she's committed. She has a son. A *teenage* son."

"No. She's not touched him."

"Oh, please. They all have. They all do. That's why they're being punished. One by one, they're being punished."

However futile, Nicole tried to reason with him. "Lieutenant Gregory, you're a police officer. You should know better than anyone that you can't take the law into your own hands."

His hearty laughter caused her to take a step back toward Matthew. "They teach you that in school, did they? Are you going to quote next the line about me not being above the law?" His grin was wicked. "But you see, I am above the law. As McCoy likes to say—no prints, no fibers, no nothing." He laughed again. "And they'll never find anything." He walked closer. "And you know why? Because I'm a cop, and I know what they look for. How ironic is that?"

Matthew again stepped between them. "You've got to stop this."

"Shut up," Gregory said as his fist connected with Matthew's face, causing him to fall back against Nicole. "Fucking pervert." He looked at Nicole. "Do you know what he did? He fucked his own mother. Not just once, but for *years*. Fucked his mother. How sick is that?"

"Matthew was a victim of child abuse. How can you possibly blame him?"

"He was seventeen years old!" Gregory yelled. "Not a fucking child." He pointed his gun at Matthew. "Tell her how you fucked your mother."

Matthew wiped at the blood dripping from his nose. "I've already told her. You couldn't satisfy her so she turned to me."

Nicole pushed Matthew out of the way as Gregory swung at him. Her punishment was an open palm slap to the face. The force knocked her to her knees.

"Goddamn bitch! Oh, I'm going to enjoy you. Yes, I am."

Jake crept between the trees, her boots kicking blindly at the rocks that littered the forest floor. To her ears, it sounded inordinately noisy, and if not for the loud voices coming from the cabin, she was certain they would hear her approach. She heard her lieutenant's angry voice, and then heard Nicole. The tension that had gripped her for most of the afternoon eased somewhat. At least she knew Nicole was alive.

But her first step on the wooden deck screamed loudly in the night as the old wood creaked beneath her weight. She held her breath, waiting, but the voices continued. She squatted down below a window, making out Lieutenant Gregory, watching as he moved his weapon from his son to Nicole.

What the hell?

Instincts told her to break in and end this before he did something crazy. However, the tiny bit of rational thought she still clung to urged her to wait for backup. She didn't think Nicole was in immediate danger and with luck, her backup was on the way. Rick would be proud of her. She was operating somewhat by the book.

But when she saw her lieutenant hit Nicole and knock her to the ground, she stood, her anger bubbling to the surface. She walked purposefully to the side of the cabin and kicked in the door, tumbling on the floor to avoid the shot Gregory fired her way. She rolled up, her weapon ready. She found herself face to face with Lieutenant Gregory.

"Drop it, McCoy . . . or I'll drop you."

She grinned. "Right back at you, Lieutenant."

"You're not going to shoot me, McCoy. Everyone knows you're gun-shy."

Jake mirrored his movements as they circled the room. "No, sir, I'm not."

"Yeah, you are," he said. He fired the next instant, the bullet hitting her in the shoulder and knocking her weapon out of her hand. "See? Sharpshooter, my ass."

Jake stumbled backward against the wall. "No!" she yelled when Nicole would have run to her. Nicole sunk back down to the floor beside Matthew, her eyes wild with fright. Jake's right arm hung limply at her side and she fought against the pain.

"Well, well. We've got a houseful of people here now, don't we?" He paced, his weapon waving out in front of him. "What to do, what to do?" He stopped pacing and looked around. "You know what, McCoy? There are only two people in this room that I want to play with. And you're not one of them. Neither is the pervert."

"Sorry to crash your party," she managed.

He cocked his head. "By the way, where's that useless partner of yours?"

"Hospital."

"Oh yeah? What happened?"

"He's got a little headache." Jake shoved away from the wall, trying to turn her body. Her weapon lay next to the fireplace, too far away. Her spare gun was tucked behind her back. Unfortunately, it was positioned so that her right hand could reach it. Her now useless right hand. "Oh yeah, Captain Zeller was quite amazed at the tale we told him. You know, how you doctored the dispatch records six years ago. How four officers responded to a non-existent 911 call, three of whom are now dead. He was pretty interested in that part."

"You don't know what the fuck you're talking about."

"Computer geeks. They can find out so much shit, Lieutenant." Jake flicked her glance to Nicole. "Matthew knows all about that."

"Shut up! You didn't tell Zeller anything!"

Jake smiled. "Backup's on the way. You're done."

"The hell I am," he hissed. He grabbed Nicole and jerked her to her feet. Matthew tried to stop him, tugging at Nicole's arm. Gregory turned the gun on his son and pulled the trigger. Matthew clutched his chest, blood seeping through his fingers as he sunk to his knees. Nicole screamed, reaching for Matthew as he slipped away. She instinctively used her elbow to pound into Gregory's midsection as she fell to the ground.

Jake dove for her gun, picking it up the instant Gregory fired. She felt the pain shoot through her and she squeezed her eyes shut for a second, trying desperately to hold on to consciousness. She saw Nicole fall away and she fired, sending Gregory backward. But it wasn't a clean shot. He sat up, taking aim again. Jake tried to shoot but her right hand gave way and the gun fell harmlessly to the floor. She watched, helpless, as he pointed his weapon at her.

When she heard the shot, she braced herself, but she felt nothing. Instead, she watched as Lieutenant Gregory sunk lifelessly to the ground. Behind him, a wild-eyed Steven stood, hands shaking so badly, the gun fell from his hands.

Jake's eyes slid closed as the world faded away.

Nicole ran to Jake, falling to her knees beside her. "Steven! Help me," she yelled. There was so much blood, she didn't know where to start. She pushed open Jake's coat, finding her shirt nearly spotless. *Oh God, her leg again.* She saw the dark spot on her jeans as blood seeped through at an alarming rate. She lifted Jake's shirt. She wore no belt.

"Give me your belt," she said to Steven. He quickly took it off and Nicole snatched it from him, tying it tightly above the wound, trying to stop the blood loss. "Ambulance?"

"Yes. I called for backup. They should be here by now."

Nicole motioned to the woman still tied and gagged. "Check on her. Her name is Joni."

When Steven moved away, Nicole bent close to Jake, whispering in her ear. "Please don't leave me, Jake. Please don't go."

She listened for a moment to her shallow breathing, praying the ambulance would hurry. She heard moaning behind her and looked up, seeing Matthew's hand twitching. She kissed Jake softly, then moved to Matthew, surprised that he was still alive. She took his hand and felt his gentle squeeze.

"Hang on, Matthew. It's all over now." His eyes fluttered open, and Nicole couldn't stop the tears that escaped. She squeezed his hand harder. "It's going to be okay."

"I don't . . . think so." He tried to swallow, but blood came out his mouth. Nicole smoothed the hair on his handsome face, trying to comfort him. "Remember me once in awhile," he whispered.

"I'll never forget."

His last breath came quickly, and Nicole wiped away her tears with blood-stained hands. She moved back to Jake, gently cradling her head in her lap, brushing her hand through Jake's hair over and over again. Joni was huddled in one corner, in shock, no doubt. Steven was on the phone, asking where the goddamn ambulance was. Nicole felt a brief smile touch her face. Steven had been hanging around Jake too long.

CHAPTER FIFTY-NINE

Nicole knocked gently on the door, then walked in. Rick slowly moved his head, his eyes lighting up when he saw her.

"Damn. You're okay?"

She nodded and managed a smile.

"I'm sorry, Nicole. He got me from behind."

"It's okay. I'm fine."

He looked behind her. "Where's Jake?"

Nicole moved closer, finally taking his hand, needing some physical contact. "She is . . . she's here, actually."

"Here? Admitted?"

"Yes, here."

Nicole closed her weary eyes for a second. She and Steven had taken Cheyenne to Jake's duplex, and she'd showered and changed, but she still felt totally exhausted.

"Is she . . . okay?"

"She's in surgery. She was shot . . . oh, damn Ricky, in her leg again."

"Oh no. Same leg?"

"Yes. Almost the same spot, about an inch higher. She lost a lot of blood." Nicole raised her hand to her right shoulder. "She also got hit here, but they said it was clean, no bone damage."

"Did she get the bastard?"

Nicole nodded. "She and Steven, yeah, they got your lieutenant."

"Steven? The lieutenant?" He squeezed her hand. "What about the son?"

Nicole shook her head. "He wasn't the killer. He was . . . a victim. But he's dead, too. His father shot him in the chest," she said matter-of-factly, somewhat pleased that she was able to keep her emotions in check. She'd broken down earlier in front of Steven, and he'd wrapped his long arms around her without hesitation.

"Jesus Christ, Nicole."

Nicole nodded. "So how are you feeling?" she asked, changing the subject.

"They tell me I have a super-duper concussion. If I keep still, I can't feel my brain moving from side to side."

She smiled. "I can't believe you let them buzz your head."

"They shaved around the wound first. I looked ridiculous."

Nicole touched the fine hair on Rick's head. "I'm glad you're okay. I was really worried."

"Yeah. I'm going to be fine. Say, where's Cheyenne?"

"She's at home. I think Steven is going to get her tonight. He lives in an apartment though, so we'll need to make some arrangements."

"No, it's okay. I'm getting out tomorrow. I'll take care of her."

"Are you sure?"

"Yeah. I'll just bunk at Jake's place." He shifted on the bed. "How long before we can see her?"

"They're going to keep her sedated. If this surgery goes well, they're going to do her shoulder tomorrow. I'm guessing Tuesday before she's awake enough for us to see her."

"Damn. Being laid up the first time just about killed her."

"At least she won't have the haunting image of a little boy this time," Nicole said quietly.

"She told you about that?"

"Yes." Nicole finally let go of his hand and moved away. "There's a patient of mine in here that I want to go visit. Do you mind?"

"No, of course not. Is it someone—"

"Yes. She was involved." Nicole swallowed. "She was to be the next victim," she whispered. "I just want to check on her."

Nicole knocked lightly on the door then pushed it opened. Joni lay curled on her bed, covers pulled to her chin. Her eyes blinked several times as Nicole walked into the light.

"Joni? Feel like talking?"

Joni sat up and nodded, but still, pulled the covers up with her. "Dr. Westbrook, are you okay?"

"I'm fine, Joni. But I was worried about you."

She shrugged. "A few bruises. Nothing I ain't used to." She pointed to Nicole's face. "Your cheek is swollen."

Nicole raised a hand to her face, lightly touching her bruised cheek. "Yes. It's nothing compared to what others suffered."

"That policewoman, did she live?"

Nicole closed her eyes for a moment and nodded. "Yes, she did. She's in surgery."

"I felt like I was on a movie set."

Nicole smiled. "But a lot scarier."

"Yes. I was scared. I knew for sure he was going to kill me. He told me so. But when I saw you, I felt . . . hope."

Nicole took her hand, feeling the need to explain. "Joni, the man who did this, he had killed others. Other patients of mine."

"Why?"

"He was trying to kill his wife. He was trying to kill her again and again."

"I don't understand."

"He murdered his wife years ago. She was a patient of mine before that." Nicole shrugged. "I'm not sure of his reasoning. I don't know what triggered him to start again." She released Joni's hand. "But I want you to know, if you'd like a referral to another doctor, I wouldn't blame you. It's your choice."

"Leave the group session?"

"Yes."

"No, Dr. Westbrook. I like the group. I feel good when we meet. I don't want to stop."

"Okay. I just wanted to give you the option."

"This guy is dead right? He won't hurt us anymore?"

Nicole nodded. "Yes, he's dead."

"Then I want to stay with you."

CHAPTER SIXTY

Wednesday morning, Nicole opened Jake's door, not surprised to find Rick sitting beside her bed. Jake was much as she'd left her the night before—pale and unconscious.

"Hey, Rick."

"Hey. I didn't expect you back already. The nurse said you'd been here most of the night."

"Yes. I didn't want to leave her." Nicole moved closer to the bed. "Shouldn't she be awake by now?" she whispered. "It's going on three days."

"Soon, they say."

"That's what they said last night."

"They said all her vitals are good."

Nicole picked up Jake's limp hand, wrapping her fingers around it. "She's so pale. She looks so fragile."

"Yeah, I know. She didn't look like this the first time. She came to right away, and she was cranky as hell."

"She lost a lot of blood. I hope—"

"No. They said she was fine. They told me earlier that it'd probably be another couple of hours before she woke."

Nicole touched Jake's face once, then bent quickly and placed a light kiss on her dry lips. "I should probably get going then. Get some work out of the way while she's out."

"Yeah, I see you're back to the suits," Rick said, pointing to her outfit.

Nicole smoothed her hands over her gray skirt. "Catherine didn't waste any time in getting my appointments scheduled. I'll come back this afternoon to see her. If she wakes, please tell her I was here."

Rick nodded. "Of course. I'm just going to hang out for awhile. I don't want her to come to and there not be anyone here, you know."

Nicole felt a blanket of guilt cover her. She should be here when Jake woke. She owed Jake her life. Part of her wanted to say the hell with her practice. The appointments would just have to wait. But then she heard Dorothy's voice, her words from last night echoing in her brain.

"It's time to put this in the past, Nicole, and get on with your life. You've got to get your appointments scheduled again. When the full story hits the paper, God knows what will happen. You could lose half your patients."

So, Nicole had called Catherine at home last night, told her to be at the office. A handful of appointments today. The group session tomorrow. Despite everything that had happened, nothing had really changed.

"By the way, how was Cheyenne last night?"

"Restless. She's one smart dog. I swear, I'm talking to her like she's human, telling her Jake was in the hospital. She looked right into my eyes. I do believe she understood every word."

"You may be right." She squeezed Rick's shoulder as she turned away. "I'll be back this afternoon, as soon as I've got the office squared away."

Rick just nodded, his eyes still focused on Jake.

346

Nicole rounded the corner on her way out and bumped into Steven, literally. He grabbed her arm to steady her, then laughed.

"High heels will get you every time."

"Hi, Steven. Yes, a week out of them. I am a little wobbly." She bent to sniff the flowers he held. "Beautiful."

"Is she awake yet?"

"No. Rick's there. He said a few more hours."

"Oh. Well, I'm still on forced vacation, so I thought I'd come and sit with her."

Nicole affectionately squeezed his hand. "Are you okay about . . . everything? I know you met with the police psychologist yesterday."

"Yes. And I've got to meet with him again this afternoon."

"And?"

He looked away. "It's still hard for me to come to terms with what I did." His voice lowered. "Nicole, I took a man's life."

"Steven, listen to me. You did not take that man's life. His life was over, one way or the other. What you did was *save* three people's lives." She felt tears gather in her eyes and watched as Steven's misted over as well. "We wouldn't be here today visiting Jake, we'd be at a cemetery burying her, Steven, if you hadn't been there." She squeezed his hand again. "Don't forget that."

"I shot him in the back."

"You did what you had to do. I would have done the same thing, Steven. He was about to kill Jake," she whispered. "If you hadn't been there, I would have been next, then Joni." She bent closer and kissed him lightly on the lips. "So I thank you with all my heart for being there." She pulled away from him, gently wiping at a tear that escaped his eye. "You're a good guy, Stevie. Your wife is very lucky."

He stepped back and cleared his throat, but the blush on his face was still bright. "Thank you. I just might be able to live with this now."

Rick looked up when the door opened, smiling slightly when Steven stuck his head inside.

"Hey, man."

"Rick."

"She's still out."

"Yeah, I talked to Nicole." He pulled the other chair from against the wall and sat down, sliding his roses onto a table. "They won't let me go back to work yet so I thought I'd hang out here."

"Internal Affairs?"

Steven nodded. "I've got to meet with the shrink again this afternoon."

"I've never had to do that. Jake says it's a bitch."

"I'd much rather talk to someone like Nicole, you know. She has this compassion about her. Dr. Rinehart is just so . . . clinical."

"Nicole was back in her power suit today."

"Yes. She looked nice."

"That's Jake's gauge."

"What?"

"The bigger the power suit, the less Jake fits in her life."

"What do you mean? I thought they were a couple," Steven said.

Rick shook his head. "No, not really. This case kinda threw them together."

"But that night, Jake told me she loved Nicole, that's why she went in without backup."

"Damn stubborn woman," Rick murmured. "But yeah, Jake's got it bad for her. I don't think Nicole feels the same."

"That's too bad. Jake, she's . . . she's something special."

Rick nodded. "Yeah, she is."

Steven cleared his throat. "I think they're really cute together, though."

Rick laughed. "Jesus, we're sitting here discussing two lesbians. How pathetic is that?"

But Steven didn't answer. He was staring at Jake. "She moved her hand, Rick."

Rick watched Jake and sure enough, the fingers on her left hand moved against the white sheet of her hospital bed. Rick stood quickly, taking those fingers in his hand.

"Jake? You back with us?" He touched her cheek, urging her to wake. "Come on, Jake. Talk to me. Wake up." He saw her eyelids flutter, but not open. Finally, a low moan and a squeeze of her fingers.

"Thirsty," she breathed.

"Oh, thank God." Rick reached for the water that the nurse had placed beside the bed. "Tiny sip, Jake," he said, placing the straw against her dry lips. She managed one sip before turning her head away.

"Ricky?"

"I'm here."

"Nicole? Okay?"

"Yes, she's fine. She was here earlier. She had appointments today." Rick watched as Jake's eyes tried to open, but failed.

"Steven okay?" she murmured.

Steven stood and walked to the bed, squeezing Jake's good shoulder. "I'm here, Jake," he said.

"My own James Bond. Thank you," she whispered, before drifting back into unconsciousness.

Steven turned away, trying to hide his tears from Rick. He wiped them away quickly.

"You okay, man?"

"Yes."

Rick grabbed his arm and turned him around, shocked by the tears in his eyes. "Steven?"

"It's nothing."

"James Bond?"

Steven managed a smile. "Private joke."

CHAPTER SIXTY-ONE

"Two have opted to stay with Dr. Andrews," Catherine said, as she went over her notes.

Nicole nodded. "That's fine." She twirled her pen absently between her fingers, wondering what she was doing here. Wondering why she wasn't at the hospital, sitting with Jake. Wondering why she was listening to Dorothy yet again.

"I've pretty much booked you up for the next two days. The group session will be tomorrow. Everyone is anxious to get back at it."

"I can't believe, after what was in the paper this morning, that they're still willing to see me."

Catherine shrugged. "Well, he's dead."

"Yeah. And I should have taken a week or two off," Nicole murmured.

"Do you want to?"

Nicole sighed. "Dorothy says I've taken enough time off the past few weeks."

"Well, she knows best, of course," Catherine said a little sarcastically.

"What do you mean by that?"

"Nothing." Catherine flipped a page on her notebook. "You've got a dinner scheduled Saturday night with Dr. Henson's group. It's been set for months, but I can try and change it if you'd like," Catherine offered.

"No, that's fine."

"Patrice Kane called to remind you of the luncheon at the crisis center next Tuesday. She said to tell you that it will be a media event, with Deb Fisher scheduled to make an appearance."

Great. Deb Fisher. Nicole rubbed her forehead, wishing she could find some enthusiasm for these events that used to be so routine for her. A routine she used to be content with, but now it only seemed arduous and taxing. And depressing. She could find little joy in it all. In fact, it was very disheartening. Because now that the case was over, now that she could resume her practice, her life, there was really no place for Jake. Despite the fact that they both knew this would happen, even though they never discussed it, didn't make it any easier to accept. The reality was, Jake was out of her life. She could prolong it by going to the hospital, staying with her. But it didn't change the fact that Jake didn't fit in her life.

"And it hurts," she murmured.

"What?"

Nicole opened her eyes, meeting Catherine's frown head on. "Nothing. I was just . . . nothing." Nicole cleared her throat. "Is that it?"

Catherine tidied her file and placed it in her lap, finally looking up at Nicole. "So, how is she today?"

Nicole didn't have to ask who Catherine referred to. "She still wasn't awake this morning. Rick and Steven were there."

Catherine shook her head disapprovingly. "You should be there when she wakes up."

Nicole leaned forward. "Yes, I would love to. Except *someone* scheduled appointments for me."

"Well, *someone* told me to get on the ball."

Nicole nodded. "Catherine, I think perhaps I wanted to jump back in full force, because if I didn't, I'd just put it off and want to stay . . ."

"With Jake?" Catherine guessed.

"I thought it would be easier to break away now, while she's . . . out of it," Nicole confessed a bit guiltily.

"Why do you need to break away?"

Nicole stood and paced behind her desk, absently noting the snow flurries hitting her eighth-floor window. How did she tell Catherine that she was in danger of falling hopelessly in love with the woman? And the longer she stayed with her, the harder it would be to leave, the harder it would be to get back to her life.

"Nicole?"

Nicole stopped her pacing, her eyes sad as she looked at Catherine. "We had a good time together, Catherine. But we both knew it was temporary." She waved her hand at her office. "This is my life. Appointments, group sessions, arranged dinners and luncheons." She sighed. "And blind dates and outings with Dorothy's powerful group of women." She shrugged. "It's my life, but it could never be Jake's."

Catherine stared, shaking her head disapprovingly. "This has nothing to do with your so-called life. You're in love with her, and you're running from it."

"No. I'm not in love with her," Nicole said forcefully, and she wondered if she was trying to convince Catherine or herself. "This is best. There's no need to prolong it."

"She's been shot, and she's in the hospital." Catherine stood and clutched the file to her chest. "I just can't believe you."

She turned and left, leaving Nicole staring after her.

When Nicole quietly opened the door to Jake's room, she was surprised to find the bed empty. She had a moment of panic and rushed back out. She grabbed the first nurse she could find.

"Detective McCoy? In room 1288?"

"Yes ma'am?"

"She's not in there."

"No. I believe she's in surgery."

"What happened?" Nicole demanded.

The nurse smiled reassuringly. "I'm sorry. You'll have to be in touch with her doctor or a family member."

"Where's Detective Chase?"

"He's been here all day. I would assume he's in the third floor waiting room."

Nicole nodded and hurried off, chastising herself. She should have been here. She should never have scheduled appointments this week until she was sure Jake was going to be fine. My God, she'd acted as if Jake meant nothing to her, as if the woman hadn't saved her life. As if . . . as if she didn't love her. *Damn.*

She hurried off the elevators on the third floor and walked down the familiar hallway. Rick sat alone, slumped down in the corner of the sofa. His eyes opened when she approached.

"What's going on, Rick?" she asked, not bothering with pleasantries.

He sat up and rubbed his eyes. "I'm not really sure. They wouldn't tell me much." He smirked. "Not family, you know."

"What *did* they tell you?"

"She had a lot of swelling in her thigh. Something about her artery not being clear."

"Blood clot?"

He shrugged.

"What about her parents? Has anyone tried to contact them?"

"No. For one thing, who knows where they are? I think Jake said they were going to Florida this winter." Rick sat up and stretched his back. "Anyway, she never called them this summer when she was laid up, either."

Nicole shook her head. "That makes no sense."

"She didn't want to worry them, didn't want them to feel like they had to come and stay with her."

"Are they just not very close?"

"I don't know. She doesn't talk about them much. I know they call and check in every once in awhile."

Nicole knew Jake was a loner and wasn't surprised that she didn't want anyone hovering over her while she was recuperating. She and Cheyenne had managed just fine. And no doubt, they would do it again. So, she sunk down on the worn sofa next to Rick and crossed her legs, wishing she'd taken the time to change into some comfortable clothes.

"I heard someone say it was snowing," Rick said.

"Just flurries. But it's quite cold."

"I feel bad. I left Cheyenne outside this morning."

"I'm going to stay, Rick. Why don't you run to Jake's and check on her?"

"No, I don't want to leave."

"I'm sure you'll be back long before they even bring her out again."

Rick hesitated, knowing how much that dog meant to Jake, but not wanting to leave in case something happened. He finally nodded. "You're right. It won't take me long. You've got my cell?"

"Yes. I wrote it on the back of Jake's card."

"Okay. I'll be back as soon as I can."

"Be careful."

Nicole watched the elevator doors close then glanced around her, noting the handful of people who waited for loved ones. Again, she felt a pang of guilt that she hadn't been with Jake the whole time. Sunday night, she'd feared for her life, and Jake had come busting in the front door to save her. Now, Wednesday night, and she'd still not talked to Jake, not looked into her eyes. Not said . . . thank you.

She sighed heavily and closed her eyes, wondering when her life had become so complex. And wondering why she dreaded going back to the life she had before Jake walked into it.

CHAPTER SIXTY-TWO

"About damn time, McCoy," Rick said. "I'm tired of seeing you flat on your back."

Jake grinned, shifting her shoulders higher on the bed. "I'll be lucky if I don't have bed sores."

"You need a haircut."

Jake lifted her left arm and raked her fingers through her hair, hair that was in desperate need of a wash.

"Ricky, I'll pay you fifty bucks if you'll shampoo my hair."

"And how do you propose I do that? You're not allowed out of the bed."

Jake arched an eyebrow. "Grab an empty bedpan and a pitcher of water. How hard can it be?"

"You're trying to get me kicked out of here, aren't you?"

"You're my only visitor. Why would I want you kicked out?"

"Hardly your only visitor. You're just not awake when she comes by."

"Funny how that is, isn't it?"

"She's got her practice going again, Jake. She's busy."

Jake nodded. "Yeah, I know. I know."

"She's been here every day."

Jake touched her injured right shoulder and rubbed it lightly, eyes closed. She tried to push away the hurt feelings and not dwell on it. The case was over, and Nicole had every right to resume the life she had before Jake became a part of it. And by all accounts, she had resumed it. And, eventually, Jake would resume hers as well.

"How's Cheyenne?" Jake asked, changing the subject.

"She's spoiled rotten, that's how she is. I can't make her go outside when I leave, so I assume she spends her days on the couch. She's there when I leave and there when I get home."

"Do you think she misses me?" Jake asked quietly.

"Yes, she asks about you every night."

Jake laughed, then grabbed her shoulder from the pain. "Damn, Ricky."

"Not my fault." Rick slid his chair closer. "By the way, Steven got a promotion."

"No kidding?"

"Yeah. They moved him over to Internal Affairs."

"Internal Affairs? Good God, you call that a promotion?"

"Apparently, his hacking skills were needed over there. I think they were quite impressed with him."

"He's a good guy," Jake said.

"Yeah. And what's with this James Bond shit?"

Jake smiled. "It's . . . private."

"Private? Well, he's got a bad case of hero worship going on."

Jake met his eyes. "I thought I was dead, Ricky. Gregory had his weapon pointed right at me. When I heard the shot, I couldn't figure out why I wasn't hit. Then Gregory fell to the floor, and Steven stood behind him, eyes wide open. He started shaking and the last thing I remember is his gun falling from his hands."

"Yeah. He was pretty shook up. I think he and Nicole have had a couple of talks about it, and that's helped. He was having a pretty hard time with the shooting."

"Yeah, I can imagine. I'm glad she talked with him. She was there, she knew the situation."

Rick cleared his throat. "And when are the two of you going to talk?"

"Not much to talk about, is there?" Jake absently rubbed her injured shoulder again. "The case is over, time to get back to real life."

"I think you should tell her how you feel, Jake."

"What would that accomplish? It would just make her feel uncomfortable. Hell, it'd make *me* feel uncomfortable." She shook her head. "No, it's over, whatever *it* was."

"You don't know that."

Jake waved at the empty room. "It's been a week, Ricky. We've yet to see each other."

"You know good and well she's been here."

"So it's a coincidence that she comes when I'm in PT? Or sleeping?"

"Yeah."

Jake lifted an eyebrow. "I don't believe in coincidences."

"Whatever. I swear, you're so stubborn," he said, grabbing his coat.

"Where are you going? It's Sunday. You don't have to be anywhere."

"It's one hour to kickoff and we have no munchies, not to mention beer. I'm going on a run."

"Ricky, you can't bring beer in here."

He grinned mischievously. "Watch me."

Nicole stuck her head in, actually surprised to find Jake sitting up in the bed. Every time she'd come, the room was either empty, or Jake was asleep. Of course, there had been nothing preventing her waking Jake up, but she'd found it easier to just sit with her for a few moments and slip quietly from the room.

Today, however, Jake was sitting on the edge of her bed, her face etched with pain. Nicole could see perspiration on her forehead.

"What's wrong?" she said, moving into the room.

Jake looked up, surprised.

"Hey, stranger," she said.

"Are you okay?"

Jake nodded. "Just got back from PT. I swear, the bastard is trying to kill me."

Nicole smiled, then couldn't stop herself from reaching out and lightly grasping Jake's arm. "Every time I've come, you've been asleep or gone."

Jake nodded. "He's had me doing PT twice a day since Friday."

"So when's the jail break?"

Jake smiled. "Tomorrow. I can't wait to see Cheyenne."

Nicole nodded. "I bet."

Jake picked up the towel and wiped her forehead, her eyes moving from Nicole's power suit to her face. "So, everything okay with you?"

Nicole took a step backward, feeling as if they were strangers and never lovers. She felt the pain immediately. "I'm doing . . . good. Catherine's got the office running at full steam again. Surprisingly, the publicity of the case has brought more inquiries, not less."

Jake gave a humorless smile. "Great. I'm really glad your practice didn't suffer."

Nicole nodded and clutched her hands together. "So, how long will you be off?"

"For awhile."

Their eyes met, and Nicole resisted the urge to go to Jake, to hold her. Apparently, Jake had moved past what they had. So she squared her shoulders, hoping desperately to keep her tears at bay.

"Well, I should run. I've got a . . . dinner date," she said.

Jake felt as if her heart would burst in her chest, but she simply nodded, hoping her facial expression didn't give her away. "I understand. Thanks for coming by."

"I'll . . . I'll see you later."

Jake nodded, but kept quiet as she watched Nicole flee from the room. With a heavy heart, she closed her eyes, falling blindly back onto the bed. *A dinner date?* Damn, that didn't take long.

CHAPTER SIXTY-THREE

"Jake, you can't just up and leave," Rick said for the fourth time.

"Why not?"

"What the hell are you going to do at your cabin? It's fucking winter."

Using her cane, Jake eased down onto the sofa, handing Rick her drink to hold. The pain in her shoulder was nearly gone, only bothering her when she overdid walking, which caused her to rely too heavily on the cane and her right arm.

"I know it's winter, Ricky. But I'd rather be stuck inside at my cabin than stuck inside here."

"You've got to do your physical therapy. How are you going to do it up there?"

"Gunnison has a hospital, you know. It's not like it's just a dot on the map."

"You'd be by yourself. Anything could happen, Jake."

Jake laughed and took her drink from Rick. "You said the same thing last summer, if you recall. Besides, if I stay here, you'll come over every night and want to drink bourbon and watch ESPN. Where's that going to get us?"

"Well, what else is there to do in the winter?"

Jake lowered her voice. "I need some time, Ricky. I need some alone time. I'm beat up, I'm tired." She cleared her throat. "And my heart hurts. The cabin is my . . . my solace."

"I'm afraid you won't come back this time," Rick said, his voice equally as quiet.

Jake nodded. "I may not. My leg is shot to hell," she admitted. "I'll never pass a physical. Taking disability and retiring is the logical choice."

"You came back before, Jake."

"Yeah. And if it was the other leg, I'd do it again. But it's nearly the same damn spot, Rick. The muscle is practically shredded."

"What are you going to do up there, Jake?"

Jake smiled as Cheyenne moved closer to her, laying on the floor, her body pressed flush against Jake's good leg. The dog knew, Jake realized. She knew what was going on, knew Jake was injured again. Knew they were going to head to the mountains again.

"We're going to sit and watch the snow fall," she said quietly. "We're going to strap on snowshoes and try to walk to the clearing to catch the sunrise. We're going to drive down to Mirror Lake to watch the sun reflect off its surface as it sinks over the mountains. Hell, we're going to listen to John Denver music until we're sick of it." Jake turned and affectionately grasped Rick's hand. "We're going to catch up on some reading, and we're going to drive to Gunnison twice a week for PT." She squeezed Rick's hand. "And we're going to be just fine."

CHAPTER SIXTY-FOUR

Catherine looked up as the door opened, her eyes brightening as Jake walked through the door, still leaning heavily on her cane. In her left hand, she carried a potted plant.

"Jake! What are you doing here?" Catherine said, getting up quickly to take the plant from Jake.

"How are you, Catherine?"

"I'm good, thanks. You seem to be getting around okay."

"Managing." Jake pointed at the plant. "Thanks for that. It was a pleasure to look at when I was stuck in the hospital." Jake shifted, then leaned against Catherine's desk. "I want you to have it. I'm heading up to my cabin for awhile, and I didn't think it'd make the trip."

"Of course, Jake. When will you be back?"

Jake shook her head. "Don't know yet. Depends." She motioned to Nicole's door. "The doc in?"

"Yes. She and Dr. Peterson are in conference."

Jake nodded. "I see. Well, tell her I stopped by, will you?"

"No! It's just Dr. Peterson. I can interrupt." Catherine quickly picked up the phone, waiting until Nicole answered. "Nicole, Jake is here. Do you have a minute?" Catherine smiled and nodded, looking up at Jake. "She said for you to go right in."

"Thanks."

Jake moved steadily across the carpet, fear more than pain slowing her pace. She'd almost driven out of town without seeing Nicole but at the last second, she turned, heading to downtown, wanting to at least say good-bye. In the last three weeks, they'd talked a couple of times on the phone. That was all.

As soon as she reached for the door, it jerked open, and Nicole stood there, a smile on her face.

"Jake! What a surprise," she said, holding the door open.

"I hope I'm not interrupting."

"Of course not. Come in." She pointed to the older woman sitting on her sofa. "Jake, this is Dr. Peterson, a colleague." She looked at Dorothy. "This is Detective McCoy."

The older woman rose and walked to Jake, offering her hand. "A real pleasure, Detective. I understand we have you to thank for Nicole's safety."

Jake raised an eyebrow. "Just doing my job." Jake looked at Nicole, noting her amused expression. "You got a minute?"

"Of course. Dorothy, we'll continue this later?"

"Sure. Call me." She nodded at Jake. "Nice to finally meet you."

"Thanks."

Nicole closed the door, leaning against it as she watched Jake. "In the neighborhood?"

"No, not really," Jake admitted. She turned, leaning on her cane as she surveyed the office. It looked as she remembered— neat, organized, and blinds raised to let in the afternoon sun. "Actually, I came to say good-bye."

Nicole shoved off the wall. "What do you mean?"

"Cheyenne and I are moving to my cabin."

"Moving? For good?"

Jake shrugged. "Most likely. Rick's moved to my place since they're selling their house, so I don't have to worry about that. He's just going to pick up my lease."

Nicole struggled to find words. "But . . . but why?"

"Well, it saves him having to find a place."

Nicole shook her head. "That's not what I mean, and you know it."

Jake shifted her weight, still leaning on her cane. A part of her wanted to tell Nicole the truth, that she was leaving to get away from her feelings, having convinced herself that once she was at the cabin, she'd realize that what she felt for Nicole wasn't really love, it was just a physical attraction that got away from them. But of course, she'd never been one to share her feelings easily, and there was really no need to start now.

"The cabin's home. You've seen my place here, you know that. Besides, I'll never be at full strength, so I'm going to take the disability this time."

"And do what?"

"Rehab up there, then . . . I don't know. I'll find something to keep me busy." She tried to smile. "I'll have a lot of time to soak in the hot springs."

Nicole met her eyes, hoping Jake didn't see the panic in her own. Despite her vow to end things, she was scared about Jake leaving. Worse, she was terrified of the possibility of never seeing Jake again. "But Jake, are you strong enough now? I mean, just you and Cheyenne? Anything could happen."

"Worried about me?"

"Yes, actually."

Jake looked away. "I'll be fine. It's my second go-round, you know."

Nicole took a deep breath. "This is just a shock, I guess."

Jake lowered her head. "Nicole, it's not like we've seen much of each other the last month. You won't even know I'm gone."

364

Nicole felt the pain in her heart, and she tried hard to conceal it. "I'll know you're gone."

Their eyes met, and Jake tried desperately to read Nicole's, hoping to find some sign that Jake was important to her, that she cared for her. But the blue eyes that met her own were nearly expressionless, as if it wasn't the same Nicole. And of course, it wasn't. This Nicole was decked out in a dark suit and pumps, even her makeup was impeccable. No, this wasn't her Nicole.

"Anyway, I just stopped off to say good-bye and to wish you well." Jake moved toward the door, hoping to make a graceful exit. "Take care of yourself, Nicole."

Nicole finally moved, walking to Jake. "Take care of yourself, too." She leaned closer and gently placed a kiss on Jake's cheek. "I'll never forget you," she murmured, before turning away, hiding her eyes from Jake.

Jake escaped before she embarrassed herself totally by the tears that were threatening to fall. She knocked lightly on Catherine's desk as she passed, not stopping to look at her. "See you around, kiddo."

" 'Bye Jake."

Once safely inside the elevator, Jake allowed her emotions to take over, and the tears flowed by the time she walked out into the cold November day.

Nicole covered her mouth, trying to keep back her tears. She walked to the window, staring down at the street, looking for Jake and not finding her.

"Oh, God," she murmured, finally giving in to her pain and letting her tears fall unchecked down her face. Her hands were shaking badly as she fumbled in her desk drawer for a tissue. Was she making a mistake by letting Jake walk out of her life?

She knew it was totally her decision. She could see that in Jake's eyes. After all, she was the one who had simply stopped seeing

Jake, stopped going to the hospital, stopped calling her. But as Dorothy had said, it was time to get her life back to normal, her practice back to normal. And as long as she continued to see Jake, continued to pretend they might have a future together, then nothing would be normal.

Then why does it hurt so much? *Because you're in love with her.*

"No," she murmured as she blew her nose. No, no, she wasn't in love with her. At least she'd held on to her sanity enough not to do something as foolish as that. No, she would be fine. Jake was gone, and Nicole had to move on. In fact, the dinner party at Irene's tonight would be the perfect cure for her heavy heart. And of course, Irene had a new attorney friend she wanted Nicole to meet.

So, she cleared her throat and squared her shoulders, wondering how badly her makeup was damaged. It wouldn't do for Catherine to see her tears. Despite her earlier assumptions that Deb Fisher was her type, Nicole knew Catherine adored Jake, knew that she thought Jake was . . . was the best thing that had ever happened to her.

Nicole closed her eyes for a moment, remembering Jake's gentle touch and her torrid lovemaking. Unconsciously, she brought her right hand to her chest, rubbing lightly against her heart.

CHAPTER SIXTY-FIVE

As the bitter cold of February gave way to brilliant sunshine in March, Jake laced up her hiking boots, deciding to chance a midday walk without the snowshoes she'd used for most of the winter. And instead of the ski poles she'd been using, she grabbed her cane. Common sense told her she shouldn't risk it, the trail would still be slippery, but she nearly ached to put some normalcy back into her life.

"Ready?"

Cheyenne's ears perked up, and she bounded off the sofa, waiting impatiently at the door for Jake to slip a water bottle into her waist pack. As soon as she was outside, Cheyenne leapt off the deck and into the snow, chasing a squirrel that had ventured too close to the cabin. Jake smiled as the squirrel found the nearest branch to perch upon, fussing incessantly at the dog that sniffed along the base of the tree.

Jake glanced up once into the sun, then slipped on sunglasses before stepping gingerly off the deck. She rarely ventured outside without snowshoes, feeling that her balance was better in the snow with the extra large shoes. That and the ski poles she always used.

But today, in the forty-degree temperatures and bright sunshine, she'd attempt a normal hike, without the cumbersome poles. They hadn't had snow in the last week, and the path they normally took into the forest was well-worn and nearly snow-free. She let Cheyenne take the lead, as she always did, and followed behind slowly, not wanting to push herself too hard.

She'd finished her physical therapy in late January and had been diligently continuing the exercises she'd learned. Her leg felt better, not great, but better. She endured the throbbing pain after each hike, occasionally having to resort to the pain pills she still kept by her bed. As before, the pain pills helped her sleep, helped her keep her dreams at bay. But instead of a little boy visiting her dreams, this time it was the touch of a woman she couldn't seem to shake. Nicole's face, her voice—they were as fresh in Jake's memory as if she were right here with them. But in her mind, Nicole was as Jake loved her, in jeans and boots, and the baggy sweatshirt she'd worn that last morning. Not in one of her neat suits, dressed for the office and her powerful friends.

She closed her eyes for a moment, trying to chase Nicole from her mind. During the dark nights of winter, she'd literally ached for her. At the very least, she'd expected a phone call or two, just to check up on her. But Ricky and Steven were the only ones who called, never Nicole. Jake had finally stopped hoping to see her name come up on caller ID.

Jake opened her eyes again, pushing back the sadness and trying to find peace in the bright sunshine and clear blue sky. She listened, hearing the chatter of a mountain chickadee. She let her mind go blank, absorbing the sounds around her—the wind as it carried the hint of spring through the trees, the squirrel that barked at her from a low-hanging spruce branch, the screaming call of a Steller's jay farther along the trail.

Jake smiled as Cheyenne came back down the path, looking for her. Her intelligent eyes met Jake's, and she cocked her head sideways, waiting.

"I'm fine," she told the dog. "Let's go."

CHAPTER SIXTY-SIX

Nicole moved between the throng of guests that crowded into Dorothy's spacious living room. She had expected a small dinner party, not this lavish affair with nearly thirty women. She smiled politely at a tuxedoed waiter who offered her a glass of wine. She found Irene, her red hair standing out in the crowd, and made her way toward her friend.

"You're late," Irene accused. "Dorothy was afraid you'd be a no-show."

"I'm surprised she missed me in this crowd." Nicole leaned closer. "I don't know half these woman. Who are they? New recruits?"

Irene laughed. "You still view Dorothy's group as somewhat of a cult, don't you?"

"Isn't it?"

"Well, if so, you're a member, too."

Nicole looked around her, seeing a few familiar faces, most of whom she'd been out to dinner with. She spied Cheryl across the room, the surgeon's hair now platinum blond. Deb Fisher stood talking to Dorothy, her arms moving animatedly. The election was only a week away, and Deb had a slight lead in the polls. Although Nicole would never voice this to anyone here, she secretly hoped Deb Fisher lost the election. Her interest to run for mayor had nothing to do with bettering the city and its people. Her interest was for her own political gain and that of her very powerful friends.

"You came alone, I suppose."

Nicole nodded and sipped from her wine.

"Cheryl's here. She came alone, too."

Nicole rolled her eyes. "How many times do I have to tell you? I have zero interest in Cheryl."

"But why? She's beautiful, she's a surgeon, and she's available."

"I don't like her, Irene. She's one of the most conceited women I've ever met. I don't like her as a person. I certainly don't want to date her."

"You know, you're getting older, Nicole. You're fast approaching the age where you can't afford to be so . . . picky."

Nicole's eyes widened, not believing what she'd just heard. "Are you serious? Irene, I'm thirty-six, and I don't care if I was forty-six. I'm not going to date someone I don't like just because I'm getting older. Besides, there's nothing wrong with being alone."

"Nicole, you've not been out on a date in *months*. Dorothy seems to think you're still hung up on that cop."

Nicole swallowed with difficulty, the unexpected mention of Jake causing her heart to tighten painfully. She couldn't seem to get the woman out of her mind, out of her heart. At night, each and every night, her mind would fill with images of Jake, and Nicole would struggle with sleep as she tried to push Jake away, only to end up giving in and embracing the images. At night, she allowed herself to become the Nicole she longed to be, free and unencumbered with her position and her practice. Free to be who she was and free to be with the woman she loved. But the light of day brought back the reality of her life, and each morning, she dressed the part, donning an expensive suit and decorating her face perfectly. Only Catherine seemed to be able to see through her facade, but she'd long ago quit mentioning the sad look in Nicole's eyes.

"I don't know why Dorothy feels the need to be so involved in my life. And if I choose not to date, Irene, I don't feel that necessitates a major discussion among you all."

Irene only smiled and patted her arm. "So, you did feel something for the cop." Irene shrugged. "Patrice said she was a knockout. But a cop, Nicole? *Please.*"

Nicole felt no need to argue. It was a moot point, really. Jake was gone. Nicole had let her walk right out of her life without a fight, pretending that all she felt for Jake was a physical attraction. Just sex. But four months had passed, and Nicole was no closer now to forgetting Jake than she'd been at Thanksgiving.

Taking a step away from Irene, Nicole looked around the room, wondering at the sudden isolation she felt. These people were acquaintances, not really friends. Even Dorothy, a woman she'd known nearly twelve years, wouldn't be considered a good friend. Nicole had always considered Irene her closest ally in the group, but now, she realized that Irene was just playing the game, too. Nicole nearly laughed. All the beautiful, closeted lesbians in one house, all pretending to be ecstatically happy in their lives. And no doubt, some truly were. Dorothy, for instance. She'd lived this life for so long, she knew none other. Deb Fisher, too, seemed immune to the trappings of living this way. She'd embraced the lifestyle and the benefits that went with being in Dorothy Peterson's inner circle.

It was suddenly all too much for Nicole. She'd sacrificed her independence by catering to Dorothy all these years. Dorothy had taken her in, had given her a start. Dorothy had funneled clients her way over the years, helping to build her practice. She'd always felt like she owed Dorothy. But something Matthew Gregory had said that fateful night still nagged at her. On the pretense that

Dorothy couldn't help them, but perhaps Nicole could, she'd shoved off patient after patient to Nicole, those whose insurance had run out, those who were about to end their counseling anyway. No loss for Dorothy, but no gain for Nicole, either. Only unpaid bills when she found their insurance cancelled. But still, she stuck with Dorothy, afraid to alienate her, afraid to be banished from the group. She'd sacrificed her professional life, but worse, she'd sacrificed her personal life. She let the one person she truly cared about walk out of her life, just because someone told her that Jake didn't fit in her life, in *their* life.

"Well, fuck that," she whispered.

"What?"

Nicole blinked, not realizing she'd spoken out loud. She met Irene's questioning gaze and smiled. "I said, 'fuck that,'" she repeated.

"Are you okay?"

"Actually, I feel great. See you around, Irene," Nicole said as she turned away.

"Wait? Where are you going?"

Nicole smiled. "Home. I'm going home."

"But we haven't eaten. Are you ill?"

"Not ill, no. I just came to my senses is all. Give Dorothy my regards, would you?"

Nicole blindly set her wineglass down, ignoring the curious stares as she snatched up her purse and coat from the spare bedroom. She heard Dorothy calling her name as the front door slammed shut, but she didn't stop. It felt too good to be escaping like this and, little by little, she felt the tension leave her, felt the tightness she'd been living with ease up. She looked up into the cold night sky, seeing the twinkling of stars overhead. Free. She always wondered what it would feel like to break away from them. She laughed as her breath frosted around her. She was going to the mountains.

CHAPTER SIXTY-SEVEN

Jake stood with her back to the fire, smiling as she watched Cheyenne attempt to curl into a tiny ball on one corner of the sofa. After three days of spring-like weather, winter had shown itself again, and they'd been buried by ten inches of fresh snow. No doubt the folks at the ski resort in Crested Butte were elated at the late-season storm, but Jake would just as soon get winter over with.

Common sense told her it was just as well. She'd overdone it the last few days, suffering each night with the pain in her leg. But the sunshine and warm temperatures couldn't keep her inside. She'd even chanced a hike to the ridge, trying to catch the sunset yesterday evening. She was disappointed when she couldn't make it all the way up, but her leg simply wouldn't support her weight as she tried to climb. She'd soaked in the tub and had taken two pain pills before the pain had eased up.

So now, she simply watched the snow falling in the late afternoon, watched as it covered up their trail into the forest. She had a stew simmering on the stove for most of the afternoon, and the smell made her stomach rumble, reminding her she'd skipped lunch. She smiled. She'd skipped lunch because she'd been taking a nap, still trying to ward off the effects of two pain pills.

Well, it would do her good to rest for a few days. She pulled back the screen on the fireplace and added another log, then limped heavily as she walked into the kitchen to get a bowl of stew. Cheyenne's ears perked up as she heard the spoon hit the bowl, but she didn't raise her head.

"I know you're listening," Jake said. "Don't pretend you don't want any."

With that, Cheyenne jumped off the couch, tail wagging as she stood next to Jake, doing her version of a pitiful beg. Jake dutifully filled a second bowl, setting it aside to cool. "Got to wait. You're still a dog, you know." Jake laughed at the high-pitched bark Cheyenne gave her. She sat down, putting most of her weight on the table as she eased into a chair. She rubbed her thigh, noting that the numbness wasn't quite as pronounced as it had been. The doctors had assured her that the pain would subside as her muscle grew stronger, but some days, like now, she wondered if she would ever be pain free. A limp, she could live with. But the sharp, throbbing pain that remained after each hike was threatening to bring her down. She wondered how long she would be able to fight through the pain. She wondered if she would eventually give in and quit hiking, quit trying to get stronger. Or would she simply give in and rely on the pain pills to get her through? A hermit and a junkie? God, that would be rock bottom. She shook her head. A hermit, maybe.

CHAPTER SIXTY-EIGHT

Nicole hesitated before walking inside. What would she say? She'd purposefully avoided any contact with them since Jake had left the hospital. Rick and Steven had both called her, but she'd refused to take their calls. She wondered how Rick would view her presence.

"May I help you?"

Nicole smiled politely at the uniformed officer who had walked up to her. She nodded. "I'm looking for Detective Chase."

"Second floor. Stairs and elevator are just around the corner there."

She nodded again, remembering. "Thanks."

While she waited for the elevator, she thought she should have called first. There was no assurance that Rick would even be here. She could always look Steven up, but she doubted he knew where Jake's cabin was.

She needn't have worried. As soon as the elevator opened, she saw Rick sitting across the room, chatting with an attractive woman at the next desk. His new partner? She walked closer, finally clearing her throat to get his attention. His eyes widened in surprise, then that charming smile she remembered flashed across his face.

"Nicole! What are you doing here?"

"Hi, Rick." She nervously tucked her hands into the pockets of her jeans. "You got a minute?"

"Sure. Everything okay?"

Nicole considered the question, then shook her head. "No. Not really. Can we talk?"

He looked at the other woman. "Be right back." He then led Nicole down a hallway and into an empty room. He politely held out a chair for her, then sat down beside her. "You want some coffee or something?"

"No, thanks." She clutched her hands together on top of the table, wondering how to begin. For all she knew, Jake had moved on. It had been four months, nearly five. Plenty of time for her to meet someone up in the mountains, someone who shared her love of the forest. Nicole hadn't allowed herself to consider that possibility before. She wasn't sure what she would do if that were the case.

"Rick, do you hear from Jake?"

Rick smiled. "We talk every Sunday. Well, unless the weather's bad and she doesn't have service. She only has her cell phone."

"So, she's doing okay?"

"I suppose. Although once her therapy ended, she's only left that cabin twice in the last two months."

"Does she . . . does she ever ask about me?"

The smile left Rick's face, and Nicole could see a hint of anger in his eyes. "At first, she asked about you all the time." Rick shrugged. "But I told her we never heard from you, and she finally quit asking."

Nicole nodded, feeling every ounce of guilt that Rick was unknowingly piling on her. "I'd like to go see her," Nicole said quietly. "Do you think she'd mind?"

Rick stood and pushed his chair away, pacing. "Why?"

"Why what?"

"Why do you want to go see her?"

"Because I . . . I miss her."

"You miss her," Rick repeated. "Well, I don't think that's a good idea."

"Why not?"

Rick hesitated, wondering how much to tell. But hell, it didn't matter, did it? "She's finally gotten over you, Nicole. If you go up there, she's just going to get hurt all over again."

Nicole's heart hammered in her chest. "What do you mean, hurt?"

"Oh, hell, Nicole, Jake was in love with you. It just crushed her when you didn't come to the hospital, when you didn't go see her afterward. Hell, you just faded away, as if she was nothing to you."

Nicole couldn't stop the tears, and she didn't try to hide them. Rick's words went straight to her heart.

"Don't get upset, Nicole. Jake knew the score. She knew she wasn't good enough for you."

"What do you mean?"

"That night at her place, when I found out about you two, she walked me out, she told me she was in love with you. But she said she knew it wouldn't go anywhere because you were a doctor, and she was a lowly detective."

"Oh, God," Nicole whispered. "But that's not true."

"Isn't it?"

Nicole stood, too, pacing opposite Rick. She wiped at the tears on her cheeks, wondering how she could have been so blind. Yes, that was exactly how it was. She was a psychologist, her so-called friends were doctors and lawyers. And yes, Jake was a cop. As Dorothy once told her, a couple of notches below them. So Nicole had believed her, instead of believing what was in her heart. And yes, she had treated Jake as if she wasn't good enough for her. *Goddamn it all.*

Nicole turned her tear-stained face to Rick, meeting his eyes. "Rick, I love her. I tried not to. I tried to push her away. But the fact remains, I'm miserable without her." Nicole swallowed. "And I suspect she's just as miserable." She took a deep breath. "Please tell me where she is. I've got to see her."

Rick shook his head. "Why don't you call her and see if she wants you to come?"

"Ricky, I'm in love with her. I want to get in my car right now and drive up there. Now tell me where the *hell* she is."

CHAPTER SIXTY-NINE

Nicole made the drive along the Taylor River with wide eyes, yet she saw little. When she realized she had a death grip on the steering wheel, she made herself relax. She was as nervous as she'd ever been and again, she was second guessing herself, wondering if indeed, she should have called first. What if Jake didn't want to see her? What if Jake really had gotten over her, as Rick said? Well, she would find out for herself. She'd made Rick promise he wouldn't call Jake, and Nicole believed he would keep that promise. She didn't want to give Jake any warning, she didn't want Jake to have time to prepare a defense. She wanted Jake as raw and exposed as she felt herself.

Raw and exposed . . . and God, so free. She'd left Catherine to figure out what to do with her appointments. She'd told her not to schedule anything for the rest of the month because honestly, she didn't know how long she'd be gone. She would stay for as long as it took. She and Jake needed some time, some real time alone, without a murder investigation hanging over their heads. They needed time to be together to see if what they had was indeed love.

Of course, this was all Nicole's thinking. Jake may have different ideas. She may actually send Nicole away, not wanting to pursue this. But Nicole knew in her heart that wasn't the case. That last day, when Jake had come to her office to say good-bye, Nicole knew then. She could see it in Jake's eyes. But she let her walk away. She shook her head. But not anymore. They would talk. They would get it all out. Then they would decide where to go from there. They were not going to hide from this any longer. And she blamed Jake just as much as herself. Jake could have said something, could have told her how deep her feelings were. But Jake kept quiet, just as Nicole had done. They were both to blame.

Nicole gasped when she topped the last hill and the Taylor Reservoir spread out before her, the snow-lined edges contrasting sharply with the deep blue open water. She had her first unobstructed views of the Collegiate Peaks, and she smiled from the sheer beauty of it. Yes, this was Jake's land. No wonder she called this place home instead of a tiny duplex in Denver.

She saw the sign for Tin Cup and turned right, thankful she'd rented a four-wheel drive SUV for the trip. The snow glistened in the bright sunshine, and she slowed, following the tracks made by previous cars. Rick could only get her to the general store in Tin Cup. After that, he said he didn't have a clue as to where Jake's cabin was. Nicole hoped someone at the store could give her directions from there.

However, the town of Tin Cup consisted only of the general store and a handful of cabins. There were two trucks parked out front, and she pulled along side them, her boots crunching on the snow as she walked up the wooden steps. It was warm and inviting inside, the huge, black cast iron stove hot and glowing.

"May I help you, miss?"

Nicole smiled, pausing to warm her hands by the stove. "I'm looking for Jake McCoy."

The man frowned and scratched his temple. "Don't believe I know him. Does he live around here?"

Nicole shook her head. "He's a she. Drives a dark green Land Cruiser."

The man's eyes widened. "Got a dog that hangs out the window all the time?"

Nicole smiled. "That would be her."

"Oh, yeah. She lives up toward Cumberland Pass, past Mirror Lake."

"I don't suppose you could draw me a map?"

Jake stood by the fire, staring out into the bright sunshine. She'd made herself stay inside today and rest. Her leg felt better, and her limp was less pronounced than it had been yesterday. So, she'd sit by the fire and read, although the book she'd started last night wasn't holding her interest. She sighed. She'd read more damn books in the last few months than she had in years. Maybe she needed to reconsider a satellite dish. Not only for television, but a computer as well. She didn't realize how much she would miss having access to the Internet.

She sighed again. She felt restless. Nervous, almost. Cheyenne lay on the rug by the fire, watching her. She tilted her head. Maybe a short hike wouldn't hurt. But not now. She'd let it warm up some. She suspected it was still in the low thirties outside.

Cheyenne startled her by jumping to her feet, a low growl coming from her throat. She stared at the door, and Jake did the same.

"We got company?" Jake asked quietly. Cheyenne stopped growling and cocked her head. Before long, her tail started wagging and Jake frowned. "What is it, girl?"

A light tapping on the door and Cheyenne's excitement caused Jake to wonder who had found her cabin. And walked from the road, no less. The gate was closed and locked.

"Come on in," she called, as she leaned on her cane, waiting. The door creaked open, and she couldn't hide the shock on her face. Cheyenne danced around their visitor, then blue eyes looked up and met her own. Jake finally found her voice. "You lost?"

Nicole swallowed nervously. "Actually, I've been lost for the last four months. I thought maybe . . . maybe you might have been, too."

Jake's heart was hammering so hard in her chest that she couldn't speak. She just stared, drinking in the vision before her. A forest-green fleece jacket covered a flannel shirt that was tucked into faded jeans. Snow still clung to her hiking boots and Jake's eyes moved up Nicole's body, resting on her mouth before locking gazes with her.

Nicole's breath caught, as it always did when Jake looked at her that way. She waited patiently for Jake to answer her.

"Lost?" Jake tilted her head. "Miserable, dead inside, yes."

"I . . . I miss you terribly," Nicole confessed. "And I feel dead inside, too," she whispered.

Jake found it difficult to breathe, and she finally looked away, wondering what this meant. Wondering what Nicole was doing up here. "How did you find me?"

"I beat it out of Rick. He told me that I should leave you alone, that you were finally . . . over me."

Jake smiled. "Little does he know, I'll never be over you."

Nicole took a hesitant step toward Jake, then stopped. "I'm in love with you, Jake. Please, can we try this again?"

Jake bit her lip, trying frantically to keep her emotions under control. A part of her wanted to cry like a baby and bury herself in Nicole's arms. And a part of her wanted to yell with elation at the top of her lungs. But she did neither. She met Nicole's eyes head on, seeing nothing but truth and honesty in her words, and the love that Jake so desperately needed to see.

She finally gave in and let the tears form and fall. With the arch of one eyebrow, she grinned. "Forgive me if I'm a little . . . sappy," she said. "I've been listening to John Denver for the last few months."

Nicole closed the distance between them, sliding her arms around Jake's shoulders as she pulled her close. "You can be as sappy as you want. I happen to love John Denver."

"Nicole, please, I'm dying here."

Nicole laughed as she slipped the robe off and let it fall to the floor. "You're not dying. I swear, for someone with an injured leg, you sure have stamina."

"I've been saving up," Jake murmured. She pulled Nicole to her, relishing the feel of Nicole's naked flesh against her own. For so long, she had dreamed of this, and now it was a reality. Nicole was here, finally. She relaxed as Nicole's mouth found hers, soft, gentle kisses that spoke of love.

"I'm not going anywhere, you know," Nicole said for the third time. She moved to her side, shifting her weight off Jake. With a gentle touch, her fingers moved down Jake's body, pausing to lightly caress the tender scar on Jake's thigh.

Jake closed her eyes, wanting to believe Nicole. They spent two days talking, and loving each other. They'd taken time for short hikes, and they'd taken time to make love. But the fact remained that Nicole's life was in Denver. And Jake, with her career over, had no desire for the city. She was right where she wanted to be. Yes, there was no doubting the love between them. What they were going to do with it remained a mystery.

Nicole's mouth moved lower, suckling Jake's breast. She smiled as Jake drew in a sharp breath. Her hands moved across Jake's flat stomach, pausing when they reached her hips.

"Tell me you love me," Nicole whispered against her skin.

"I love you," Jake murmured.

"And you can't live without me," Nicole breathed as her mouth moved lower.

"I'd die without you," Jake whispered as her eyes slammed shut. Her hips arched against Nicole's mouth, giving in to the pleasure that the other woman gave her. "God, Nicole," she murmured as she opened wider.

"I love you, Jake," Nicole murmured as her mouth finally

claimed her. Her hands spread Jake's thighs, holding her down on the bed when Jake would have arched against her.

Jake's hips raised off the bed, her injured leg screaming in protest as her muscles clenched. She ignored the pain, instead she embraced the love she felt for Nicole and the love that Nicole showered her with. Her hips pressed firmly against Nicole's mouth and she didn't try to hold back the cry that escaped as she climaxed.

Then Nicole was there, brushing soft kisses across her face. Jake finally opened her eyes, pulling Nicole close.

"I love you so much," she whispered.

"Oh, Jake . . . I love you, too. I'm sorry I wasted all these months."

Jake leaned back, pulling Nicole with her. They settled against the pillows, arms wrapped around each other.

Jake knew they couldn't put it off forever. They'd talked about everything except their future. "What now?"

"What do you mean?" Nicole asked.

"You've got your office in Denver. I'm here. That's what I mean," Jake said. She kissed Nicole and gathered her closer. "We've talked about everything but that. What are we going to do?"

Nicole smiled as she burrowed against Jake. "I'm thinking maybe I could get a teaching job at the college in Gunnison," she said.

Jake sat up. "Are you serious?"

"Yes, I'm serious."

"But what about your practice, your clients? What about Catherine?"

Nicole laughed. "Catherine adores you. I'm sure at this very moment, Catherine is assigning my patients to other doctors, knowing that I won't be returning."

Jake took both of Nicole's hands and pulled them to her chest. "Are you sure, Nicole? I mean, Gunnison is hardly Denver."

"Jake, the only thing I'm sure about is that I love you. Whatever happens, happens. I just want to be with you."

Jake reached out, cupping Nicole's face with her palm, rubbing her thumb lightly across Nicole's lips.

"I love you . . . totally, completely," she whispered. "I want to spend my life with you, Nicole. If you need to be in Denver, I'll go with you. This little cabin, Gunnison, it's hardly what you're used to."

"What I'm used to is pretending to be someone I'm not. This is real, Jake. Right here, with you. This is real." Nicole lay back, pulling Jake on top of her. "You know what? I think I've had my fill of Denver, anyway. I think I'm ready for a little . . . mountain living. It's hard to find secluded hot springs in the city, you know."

"Ah. So it's the lure of your own private hot springs that has you wanting to move here, huh?"

Nicole kissed Jake softly, then smiled against her mouth. "Well, that . . . and the prospect of seeing you naked in the hot springs, making love to me."

"That can be arranged, you know." Jake pulled Nicole on top of her. "In a few months, that is." Her kiss was lingering, promising more. "For now, you'll have to settle for this bed and the fireplace."

"And I like this just fine."

Publications from
BELLA BOOKS, INC.
The best in contemporary lesbian fiction

P.O. Box 10543, Tallahassee, FL 32302
Phone: 800-729-4992
www.bellabooks.com

PASSIONATE KISSES by Megan Carter. 240 pp. Will two old friends run from love?
1-59493-051-1 $12.95

ALWAYS AND FOREVER by Lyn Denison. 224 pp. The girl next door turns Shannon's
world upside down.   1-59493-049-X $12.95

BACK TALK by Saxon Bennett. 200 pp. Can a talk show host find love after heartbreak?
1-59493-028-7 $12.95

THE PERFECT VALENTINE: EROTIC LESBIAN VALENTINE STORIES edited by
Barbara Johnson and Therese Szymanski—from Bella After Dark. 328 pp. Stories from the
hottest writers around.   1-59493-061-9 $14.95

MURDER AT RANDOM by Claire McNab. 200 pp. The Sixth Denise Cleever Thriller.
Denise realizes the fate of thousands is in her hands.   1-59493-047-3 $12.95

THE TIDES OF PASSION by Diana Tremain Braund. 240 pp. Will Susan be able to hold
it all together and find the one woman who touches her soul?   1-59493-048-1 $12.95

JUST LIKE THAT by Karin Kallmaker. 240 pp. Disliking each other—and everything they
stand for—even before they meet, Toni and Syrah find feelings can change, just like that.
1-59493-025-2 $12.95

WHEN FIRST WE PRACTICE by Therese Szymanski. 200 pp. Brett and Allie are once
again caught in the middle of murder and intrigue.   1-59493-045-7 $12.95

REUNION by Jane Frances. 240 pp. Cathy Braithwaite seems to have it all: good looks,
money and a thriving accounting practice . . .   1-59493-046-5 $12.95

BELL, BOOK & DYKE: NEW EXPLOITS OF MAGICAL LESBIANS by Kallmaker,
Watts, Johnson and Szymanski. 360 pp. Reluctant witches, tempting spells, and skyclad
beauties—delve into the mysteries of love, lust and power in this quartet of novellas.
1-59493-023-6 $14.95

ARTIST'S DREAM by Gerri Hill. 320 pp.When Cassie meets Luke Winston, she can no
longer deny her attraction to women . . .   1-59493-042-2 $12.95

NO EVIDENCE by Nancy Sanra. 240 pp. Private Investigator Tally McGinnis once again
returns to the horror filled world of a serial killer.   1-59493-043-04 $12.95

WHEN LOVE FINDS A HOME by Megan Carter. 280 pp. What will it take for Anna and
Rona to find their way back to each other again?   1-59493-041-4 $12.95